William Wyatt Gill

From Darkness to Light in Polynesia

With Illustrative Clan Songs

William Wyatt Gill

From Darkness to Light in Polynesia
With Illustrative Clan Songs

ISBN/EAN: 9783337179458

Printed in Europe, USA, Canada, Australia, Japan

Cover: Foto ©Andreas Hilbeck / pixelio.de

More available books at **www.hansebooks.com**

FROM DARKNESS TO LIGHT IN POLYNESIA

WITH

ILLUSTRATIVE CLAN SONGS

BY THE

REV. WILLIAM WYATT GILL, LL.D.

AUTHOR OF 'MYTHS AND SONGS FROM THE SOUTH PACIFIC,'
'JOTTINGS FROM THE PACIFIC,' 'LIFE IN THE SOUTHERN ISLES,' ETC.

LONDON
THE RELIGIOUS TRACT SOCIETY
56, PATERNOSTER ROW, AND 65 ST. PAUL'S CHURCHYARD
1894

PREFACE

A FEW years ago (at the suggestion of Sir George Grey, K.C.B., and Sir James Hector, K.C.M.G., M.D., etc.), the New Zealand Government printed the earlier part [1] of the present volume for the use of scientists. A few copies were forwarded to the great public libraries of the United Kingdom. In New Zealand itself considerable interest was thus awakened by the discovery of the near kinship of the Hervey Islanders and the Maoris.

It has occurred to me, that intelligent friends of Christian missions might be interested in comparing the past with the present. The present volume is intended to assist such an inquiry.

In 1888 Her Majesty's Government 'assumed a protectorate over the group of islands known as the Hervey Islands, situated in the South Pacific Ocean between 18° and 22° south latitude, and 156° and 160° west longitude.' Frederick Moss, Esq., has been appointed the first British Resident.

The Hervey Group consists of seven islands, viz. Rarotonga, Mangaia, Aitutaki, Atiu, Mauke, Mitiaro, and

---

[1] Under the title of *Historical Sketches of Savage Life in Polynesia ; with Illustrative Clan Songs.*

Manuae. The population is small, being about 7000. The island of Mangaia is about as large as Jersey, with a population of 2000. The present writer spent the whole of his missionary career—thirty-three years—on the islands of Mangaia and Rarotonga. The political capital of the group is Rarotonga, the home of the British Resident.

Mangaia is in 21° 57′ south latitude, and 151° 7′ west longitude. It is twenty miles in circumference, and not more than six hundred and fifty feet above the sea. It may be seen, in clear weather, at a distance of thirty miles. Mangaia is a complete coral island ; it rises from deep water as a ring of live coral. The unbroken fringing reef is covered at half tide ; beyond it, landward, are broken masses of dead coral rock. At the distance of some two hundred yards from the rugged beach rises gradually a second or inner ring of dead coral, which, towards the interior, is perpendicular. This remarkable belt of uplifted dead coral, surrounding the island like a cyclopean wall, is from one to two miles across. In some places to cross it is like walking over a few millions of spear-points. Many ghastly wounds are occasioned by foot-slips. Numerous sea-shells of existing species are imbedded in the highest parts. It is honeycombed with very numerous and extensive caves, formerly used as habitations, cemeteries, places of refuge, and stores. Scores of them are filled with desiccated human bodies. Stalactite and stalagmite abound, and form thick and fast-growing layers of lime rock. The largest and most famous of these caverns is known as Tuatini, 'the Labyrinth.'

The interior of the island is formed of dark volcanic

rock and red clay, descending in low hills from a flat-topped centre, known as 'the crown of Mangaia.' There is no lagoon. Streams of water, after fertilizing thousands of taro plantations, find their way to the ocean by subterranean passages through the second or inner ring of dead coral, to which reference has been made.

The population of Mangaia is now gathered into three villages : the principal one being on the west, the second in size and importance on the south, and the third on the north-east.

It is a very interesting circumstance that songs still exist in the native language, describing the visit of Captain Cook to the Hervey Group in 1777. The originals, with a translation, are given in the present volume. These Historical Sketches with Illustrative Songs may not be without interest to students of ethnology and others. During a long residence on Mangaia, shut out to a great extent from the civilized world, I enjoyed great facilities for the study of the natives themselves and their traditions. I soon found that they had two sets of traditions —one referring to their gods, and to the supposed experiences of men after death ; another relating veritable history. The natives themselves carefully distinguish the two. Thus, historical songs are called *pe'e ;* the others, *kapa*, etc. In the native mind the series now presented to the English public is a natural sequence to *Myths and Songs ;*[1] the mythical, or, as they would say, the spiritual, necessarily taking precedence of the historical or human.

---

[1] *Myths and Songs from the South Pacific*, with a preface by Professor Max Müller.

In such researches we cannot be too careful to distinguish history from myth. But when we find hostile clans, in their epics, giving substantially the same account of the historical past, the most sceptical must yield to the force of evidence. I say substantially, as in some of the earlier stories there is a great air of exaggeration—*e.g. The Story of Moke̓, The Twin Kites,* and *The Expelled God.* But the reader will observe that in all three stories the national feeling was invoked against other islanders. In the great mass of song and story there exists the wholesome corrective of clan rivalries to prevent such self-laudatory exaggerations. I have endeavoured to relate the stories as the natives give them, without improvement or elimination.

When first we settled down amongst these islanders and attempted to acquire their language, I was often puzzled by references to past events, scraps of song, myths, and proverbs—the force of which depended upon an accurate acquaintance with the circumstances which originally led to their utterance. Two courses lay open to me—either to ignore their ancient religion and their undoubted history, or to study both for their own sake, and especially with a view to understand native thought and feeling. I chose the latter course.

The ignorance of these islanders of the art of writing fully accounts for the absence of many really ancient compositions. It was not that they were deficient in natural ability, or in desire to perpetuate the knowledge of the remote past. What race unacquainted with the use of metals ever invented an alphabet or made any considerable stride in civilization ? Each clan, as it rose to importance, was assiduous in composing and preserving its own songs and history, but was willing enough to cast into the shade those of its fallen rivals. A few of the prayers in *Myths and Songs* are believed to be of great antiquity, being independent of clan jealousies ; constituting, in fact, the liturgy of each succeeding generation. I have been the more anxious to put these things on permanent record, as the correct knowledge of the past is rapidly fading away, and will probably soon become extinct.

'Are the Polynesians worth the saving ?' inquired an eminent preacher and author of the writer, when on furlough at home. I think the perusal of the following pages will be a sufficient answer to that question. Our Master came 'to seek and to save them that are *lost*.' Christ's pity for the downtrodden and outcast of all races is the sure evidence of His divine mission.

The successful introduction of Christianity into New Guinea and the adjacent large islands, together with the multitudinous islets of the Pacific, is mainly due to the labours of native pioneer evangelists from the older mission fields. Led by the Revs. W. G. Lawes, James Chalmers, Dr. George Brown, and many other brave European workers, they have done wonders. One hundred and sixty students (male and female) of the Rarotongan Institution alone have died at the post of duty ; some kidnapped and sold (with their flocks) into slavery in Peru, etc. ; others martyred in the New Hebrides and in New Guinea ; but the greater number victims of deadly fever.

'Blessed are the dead which die in the Lord.' I am persuaded that these noble men and women who fell on the battle-field were comforted by the thought that they were winning a new empire for their Divine Master! May British Christians emulate their apostolic zeal!

WILLIAM WYATT GILL.

CONTENTS

PART II.

LIGHT.

LIST OF ILLUSTRATIONS

PART I

DARKNESS; OR, INCIDENTS OF SAVAGE LIFE

A MAT HUT IN MANGAIA.

DARKNESS

OR

INCIDENTS OF SAVAGE LIFE

—◦◦◦—

CHAPTER I

SUMMARY REVENGE

ANA-NUI, or the Big Cave, is celebrated in the annals of
the Aitu, or god tribe, as the scene of the first great
misfortune which overtook them in the latter days of
Rangi.

Their ancestors came from Iti (Tahiti), and settled
down on the eastern part of the island where they first
landed. On one occasion a grand feast was to come off
in honour of the gods. As this tribe were noted fishermen,
they were all busy. After spending the day in the sea,
the entire tribe, with their wives and children, slept on the
sandy floor of the Big Cave. This cavern, as the name
implies, is very spacious, but has this drawback: the centre
is open to the dews and rains of heaven. The entrance is
very narrow, admitting only one person at a time. Near
this entrance are great boulders, which render access and
egress alike difficult.

B

A large turtle having been caught, custom required that it should at once be presented to the king, who lived near Rongo's *marae*, or sacred grove, on the western part of Mangaia. This king was Tama-tapu, whose father Tui came from Rarotonga, where the name is still one of dignity and power. By courtesy Tui shared regal honours with Rangi, sitting with him on 'the sacred sandstone' (*kea inamoa*), and being appointed by him to guard by his prayers the sea-side from evil-minded spirits coming from the sun-setting, whilst Rangi kept a sharp look-out against bad spirits from the east. Tui was dead, and his regal duties descended to his son Tama-tapu, who set the first example of wanton blood-shedding in war.

When about a mile from Orongo, the two turtle-carriers perceived a strong fragrant smell. The fact was, Tama-tapu, dressed up to the height of heathen extravagance, and highly scented, had that morning gone into the interior. Hearing footsteps approaching, he hid himself in the bush at a spot known as Okara. Said one of the Aitu, 'It must be the fragrance of that villain's clothes,' little thinking that Tama-tapu was listening to the disparaging remark. On they walked to the residence of the sea-shore king, and, depositing the turtle, immediately returned.

Tama-tapu was stung to the quick. Slowly returning to his home, he gave vent to his feelings, weeping long and loud, and then planned his revenge. Triton-shell in hand, he started off to the south-west part of the island, where his mother's clan (she was a native of Mangaia) resided. This clan was called Te-tuikura—'The red-marked ;' they worshipped Tekuraaki, a god introduced by Tui from Rarotonga.

He quickly assembled his royal clan by blowing his triton-shell. They were indignant at the story of the humiliation he had undergone. A hurried feast was at once prepared for Tama-tapu; each person partaking of it was thereby pledged to avenge his quarrel. It was arranged that they should divide themselves into two parties, one to prepare candle-nut torches, and the other to cut green calabashes, to serve, when hollowed out, as dark lanterns. The rendezvous was the *marae* of Motoro, in the interior, at dusk.

At the appointed time every warrior belonging to 'the red-marked' tribe was at the appointed place of meeting. Their first employment was to clothe the incensed Tama-tapu; each individual came forward with a piece of the finest cloth, which was wrapped round his person. It is said that in all as many as two hundred pieces were thus collected about him, so that he was almost buried under the pile.

Torrents of rain now fell—a good omen in their estimation. But the irate king never moved, as his presence at the *marae*, as well as his incantations, were deemed necessary to the success of the expedition. The expedition now started, under the guidance of the warrior chief Matataukiu. Each warrior carried in his left hand a green calabash, scooped out in such a way as to admit a candle-nut torch; but these torches were on no account to be lit until they should get near the scene of slaughter. For the present, a single torch was to guide the warriors on their way.

They first halted at Tevaenga, a distance of two and a half miles, to slay Turuia, the original priest of Tane-Ngakiau, god of the devoted tribe. The old man was clubbed in his sleep, and on the following day laid on the altar of Rongo. Passing on another two miles to the district of Karanga, they slew two more chiefs of the tribe they were intent on annihilating. Elated with these successes, they hurried on to the Big Cave, where the devoted tribe slept on during the tempest of rain without sentinels or the least presentiment of danger.

On nearing the cave, some of the assailants made their way over the rocks to guard the opening at the roof of the cavern, lest any should mount the rugged path and so escape; but the main body went along the sandy beach to the proper entrance to the cave. When tolerably near they lighted their torches with difficulty, and carefully covered them with the green calabashes, taking precaution that the light should fall only on the ground, like the dark lanterns of police at home.

Silently, yet rapidly, they approached their victims. Their leader, Matataukiu, on arriving at the narrow entrance, gave the signal to his followers by throwing away his calabash, thus gaining the advantage of a bright light to enable him the more effectually to execute his bloody purpose. The overhanging rocks sheltered their candle-nut torches from rain.

'The red-marked' tribe now rushed pell-mell upon these poor defenceless Aitus, who in many instances were despatched in their sleep. Like sheep penned up in a fold, they were slaughtered at the will of these cruel men, without regard to age or sex. One powerful man, Pāpākea, the chief warrior of the devoted tribe, darted through the ranks of the attacking party and made for the ocean, intending to swim out a short distance, and then, under cover of darkness, to come ashore again at another part of the island. Although closely pursued, he would certainly have escaped but for a deep hollow in the reef, into which he unfortunately fell. As Pāpākea rose to the surface, his skull was cleft by his foe. The place where he fell still bears his name. Of the large number cooped up inside that cave, only one—a man named Teruatonga—escaped, by climbing up to the opening in the roof. The pathway by which he climbed is not very difficult. At the top he saw an ironwood sword ready to descend upon his head. But as the light of the torch fell upon the trembling Aitu, who had given himself up as lost, the chief of that detachment of 'the red-marked' tribe saw the face of an old friend, and permitted him to escape.

It is said that the blood of the massacred tribe tinged the waters of the reef, and even extended to the ocean.

In Mangaian story the slaughter of the god (Tane) tribe, at the Big Cave, ranks as the first bloody surprise of which subsequent history furnishes endless instances. The engagement which followed at Tangikura is the second battle fought on this island. The most careful consideration of the entire stream of their history convinces me that this never-forgiven and cruel attack took place about 470 years ago. It is curious that all the prominent names in this story—Matataukiu, Rautakanini, Pāpākea—are still kept up in their respective families.

THE WRONGS OF THE AITU TRIBE; COMPOSED BY KOROA, *Circa* 1817.

A 'crying' (*tangi*) song pertaining to the 'death-talk' of Arokapiti.

TUMU.	INTRODUCTION.
Solo.	*Solo.*
Tiō ra, kotia te ue i Tangikura, Ei pueke ia Ana-nui, Ko te Aitu te atua ū !	Sing we the dark lanterns made at Tangikura To light up the Big Cave, Where the god tribe was wrapt in repose.
Chorus.	*Chorus.*
E ngaee mai e Teruatonga ē !	Alas ! Teruatonga alone did escape !

<table>
<tr><td>

PAPA.

Solo.

Pamiro te one ra, e Tevaki ē !

Chorus.

Pamiro te one i poro ai
Ei akapou ia tatou
I te anau oki a Tevaki ra i Tekuti-
kuti.

Solo.

I Tekutikuti Takiri, e ua kapitia
Tuarau
E te tueru, tei Ruaoata i te vairanga.

Chorus.

Ua motu au ki Aratangaroa ē !

UNUUNU TAI.

Solo.

Te umu aitu, na veravera o Iti ra ē !

Chorus.

Te umu aitu, na veravera o Iti.
　　Tei Ana-nui na tauna,
　　Na pururua a Matataukiu,
'Tae a kauvai te pera i Avaavaroa.
　　Tei Okara na tara koumu,
　　Kua akarongo te ariki Tama-
　　　tapu,
　　Auā e kai i te ua i te ika
　　　　I te onu a Rongo:
　　Kua vaia i te aunga puāriri paoa
　　　　No taua tae ra.
Te vai ra i Pāpākea, e ake karea i
taruarere.

</td><td>

FOUNDATION.

Solo.

At Pamiro[1] was the hiding-place of
Tevaki.

Chorus.

At Pamiro he adjured his sons
　　To die a brave death—
A death befitting the children of
Tevaki.

Solo.

The eldest, Takiri, was speared ; the
next, Tuarau,
Was hunted to death, and lies deep
in the cave Raupa.

Chorus.

The sire was with difficulty saved.

FIRST OFFSHOOT.

Solo.

The flaming ovens[2] devoured the
god tribe.

Chorus.

The flaming ovens devoured those
from Iti.
At the Big Cave perished a multitude,
Deceived by Matataukiu's dark
torches :
Torrents of blood flowed into the
ocean.
　　By the roadside at Okara,
The royal Tama-tapu heard the
whisper,
' Why should *he* taste the daintiest of
morsels—
　　The turtle sacred to Rongo ?'
Ah ! I perceive the rich perfume
From the dress of that fool !'
Pāpākea stumbled on the reef ; the
brave was utterly undone.
　　Sing we, etc.

</td></tr>
</table>

---

[1] Pamiro is the name of a spot where, in the days of Mautara, Tevaki took refuge after the slaughter of his first family. Twice in the history of this tribe *the entire race was exterminated all but one member ;* Teruatonga was the favoured individual in the first instance at the Big Cave, and Tevaki in the comparatively modern age of Mautara.

[2] A subsequent atrocious murder of this devoted Aitu tribe, twice enacted against them.

Unuunu Rua.

Solo.

Veroia Matakere i te ngau roa ra ē !

Chorus.

Veroia Matakere i te ngau roa,
I turanga rāui i Teueue i raro io
   Moana,
Tei Kurupeupeu te ariki paa
O Tevaki nei, O Tenau ariki,
O Temoeau te ivi i akamocia i
Ia Tirango i te are korero.
    Na Ivi paa tei akaō?
    Te manga i kai ai.
Te vai ra i Pāpākea, e ake karea i
   taruarere.

Unuunu Toru.

Solo.

Pokia Ana-nui e !

Chorus.

Pokia Ana-nui e te matakeinanga,
O Rautakanini ra, e ngati i Te-tui-
  .kura
    E ariki Tama-tapu.
Kua kapi te rangi ia Iva,
Takaia e Rongo ia ē te enua.
O te kautuarau, e ko te ua e pa,
    Kua ki te roto i Mangaia.
Kavea i uta i te tukono i te mana o
   te ariki.
Te vai rai Pāpākea, e ake karea i
   taruarere !

Second Offshoot.

Solo.

Matakere was speared in the open
   plain.

Chorus.

Matakere was speared in the open
   plain,
Amongst the rocks not far from the
   sea,
Condemned to wander from place to
   place
Was the childless old man Tevaki.
Was not his mother, ' the Soft-
   sleeper,'
Descended from the great Tirango,[1]
    Daughter of Ivi the priest ?
    Hence the wisdom of the son.
Pāpākea stumbled on the reef; the
   brave was utterly undone.
    Sing we, etc.

Third Offshoot.

Solo.

They were caught in the Big Cave.

Chorus.

They were caught in the Big Cave by
   their foes,
By Rautakanini and ' the red-marked '
   tribe,
    Sent by King Tama-tapu.
The heavens became as black as
   Hades :
By the fiat of Rongo the island was
   flooded.
The fine cloth was all soaked in the
   storm.
    The valleys of Mangaia were
    covered,
Only hills could be seen : O thou
   wonder-working king !
Pāpākea stumbled on the reef; the
   brave was utterly undone.
    Sing we, etc.

---

[1] Tirango was the famous warrior of the Tongan clan who exterminated
the Tekama tribe ; but was eventually slain in battle. The spot where he fell
is well known.

CHAPTER II

A DRESS OF FEATHERS

IVITU, nephew to Rangi, collected a number of friends, and at Tangikura, the head-quarters of the 'red-marked' tribe, gave battle to Matataukiu and Tama-tapu, in the vain hope of avenging the treacherous slaughter of the Aitu or god tribe. Ivitu's party of one hundred and forty was defeated ; the leader and most of his warriors perished.

In the heat of the conflict two of the vanquished escaped unhurt to the rocks of Tevaenga, on the north of the island, which, unlike the wild home of Rori, in after days, in the east, are everywhere covered with the densest tropical vegetation. Lofty forest trees of various kinds overshadow smaller plants, and beautiful creepers everywhere hide the naked rock from view. At mid-day it is twilight, and the painful silence of the primeval forest is pleasantly relieved by the occasional twittering of drowsy birds. On one occasion the writer, having lost his way, wandered about for hours amongst these rocks and trees, and only gained the interior by walking opposite to the setting sun. In the patches of soil between the stones a considerable variety of wild food grows. Amongst these is the *mārarau*, or sweet yam, which tastes like the sweet potato ; also the noble indigenous true yam (*ui parai*), in addition to the ordinary pandanus, *nono*,[1] and other edible but inferior fruits.

[1] *Morinda citrifolia.*

This magnificent hiding-place, nowhere less than two miles wide, extends for several miles; but there are only two places where fresh water can be obtained. One of these is so exposed as to be of little use to a poor fugitive. The well-protected perennial fountain was close to the hiding-place of Uriitepitokura and his father Temoaakaui. Any one may trace the course of the stream under the vast pile of rocks from the neighbouring valley; but the secret pathway by which the fugitives descended from their eyrie to fill their calabashes is unknown, having been built up so lately as 1846. The sense of security induced by Christianity causes such knowledge to die out, save in tradition.

The home of these hermits, which bears the name of the son, is a tolerably wide cleft between the rocks, close by the secret road to the deep fountain. The overhanging rock forms a convenient roof, whilst the dried leaves of the *Barringtonia*[1] and other trees made a soft bed for father and son. From the extreme end they could, by moonlight, feast their eyes with a view of the fertile valley of Tevaenga, with ranges of pleasant hills in the distance. The cave is at a considerable height from the ground; the rocks being perpendicular, they were safe from surprise on that side.

They had one faithful friend—an aunt of Uriitepito-kura. She alone was in the secret of their hiding-place, and at dusk would occasionally bring a basket of cooked food, which was hoisted up by means of a long rope made of hibiscus bark. It is a wonderful thing that for the period of *four years* she should have continued to feed these fugitives without betraying her secret.

---

[1] The flowers of the *Barringtonia speciosa* are very beautiful. Its broad, glossy leaf is used for dressing wounds; the fruit, when grated, furnishes a powerful fish poison; the timber makes the best canoes.

These occasional supplies were, of course, supplemented by what they could collect in the forest. During those four weary years of exile they did not once venture into the interior.

Amongst the rocks of that part of the island there was at that time abundance of beautiful birds; two or three varieties of the pigeon; several sorts of sea-roving birds, who incubate in the stones and hollow trees of that part of the island; beside the true woodpecker and the linnet. The bird most easily caught by Uriitepitokura and Temoaakaui was the *titi* (so called from its cry). In the month of December it leaves its burrowings in the red mountain soil, and comes to the rocks near the sea to fatten its young on small fish. By day it hides in holes, and sleeps. The hunter has only to call at the entrance to the dark cave, in a plaintive voice, *E titi e*, when the foolish bird, imagining it to be the voice of its mate, comes out of its secure hiding-place, and, dazzled by the unwelcome light, allows itself to be caught by the hand. In size and colour it closely resembles the dove, but the breast is of a light yellow.

Unlike Rori, they ate[1] all they could catch, carefully collecting the best feathers in the driest part of their cave. They were in great want of warm clothing, but dared not beat out the bark of the banyan tree growing on the neighbouring rocks, for fear of being discovered by their foes in the interior. A noble substitute was at length devised—they would manufacture dresses of birds' feathers! Of feathers they had abundance; but how to work them into a dress? In the rocks of Tevaenga grow the best and

---

[1] Rori regarded these same birds as minor divinities. To one family the *land crab* was sacred, to another not. To one the *centipede*, to another not. To one the pretty blackbird was an embodiment of his god, to another the same bird was food.

longest *oronga* (*Urtica argentea*) for the manufacture of fish-nets. This nettle-tree[1] usually grows out of the very stones under the shadow of lofty trees. They stripped off a quantity of the bark, and, carefully scraping it, exposed it to the sun by day and dew by night until fit for use. The custom of the natives is to twist this fibre into twine with the palm of the hand upon the bare thigh. With this string the hermits of Tevaenga ingeniously wove together the beautiful white, green, blue, and yellow feathers of the birds they had eaten. This cloth was doubled, in form like a sheet, with a slit to admit the head of the wearer. Such a dress would be called a *tiputa* of feathers. Thus clothed, father and son could defy the cold of winter, and the frequent heavy showers of the tropics.

Two grand head-dresses were subsequently made of feathers. The shape was conical, and bore the name of *pare piki*. This was the nearest approximation to our 'crown' existing in their language. Captain Cook refers to these head-dresses of gay feathers interwoven with fine sennit.[2] The finishing touch was the insertion of a number of the long red tail-feathers of the tropic bird. Such a prize was considered to be well worth fighting for.

Rori worked in wood and stone; these fugitives excelled in the manufacture of fine and valuable fish-nets. The palm was given to the *nariki*, which is invariably six yards long and four wide. The meshes are so small that only the very tip of the finger can be admitted. Such valuable heirlooms are only used on grand occasions. The making of one such net might well occupy father and son for a whole year.

---

[1] Attains the height of eighteen feet. The fruit is like a small mulberry, but of a *white* color.

[2] Platted string of coco-nut fibre.

It is said that two *nariki* nets were completed by Uriitepitokura and his father, with the express purpose of purchasing the protection of some powerful chief. No serf dared possess such valuable property. Their commendable diligence was shown by the preparation of *five* other fine nets, of inferior value and only two yards long, called *kukuti*. They then set to work upon a coarse long net (six yards in length) known as a *tata*, and used daily in times of peace to catch larger fish. The making of all these nets, a fortune still in the eyes of a Mangaian, might well occupy two men for a period of four years.

The drum of peace had sounded, so that the fear of being clubbed to death at their first appearance in the interior was removed. But of what avail would this be without the friendship of some chief to supply them with food and a plot of land? Their surviving relatives were slaves of the conquerors, and could only pity them by stealth.

But Temoaakaui was not destined to enjoy the reward of his incessant toil ; for in the last year of their residence in the *makatea* (rocks) he sickened and died of privation and anxiety, for their supplies came no more. Ere he died he revealed to his son a plan he had devised to insure his safety. About a mile from their solitary home on the margin of the forest was the principal pathway to the beach, by which those in the interior obtained their occasional supplies of sea-water and fish. Midway lay a pile of rocks close to the narrow and rugged path where Uriitepitokura should conceal himself and watch patiently those passing, until a suitable young person should attract his notice. Two small eye-like apertures[1] in the stone

---

[1] A native of this district, accustomed with his friends to use this pathway to the beach by night for the purpose of fishing, was so irritated by the apt resemblance of the rock to human eyes that he one day borrowed a sledge-hammer and utterly demolished this natural curiosity.

would enable him to see without being himself observed. To the girl that pleased his fancy he should offer marriage, and the possession of all their accumulated treasures.

In the interior lived Akamārama, considered to be a great beauty. Her parents were very proud of her, and compelled the fair one to *noo are pana, i.e.* to live entirely inside a house specially erected for the purpose, in order to blanch her complexion and fatten her against the day when a certain grand dance should come off. The object contemplated by the parents was an eligible marriage with some young chief.

The great requisites of a Polynesian beauty are to be fat, and as fair as their dusky skins will permit. To insure this, favourite children, whether boys or girls, were regularly fattened and imprisoned till nightfall, when a little gentle exercise was permitted. If refractory, the guardian would even whip the culprit for not eating more. Songs were made in honour of the fair one on occasion of her *début*.

Now Akamārama had grown tired of this fattening process. One day she was left in the care of an easy-going old uncle. The wilful girl thought this a favourable opportunity to obtain a little liberty, though perchance at the expense of her complexion. Seizing the empty calabashes, she contrived to elude her guardian's notice, and darted through the forest by the accustomed pathway to the sea.

Here was Uriitepitokura's opportunity; for, finding her alone, he emerged from his curious hiding-place and followed the fair fat girl. Imagining that she was pursued by her uncle, she looked back, and, to her astonishment, saw a tall strange youth dressed in a magnificent *tiputa* of feathers of many colours, surmounted by a magnificent head-dress. She had never before seen anything half so fine, and was lost in admiration, whilst the young hermit in a few words told his sad history and entreated her protection. He had priceless treasures ; they should all be the property of Akamārama and her father, if she would marry him.

She returned to her home and received the scolding she deserved for thus endangering her complexion ; but Akamārama flatly refused to go on with the fattening process. Daily altercations now took place with her parents, who were amazed at the sudden change that had come over their daughter. To various suggestions of marriage from her parents she invariably turned a deaf ear. In despair they begged her to say whom she would marry —for a proposal of marriage may emanate with propriety from a woman of rank to an equal or to an inferior. She now revealed her attachment to an exile in the rocks on the outskirts of their own forest ; not forgetting to dilate on his wonderful dress of variegated feathers, and the hint of still more precious treasures of fish-nets. The astonished parents gave their entire but not unselfish consent.

To-morrow, guided by their pretty daughter, they would fetch the hermit and arrange the marriage with him. A secret visit from Akamārama told all that had so auspiciously occurred, and removed all his fears. At the time appointed, Uriitepitokura boldly showed himself to the friends of the future wife, dressed up with special care in all the finery bequeathed to him. The fugitive was nothing loth to leave his old dwelling in the cleft of the rocks for a comfortable dwelling in the interior. But first, he conducted his new friends to his eyrie to fetch the nets, and the other dress of feathers, not forgetting the wonderful conical hats.

To remove these treasures required the assistance of several strong men. At the home of Akamārama numbers had collected to see a man who had seemingly dropped down from the clouds. Uriitepitokura now formally made a presentation of the nets, etc., to the father and uncle of his bride, as an equivalent for protection and food in the future. The gift was graciously accepted, and a small return present made to him as an inferior, in token of ratification of the agreement. One or two of the nets were that same day given to the paramount chief, to secure his good-will and powerful aid in protecting the slave.

Akamārama was led by her parents to the side of the bridegroom, who wished to put on her the beautiful dress that had been prepared for the happy occasion. But she would not consent; she, however, gladly put on one of the *pare piki*, or glorious head-dresses so coveted in ancient times. They sat together on a piece of the finest whitest native cloth, to receive the presents of admiring friends to husband and wife separately. They then both partook of food, in symbol of their future union, all present rejoicing in the good things provided for the occasion. Such only was the marriage ceremony of those days. Finally, tradition asserts that Uriitepitokura and Akamārama had no reason to repent their union in after-days, although denied the greatly coveted gift of offspring.

Such is the old story connected with the well-known Cave of Uri-i-te-pito-kura, called in short To-uri.

In this cave is still hidden the god Mokoiro, *consisting merely of a small roll of sennit !* It had no human likeness whatever, and therefore found no place in the king's idol-house.

CHAPTER III

THE GIANT MOKÈ

ON the southern part of Mangaia is a small lake named Tiriara, which receives all the streams from the valleys on that side of the island. It discharges its superfluous waters into the sea through a narrow passage under the vast belt of rocks which, like a massive wall, surround the fertile portion of the island. The distance from this lake to the ocean in a straight line is about a mile. Amongst the gloomy rocks and chasms which occupy this intervening district there loves to wander, according to ancient story, a female named Tumuteanaoa, or Echo. Though rarely seen, one cannot doubt her presence, for, say what you may, Echo delights to repeat your words with singular distinctness. This rock-nymph has a numerous offspring, which have the visible form of *rats*. In later times they gave birth to the common rat which now everywhere infests the island. Tumuteanaoa is likewise the mother of fresh-water eels, shrimps, and a small delicious fish called the *kokopu*, which abounds in this little lake.

The renowned Mokè was the son of Tavarc, the profound sleeper, so named because she was in the habit of sleeping from the month of Pipiri (July) until the bread-fruit was ripe and crabs were plentiful (February).

During all these months her limbs were rigid ; but at length the fervid rays of the sun relaxed her muscles and put an end to her sleep. Her illegitimate son first saw the light at a spot called Ukuroi, in one of the most sequestered and picturesque valleys on that side of Mangaia. He was excessively small and feeble at birth, so that he was left on the greensward near the fountain-head to perish. A sudden freshet swept him from his native valley to the lake, and bore him right under the rocks, where in semi-darkness, and unknown to all beside, Echo fed this waif on frothy bubbles collected from the little eddies on the surface of the lake. Mokè grew apace under this careful nurture. At length he was permitted to drift on with the waters of the lake through the unexplored fissures and caves until he reached the sea. A slight hollow in the rocks near the reef is still known as the Cave of Tavare. Here the profound sleeper happened to be resting one day after fishing, when she joyfully recognized her now noble boy fearlessly drifting out into the main ocean. She rushed to detain Mokè, and, after swimming a considerable distance, succeeded in bringing him ashore to her temporary abode. In this cave by the shore she fed him bountifully with fish, and other substantial food, until he grew up to be a man of gigantic proportions, actually attaining the height of sixty feet !

He now made his way into the interior of the island, and astonished his countrymen, hitherto unaware of his existence, with many proofs of his enormous strength and bravery. On the western shore, on the sandstone rock, often washed by the sea, are two hollows in the shape of a man's foot, designated 'the Footprints of Mokè.' They are half a mile apart. The left footprint is two feet eight

inches in length ; width of heel nine inches, the broadest
part being sixteen inches.   The right footprint is somewhat
smaller.

One memorable day a fleet of double canoes arrived
from Rarotonga, with no less than two hundred warriors
on board, led on by the brave Kateateoru.   The place
where they landed is in a straight line from Rarotonga,
and is named Avarua, because these formidable visitors
started from a part of Rarotonga so named.   The
Rarotongan warriors lived peacefully enough at first, but
eventually enraged Mokè by the murder of Tepuvai, the
third king of Mangaia.   The giant resolved upon obtaining
revenge, but for the present concealed his purpose.   Under
the guise of friendship Mokè induced the strangers to
visit the south of the island, where he lived.   They did
so ; and, led by their favourite the giant, they made their
way to the neighbourhood of the lake, of course helping
themselves to all the food they could find.   Not the
slightest opposition was offered to their rather unceremonious proceedings.   On a hill overlooking the lake was
the dwelling of Mokè ; and farther on lay the district of
Tamarua, where he resolved to fight the invaders.   On
the morning of the fatal day he selected two beautiful
ariri shells (*Turbo petholatus*), one for himself, and one for
his adversary Kateateoru.   Secret instructions were given
for his forces to hide themselves in a certain spot at
Tamarua.   The narrow pathways between the deep *taro*
swamps were obliterated.   This done, Mokè returned to
look at his shells : to his joy, the one representing his foes
was turned upside down.   He interpreted this as a sure
omen of their destruction.   He forthwith went after the
Rarotongans, who had no idea that he was playing them
false.   Apparently they had little to fear, seeing that the

giant was quite alone, and carried only a stout walking-stick. He led them in a very friendly way to Tamarua, so that the visitors might enjoy the good things of that district. In a short time they scattered themselves all over the broad and fertile valley, climbing coco-nut trees along the edge of the *taro* swamps. While thus employed the whole male population of the island rushed out from their ambush, and speared their visitors without mercy. In attempting to escape from the morass, numbers sunk up to the middle, or deeper still, and were picked off by their foes. Under such circumstances the utmost bravery could effect but little. Mokè killed all who attempted to return by floundering through the swamps, hoping to gain *terra firma*. The stout walking-stick of the giant proved to be a truly formidable weapon. Some assert that it was in fact Timapere, 'the whisker-away,' whose blows were ever fatal. Be that as it may, twenty Mangaians fell that day ; whilst, of the two hundred Rarotongan warriors who landed on these shores, only one escaped with his life. Kateatcoru was expressly spared, in order that he might convey to his native land the fame of Mokè.

A great double canoe sailed back to Rarotonga with a fair wind, with Kateatcoru as the only voyager. Great was the grief and indignation of his countrymen upon learning the tragical fate of the warriors. Immediate preparations were made for a second descent upon Mangaia.

Nor was Mokè idle. Certain that so brave a race as the Rarotongans would speedily return, in order to be revenged for the slaughter of their friends, he built a fortification consisting of rough stones, 162 feet in length, on the hill opposite to the ancient landing-place. Every bush near the edge of the cliff was cut down, so that the expected invaders might see that Mokè was not unprepared for the contest.   The giant next lopped off the tops of the dense growth of ironwood trees which at that time covered the sandy beach.   Their bare limbs, reduced to the height of ordinary men, were carefully wound round and round with native cloth, so as to give the appearance of human heads.   On the short lateral branches long native dresses were suspended ; spears were carefully poised, as if in human hands ; so that at a little distance there seemed to be on the beach, close to the landing-place, a strong army drawn up in battle array.   Not a leaf was permitted to grow up, to prevent the full effect of this harmless demonstration.   The reason for it seems to have been that in ancient times the population of this island was far inferior to that of Rarotonga ; so that in a fair fight they would have been utterly unable to repel the invaders.

At length the Rarotongan fleet of war canoes hove in sight.   Kateateoru acted as pilot ; but the famous Teuaopokere, full thirty feet in height, was their leader and chief warrior.   Upon approaching the place of de-barkation, they were greatly daunted by the sight of the fortification, and especially at the seemingly formidable army drawn up to oppose their landing.   Behind the sham warriors there was a small band of veritable combatants. But Moke could nowhere be seen.   Teuaopokere at first felt excessively mortified at the non-appearance of the giant he had come so far (120 miles) to destroy in single combat.

All this time Moke concealed his enormous person by standing in the ocean near the landing-place, where the water is many fathoms deep.   His long locks floated in the breakers ; a large pearl oyster-shell concealed his face. At last the pilot caught sight of the head of the hidden warrior, and bade him show himself to Teuaopokere.

Mokè shouted, 'Let t he great Rarotongan chief first show himself!' which he willingly did, standing well armed on the deck of his great canoe, full thirty feet high! Mokè now slowly emerged from his briny hiding-place, and stepped on a projecting point of the reef, holding an enormous stone in his right hand. To the eyes of the terrified invaders his gigantic form seemed to pierce the skies, being twice the height of Teuaopokere. Without a moment's delay the invading fleet turned their canoes, and sailed straight back to Rarotonga. To hasten their flight, the giant Mokè hastily broke off three points of rock, and hurled them after the retreating fleet. They fell short of the mark on the reef with the noise of thunder, causing the entire island to tremble.

These legendary stones are pointed out on the reef, each standing about a mile apart, and weighing about twenty tons apiece! As one might suppose, Mangaia was never again troubled with warlike visitors from the sister island. Mokè is said to have charged Amu, the fourth king, to despatch all strangers on landing.

On the eastern part of the island, close by the scene of the slaughter of the Rarotongans, is a strong but rough wall, also built by the giant. In front, towards the interior, is a beautiful piece of rising ground, very gently undulating, and terminating in a grassy knoll. It is fabled that the giant lies buried, face downwards, here, close to the scene of his signal victory, the undulations of the soil exactly corresponding with the natural curve of his back.

Such is the wild story of Mokè. That a brave and gigantic man of that name once lived and repelled a formidable band of Rarotongan warriors is borne out by the traditions of the sister island. In fact, they assert that his notable device to augment the slender ranks of his army was afterwards imitated at Rarotonga.   One of Iro's party of exiles, named Auau, married into the Makea clan, and told them how Mokè had once frightened away a superior invading force.   The story of Iro is related in a subsequent chapter.   In the reigning family at Rarotonga the memorial name Takau,[1] *i.e.* twenty, is still kept up, with reference to the number slain by *their* warriors.   In a similar way the feats of the Mangaians were commemorated by the name Te-upoku-rau, *i.e.* 'the two hundred heads.'   Each generation of admiring Mangaians doubtless added some new marvel to this famous warrior of remote times.

Opposite to one of his fortifications is a wall.   The intervening space of seven feet four inches is said to be an accurate measurement of the breadth of the shoulders of the giant !

Mokè was the third warrior chief of Mangaia ; he flourished about four hundred years ago.

---

[1] The present Queen of Rarotonga is Makea *Takau*.   Makea is merely a hereditary title (like Pharaoh, Candace, etc.) ; the true name is Takau.   See frontispiece.

CHAPTER IV

THE TWIN KITES

In 1865 I visited for the first time the pretty island of Mauke, about one hundred miles to the north of Mangaia. A chief and a deacon who accompanied me were well feasted and most kindly treated by the Mauke people. An aged man, who said that he was a native of Atiu, inquired of the visitors whether they had ever heard of Akatereariki. The deacon replied that he had heard of his visit to Mangaia in the olden time ; adding, the land which once belonged to his famous Mangaian wife was now his. The deacon forthwith chanted an ancient song in praise of Akatereariki, to the astonishment and delight of all present. As the song proceeded the old Atiuan wept freely, saying that, though now naturalized at Mangaia, it was originally derived from Atiu, and referred to *his* ancestors. Upon our return to Mangaia I wrote down the song from the lips of the deacon.

The song refers to *kite-flying*. In times of peace this was the great delight of aged men. Kites were usually five feet in length, covered with native cloth, on which were the devices appropriate to their tribe—a sort of heraldry. The tail[1] was twenty fathoms in length, ornamented with a bunch of feathers and abundance of

---

[1] The *long* tails had six bunches of leaves, to correspond with the number of the Pleiades. *Short*-tailed kites had but four, in imitation of the constellation Piriereua.

sere *ti* leaves.	Parties were got up of not less than ten kite-flyers ; the point of honour being that the kite should fly high, and be lost to view in the clouds.	Songs made for the occasion were chanted meantime.	It was no uncommon event for them to sleep on the mountain, after well securing the kites to the trees.	Of course the upshot of all this would be a grand feast, in which the victor got the biggest share.	So serious was this employment that each kite bore its own name, and tears of joy were shed by these grey-bearded children as they witnessed the successful flight.	When desirous at length of putting an end to their sport, if the wind were too strong to allow the string to be pulled in, it was customary to fill a little basket with mountain fern or grass, and whirl it along the string.	The strong trade winds would speedily convey this 'messenger' to the kite, which then slowly descended to the earth.

Children's kites were, and still are, extemporized out of the leaves of the gigantic chestnut tree.	Sometimes one sees a boy (no longer grandfathers) flying a properly-made kite.

Akē, a chief of Atiu, was famous for his kite-flying ; no kite in all the island could compare with his.	On one occasion, when a strong north wind was blowing, he let go his 'twin kites,' which bore the name of 'The Sorrowful Ones.'	A huge basket of stout string was exhausted ; the kites were the admiration of crowds of spectators, when unfortunately the string broke, and the kites were lost.	Akē, knowing that the wind was favourable for Auau (Mangaia), remarked to his son Akatereariki that in all likelihood his favourite 'twin kites' would reach that island.	The son of Akē at once prepared his *titira*, or double canoe, to sail to Auau in search of the lost kites.	With a good supply of coco-nuts for food and water, and attended by a number of Akē's vassals, he set off on his voyage. In a couple of nights Akatereariki made Auau, and landed opposite to the *marae* of Rongo, on the western part of the island. He inquired whether any one had seen 'the twin kites of Akē.' The Mangaians said that a pair of foreign kites had recently come ashore on the east of the island, exciting great interest, as coming from another land. Akatereariki went to look at them, and found that they were indeed his father's famous kites.

The real object of his visit to Mangaia was to get a handsome wife, under guise of kite-seeking. The prettiest woman on the island at that time was Matakore, only daughter of Tiaio, supreme temporal and spiritual sovereign, whose principal residence was in the sacred district of Keia. Akatereariki was deeply smitten by her charms, but could obtain no response. Nor was he the only suitor for the hand of the lovely girl. The famous Tairiiterangi had sailed in his big canoe from Rarotonga to fetch her as his wife, but she would not deign him a smile. It was known that he had gone back with his friends in order to seek enchantments and love charms to enable him to win the obdurate Matakore.

Tiaio did not permit strangers to enter his dwelling. But one evening, when the doors were secured, and the candle-nut torches of the supreme chief cheerfully burning inside, the crafty admirer of Matakore hid himself under the eaves of the thatch, and softly recited or chanted the subjoined song. The astonished girl was greatly delighted, and coaxed her father to open the door and allow the musical stranger to come in. Tiaio that night feasted Akatereariki, who at length avowed his love to Matakore, and entreated the consent of her parents.

Akatereariki's suit was successful; the beautiful girl

became his wife. After some time Akatereariki intimated to Tiaio his wish to return to Atiu with his wife. The supreme chief consented, but his brother, Pukenga, was violently opposed to their going. But go they did, and that by way of Rarotonga. When about half way to Rarotonga they fell in with a great decked double canoe, bound to Mangaia. It was Tairiiterangi and his warrior friends, about to solicit for a second time the hand of the fair Matakore.

The canoes were laid alongside of each other. As soon as Tairiiterangi saw the lovely girl quietly sitting behind her husband, he became mad with anger. A fight ensued. The Rarotongans slew Akatereariki and most of his companions—even Matakore perished. The bodies of the slain were thrown to the sharks, excepting the unfortunate bride. Ere long the great canoe of Tairiiterangi sailed into the harbour of Ngatangiia ; the body of Matakore was carefully anointed with oil, and kept on one of the *maraes*.

Those spared by the victorious Tairiiterangi succeeded in getting back to their homes in Mangaia, and told the sad tale of the death of Matakore and her husband and others. Burning for revenge, her uncle Pukenga, a man of great strength, with a number of his followers, set sail for Rarotonga. Landing at Ngatangiia, he marched straight up to the *marae* where the body lay exposed, and bewailed the unhappy end of his pretty niece, without any active opposition on the part of the Rarotongans. The corpse was now enveloped in a *paoa*, or sort of mourning used only for the best-beloved.

Pukenga publicly challenged Tairiiterangi to compete with him in a race. The challenge of the Mangaian chief was accepted, and a long plot of ground was cleared for the purpose. Numbers assembled to witness the race. Four times they ran the entire distance, when Tairiiterangi was completely exhausted, and lay panting on the ground. Pukenga continued to run alone without any apparent sign of weariness. After having for the eighth time traversed the whole distance with seeming ease, to the amazement of all, he suddenly seized his club, and with one blow dashed out the brains of Tairiiterangi.

Pukenga and his party succeeded in making good their retreat to their canoe, and even carried off the body of his beloved niece. They eventually reached Mangaia in safety. But from that day it became customary to murder all visitors touching the reef. The fierce hostility towards strangers which was manifested in 1823, when the Rev. J. Williams first endeavoured to land Christian teachers, is attributed to the battles in the time of Mokè, two generations prior to the death of Matakore, and to the contests with Tairiiterangi.

When referring to any one of unusual strength, it is to this day usually said, *Pukenga oai e ngi ai raua?* ('Who can compare with Pukenga?')

Tiaio reigned about 360 years ago ; he was the fifth sovereign of Mangaia.

The father of Matakore is the Tiaio who was clubbed to death for wearing in his ears the flower of the scarlet *Hibiscus* in front of the *marae* of Motoro, and was afterwards deified, and associated with Motoro in worship. Tiaio was believed to be enshrined in the eel, and especially in the shark.

THE SONG OF THE TWIN KITES.

Adapted by Paī, circa A.D. 1770.

Tumu.	Introduction.
Kua rere te pa manu naau, e Akē, No nunga i Atiu, Ei akaariki i to tere ē ! Te ui tōkere i tangi reka ē !	Thy kites, O Akē, have sped their flight Far away from Atiu. Thine is a peaceful errand. How softly sounds that drum !

PAPA.

Tangi reka mai, e reira e,
   O te pau i karavau
   Na Akatereariki.
   Naai e rutu ē?
Na te mana o Manii kake mai ei?

FOUNDATION.

Ah! soft indeed its notes;
The drum which ever sounds
   Is Akatereariki's.
   Who shall beat it?
Who has the skill of Manii[1] to
   attempt it?

UNUUNU TAI.

I rere, i rere ki te matangi ē!
I te matangi o te pa manu a Rongo,
  O te pa manu a Rongo ai,
   Ko te manu i rakei,
   Ko te kiakiato rai,
  Ei moenga i ka oro ei.
O te taupiri tau ki te manu ē!
Te ui tōkere i tangi reka ē!

FIRST OFFSHOOT.

They sped, they sped on the wind.
The winds favoured the kites[2] of
   Rongo;
Those beautiful kites of Rongo;—
   Kites gaily decked out,
   Strengthened on the back,
   And covered with devices;—they
   fly!
Wonderful tails have those kites.
How softly sounds that drum!

UNUUNU RUA.

Turua te manu o tai enua ē!
   O tai enua' i!
Kua piri te arorangi o tai enua;
   Kua piri te arorangi.
Taku manu, taku manu,
Miria e te matangi, parea e te
  matangi.
   Kua motu paa i Ruaunga.
  'Mata-ruerue' nga tama ē!
O te taupiri tau ki te manu ē!
Te ui tōkere i tangi reka ē!

SECOND OFFSHOOT.

A second time thy kites reached other
   lands;
   Ah, distant lands!
A strange horizon has encompassed
  them.
   Clouds hide them from view.
Alas! my kites, my kites, ill-treated
And hurried far away by the winds,
May fall perchance on Mangaia![3]
Ye 'sorrowful children'[4] of mine!
Wonderful tails have those kites.
How softly sounds that drum!

AKAREINGA.

Ai e ruaoo ē! E rangai ē!

FINALE.

Ai e ruaoo ē! E rangai ē![5]

---

[1] Manii, an Atiuan chief slain in Mangaia because he would not part with his beautiful breast ornament. The spot where he fell is a place of pilgrimage even now to his countrymen; it is called Matatia.

[2] Rongo presided over peace and war, the dead, and *kite-flying*.

[3] I have substituted the name of the island for that of the particular spot where it is pretended that the kites fell, after coming a hundred miles.

[4] The name of these 'twin' kites; they are regarded as the '*children*' of Akē. The tragic fate of Matakore is doubtless a fact. It is universally believed to be such by the natives. The song, in its original form, must be over 340 years old.

[5] Meaningless, like our 'Fal, lal, lal.'

CHAPTER V

WEEDING BY MOONLIGHT

THE Tekama clan anciently dwelt at Karanga, on the north-east of Mangaia. They originally came from Vaiiria, an inland district of Tahiti. The first resting-place of these fugitives was Atiu; but, being expelled that island, they sailed for Mangaia, where they were well received. Marrying women of the island, they ultimately became formidable in point of numbers. At last they devised a notable expedient for obtaining possession of the entire island.

Close to the frowning rocks, some hundreds of feet high, was a large taro[1] patch called Puamātā. It should be weeded, and the weeding should be done by moonlight —a favourite time with the natives on account of the delicious coolness after a sultry day. The leading men of the different districts were invited to assist. None refused the invitation, as it was announced that a great feast was in preparation, and no native neglects to attend to eating and drinking.

The preparation for the feast went on day by day; but it afterwards transpired that the fish was secretly devoured by the Tekama tribe, pieces of green wood instead being cut into the shape of fish, well wrapped up in leaves, and ostentatiously baked in the oven. So, too, of native puddings, usually made of banana, taro, and coco-nut.

---

[1] Taro (*caladium petiolatum*) is usually planted in swamps. It is a most nutritious root; far superior to our potato. The leaves, when cooked, taste like spinach.

Hundreds of new coco-nut-leaf baskets were plaited, to enable the guests the more conveniently to carry away their respective divisions of food. Such a feast had not yet been seen.

On the appointed beautiful moonlight night the visitors from the different districts slowly assembled for the proposed weeding. But the real purpose of the Tekama was a very different one, each individual being secretly armed with a light club or a small war-axe easily hidden in the dress. When the first party of six or eight made their appearance the men of the Tekama clan feigned to be diligently weeding. Under the pretence of a cordial greeting they went through the *reru tāki*, or frightful Mangaian war-dance, in which the performers leap wildly into the air, slay imaginary foes, and wind up with a wild prolonged yell. In doing this they contrived to surround their guests, and then, without the slightest warning, dealt them death-blows on the head. The screams of the victims were lost in the prolonged final yell of the war-dance.

In this novel fashion, under the mask of warm friendship, several arrivals were entirely disposed of. It is believed that a great number were killed that night. The slain were either hastily covered with the long grass of the taro patch, or summarily trodden down in the mire.

Unluckily for the murderers, as one party arrived within a hundred yards of the tragic scene, a bit of rising ground concealing them from the sight of the Tekama, they distinctly heard a death-shriek after the cessation of the war-dance. They immediately turned back and fled to their homes, everywhere spreading the news of the treachery of the Tekama.

Next day the surviving male population of the island under Tirango assembled to avenge the death of their friends. They did not find the Tekama unprepared for battle. The spot chosen by them is excellent for the purpose of defence. On either side of their entrenchments were miry taro patches. At the back is the narrow path for flight to the desolate rocks, where they would be safe for a while, if defeated. But despite these natural advantages the Tekama were routed in this fight, known as the Battle of Rangiue. In their flight to the rocks they threw aside all their valuable ironwood weapons. The first anxiety of their chief, upon collecting his now broken clan for a second engagement some time afterwards, was to provide a new supply of spears and clubs. Unable to obtain ironwood of the requisite size and length, they cut down *māriri* trees, spears made from which are as sharp-pointed as the best ironwood, but exceedingly brittle. This great undertaking accomplished, they gave battle again at Putoa, but lost great numbers, on account of the bad quality of their weapons.

Once more the scattered remnants of the fallen tribe made a desperate stand. This time it was at Maungarua ; the attacking party divided themselves into two companies, so that, whilst the fragment of the Tekama was engaged in front, the others, taking an apparently impracticable path, attacked the bewildered foe in the rear. Thus there was no chance whatever of escape. Almost every male of the tribe was slain, the women being, according to custom, reserved for the victors. Thus the famous weeding, with which the name Tekama is indelibly associated in the Mangaian mind, became the cause of the speedy and utter destruction of the clan.

The bodies of those treacherously slain by the Tekama were allowed to rot in the mud of the taro patch. The one great taro patch now forms two, and is kept well planted, as though it had never been a graveyard. But the natives of that district superstitiously believe that at the full moon, when the unsuspecting guests were slain and sunk there, the water assumes a blood-red appearance! At my visit I noticed a quantity of curious grass with a deep red tint. My aged guide remarked that this grass grows rankly only where human blood has been shed! Since. that day I have seen abundance of the same sort of grass in various parts of the island where no such crime as *te tauna i Puamātā* ('the slaughter at Puamātā') was ever committed.

The date fixed for these events by the most intelligent natives is the period immediately preceding the first *umu Aitu* for the extirpation of the worshippers of Tanè, which would be about three hundred and twenty years ago.

It is said that one or two young children survived the destruction of the tribe, and amalgamated with their mothers' clan, the Tongans.

The following extract from the war-dirge in honour of Tuopapa (*circa* A.D. 1790) refers to this moonlight weeding, and to the two ovens for the destruction of the Aitu :—

Pokia, e Tanè-kai-ai, te tāuna i Puamātā,	Alas for Tanè-devoured-of-fire; and those at Puamātā,
Pokia, pokia, pokia e! Era tokovaru!	Caught, slain, and buried in the mud, eight at a time!
Kua pau ua te tāuna o Tekama I te umu Aitu.	Hence the overthrow of the Tekama. Weep for the fiery ovens!
Takina, e Tongaiti, te vairakau, A ngaa te kano i te kava. A mate! a mate!! Rumakina e! Era tokoiva!	Lead on, brave Tongan,[1] thy warriors. Break through the centre of the enemy. Death to you! death to you!! Hurl them in, nine at a time!
Kua pau ua te tauna o Tiroa I te umu Aitu.	The entire tribe of Tiroa[2] has perished In those fearful ovens.

---

[1] Tiranga, the leader of the attack in the battle on the following day. For his bravery he was afterwards declared temporal 'lord of Mangaia.'

[2] Priest of Tanè Ngakiau, offered in sacrifice to Rongo about the time when the tribe to which he ministered was thrown 'nine at a time' to the flames.

It was evidently believed in 1790 that the destruction of the Tekama and the fiery ovens were events not far apart.

CHAPTER VI

TWO MEMORABLE OVENS

ON a gentle slope at Putoa, on the east of Mangaia, just where the mountain fern—that unerring token of barrenness—gives place to coarse long grass, and almost under the shadow of the high rocks, is a circular hollow, now only thirty-four feet across and comparatively shallow. It has evidently been the work of man in some former age. Tradition says this hollow was once of great extent and depth, but successive displacements of clay and stones from the neighbouring hills during the heavy floods of summer have well-nigh filled it up. In 1854 a rainstorm of terrific violence brought down a vast quantity of *débris* upon the lower and fertile grounds in that entire district, almost depriving many families of the means of subsistence.

At first sight an individual accustomed to South Sea Island life would pronounce this to be a monstrous oven for baking the *ti* root (*Cordyline terminalis*). But on closer investigation this would seem incredible, as no *ti* ovens were ever half so large as this must originally have been. The real purpose for which this vast hole was dug is a topic of unfailing interest to every Mangaian.

The Aitu or god tribe was, as we have seen, almost extinguished at the Big Cave, for speaking ill of the king Tama-tapu. In the battle which followed, most of their connections and friends perished. And yet in a few generations afterwards the Aitu tribe reappears in history. Possibly a few escaped the hand of Matataukiu, by not sleeping at the Big Cave.   But the received explanation is that six canoes full of the worshippers of the same god drifted here from Iti (Tahiti).   Thus this tribe again grew really formidable for numbers, and spread themselves all over Putoa and the contiguous district of Ivirua.

The god of this tribe was Tanè ; but there were many Tanès or lesser divinities included under that name. Nevertheless all worshippers of Tanè were regarded as forming one great tribe.

These driftaways from Iti, whose names are preserved, brought no wives with them, but intermarried with the older families on the island.   So strong did they feel themselves to be that Pauteanua resolved to set up a grand *marae* shaded by a noble grove of trees at Ivirua. The site of the grand *marae* was well chosen, being on rising ground overlooking the fertile valley.   The *marae* itself—the best-built on the island—was 100 feet long and 25 feet broad.   It is now in ruins, and planted with paper mulberry (*Broussonetia papyrifera*), for the manufacture of native cloth.   Great stones are buried deep in the soil, three feet, however, being exposed to view on all sides.   In all other *maraes* the centre is filled with earth, a thick layer of snow-white pebbles covering the whole.   But the ' god tribe ' resolved that this should excel all other *maraes;* they therefore *determined to fill Maputū* (as it is called) *with human heads cut off for the purpose !* and this they did !

Revenge for the many cruelties practised upon their tribe was doubtless the motive for this bloody consecration. Night attacks were made upon the older settlers, for the purpose of securing a number of heads.

Coco-nuts are tied together by fours, for the convenience of carrying.   A man usually carries two or three such bundles on one end of an old spear, and an equal number on the other. The Aitu tribe substituted human heads reeking with blood, tying them together by the hair. Entire families were slain when assembled at their evening meal. Hence the proverb, ' Hasten our meal, or the Aitu will be upon us, bringing terror, chilliness, and death.' Hence the custom [1] of eating the evening meal *before* the setting of the sun, to avoid a surprise.

The *marae* was at last filled up ; a covering of earth was laid on the human heads ; sea-pebbles (still traceable) ornamented the surface ; and the whole was dedicated to Tanè-ngaki-au (Tanè-striving-for-power).

The Aitu had triumphed ; but the relatives of the murdered did *not* forget what had occurred. Several years elapsed ere they dared to wreak their vengeance upon the wrong-doers. The mode of revenge adopted was novel and fearful.

In the dry season (from July to December) taro [2] roots are scarce. In the olden times these islanders subsisted on old coco-nuts and wild yams during these months. But nuts alone are too rich, so that it became customary to dig up roots of *ti*.[3] These roots were cooked in great ovens dug for the purpose, and afterwards kept in store for the winter months to eat with hard coco-nuts. *Ti* is remarkably sweet and agreeable to the European palate.

The chief of the primitive tribe of Ngariki at that time (*circa* A.D. 1620) was Ungakute, who announced an extraordinary oven of *ti*. It was dug in the midst of the little homesteads of the Aitu clan, on the boundary line dividing Tamarua from Ivirua, the original settlement made by their ancestors. The *ti* tree was usually planted in avenues near their dwellings, so as to be ready for cooking whenever the chiefs might give the welcome order to their people.

---

[1] They now eat by lamp-light.   [2] *Caladium petiolatum.*
[3] *Cordyline terminalis.*

Ungakute's oven was professedly for *all Mangaia*, in place of the twenty or thirty ovens usually prepared. The proper parties to dig and get ready ovens of this sort were the Aitu clan, as the original Tanè was Tanè-papa-kai = 'Tanè-giver-of-food,' and under his wing all subsequent Tanès took refuge. On a given day great logs of firewood and firestones were collected. Next morning an enormous hole or oven was dug. All being ready, on the third day a great crowd of men, women, and children came bearing great uncooked *ti* roots. The firewood was at a given signal carefully piled up so as completely to fill the hollow ; and on the top enormous stones of black basalt were laid, so as to cover the whole. The wood was now lighted in different places, and speedily the whole was in a fierce blaze. When the wood (more than half of which was green) was burnt out, the firestones, now red-hot, sunk to the centre of the deep hollow. Now was the moment of danger, when the bravest and most adept selected long *green* branches of the chestnut with a hook at the end, in order to pull these heated stones into proper order, so as to form, in fact, a red-hot pavement, on which the *ti* roots might be thoroughly and equally baked. This dangerous feat accomplished, laminæ stripped off banana stalks with abundance of the juiciest leaves were thickly strewed over these glowing stones. Green limbs of trees were then laid over the oven, to enable men carefully to pack the roots without burning their feet. As the oven was filled with *ti*, these sticks were gradually withdrawn.

In packing these roots the least valuable part is placed downwards, the slender juicy tops upwards. Each person ties something on his own half-dozen or more big roots, so that there may be no confusion when the oven is opened. The roots require to be packed closely, to prevent heat from escaping upwards. When the oven is at last completely filled up with *ti*, the biggest roots being in the centre, the whole is covered over with a vast quantity of leaves. Finally the oven is covered in with earth to the depth of three feet. A large oven requires two whole days and nights for the contents to get thoroughly done. Upon opening the oven, each person is careful to take only his own bundle of *ti* roots. This is, strictly speaking, a steaming oven—the very best mode of cooking this sort of food. The process, however, is very laborious ; hence *ti* ovens were made only by order of the chiefs.

The foregoing is a description of an ordinary *ti* oven. But Ungakute intended that his should be of a very different character. The greater portion of the Aitu clan attended, and, as in duty bound, lent their aid in digging the oven, it being a time of peace. The only possible ground of suspicion was the gigantic proportions of this oven, the smoke of which, according to the tribal songs, 'blackened the entire heavens.' As soon as the tremendous fire lessened, the Aitu and others approached the edge of the oven with long green hooked sticks, apparently ready at the giving of the word to arrange the firestones in order.

Ungakute shouted in stentorian tones, *Ka uru te umu !* = 'Rake the oven !' At this each member of the devoted tribe found himself suddenly seized by his neighbour, and hurled down into the deep oven, lurid with red-hot charcoal and stones ! Two of them in falling succeeded in dragging down each his man. *But none of those who fell ever got up again ;* for those who had planned this fearful tragedy had taken care to have at hand the heavy ironwood spades used the day previously in digging the oven, and kept professedly for the purpose of closing it over with earth, in reality in order to force back into the burning mass below those who might struggle to get up the sides. Even the half-grown lads belonging to the Aitu tribe were hurled into the oven, and perished miserably with their parents. The bodies of this unhappy tribe were left to be totally consumed in the fire of this memorable oven, which was of course at once abandoned.

The wives and mothers of the dead fled in horror to the rocks, and remained there until some few months afterwards, when the drum of peace was beaten. Several Aitu who were not present at the dreadful oven survived this wholesale destruction of their tribe. The sovereignty of the island reverted to the original clan of Ngariki, Ungakute being formally declared 'temporal lord of Mangaia.' The remnants of the 'god' tribe became slaves to those who had cooked their nearest relatives.

Most incredible does it seem that in a subsequent age, when the remnants of the Aitu clan had again increased in numbers, this trick should have been successfully repeated. *Yet such was the case* (*circa* A.D. 1660). No new offence had been given ; but the *marae*, filled up with the heads of their ancestors, had not yet been forgiven. Nothing but the utter extinction of this Aitu tribe would satisfy the malice of the clan who boasted to have sprung out of the shades.

The leading chief amongst this dominant tribe, the worshippers of Motoro, was Kaveutu, who emulated the fame of Ungakute. This time the oven was dug at the foot of a hill near the rocks on the north of the island. This wild and desolate neighbourhood is called Angaitu. As the crest of the hills is further removed, this second oven is much larger than that at Putoa, being more recent, and from its position less liable to be filled up with stones and clay. At the present time it is forty-eight feet across, quite round, and much deeper than the older one.

Like that at Putoa, it is said to have been originally much larger and deeper. This second oven was also dug at a boundary line, dividing Tevaenga from Karanga. Again the services of the ill-fated tribe were called into requisition to dig another monstrous oven to their own destruction. In all respects the second catastrophe was similar to the first, except that in the latter instance none of the dominant tribe perished with their victims. Moreover Kaveutu and his friends so arranged their plans that nearly all the ramifications of the doomed tribe worshipping Tanè perished in the flames, women and children included.

As Koroa sang in modern times (A.D. 1817)—

Te umu Aitu, na veravera o Iti ra ē !	The flaming ovens devoured the Aitu ;
Te umu Aitu, na veravera o Iti.	The flaming ovens devoured those from Iti.

The known survivors were the priest Tepunga, Tevaki, and Teko, wife of the famous Mautara. Kaveutu was proud of having become in his turn despotic temporal sovereign, and especially proud of having wreaked full vengeance on the defenceless remnants of the Aitu.

To this day these gaping holes in the clayey soil are known as *nga umu Aitu* = 'ovens for the Aitu tribe.' Truly the heathen are 'hateful and hating each other.'

At the 'death-talk' of Arokapiti (A.D. 1817), Koroa recited a song (his own), of which I give a verse :—

Mani nga toa o te Aitu ;	Hail to (the memory of) the warriors
O te Aitu, ei kaunio ia Maputū	of the Aitu tribe,
I te kapua anga mai,	Who filled up the marae of Maputu
O nga kapu o Tetuma ē !	Against the day of its dedication !
E aaki mai nga ponga ē !	What rows of human heads !—
Kua tae oki i te tuuri karaii[1]	A crime ne'er to be forgiven,
E te tatakanini.	For which men, women, and children
Kua piri ake, e Tevaki e, ei Putuputu, kiau	Were in after-days exterminated.
	None were saved but Tevaki,
Eiaa ra o te ata kura i iti ē !	Who worshipped the red light in the east.

---

[1] *Tuuri karaii* = turning up stones under which little crabs (serfs) hide—extermination.

i.e.

CHAPTER VII

THE EXPELLED GOD

CIRCA A.D. 1660

IN the interval between the vast ovens by which the Aitu tribe was consumed, the priest Ue landed at Karanga, on the north-east part of the island. He came to Mangaia in a double canoe, professedly in search of his god Tanè. His original home was on the eastern side of Taiarapu, the peninsula forming the southern part of Tahiti, where Tanè was once worshipped, but was ignominiously expelled on account of his 'man-devouring' propensities—*i.e.* great numbers of persons wasted away in consequence of his anger. Tanè was known by the appellation of *the yellow-toothed god—yellow with eating mankind!*

The sacred sennit, or finely-plaited coco-nut fibre, was the supposed shrine of this ferocious deity. A strong feeling of opposition having arisen to the worship of Tanè at Tahiti, the priest carefully hid the unpopular god in an empty coco-nut shell, securely plugged the tiny aperture, and threw it into the sea, adjuring Tanè to seek a new home in some distant land.

After a few weeks the sorrowing priest resolved to abandon his ancestral lands, and go in search of the expelled god. Launching his canoe and spreading the mat sail, Ue started off on his eventful voyage with a steady trade breeze. He touched at several islands on his way, without hearing anything of Tanè hidden in an empty calabash. At last reaching Auau (Mangaia), he resolved to rest himself awhile after a voyage of some four hundred miles.

Ue's first care was to set up a *marae* to Tanè at a spot about a mile from where he first set foot on the soil. Noticing, however, that the planet Anui, 'Tanè's eye,' *i.e.* the morning star, rose a little on one side of *marae*, Ue was dissatisfied. He sought carefully for a new site, eventually fixing upon the slope of a hill, now covered with coco-nut trees, known as Maungaroa, due east. Here the anxious priest built a new *marae* to his expelled divinity, and was delighted to find that 'Tanè's eye' rose directly over it, just as had been the case at his old *marae* at Taiarapu.

Ue now started off to the place where he had originally landed, with a large scoop-net to get fish for the dedication of his new *marae*. After the most diligent fishing he obtained only a minnow. Advancing, however, towards the due east part of the reef in a straight line with Maungaroa in the interior, when despairing of his errand, he noticed something floating towards him on the sea. It proved to be merely a coco-nut-shell well stopped. On opening it he heard a chirp ; it was his long-lost god Tanè, who henceforth was known as Tanè-kio, or 'Tanè-the-chirper.'[1]

The delighted priest at once carried off the coco-nut-shell and the still imprisoned god to his subsequently famous *marae*, and carefully deposited his new-found treasure there. Tanè, an outcast from Tahiti, and long a

---

[1] The Revised Version of Isaiah viii. 19 uses the word 'chirp'—the exact equivalent of the *kio-kio* of the Rarotongan version. The heathen priests were most skilful ventriloquists.

waif on the illimitable ocean, had found a new and congenial home!

But the troubles of Ue were not over. When all was completed, he found that the older driftaways from Iti (Tahiti), who worshipped Tanè-ngaki-au (Tanè-striving-for-power), looked upon this new Tanè and his temple with no favour. *Their* great *marae* at Maputū had been solemnly dedicated with human heads recking with blood —the new *marae* with a minnow, and a coco-nut-shell containing only a bit of sennit! As for the alleged 'chirping,' who but Ue and his insignificant clique had ever heard it?

Ue desired to settle down in the neighbourhood of his god; but the land thereabouts had long ago been all parcelled out amongst the older settlers. Eventually the worshippers of Tanè-striving-for-power drove the unfortunate priest to seek refuge on the margin of the sea, at a most sterile and desolate spot near the hiding-place of Rori in later times. Almost dying of hunger in this most barren place, where scarcely a leaf can be seen, Ue made up his mind to leave this inhospitable island for ever.

A single friend, Mataroi, celebrated for his skill in manufacturing stone adzes sacred to Tanè, volunteered to share the fortunes of Ue. These two kindred spirits crossed the island, seeking the point due west, where Ue set up his third and last *marae* in honour of his god. A more useful memorial was the enclosing of a spring with large smooth stones, still known as the Fountain of Ue. Within the past few years the stones have been removed for building purposes. Ue and his friend set sail and left the island for ever.

Such is the story of Ue and his *marae* at Maungaroa. The persecutors of Ue all perished (save two) in the second fearful oven at Angaitu. Tevaki, one of the survivors, worshipped at Maungaroa, a spot most sacred in the eyes of all his numerous descendants, until idolatry was finally subverted by God's blessing upon the labours of Davida and Tiere.

THE EXPELLED GOD.
INTERLUDE TO THE FÊTE OF PARIMA.
By Tuka.—Circa 1816.

FIRST BAND.

Ia Ua te vari i te marae ;	Ue set up the first altar ;
Te vari i Putoa, na itiki o Tanè ē !	His home was at Putoa,
Uia, uia Tanè e, ei ata ē !	Where the morning star stood o'er him.

SECOND BAND.

Tiroa te pia i Itianga ;	Tiroa was offered in sacrifice ;
Kua kapitia Matariki,	Matariki, alas ! shared his fate ;
O na pia o Tanè ē !	Both were priests of Tanè,
E rua katoa i āriki nei.	Offered to their relentless gods.

FIRST BAND.

Pangeara Tepunga i Ngaua.	E'en Tepunga was laid on the altar.
Te kapu i te upoku,—	The sacrifice was headless !
Kua rika te kiri o Mautara,	Mautara himself was horror-stricken
O na raverave na Ngariki nei.	At the atrocities of the tribe Ngariki.

SECOND BAND.

Kua ora Tevaki ia Raumea,	Tevaki alone was saved by Raumea ;
Ei tamaru na Mautara,	Under the shadow of the great Mautara
E ora'i Kaukare nei.	His only son Kaukare was secure.

FIRST BAND.

Kua ora Iva-nui-tarava etu,	The band of Orion now shines brilliantly,
E Mere, kua kake oa te pa etu nei.	Sirius too, and all the stars of heaven.

SECOND BAND.

Kua kake te uri a Vairanga	The posterity of Vairanga [1] yet survive ;
O ngati Kāki, tei takina i te rā nei.	The descendants of Kāki now prosper.

FIRST BAND.

Taki na i te ra iā iti,	Prosperity now smiles upon Mataroi,
Te rā ia Roi, ei tukirua	Despite the two great attempts
Ite pou tai o Tanè ē, reiā !	To destroy the tribe of Tanè.

---

[1] Vairanga, Kāki, Mataroi, are the names of three chiefs of the original drift canoes from Tahiti. Ue came later.

SECOND BAND.

Reia e te utu, paoa e Aumea,
Na Mere te vai e vā 'i mai,—

Te vai ia atea : *na umu Aitu*
Na Kaveutu te amo ia Ngati Tanè nei

Once the stars [1] fought, valiantly did Aumea (Aldebaran)
And Sirius fight the Pleiades,
And were victorious. *Thus were the Aitu*
Consumed in the fiery ovens of Kaveutu. [2]

CHORUS.

Taki na ake Ngariki ē !
E maunga i te rā nei.

Mighty is the tribe of Ngariki !
A mountain touching the sun ! [3]

Towards midnight the music and dancing ceased. The performers arranged themselves into two bodies, reciting alternately stanza by stanza until the last, when both parties met and recited the final verse with tremendous emphasis. The drum was again beaten, and the *kapa*, or semi-drama, proceeded. This chanting or plaintive recitation was the true Polynesian mode of singing. Singing, as we understand the term, is in the native mind indelibly associated with Christianity.

[1] Star-worship was indelibly associated with this tribe. Aldebaran and Sirius are *red* stars, as if shadowing forth the lurid ovens which in a former age consumed their worshippers.

[2] Both ovens are, for poetical purposes, attributed to the author of the second. Kaveutu was of the same tribe as Ungakute, and possibly a descendant of his.

[3] A delicate compliment to Pangemiro, the warrior-chief of Mangaia at the time, as being a member of that tribe.

CHAPTER VIII

THE EXPELLED GOD

(CONTINUED)

LATTERLY, inquiries have been made at the neighbouring islands to ascertain the fate of Ue after leaving Mangaia. He reached Aitutaki, where his descendants, the Ngati Ue = 'the clan of Ue,' still flourish. In extravagance the story of his subsequent adventures, as told by his descendants, exceeds all others. It is as follows :—

A fleet of warriors from Samoa once invaded Aitutaki, destroying the entire island. These fierce Upolu men reserved the king, Temaeva, for eating long after the fighting men of Aitutaki had been devoured. As escape was deemed impossible, the unhappy king was allowed a little liberty. One evening he saw Tuoarangi—a man who was supposed to be dead—steal out of his concealment in the bush, and launch a small canoe in order to escape to Rarotonga. Temaeva entreated the fugitive, should he arrive in safety, to proceed at once to Arorangi, and inquire of his daughter Maraerua (who had married the king there) whether she had a brave son willing to avenge the wrongs of his grandfather. 'For,' added the captive Temaeva, 'I shall be eaten up to-morrow ; already the firewood and wrapping-leaves are gathered for my oven, and the taro to be eaten with my poor body has been taken up.'

In those times the nights were unusually prolonged, unlike the brief nights of a degenerate age. Tuoarangi safely reached Rarotonga, and, proceeding to the home of Maraerua, told his mournful tale. At once her grown-up son, Marouna, resolved to go to the help of his unfortunate grandfather. Taking off his magnificent head-dress, he therewith purchased a large double canoe, which he named Rautiparakiauau = 'The fading *ti* leaves of Auau,' *i.e.* 'Ripe for destruction.' ·A number of brave Rarotongan warriors accompanied Marouna. Ere starting on his voyage, he slew two or three men with his own hand, to evince his bravery and as an omen of success.

That same night Marouna reached Mangaia! On proceeding to the interior, his further progress was opposed by Ue at the fountain called by his name. These men being of equal strength and cunning, neither could get an advantage over the other. They therefore saluted by pressing noses, and became the best of friends. Marouna now invited Ue and Mataroi to accompany him to Aitutaki to avenge the wrongs of his grandfather, King Temaeva. This being agreed to, they all started off in that famous craft 'Ripe for destruction,' and, in that night of wondrous duration, reached Atiu, where the redoubtable Kaurā and Tara joined the expedition. Long ere break of day they reached Aitutaki, the final goal of their midnight wanderings. The Samoan sentinel at the entrance to the lagoon was at once despatched; a second sentinel, guarding the sandy beach, likewise fell. Further on, a vast block of sandstone is pointed out, where two more were destroyed; so that the slumbering warriors in the interior received no intimation of impending danger. The canoe was dragged up amongst some neighbouring taro patches, and there hidden in the mud, defiling the stream, which to this day is, in consequence, called Vaieu, or ' Muddy Brook.'

Temaeva was still alive, and expecting to be cooked in the morning. After greeting his brave grandson for the first time, he gave them some ripe bananas to eat. Marouna and his followers now proceeded to the houses where the successful invaders from Upolu were sleeping. Each head was gently lifted up : if heavy, being clearly the head of a warrior, it was immediately clubbed ; but if the head proved to be light, the owner was permitted to sleep on till daylight, as it was evidently the head of a coward. In this way the leading enemies of Temaeva were quietly disposed of. At daylight the astonished and affrighted survivors made a feeble defence, and were to a man put to death.

In the division of lands which followed, the enfranchised king bestowed great possessions upon Ue and Kaurā. At the present time their respective clans form a considerable portion of the population of that beautiful little island ; but, unhappily, in after days these clans fought fiercely against each other, the tribe of Ue gaining the victory. In the fifth generation from Ue, Christianity was introduced to Aitutaki.

That a descent was made upon Aitutaki by a hostile fleet from Upolu is doubtless true : that Temaeva, in the last extremity, gained help from Rarotonga, Mangaia, and Atiu, is very probable. But the Polynesian love of the marvellous is excessive ; hence a complete voyage of the group, which might well occupy a fortnight, is made in a single night of unheard-of duration.

The Mangaian story makes Ue and Mataroi start off alone in search of a new home. The Aitutakian account represents Ue and Marouna as becoming friends after a smart trial of strength.

In 1864 the late Rev. C. Barff told me that the tutelar god of Huahine was Tanè, whose worship once prevailed over Tahiti, and that people and god came originally from Manuā, the eastern portion of the Samoan group. The proof of this, he remarked, was found in ancient traditions and songs pointing to Manuā. These dovetailed with the statements of the old men of that island, or cluster of islets, when, in company with the lamented Williams, he introduced Christianity to Samoa in 1830.

The original Tanè of Mangaia was 'Tanè-giver-of-food,' deified by his son, Papaaunuku. Then came 'Tanè-striving-for-power,' whose worshippers were all condemned to furnish sacrifices to Rongo, tutelar god of Mangaia. Next in order came 'Tanè-the-chirper,' often called 'Tanè-of-the-shadow' (Tanè-i-te-ata), in allusion to the star of day appearing directly over the head of Ue at Maungaroa.

There is a close analogy between these Tanès of Polynesia and the Baals of Phœnicia. Tanè, like הַבַּעַל *habbaal*, means 'husband;' both undergo numberless modifications; Tanè and Baal are invariably associated with the worship of heavenly bodies. Tanè is the fifth son of Vātea and Papa, *and is enshrined in the sun* (= *Rā*). Sometimes the morning star is lauded as ' the eye of Tanè ; ' at other times Jupiter, by mistake for Venus, attained this distinction. Of course the older colonists adhered firmly to their myth concerning the sun as ' the *right* eye of Vātea ' (= noon), parent of gods and men ; his *left* eye being the moon.

Tanè is invariably regarded as a male divinity, and had innumerable modifications, הַבְּעָלִים (*habbaalim*), a few of which I subjoin :—

1. Tanè, *i.e.* Tanè-papa-kai.	Tanè-piler-up (*i.e.* giver) of food.
2. Tanè-ngaki-au.	Tanè-striving-for-power.
3. Tanè-kio, or Tanè-i-te-ata.	Tanè-the-chirper, or Tanè-of-the shadow; also known as Tanè-of-the-yellow-teeth.
4. Tanè-i-te-utu.	Tanè-of-the-Barringtonia-tree.
5. Tanè-i-te-kea.	Tanè-consecrator-of-kings.[1]
6. Tanè tukia-rangi.	Tanè-the-heaven-striker.
7. Tanè-kai-aro.	Tanè-the-man-eater.
8. Tanè-i-te-roa.	Tanè-the-tall.
9. Tanè-marō-uka.	Tanè-shearer-of-thatch (for dwellings).
10. Tanè-mata-ariki.	Tanè-of-the-royal-face.
11. Tanè-arua-moana.[2]	Tanè-guardian-of-the-ocean.
12. Tanè-ere-tue.	Tanè-the-storm-wave.
13. Tanè-vaerua.	Tanè-the-spirit.
14. Tanè-i-te-io.	Tanè-inspirer-of-bravery.
etc., etc., etc.	

The first four only possessed ironwood representations admitted to the king's god-house.

The natives of Atiu lived in dread of Tanè-mei-tai, *i.e.* 'Tanè-out-of-the-ocean.'

The Mitiaro people believed that their island was beautified by Tanè-tarava, or 'Tanè-the-all-sufficient.'

The tribe of Tanè, discarding the myth of Ina, regarded thunder as '*the voice of Tanè*.'

UE FINDING HIS GOD TANÈ; COMPOSED BY TUKA, *CIRCA* A.D. 1817.

For the ' Death-talk of Arokapiti." [3]

TUMU.	INTRODUCTION.
Te etu tangi a Terangai,	'Twas the loved star of Terangai [4]
E vā'i mai i Maungaroa,	That stood o'er Maungaroa,—
Na Ue e akatere !	The guide of Ue.
Ua karo i te ata e kake ē !	How he gazed on its rising !

---

[1] Literally Tanè-of-the-sacred-sandstone.

[2] To whom libations were offered of chewed *Piper mythisticum*, that he might send abundance of sprats, etc.

[3] Arokapiti was a famous modern chief of the tribe of Tanè. His god was Tanè-kio; hence the burden of the preceding song is the arrival and settlement of his god at Mangaia.

[4] Terangai was the original founder of the existing tribe of Tanè. He came from Iti, *i.e.* Tahiti.

PAPA.

Terau oki to tama rā rire
I ravea'i e Tanè nei,
Ei koatu i Maungaroa na Ue,
No vara nei te pia.
Ei vari au ki Maungaroa ra ē !

FOUNDATION.

Terau,[1] too, was thy son,
Adopted by the tribe of Tanè.
To pray at Maungaroa on behalf of
  Ue (*i.e.* the tribe of Tanè)—
He the priest of (the tribe of) Vara.[2]
My boast is of Maungaroa !

UNUUNU TAI.

Te etu tangi ē a Terangai ē !
A Terangai, tei Tupuaki enua,
Ua ketu aere mai !
Ua ketu aere mai.
Mei ia Ue mai te atua
Eiia koe tau ai ē?   Ei Avaavaiē.
Ua akatere e Tanè ē !
Ua karo i te ata e kake akē !

FIRST OFFSHOOT.

The loved star of Terangai—
Of Terangai whose home was at
  Tupuaki,
He earnestly sought—
Ah ! how earnestly did he seek
A new home for his god.
At what place did it land?   At
  Avaavaie.
Behold the guide of (the tribe of)
  Tanè !
How he gazes on its rising !

UNUUNU RUA.

Akatere atu ē i te kavainga ē !
I te kavainga tei mua i te marae,
I te titara tapu ra,
I te titara tapu ra'i !
Taii te pipi i to marae,
O te ara patu i Maungaroa
Tei takina e Ue ē.
Ua akatere e Tanè ē !
Ua karo i te ata e kake akē !

SECOND OFFSHOOT.

Be thou the guide, thou harbinger of
  day !
Yes, thou harbinger of day, guide to
  the marae.
To the sacred shrine itself,—
E'en to the sacred shrine itself !
Let wild vines cover thy marae,
So well-built on Maungaroa,
The result of the toil of Ue.
Behold the guide of (the tribe of)
  Tanè !
How he gazes on its rising !

UNUUNU TORU.

Tiria mai ē, no kai maki ē,
No kai maki i te tama takitai ē !
I te tama akaaroa ! I te tama akaaroa'i,
Ua kaukau i te tai ē !
E atua nio renga ra ia Iti.

THIRD OFFSHOOT.

Expelled for occasioning sickness,
For occasioning sickness amongst
  children—
E'en amongst the best-beloved,
Thou didst float o'er the ocean,
A yellow-toothed god from Iti (*i.e.*
  Tahiti).

---

[1] Terau was the son of Vara, priest of Motoro. His own god was Tanè.
As priest of Motoro he swayed the island. Hence the introduction of his name
into this song.

[2] Vara is here evidently put for the priestly tribe, of which he was the
founder.

Eiia koe tau ai? Ei Avaavaiē.
Ua akatere e Tanè ē!
Ua karo i te ata e kake akē !

At what place did it land? At Avaavaiē.
Behold the guide of (the tribe of) Tanè !
How he gazes on its rising !

UNUUNU A.

Eketia i raro ē, i Karangaiti ē !
I Karangaiti, i te tautai ngere ē !
Aore e mataika.   Aore paa e taia,
      Aore paa e taia'i.
Ngaro atu ai, e Ue e, i te taruku
Tei Poiritama rai ; tei Avaavaiē.
Ua akatere e Tanè ē !
Ua karo i te ata e kake akē !

FOURTH OFFSHOOT.

He[1] went on the reef at Karangaiti ;
Yes, at Karangaiti he fished in vain,
He failed to obtain an offering, utterly failed ;
      He obtained nothing.
Ue put down his net
At Poiritama, and (successfully) at Avaavaie.
Behold the guide of (the tribe of) Tanè !
How he gazes on its rising !

AKAREINGA.

Ai e ruaoo !   E rangai ē !

FINALE.

Ai e ruaoo !   E rangai ē !

[1] 'He,' *i.e.* Ue.

CHAPTER IX

ADVENTURE OF THE SURVIVOR OF THE AITU TRIBE

ONE day the accustomed present of food from the chiefs was brought to Mautara, as priest of Motoro, garnished by the cooked head of Tepunga. Now Tepunga was priest of Tanè, the god worshipped by Mautara himself. Of course this was a studied insult to the wily priest of Ngariki, who for the present dissembled his anger. Mautara did not taste the head of Tepunga : not, however, as objecting to such diet, but because it would draw down upon him the anger of his own divinity. The corpse had first been offered to Great Rongo ; and then, contrary to all precedent, the offering had been despoiled of its head.

Mautara thirsted for revenge. At a meeting of chiefs at the grand *marae* of their god Motoro, Mautara fell into an ecstasy produced by swallowing an unusual quantity of *Piper mythisticum*. With eyes ready to start out of their sockets and in great agitation, he said in unearthly tones, ' I, Motoro, require of So-and-so, my faithful worshippers and distinguished chiefs, a most costly offering. On a given day the first-born of each must be slain and eaten in my honour by the tribe of Ngariki, descended from Great Rongo ! '

From this fearful command no appeal lay. Mautara professed to be horror-stricken, but he had merely been the mouthpiece of their god. *On the day appointed, these children, the flower of the ruling clan, were killed, cooked, and eaten by the assembled tribe,* in supposed obedience to the will of Motoro! Tepunga was amply avenged. Mautara in after years confessed that it was all a trick of his own, to wreak his vengeance upon those who had so barbarously insulted him.

Tevaki, uncle of the crafty Mautara, now became priest of Tanè, the last of his race. It was he who put the priest of Motoro up to the cruel trick of demanding the first-born of the ruling tribe. Four preceding priests of Tanè had all been laid in sacrifice on the bloody altar of Rongo. Tevaki and his four grown-up sons must be slain. The sons fell fighting, the eldest, Tuarau, at Tamarua, where for some days he was concealed in a dense growth of brushwood. The spot where he was clubbed is now the site of the schoolhouse of that village.

The now childless Tevaki hid himself in the rocks of Tevaenga. Daily search was made for him by his foes. One rainy night he descended from his lofty and almost inaccessible hiding-place into the interior, in the hope of meeting his nephew Mautara, whose priestly duties detained him a few days at that part of the island. A venerable chestnut-tree is pointed out as the place where he took shelter during the storm, until he believed that his foes were all wrapped in sleep. At length he started a second time for the hut of Mautara, which was surrounded by the members of the hostile tribe. The trembling old man succeeded in reaching the house unobserved. After a weeping welcome, the hungry fugitive ate a good meal, and consulted with Mautara as to the best means of securing his safety. That his foes would relent was out of the question, his offence being that he was the last of the hated tribe of Tanè, and priest of that rival god.

It was resolved that Tevaki should start at once for

Putoa, and hide in the rocks and thickets of that neighbourhood. The rain still fell in torrents. With leaves of gigantic taro (*Alocasia Indica*, Seeman) for umbrellas, the elder sons of Mautara (Teuanuku and Raumea) led the childless old man to a cave in the district indicated. A quantity of cooked taro left with him sufficed for the present. Fortunately, the two young men got back before dawn, so that their nocturnal travels were unsuspected.

Mautara soon afterwards returned to his own hereditary lands on the southern part of the island. The house of the priest was set up at the head of the valley, where six minor valleys open to view in lovely perspective. Tevaki's residence at Putoa becoming suspected, under cover of a dark night the same young men conducted the hunted hated priest of Tanè to the well-built reed dwelling of Mautara.

Upon his arrival, Tevaki was hidden inside the *pa tikoru*, or that part of the dwelling curtained off with a piece of sacred cloth. On no pretence whatever could this sanctuary be invaded. His presence there was for a long time kept a profound secret. Meanwhile, the rocks of Putoa, which he had just left, were thoroughly searched by the foes of Tevaki. Eventually the truth leaked out, and constant watch was kept near the dwelling of Mautara for the old man, should he unwittingly put himself in the power of his foes by leaving the charmed dwelling of the priest. Even Tokoau, the factotum of Mautara, proposed again and again that Tevaki should be eaten ; for Tokoau was passionately fond of human flesh. A minute's walk outside the house would have cost Tevaki his life. Such was the wonderful ascendency which Mautara maintained, that his old uncle lived a *whole year* inside the curtained partition. Namu was concealed with difficulty for *one month* by his father-in-law, and at last had to run for his life when the sanctuary was invaded.[1]

At the expiration of the year (*circa* A.D. 1720), the battle of Arira was fought, putting an end to the supremacy of the original tribe which had so persistently sought the life of Tevaki. The utter rout of Ruanae at Pukuatoi, some two years later, removed all fear, as Teuanuku was declared warrior-chief of Mangaia.

Tevaki became now a man of consequence, and lived to a very advanced age. There was born to him a son, who grew to manhood under the fostering care of his cousins, and eventually became the founder of the present numerous tribe called Ngati Tanè = 'the descendants of the god Tanè,' who claim almost half the island as their own. Thus the last survivor of the Aitu became the author of a new and altogether prosperous clan.

The tribe of Tanè has the honour of first embracing the Word of God in 1824. Their honest pride is that they early gave up their idols and embraced Christianity. Parima and Rakoia were distinguished chiefs of this clan, who did all they could to aid the cause of truth and righteousness in their day. Numerous deacons and evangelists have been furnished by this family.

In 1854, Kaveriri, one of their number, 'counted not his life dear unto him, so that he might finish his course with joy, and the ministry he had received of the Lord Jesus.' He was one of five who were slain and eaten by the savage natives of the island of Fate, one of the New Hebrides.

The rival 'gods,' Motoro and Tanè, now repose quietly in the museum of the London Missionary Society.

---

[1] This 'curtained sanctuary' of Mautara has become proverbial. Native preachers love to urge poor sinners, hunted by Satan, to take *sure refuge* inside *te pa tikoru o Jesu* = 'the curtained sanctuary of Christ.'

CHAPTER X

PANAKO'S STRATAGEM

CIRCA A.D. 1666

BATHING one day in the pretty lake associated with the name of the giant Mokè, I was desirous to track the course by which its deep waters pass on to the ocean under the rocks. A dense growth of hibiscus overhangs, and in some places touches, the waters. Not being an expert swimmer, with the assistance of a native I lashed together with hibiscus bark two coco-nut troughs which happened to be at hand. Unitedly they bore my weight; a dry coco-nut branch served as a paddle. On this extempore canoe I paddled under the spacious opening. The lofty roof grew lower as I advanced, and a feeling of awe crept over me as I solitarily paddled on to the farthest part of the Cave of Tangiia, which is nearly two hundred feet in depth.

Finding my farther progress stopped, I turned and gazed upon the novel scene—the dark waters underneath, the dome-like walls of the cave, blackened with age, around, while overhead a vast mass of hardened coral sustained a most luxurious tropical vegetation. Through the spacious entrance the best view of the pretty lake was obtained, reflecting on its still bosom the rocks and trees which surround it. Beyond lay the fertile taro patches, the rich soil of which, carried by freshets into the lake, made it so black. Noble coco-nut groves adorned the base of the range of hills in the distance. The upper part of these hills was covered with slender ironwood trees, mistaken by Captain Cook for willows.

At the farthest part of the Cave of Tangiia is the gorge through which the swollen waters of the lake sullenly rush into the ocean. In the dry season, when the lake is shallow, it is easy to crawl through this opening into a spacious but gloomy cavern, ever associated in the minds of these islanders with the name of Panako, who here found a safe asylum from his foes.

The lofty open cave into which I had paddled was formerly regarded as the abode of the god Tangiia, whose name means 'a murmuring' of waters. Tangiia was supposed to be enshrined in the hideous ironwood idol now in the London Missionary Society's museum. He was regarded as the fourth son of Vātea (noon) and Papa (foundation); being one of those who accompanied Rangi from Avaiki, or the nether world, to this upper world of light. This mythical personage must be distinguished from the great historical warrior chief of the same name from Tahiti, who was one of the first settlers at Rarotonga, and whose son Motoro, drowned by his brother at sea, was afterwards worshipped at Mangaia.

On a pleasant fertile slope near the lake stood the sacred grove or *marae* of Tangiia, long since demolished, and now well planted with arrowroot.

The worshippers of this god were once numerous and powerful, but, being devoted to furnish sacrifices to Rongo, became in time almost extinct, a very few only surviving to this day.

Sixty years ago, the Christian pioneer Davida had been labouring on this island some few years with marked success. Those who had been baptized united in building a Christian village on the margin of the sea. The Sabbath was very strictly observed by these early converts. But the heathen living in the interior openly showed their contempt for that sacred day by pursuing their usual occupations. On a bright Sunday morning, Tapaivi went to the lake after *kokopu*, a fish especially plentiful in the inner cave, where Panako once took refuge. The waters being low, Tapaivi and his assistant crept in without difficulty. Their fishing greatly prospered ; but somehow they failed to notice that the waters had suddenly risen, and they were in fact imprisoned. A storm from the south had occasioned a sudden rising of the ocean, thus preventing the egress of the waters of the lake, which now rapidly filled the Cave of Panako.

Very uneasily did these poor fellows wait in utter darkness for the subsidence of the waters. Hour after hour passed, but the waters continued to rise. Dismissing all thought about fish, and anxious only to get out of their gloomy prison, they repeatedly dived for the narrow opening. Each time they rose they struck their heads against the solid rock instead of clearing the entrance. Exhausted by their efforts, they impatiently waited for help. In the afternoon of that Sabbath, their friends, wondering at their long absence, went to the lake, and finding that its waters had risen to an unusual height, at once divined the truth.

A long pole was quickly cut down. Approaching as nearly as they could in a raft, they inserted it in the opening. Two men held firmly the outer end, whilst the third crept under the water, holding on by the pole, and finally, emerging into the inner cave, he found the Sabbath-breakers very uncomfortable in mind and body. Explaining the process, all three quickly dived for the inner end of the long pole, and with its aid succeeded in finding the true opening, and soon rejoiced to see the light of day. Tapaivi and his friend shortly after joined the Christian party, being, as he assured me, effectually cured of Sabbath-breaking.

But this cave derives its name and permanent interest from the circumstance that the royal Panako, having fought a most disastrous battle under the shadow of the vast overhanging rocks close to the lake, he and the other survivors took shelter in this almost inaccessible cave, the waters of the lake being low. His force was now reduced to forty warriors, with twenty lads fit to carry stones and their fathers' spears. Most of the women remained with their relatives in the interior, to await the will of the victors—to be slain, or reduced to slavery, or to be married to the murderers of their husbands and children.

Panako and his tribe had plenty of room inside their cave. As it was the dry season, sufficient light came in through the aperture to relieve the gloom. One or two warriors kept strict watch at the entrance throughout the day, whilst the rest slept. At nightfall all hands issued forth by twos and threes to forage. Occasionally some of these were caught and slain, but, generally speaking, the poor fellows contrived to get back with their scanty spoil. To put an end to their nightly depredations, a row of long stakes was driven into the muddy bottom of the lake, and at the top firmly tied together. Death at no distant date now stared them in the face, as the vigilance of their foes cut off all further supplies of food.

Of brackish water they had a plentiful supply. They caught abundance of shrimps, eels, etc., which they cooked inside the cave. To eat with the fish they had only *maramara*, or sweet-scented black loam from the bottom of the Cave of Tangiia. This fragrant earth was thickly plastered on the walls of their gloomy abode, to be cooked and eaten at leisure when dry. Sick people with capricious appetites still send to the lake for *maramara*, which contains a quantity of vegetable matter from the valleys. I have several times tasted it, but, notwithstanding the praises of the natives, could not swallow it. Month after month passed away in this dreadful prison-house ; they must soon perish, as their foes kept away the women in the interior, who would have brought supplies. The usual result of their own foraging parties was merely the obtaining of a supply of firewood to cook their fish and *maramara*.

Panako knew that about a mile from the lake, at Tamarua, lived a warrior named Onè, whose ancestors had ever been on good terms with his own. Could not Onè help them, being on the winning side ? He determined to leave the cave and have an interview with him. That night, after considerable labour, two or three stakes were pulled out of the mud, leaving a free passage for a man, while above water nothing unusual could be seen. Being an excellent swimmer, at dawn Panako bravely dived through the opening in the palisading, and, rising to the surface, caught a sere leaf of the hibiscus (nearly round, and fully ten inches in diameter) that happened to be floating near. Holding the stem between his teeth, Panako gently swam on his back, his body hidden in the black waters of the lake. Amid the myriads of yellow leaves silently drifting on the lake in the winter season, this attracted no attention.

Fortunately for Panako a heavy rain compelled his foes to keep inside their huts during his exit across. Arrived at the farthest point of the lake, a distance of a quarter of a mile, he emerged from the water amidst some tall bushes, and put on a woman's petticoat he had brought with him firmly rolled up. He then plaited a few taro leaves for a head-dress, covering his neck and bosom with thick wreaths of the same, in the approved fashion of the women of those days.

Thus arrayed in female attire, Panako slowly ascended the hill, collecting dry sticks as if for firewood, carried, woman-fashion, under the arm. The crafty Panako was seen by several of the warriors, who sat at the entrance of their huts watching the rain ; but his disguise and imitation of female gait were so perfect that the figure slowly moving through the trees on the slope of the hill was considered to be a woman belonging to the conquering tribes. Who else could dare to move about by daylight in front of a hostile camp ?

Once screened from observation by tall reeds and trees, Panako, avoiding the usual narrow track, pressed on, tremblingly but rapidly, to the dwelling of his friend. Onè was astonished at the temerity of Panako, whom he had never expected to see alive again. Onè was disposed to succour the royal fugitive, if there were any chance at all of success. A plan of operations was agreed upon, and the night fixed when Onè should bring all his Tongan tribe to attack those who so vigilantly guarded the cave night by night.

To ratify this treaty a ripe bunch of bananas was given to Panako ; but, instead of eating it, he broke it up into little clusters, and disposing them as best he could in the folds of his petticoat, he took up his bundle of sticks, and departed by the way he came, unknown to any but Onè.

The rain still poured down. The royal fugitive got back to the margin of the lake ; doffing now his head-gear and wreaths, besides the large bundle of sticks, he provided himself, as in the first instance, with a fallen leaf of the hibiscus, and noiselessly swam on his back towards the cave. Once beyond reach of pursuit, he dived through the opening in the palisades, and soon was amongst his miserable friends. He bade them not to despair, for Onè would come to their rescue. The ripe bananas, a priceless boon to the starving fugitives, were carefully portioned out. That all might have a taste, it was needful to divide each banana into three portions.

A consultation was now held how best to secure the favour of Rongo, the divine arbiter of the destinies of war. The best blood must be spilt to secure victory. The man next in rank to Panako was Tiroa, priest of Tanè, who offered to die. On the morrow the self-devoted victim took a sad farewell of his friends, and openly left the cave, heroically entering the encampment of his foes. Of course they at once speared him, and, it is said, laid his body on the altar of Rongo, without divining why he courted death at their hands, as the visit of Panako to Onè had not transpired.

Next day Onè assembled the Tongan tribe, and made his appearance amongst the cave-watchers, who gave him a good reception. At twilight he proposed that he and his tribe should keep guard all night to cut off all stragglers from the cave. This would permit his friends to obtain a good night's rest after their incessant watching. This was at once agreed to.

Now it was the usual practice in times of war for armed night guards to play quoits,[1] in order to keep themselves awake. Onè looked about for a suitable place for his deadly purpose, and found one not far from the cavern where Panako had taken refuge. On my visiting this spot it was evident that only one person at a time could enter, whilst the interior will accommodate scores. At

---

[1] This is an ancient Mangaian game. In my time it was introduced to Rarotonga.

the opening were stationed a number of Onè's warriors, in order to cut off stragglers from the camp of the victors who might be attracted by the supposed quoit-playing. Every now and then the war-dance was performed, *as if Onè had succeeded in killing some of the poor wretches from the cave* prowling about for food, whilst in reality he had turned his spear against his former associates.

That fearful night, the fugitives, inspired with new courage, came out of their gloomy stronghold, and united with Onè in the work of slaughter. Their faces were blackened, and strips of white *tapa* wound round the forehead, to distinguish their own united force from their foes. Again and again the war-dance was performed, as they succeeded in cutting off numbers of the enemies of Panako, who had come to see what made their companions so merry. The bodies of the slain were at once dragged out of sight, so that new-comers had no suspicion of the fate of their friends, and were in their turn put to death.

In this way Panako was amply revenged upon the ancient tribe of Ngariki, the remnant of which, for the first time in their history, took refuge on the rocks. A neighbouring taro patch, Kumekume, is still pointed out as the spot where the dead bodies of their foes were trampled down out of sight in deep mire.

Wondrous change for the miserable cave-dwellers! Panako and his clan were now at liberty to move freely over the island, breathing the fresh air, and eating what little food remained. Panako was declared supreme chief of Mangaia. How long he enjoyed that dignity is uncertain, but half a dozen years would be a long time for heathen to live in peace. The chiefs whose rule lasted longer are but few, and their names well known. As long as Onè lived, the united tribes continued in harmony.

But after his death his place as chief was occupied by the warlike Ngauta, 'eight times lord of Mangaia,' who was unwilling that Panako should enjoy the supreme dignity, because everybody knew that but for the cunning and bravery of the Tongans, Panako and his associates must have perished of starvation. These quarrels were fomented by Tekaraka, at whose instigation a battle was fought at Arakoa, on the west side of the island. In this engagement Panako and many others of his clan were slain by Ngauta, who now assumed the government of the island.

The famous league between Onè and Panako is known as 'the sere-leaf compact,' in allusion to its brevity. The royal triton-shell used by Panako in his journeyings round the island is in my possession.[1] The Tekaraka who occasioned the destruction of Panako is the man of that name mentioned in New Zealand annals. Others assert that *this* Tekaraka was named after the companion of Tauai, who, expelled from Mangaia, found a home in the distant island called 'The Fish of Māui.'

The breaking up of 'the sere-leaf alliance' and the fall of Panako in the battle of Arakoa are referred to in the—

WAR DIRGE FOR TUOPAPA.

By Teinaakia, A.D. 1790.

FIRST SPEAKER.

Ka ano au e momotu i taū ivi ei ō noku;
I am resolved to put an end to our alliance;

Noou tera autua, e taū taeake o, noku tera.
Take this, friend, as a parting gift from me.

SECOND SPEAKER.

Ae, eaa to ara i vā' i ai koe ia taua?
But why thus rudely put an end to our friendship?

FIRST SPEAKER.

Oro mai, ei tara ua na taua,
Na te arekorero, a titiri atu taua.
It is the wish of the wise men of our tribe;
Perhaps 'twere better to disregard their words.

---

[1] Now deposited in the British Museum.

SECOND SPEAKER.

Ei kona ra, e Onè, ka aere au ka ēra
Ia Ngariki ia tau i runga i tai motu.

Farewell, Onè; I go to deceive and drive
The ancient tribe of Ngariki off the island.

FIRST SPEAKER.

Akaruke atu, a kitea koe.

Take care, or you will be found out.

(*Another Scene.*)

SECOND SPEAKER.

Ie ui atu te ara o Tekaraka e,
I ana mai ïa i te aa ō.
I ana mai ua au i aaki i te tamaki;
Te kotikoti a tuna ia maira korua e
Onè ma.

If any ask why Tekaraka comes here,
And what object he has in view,
'Tis to warn you of impending danger;
Eel-like you will be chopped in pieces by Onè's tribe.

FIRST SPEAKER.

E Tutavake e, tena oa te veu; teia
toku taeake.

Ye gods, a fight is at hand! How precious a friend!

SECOND SPEAKER.

Koai toou taeake i aakina'i koe?

Who is this friend that kindly put you on your guard?

FIRST SPEAKER.

O Tekaraka te toā.

Tekaraka told me.

SECOND SPEAKER.

Ae, ua kite ia i te maro?

Did he actually see the war-girdle put on?

FIRST SPEAKER.

Ae, te taeko!

He pretends that he did.

SECOND SPEAKER.

Ae, e amo oa tena iaau ia tu korua
ia ta,
Aitoa korua ia ta!

'Tis false; he wishes us to strike the first blow,
So that the blame may rest upon us.

A SINGLE VOICE.

E Tengaungau ōi, e tu ra, umea to
maro;
Inapo nei ua koe!

Brave chieftain! rise, adjust thy war-girdle;
This night may be thy last.

THE ENTIRE CLAN.[1]

Tera te ivi o Tongaiti ei ngaere ia
Tutavake:
Tukua mai te ariki o Rongo ei kave i
te puruki!
Iekōkō!
Era a pia te kaū o Tutavake,
Ei taeva i te rangi tao.
Ka eva Ngariki i te Moreikau,

Here come the Tongans inspired by Tutavake:
Sovereign appointed by Rongo, lead the attack.
(War-dance performed.)
The deadly spears are now uncovered,
And every preparation made for battle.
Ngariki has foolishly taken the initiative.

---

[1] Standing in two rows, facing each other.

<table>
<tr><td>

Ka riro oki te taeko,
  Ka ta i te ivi roa ō!
Noo akera Panako ia puruki
I te taparere i Arakoa,
I te tauenga rā i te aiai.
Karo tika ra, e Rongo, i te vaipoko!

</td><td>

The deceiver attained his purpose ;
The long-dominant tribe is doomed.
The royal Panako fought his last battle
On the hill-slope of Arakoa,
When the sun was low in the heavens.
Ah! Rongo, he was deceived to his death.

</td></tr>
</table>

The above is the commencement of this celebrated war-dirge, the extracts given elsewhere being the continuation, with occasional pauses, as new events in the history of the clan to which the deceased belonged are taken up. The chant is caught up from the lips of. the solo, who repeats a single line relating to some new disaster or success.

The destruction of Panako's foes by the aid of Onè and his clan are descanted on in Tuka's war-dirge for his relative Tuopapa, A.D. 1790.

TIAURU (WHOSE FATHER WAS BURIED IN THE TARO-PATCH).

<table>
<tr><td>

E karo mai koe iaku.
E tara ra, e Ngauta, i tai naau tara.

</td><td>

Pray have some respect for me.
Oh, Ngauta, make some peaceful settlement.

</td></tr>
</table>

NGAUTA, LORD OF MANGAIA.

<table>
<tr><td>

Eaa taku tara ka tara'i ?
Kua tara atu uao—
Tera taau, o taū rae ra !
E ariki mana koe !
Ie oro, ukea mai tei Kumekume !
    E taea ra oa ?

</td><td>

What can I say to please thee ?
Say what I may, still thou will plot
To cleave this poor skull of mine.
(Derisively)—If thou be a mighty king,
Be revenged for those buried in yon taro-patch.
    Darest thou attempt *that ?*

</td></tr>
</table>

TIAURU (FOAMING WITH RAGE).

<table>
<tr><td>

Eaa to reira !
Tena au. Tena au.
Aore e pa, aore e arai i to rae kere?
E manga koe na te araā !

</td><td>

To *me*, that were but child's play !
Here am *I*. Here am *I*.
Who dare stop me? Who shall save thy black skull ?
This club shall scatter thy brains.

</td></tr>
</table>

Despite these boasts of Tiauru, he and most of his clan were miserably slain by Ngauta, and trampled down in a neighbouring eel-swamp, in emulation of the prowess of his uncle Onè, associated with Panako not many years previously.

CHAPTER XI

A BOY'S VENGEANCE

CIRCA A.D. 1670

IN the days of the invincible Ngauta, some twenty men were fishing with a long drag-net on the northern side of the island. Late in the afternoon was, as it is still, the most favourable time for catching *kanae*—a species of mullet frequenting that part of Mangaia. At dusk a division of the finny spoil was made, each fisherman receiving one large mullet as his portion, without counting inferior fish.

Now these fishermen were all of the subject tribe; but one of their number had a young friend, named Taipiro, belonging to the then dominant Tongan clan, who helped to drive the fish into the net by beating the sea with coco-nut fronds. Taipiro had seen about a dozen summers. When the division was being made his friend said more than once, 'Let not this boy be forgotten.' But, whether from accident or design, whilst all the others received an equal share, Taipiro had nothing. His friend, grieved at this, cut his own fish in two and gave the boy the best half.

They then proceeded towards the interior by a very rugged but well-shaded path, now but little used. As it was quite dark by the time the party emerged into the valley, they concluded to sleep in a cave close by, a common practice with the islanders. The proper entrance to the Cave of Taipiro, as it has ever since been called, is very narrow, so that one has to sidle in. Near this entrance Taipiro sat down, saying to his friend, 'Here let us sleep apart from the rest.'

Some of them now busied themselves in getting a light by rubbing together two bits of dry wood. In a short time, they made a blazing fire out of the dry sticks which covered the ground ; and, in accordance with native etiquette, each broiled his own share of fish on the red-hot embers, and then supped with a keen appetite on the remainder of taro they had carried with them.

In a short time the fishermen, wearied with their day's work, fell asleep on the dry leaves which thickly strewed the floor of their ill-covered cave. The fire was dying out, when Taipiro cautiously crept through the narrow entrance and crossed the hills to Tamarua, where Ngauta and his principal warriors then lived. Aided by the light of the newly risen moon, the hurried journey could well be accomplished in an hour.

Close to the dwelling of the 'lord of Mangaia' lived Vaeruarau, the king of those days. Ngauta and Vaeruarau were both roused from sleep to hear Taipiro's tale of the dishonour put upon the dominant clan in the person of one of its youngest members. Vaeruarau at once went to a little *marae* named Ariana, where the royal war triton-shell lay, and sounded it long and loud. The warriors of that neighbourhood started out of their sleep at this summons, adjusted their war dresses in the moonlight, and assembled forthwith at the dwelling of Ngauta. Led by Ngauta and Vaeruarau they first made for the level central hill, which is about halfway to the cave. On this supposed 'crown' of Mangaia, Vaeruarau adjusted on each the girdle sacred to Rongo, invoking the aid of their raven-haired god of war. A little past midnight they set out to Tevaenga, where helplessly stretched out on the earthen floor of the cave their unconscious victims dreamed not of danger.

It was near dawn by the time Ngauta and his party arrived at the cave. The three entrances to it were closely guarded, so that escape was utterly impossible. When the meshes of the fatal net were thus drawn closely around the unconscious victims, Taipiro stealthily advanced to the principal entrance, where his friend lay sound asleep. Cautiously rousing him, the boy begged the fisherman to follow him outside the cave. The man, still half asleep, mechanically obeyed, little thinking that this was to save his life.

As soon as they were fairly out of danger a terrible war-shout was raised by Ngauta, effectually rousing the devoted sleepers. The cruel warriors rushed upon the horrified and defenceless fishermen. Upon a large flat-topped stone commanding the narrow entrance stood a fierce warrior felling the few who, dashing past their foes inside, vainly hoped for life. Of the entire party not one escaped save the friend of Taipiro!

Such is the darkness of the heathen mind that these poor fellows were believed to have been justly slain.

To this day, if a number of natives are dividing out fish, somebody will playfully say, 'Remember Taipiro, lest we be served as those were who grudged him an equal share.'

The triton-shell used by Vaeruarau on this occasion has been carefully preserved in the family of the worthy old king of Mangaia. No one but the reigning sovereign might use it. The king made me a present of it.

An amusing story was told me by the king relative to his ancestor Vaeruarau. In the incessant fighting of

Ngauta's younger days the kingly family was almost exterminated, only a royal female and her infant son surviving. The drum of peace had been beaten, and the infant Vaeruarau carried to O-Rongo, the *marae* of the god of war, as the future king and high priest. A grand feasting in honour of the gods at the cessation of war and the installation of a king was to come off.

Every preparation for the feast was completed ; all the great men of the time were waiting ; but who should perform the necessary *karakia*, or 'prayers?' Buanga, the mother of the infant king, *could not*, being disqualified by her sex, though well versed in these 'prayers.' The baby-king Vaeruarau was too young to learn. Not a creature else on the island was eligible to perform such sacred functions. What was to be done? A happy thought struck the mother. Though her child, high priest of the gods, was too young to perform the accustomed prayers, he was not too young to *cry!* She therefore gave the young king a smart blow on the back, causing him to cry lustily. This was enough ; the royal voice had sounded in the hearing of the gods, although not quite in the right way! It was to be accepted in the place of the 'prayers' or 'grace ;' and of course the feast was immediately proceeded with to the satisfaction of all parties.

Vaeruarau was eventually murdered at Ngauta's suggestion in after-days. He fell at Ariana, his little *marae*, and was greatly lamented. Divine honours were paid to him after his decease. Rori carved an ironwood representation of the murdered king. This image was duly installed amongst the principal gods of Mangaia! For some time the worship of Vaeruarau prospered ; but this god being at length accused of the crime of 'man-eating,' *i.e.* of occasioning sickness and death amongst his worshippers, he was ignominiously expelled from the house of the gods. The 'god' was secretly hidden in the rocks near the pleasant home of Rori at Ivirua. Secret visits of respect were paid to this disgraced divinity down to 1824, when idolatry was finally subverted.

Is not a counterpart of all this found in so-called Christian countries, in the canonization of saints, in the offerings, and in the inferior worship paid to them?

An allusion to Taipiro's exploit occurs in

THE WAR-DIRGE FOR TUOPAPA.

By his nephew Teinaakia, *circa* A.D. 1790.

Naai teia tutai?
Na Taipiro i aere te po, i aere te ao,
   I rauka'i tona ariki,
I pau ei te tauna i ana-nui.

Who occasioned this slaughter?
Taipiro, who travelled night and day
   To gain a great name
By destroying the sleepers in the great cave.

Era ei ia Rongo Mangaia!
Kokii o te toa a puta i te rangi.
A kako, e Ngauta, a motu o Teipe:
A motu o Paia, era tumangamanga!
Arutoa mai koe, taae atu au.

Ah! Rongo, thou art sovereign of Mangaia.
Seize the war-spears, lift them high.
Ngauta loves war, and has given over Teipe.
O Paia, these warriors must die!
If one army be brave, so too is the other.

A kai Tutavake i te aunga toto,
E kapua tangata i tera peiaa;—
   Peiaa Tongaiti i kai ai.
Na tera eretonga e mau Mangaia na Tekea.

Tutavake [1] delights in human blood,
And long rows of human heads,
Secured by the bravery of the Tongans.
Mangaia ever belongs to the bravest.

   E kapa rakau to Rongo;
    Ei au ngangare;
   Aore e tainga miro i teia.
    E ta Turanga e ta Teipe.

Rongo's dance is a dance of spears.
   Peace is but transient.
In this case no provocation [2] was given.
   Attack Turanga [3] and Teipe.

   Porutu i te rangi tao:
    Euea te rangi tao:
   Ua kaki i te rangi tao:
    Ua ka te ngakau!

Spears rain from the skies.
Reverse now these spears.
Nay; we thirst to fight,
Our hearts are burning with rage.

---

[1] Tutavake is the demon from the shades who slew Tukaitaua, the first who shed human blood in this world of ours.

[2] *I.e.* no blood was first shed by the fishermen.

[3] Turanga and Teipe are put for their respective worshippers.

CHAPTER XII

FEMALE TREACHERY

CIRCA A.D. 1674

DURING the latter part of the iron sway of Ngauta, the great Tongan and Teipe clans, long united and supreme, quarrelled. The ground of the quarrel was the belief (for it was never proved) that the head of the Teipe tribe maliciously injured the beautiful yam vines growing in front of Ngauta's dwelling, and furthermore fouled the stream of which the great chief daily drank.

A challenge was sent to Arepee to prepare for battle. Although the challenge was manfully accepted, the chief of Teipe felt that his days were numbered. A wild spot on the crest of a hill overlooking his pleasant home in better days was chosen for the final feast. But the engagement itself came off in a narrow rocky gorge, known as the Ikuari, overhung with a noble species of gigantic laurel and other trees. The reason for selecting this most extraordinary battle-field was that it was the favourite path to the sea used by his daughter Taaumārama, the real author of their troubles. The rock on which Ngauta for some time stood alone, keeping his foes at bay until his friends could come to his rescue, is still pointed out. Teipe was utterly routed, the fugitives flying in various directions for shelter in the rocks.

One band of eleven, all nearly related to each other, rushed towards the shore to a long cave with a narrow opening close to the sea. This entrance was completely hidden by trees and wild creepers, so that a stranger might pass and repass a thousand times without detecting its existence. It is now known as Tungāpi.

Here these unfortunate warriors hid themselves for a long time. The ruling party made several bootless searches for them, but, discovering no traces whatever, believed them to be all dead. During these weary months the sweet-tasted but minute kernel of the *Pandanus drupe* was their main support. Their plan was to bring the ripe fruit to the mouth of the cave and spend the livelong day in pounding the hard shells and carefully picking out the nutritious morsels so hard to get at. Now and then they got a taste of the ill-smelling and unsavoury *Morinda citrifolia*, and especially of a species of sweet yam. Fish was obtained, too, with great caution and constant fear of detection. These hungry fugitives abstained from eating land crabs, which abound in all solitary places, hiding under stones. Nor did they attempt to catch the pigeons, at that time plentiful. The reason for this was that they imagined themselves to be under the special protection of these rock-gods. The only water they drank was painfully collected from the crannies of the rocks.

One evening Inangaro, the head man amongst them, when wandering in quest of berries to satisfy the cravings of hunger, observed a basket of cooked taro temporarily left there by a woman engaged with her friends in catching fish on the reef, according to native custom. Unhappily for Inangaro, he resolved to get possession of the taro. Should he steal it? The owner would be sure to report her loss to Ngauta, a search would be instituted, detection and death would possibly result. Should he murder the owner of the basket? Of course she had companions, who would discover the crime, and vengeance would certainly follow. Inangaro resolved to make love to the fair owner for the sake of her food.

He accordingly hid himself until Inaango, the owner of the basket, made her appearance alone. He begged the astonished woman to give him a single taro. She good-naturedly emptied out for him the contents of her basket, which was afterwards equally divided to his friends inside the cave.

Inangaro, a young and handsome fellow, pretended to be smitten with the charms of Inaango, and entreated her not to reveal the secret of his existence to her companions. The dusky beauty promised secrecy, and failed not to bring her lover supplies of food from time to time. After a time her visits became a matter of course, and Inangaro very unwisely showed her the interior of the cave where the fugitives, her pensioners, were cowering over a fire roasting *nono* apples.

On one occasion, when Ngaae was roaming alone over the rocks and along gloomy ravines collecting pandanus fruit, he heard a female voice chanting a song. He drew nearer and nearer through the bush to listen, without being himself perceived, and found that it was Kurauri (better known in later days as Puiariki), engaged in stripping bark off the branches and long rope-like roots of the banyan-tree. This almost imperishable tree grows everywhere amongst the most inaccessible rocks. To collect its bark has been from time immemorial woman's dangerous employment. It is used for making coarse native cloth.

Kurauri too was provided with a small basket of taro,

greatly coveted by Ngaae. Upon showing himself she proved to be as good-natured as Inaango. They were old acquaintances, but Kurauri had imagined that the fugitives had all perished of hunger. She returned to the interior with plenty of bark, but contrived on one pretence or another to meet her lover constantly without exciting the suspicions of her friends. The best she could get was taken to Ngaae and his companions, the food being divided out with the strictest impartiality.

Now Inangaro, the elder brother of Ngaae, did not really care a rush for Inaango, but her food could not be dispensed with. Kurauri, their new lady-friend, was the real object of attraction to him. Here was an awkward predicament—Kurauri was really loved by two brothers. The younger one generously gave up to the elder, who was a poet, and in their frequent wanderings through the rocks composed for Kurauri the accompanying song, in sorrowful commemoration of the want and suffering the exiles had so long endured.

Their condition was now vastly improved, so that they scarcely ever ventured to a distance from the sequestered cave, lest they should be overtaken and slain. The two women continually visited the interior, but luckily never met.

On one occasion, however, after enjoying a scanty meal furnished by Karauri, it was prophetically remarked, ' We shall perish whenever one of our kind protectresses becomes aware that we have a second. We cannot escape, because we have shown them our asylum.'

Now it happened shortly after this that these patronesses of the fugitives went fishing with a number of other women. Karauri was very successful, and early in the evening extinguished her torch and ran to her friends in the cave with what she had obtained. To avoid detection she did not stay a minute, but, relighting her torch, resumed her fishing with her companions, who had not observed her brief absence.

The hungry fugitives at once cooked the fish in the interior of their retreat, and enjoyed their unusually good supper. The meal was scarcely over, when Inaango made her appearance with her basket of fish. The infatuated chief of the party, Inangaro, said to her, ' We have but just finished what Kurauri brought us.' At this Ngaae interposed, ' Speak gently, brother, for we owe our lives to her.'

Bitter jealousy at once sprang up in the mind of this woman, who now for the first time became aware that they had a second lady-protector. She had imagined that she reigned supreme in the affections of the noble-looking Inangaro.

On looking round, Inaango was found suddenly to have decamped. The poor fugitives now realized their critical position : she had doubtless gone to seek revenge. And who had ever received pity at the hands of the terrible Ngauta? No time was to be lost. Great stones were at once rolled to the narrow entrance of the cave, in the hope of effectually concealing it. Two of their number, Vivi and Tito, started off by themselves to another part of the island, ever hiding by day in the densest thickets near the sea, travelling, although with great difficulty, by night. Some years later, Vivi and Tito were slain by the fierce Tamangoru in the interior.

The other nine betook themselves to a noble Barringtonia-tree, hoping to be effectually hidden by its broad and glossy leaves. As soon as Ngauta heard from his cousin that a cave full of fugitives existed near the sea, he immediately summoned his warriors, and with lighted torches proceeded to the shore in search of the unhappy creatures. It was expressly stipulated that Ngaae should be spared, on account of the rebuke administered by him to his brother. The armed party wearied themselves in their search for the cave, the entrance to which had so cleverly been closed. As the morning star appeared, one of their number laid down his head on the gnarled root of a huge tree to rest himself, when he noticed a whistling of wind, as if through some hole. The man rose and sought for the supposed cave, but could discover nothing. Again he lay down to rest, and again a rush of air arrested his attention. Listening attentively, he became convinced that a cave of no ordinary size was near. He therefore summoned the whole party to relight their torches and join him in the search. And now they quickly detected the true opening to the cavern, which is very spacious inside, with an aperture for egress at the farther end. The large stones were removed, abundant evidence of the recent occupation was to be seen, but the fugitives themselves had mysteriously disappeared.

The search was recommenced with new zeal outside. It was early dawn, and yet no clue had been discovered, At last, wearied with the fruitless labour, they all gathered together under a Barringtonia-tree of enormous proportions to rest awhile. Some of the tired warriors were soon wrapped in profound slumber. But one of their number lay on his back watching the increasing light of morning. It seemed to him that there was something unusually dark in the uppermost branches of the tree; it must be the men they were in search of, hiding in the magnificent foliage.

In a second the whole party were on their feet,

brandishing their long spears. First of all the trembling Ngaae was ordered to come down, which he did. Seven poor exiles were speared to death on the branches. One of them bravely leaped down expecting instant death, but somehow managed to get off unobserved. But human footsteps covered with blood attracted the notice of some of the attacking party. For a long way they were tracked with ease, but finally were lost in the sea. The warlike clan of Ngauta returned to the interior well satisfied with their morning's work.

The last of the retreating clan lingered on the edge of the cliff over which the pathway passes, to watch the sea, when in his direct line of vision he saw a head cautiously peeping out of a great block of coral standing on the reef. The head quickly disappeared, having caught sight of the armed warrior standing against the blue sky. Guessing this to be the escaped victim, the pitiless foe at once retraced his steps to the shore, and climbing up the coral reef, clubbed the poor creature whose crouching form closely fitted the hollow where he lay. Such was the unhappy fate of Teuarāvai.

Ngaae was duly delivered up to Inaango, the author of all this mischief. He was content to marry her, although he well knew that if at any time he should have the misfortune to displease her his life would be the forfeit.

Inangaro was selected for an offering to Great Rongo. It was to obtain this suitable sacrifice that Ngauta so willingly set off in search of the fugitives. The nose and ears of this handsome man were cut off and divided out by Rauue, the king of those days, to all the landowners and chiefs on occasion of beating the drum of peace.

Ere the corpse was mutilated, the very day it was

solemnly exposed to the gaze of men and gods (according to the faith of former times), Kurauri made her appearance, carrying in her hand two pieces of dark mourning native cloth to cover the nude body on the altar. She was sternly ordered back, but refused to obey, well knowing that she, being a member of the winning tribe, would not be slain. After carefully wrapping up her dead lover, she clasped his neck in her arms, and gave vent to her grief in the song which Inangaro had composed for her in happier days. The warriors and chiefs around listened with undisguised admiration, and the song, such as it is, took its place amongst the literary treasures of the tribe.

The news of this unwonted scene spread, and Inaango, the bitter rival of Kurauri, rushed towards the sacrifice, intending to drag away her hated relative. This unseemly fray was not permitted, so that she was compelled to listen to the song in question, with the pathetic additions of her rival. She, however, gave vent to her utter disgust and contempt of the whole proceeding by repeatedly growling, *Aitoa! aitoa!* ('Serve him right! serve him right!')

Amongst those present was a young man named Iro, who, with his near relatives, was some years later driven off the island to perish at sea, but reached the south-eastern coast of Rarotonga. A year or two afterwards a season of severe scarcity occurred at that island, when the refugee Iro and the rest of his clan climbed a lofty mountain named Teroume, in the hope of obtaining a supply of wild yams. He there recollected the song of Inangaro, and through its words gave expression to his grief for the land of his birth, to the great delight of his newly-acquired Rarotongan friends. The descendants of the little Mangaian colony at Titikaveka, Rarotonga, to this day resort to the mountain referred to as an unfailing resource in time of scarcity, never omitting to recite the following song :—

THE SONG OF INANGARO.

Circa 1670.

TUMU.

Te aoa i makuku,
　Kua vai reka te tane.
Kua iri tau kakara ŭ !

INTRODUCTION.

Under yon ancient banyan tree
Was I first seen by my lover,
Covered with sweet-scented flowers.

PAPA.

Naai rai e ngaki
I te onge roa i taukauri e tu ē ?

FOUNDATION.

Who now shall gather food
For these starving, wretched exiles ?

UNUUNU TAI.

Mai tu e, e ruao, mei Kurauri,
　Mei Kurauri te ngara ē,
Ka roiroi i te ngara ia Inangaro tu ē !

FIRST OFFSHOOT.

Long has Kurauri waited ;
Wearied out was Kurauri,
Hoping again to meet Inangaro.

UNUUNU RUA.

I ngaki, i ngaki ki Kopaka ē,
Ko te uru kura ē, ko te uru kura.
Ko ara momotu rai e tu ē !

SECOND OFFSHOOT.

He was wearily gathering wild berries,
Such as grow on the rugged red cliffs ;—
Sweet-tasted pandanus kernels his only food !

UNUUNU TORU.

Naai ra e ngaki
　Ko te kumukumu?
Kura io aaki ko Ngaae e tu ē !

THIRD OFFSHOOT.

Who now shall gather food
By torchlight fishing,
When Kurauri gave the spoil to Ngaae ?

UNUUNU A.

I ngaki, i ngaki, ki Oenga ē,
Te enua tapu o Ngariki,
Enua kimi oki au ē !
Ko ara momotu au e tu ē !

FOURTH OFFSHOOT.

Sometimes thou didst venture
Into the sacred land of the kings,—
I following thee with my basket ;—
Sweet-tasted pandanus kernels thy only food !

When Christianity inaugurated the present friendly intercourse between the islands of the group, the Mangaians were not a little surprised that this ancient song had long been familiar to the natives of all the neighbouring islands. So that this irregular fragment has become a literary curiosity amongst the islanders themselves. Its rough form and unusual expressions are evidence of considerable age, as it was only at a later day that the highest development of native poetry took place, under the rule of the priestly clan of Mautara.

The spear wielded by Ngauta on this and many other occasions was thirty feet in length, and is said to be sacredly preserved in a dry cave. No consideration would induce one of the few collateral descendants of this distinguished warrior to reveal the precise whereabouts of this cavern, which is believed to be filled with memorials of the departed glory of their once-powerful clan. A lizard of enormous proportions and dreadful eyes, and a centipede of unheard-of size, are superstitiously believed to be the guardians of these hidden treasures. Woe betide the daring youth who should seek to enrich himself at the expense of the dead!

The final overthrow of Teipe at the battle of the Ikuari is alluded to in

THE WAR-DIRGE FOR TUOPAPA.

By Teinaakia, *circa* 1790.

Vāia Rongo puā akaneke atu Ngauta ia Paia,
    Ua tae Rongo vāvāia.
Era na tauokura e uaki i te parai o Tutavake.
    No Rongo tera autua :
    No Tonga-iti tera auaro.
    Ka aere Tepei i Te-ikuari.
    Ka aere Tekuru i te opunga o te rā.
Tera oa na kai-tamua a Tutavake
Oi atu korua, e au tacake, ia atea.
    Oi tika ; oi atu.
Taumaa i te uru i te tokotoko ei vaerua toa,
Ei momotu i te mokotua o Tongaiti.
    Piritoa ! piritoa !! piritoa !!!

The tribes of Ngauta and Arepee are at enmity ;
    Rongo has decreed their fall.
Here are plenty of spears for the impending fight.
    Let Rongo take the lead :
    Let the Tongans do his bidding.
    Tepei will fight at the Ikuari ;
    The battle-field is towards the setting of the sun.
Ah ! the first-ripe fruits of death have been plucked.
Alter the battle-field to some open spot.
    Move on ! Move on !
On the rough rocks brave men are fighting
And breaking the very backbone of the Tongans.
    Crash ! crash !! crash !!! I go the spears.

Taina ra !
Ka aranga oki Teipe i te ivi vaia ō !
   E varu ata i te patiakā
I koa 'i, i kiritia 'i nga rakau e varu.
   Te aoa mai na tai,
   Na tangi ravakau.
Taumaa Tevaki i te paratao ō !
    Kāreia !
   Aue te vairakau ē !
Ei kona rā Tirango e pa 'i.
   Aue te pa moa ē !
   Era te mataati.
Ka peke iia, e Paia, teia kopu,—
   Teia vakanui taae ?
Ka ati iia ? ka oro iia ?
Eea tu atu ? Eea tau atu ?
I nunga i tai motu putaonga 'tu
I Marotangiia, i Tearataukanii,
I te ara tuaririki, te ua o te rangi ē !
Era, ka ariu ! Tueruia atu Rongo
Ia tu a papa tavaki i te kopunga rā
I te avatea ; oe mate io, oe ora atu !
Ka ao Tutavake i ora ake !

Slay them !
Teipe is doomed now Ngauta attacks them,
   On a series of platforms,
Eight in number, secured with stakes and ropes.
   They were taken in the rear
   By their crafty foes.
Skulls are splitting on every side.
   (War dance performed.)
   Ah the clashing of spears !
Descendants of Tirango, destroy your foes !
   They are but ensnared birds.
   They fly for their lives.
Whither indeed shall the vanquished fly,—
   This vast host ?
Where can shelter be found, or life be safe ?
Can another stand be made ? Is all hope gone ?
The fugitives are scattered hither and thither
In the rocks and caves of Marotangiia,
Crowding the 'narrow path' in a heavy rain.
Some are hunted by Rongo[1] from rock to rock ;
Like wearied tropic birds they drop dead in the valleys.
Many perish, but few survive.
What a day of woe the day after the battle !

---

[1] Rongo, 'god of war,' is put in place of those who do his bidding.

CHAPTER XIII

THE SERF AND HIS MASTER

IN the palmy days of the clan Ngariki, Autea and his family lived in Ivirua, on the lands and under the immediate protection of a chief named Mouna.[1] Autea was supposed to be on excellent terms with his master, who was of a most genial disposition. Underneath this apparent friendship there lay concealed in the mind of the serf the bitter recollection of the defeat and slaughter of his own clan Tanè. The following well-known incident revealed the truth :

One morning Autea went fishing off a huge rent in the reef, known as Vaingatara, occasioned by the discharge of the fresh-water streams of that part of the island into the ocean. The place is famed for the abundance of *nanuè*, a fine fish common throughout the Eastern Pacific.

At mid-day Mouna started off alone in his slender *puka*[2] canoe to share the sport. Happening to lose his hook, he asked Autea to lend him one. Autea replied that he had only one of the sort required, and that was the hook he was angling with. Anxious not to return home empty-handed, Mouna set to work upon the shell of an *ariri* (*Turbo petholatus*) which he had picked up on the

---

[1] To be carefully distinguished from an earlier Mouna who slew the king Tiaio. See p. 29 of *Myths and Songs*.

[2] A species of *Hernandia*.

reef. A piece of red quartz, sharp as flint, was his only implement. (In those days a man always carried about with him in his girdle a piece of this quartz, as we carry a pocket-knife.) Knowing that there was not a breath of wind to ruffle the glassy sea, Mouna chipped away at the shell until the hook was completed. In a few seconds more it was fastened to the line, and baited. Looking up, he was alarmed to find that he had drifted out to sea ; indeed, he almost despaired of regaining the distant shore of his island home. Earnestly invoking the aid of his god Teipe, he paddled back with might and main. Happily the current turned in his favour, and he again arrived on the fishing-ground in time to secure a basket of fish ere sunset.

The serf witnessed the drifting out to sea. He returned to the interior inwardly chuckling at the apparent certainty that one of the leading warriors of the dominant and hated tribe of Teipe would never again set foot on land. Judge, then, his surprise, as darkness came on, at hearing the well-known voice of the master calling his wife to cook the fish.

Next morning Mouna desired his son to run about the adjoining premises of Autea, *as if in play*, so as to discover where his fish-hooks and lines were drying in the sun, and to be sure to bring them stealthily to him. In a few minutes the boy returned with a number of hooks of different sizes tied together. Amongst them were several intended for *nanue.* His surmise had proved correct : the serf cherished the grudge of his clan against his master. A message was at once sent by the boy to Autea, for him to depart. When it was delivered, the serf, knowing its justice and irrevocableness, wept bitterly with his wife and children. Gathering up a few portable articles, without a word of farewell or even a sight of his master, Autea made a sorrowful journey across the hills to Tevaenga, where he had two brothers living as serfs to a very exacting and disagreeable chief.

The fugitives found shelter, though a very poor one, at Tevaenga. When the brothers heard the story of ejectment from the lips of Autea, they severely blamed him. They composed a commemorative song, which they were permitted to chant at the ensuing fête of their lord. Of this song only the subjoined fragment is now remembered. The irregularity of the original attests its comparative antiquity :—

Nai tanu au i te kakara tupu.
Kia atea koe ē, e kino te karo ē !
Nai kino paa te karo e reire ē !
Autea e ! nai miri koia 'i te akamou-
  ponga ē !
Mai te are taeake ē, mai te are tae-
  ake ē !
Tatou e tokotoru katoa ē !

I was as a fragrant flower growing near the house.
'Twas thine own folly drove thee far away.
Alas, the greatness of this folly !
O Autea, thy sin led to this cruel revenge !
In early life we lived—we lived together.
Once more misfortunes unite us all three.

Scarcely a day passes on Mangaia but a serf is advised to 'remember Autea.' The fate of Autea was tragic. The three brothers went fishing with a net on the outer edge of the reef at Atuakoro, when an immense wave swept all three into the ocean. The bodies were never recovered.

It was by no means necessary, or even usual, to give a *vivâ voce* notice to a serf to quit. It was enough for the master to sit down on the ground near the threshold of the serf's hut and procure fire by the use of firesticks (*ikā ai*). At other times the lord of the soil would plant his short spear (anciently used as a staff) into the serf's taro-swamp, to signify that his gift had been resumed. For the lord of the soil to be often seen in the serf's plantation was a sure sign that he meant to eject. The ordinary method was, and indeed still is, for the master to weed the sloping sides of the serf's taro patch. The *formal* method of ejectment is to 'put down the *rāui*,' which is simply a green coco-nut frond, platted in three places on either side of the midrib, as a rough representation of the human form. This platted frond is firmly secured by pegs driven into the earth. The symbolism is, the real proprietor of the soil taking possession of it with his hands and legs ! If, as frequently happens, the *rāui* is disputed and chopped in pieces, the lord of the soil in a tempest of rage declares his *spine* (*i.e.* the midrib of the frond) has been chopped in two ! In the olden times death was the only adequate compensation for such an insult.

CHAPTER XIV

MAUTARA THE CANNIBAL

CIRCA A.D. 1666–74

AMONGST the fugitives who escaped after one of the early battles of Ngauta was a powerful fellow named Mautara, who sought shelter amid the secluded glens and vine-clad rocks of Ivirua. For several years he lived on without the knowledge of the victorious and hostile families of the interior. He subsisted upon wild fruits, which are plentiful in that neighbourhood; in the winter season he dug up a species of yam, which grows luxuriantly wherever the sun can penetrate the dense foliage. His home was an extensive, circular, deep cavern, which still bears his name. The approach to the Cave of Mautara is by a natural narrow pathway over loose stones. It is a region of perpetual humidity. One might wander for days over these moss-grown, fern-hidden rocks, without suspecting the proximity of this secure hiding-place. Most of the caverns of this island are at a considerable elevation; occasionally, as in this instance, it is needful to *descend* again by a difficult path, shaded by trees, in which the pretty *ngoio* (a species of dove) builds her nest and rears her speckled brood in safety. A feeble light struggles into this strange abode through two gloomy apertures.

Mautara was a cannibal. He chose this cave on account of its close proximity to a pathway to the sea known as Anarea. Then, as now, young folks were accustomed to go that way to the beach, in order to fish, or to fill their calabashes with salt water. Solitary stragglers were sure to disappear without a clue to their fate. These victims were conveyed to the great cave to be cooked at sunset. As the whole of the prolonged sway of Ngauta was unsettled, continual fighting being the order of the day, it was impossible for the relatives to ascertain what had become of these missing ones.

Dusk of evening and morning twilight were the only periods when Mautara deemed it safe to go in quest of prey. He slept through the day in his lair to avoid detection. His usual place for digging up wild yams was in the neighbourhood of the present Iviruan mission premises.

Like Ngako of later days, he sometimes preyed upon stragglers of his own and other tribes in adversity. Occasionally he would come upon some one asleep in the rocks ; a blow from his club would despatch the victim. At other times a slip-noose of strongly-platted sennit would enable him noiselessly to strangle the poor wretch.

He had become so accustomed to this mode of life that, having one morning secured a victim at the narrow pathway to the sea where only one can pass at a time between the perpendicular rocks, he unwisely ventured to steal some taro for a feast.

It happened, however, that at the edge of the magnificent pile of rocks at his back was a small *marae*, where, at that early hour, Kauate and his son Reketia were paying their respects to their tribal divinity. Their royal clan had been worsted in a later battle of Ngauta's at Tamarua, known as 'the fight at Punanga.' The bodies of Tiauru and the rest of the slain were sunk in a neighbouring eel-swamp. The standing-place of the victorious Ngauta is marked by two large stones.

Kauate and his son at once recognized Mautara, and resolved to intercept him. The favourite weapon of the cannibal was the *aro*, which he had planted upright in the soft banks of the taro-patch. The grand point, of course, was to secure the weapon before Mautara should be aware of their approach. Swiftly and stealthily they descended to the valley, and then crept round a great rock which lay between them and the taro-patch, in which the cannibal was busy, utterly unconscious of danger. In another moment father and son darted out from behind the rock and rushed along the narrow pathway to secure the club. Mautara, now aware of his critical position, made a desperate effort to grasp the trusty club which had so often befriended him ; and would doubtless have succeeded but for the deep mud of the taro-patch, in which he piteously floundered. When the cannibal was tolerably near the coveted weapon, Kauate snatched it out of the soil, and whirling it round, dealt his foe a terrible blow on the head. A second blow finished Mautara, whose body was hastily dragged out of the mud to the neighbouring hibiscus bush.

Hitherto Kauate and Reketia had not tasted human flesh, but they resolved now to begin upon so promising a subject. So corpulent was Mautara that they contented themselves with cutting off the thighs to cook, leaving the unwieldy carcase to rot. The place where this unholy feast was cooked is a grotto, Turuatua, formed by a curiously overhanging rock, where natives love now to recline during the heat of the midday sun.

The taro-patch where the savage met with his deserts is commemoratively called Pakā, 'Fallen,' and is in the possession of Katuke, the native pastor of the village.

Though Kauate and Reketia were exiles, they were

not friendless. They informed those who by stealth supplied their wants of the tragical end of the cannibal, who had been the pest of the neighbourhood. A careful search was instituted to ascertain the headquarters of Mautara. The red clay marks on the pointed rocks revealed the secret. In one of the dreariest recesses of that gloomy cave was found his sleeping-place of dry grass and fern, with abundant evidence of his nefarious occupation in past times.

Kauate and Reketia on more than one occasion made their way to Putoa, to consult with the afterwards famous warrior, Ngangati, and the celebrated 'mouthpiece of the god Motoro,' how to restore the supremacy of the ancient tribe to which they belonged. The true name of the celebrated priest was Rongo-i-mua = 'Rongo-the-Leader;' but, when about the time of these midnight conferences he took to eating human flesh, the priest of Motoro was nicknamed Mautara, after the cannibal slain by Kauate. Strangely enough, this nickname was far from being disagreeable to the priest, and ever after stuck to him; so that at this moment the name in question recalls to a native of Mangaia the memory not of the miserable solitary cannibal of Ivirua, but of the great man who founded a tribe which for a century swayed the destinies of Mangaia.

The priest, in a drunken ecstasy, assured the fugitives that only in one way could the worshippers of Motoro be restored to power and prosperity, and that was by the sacrifice of Kauate himself. With a strange heroism Kauate agreed to die on behalf of his tribe ! Not, however, as an altar-offering to Rongo—that were impossible ; but *Kauate should seek a violent death at the hand of his foes.*

Kauate was the tallest man of his time. He one day

wrenched off by main force a bunch of green bananas belonging to one of the hereditary foes of his clan, and buried it in the earth near the public road to ripen. A moment's glance convinced the indignant owner that no ordinary man could perform such a feat. It must have been done by tall Kauate. A careful search was made to discover where it was buried. It was soon found. As on the fifth night the bananas would be ripe, the tribe of Ngauta were on the alert and well armed. It was said that Kauate, aware of all this, begged his son to live ; but Reketia refused to leave his father. On their way to disinter the bananas they both fell at the hands of their foes.

The subsequent well-planned and successful surprise of Ngangati, in which ' every slave slew his own master,' and the invincible Ngauta was slain by his nephew, as well as all the glories of his prolonged rule, were all attributed to the costly offering of the conquered chief Kauate. This circumstance, regarded as the turning-point of their history, was commemorated in song.

FÊTE SONG OF RUAKURA.

By Tangarerua, *circa* A.D. 1790.

Reketia urunga i Mataira
Kauate te are o Ngariki.
Kua motu koe ia Motoro, ka ta ē !
   O Ngariki oki te puanga.

Reketia was slain by his foes,
With Kauate chief of the royal clan.
'Twas the fiat of Motoro that ye should
   die,
To resuscitate the fortunes of Ngariki.

Pua i Tevaenga, o te Tikute,
   O Ngati Marua :
Te ivi matakeinanga ia Ngariki ē !

Born in Tevaenga, son of Tikute,
Originally from the land of shadows,
Thou wast the proud head of our
   tribe.

Noo i Ivirua, kopu tangata o Motoro,
   Amu te tuarangi ē !]

Ye lived at Ivirua, worshippers of the
   god Motoro,
     Like the famed Amu (long ago).

Ei tauka ia Ngariki ;
O Vaeruarangi au ē !

Descendant of Vaeruarangi,
Why didst thou not live to rule
   Ngariki?

CHAPTER XV

THE CANNIBAL TANGAKA

CIRCA A.D. 1680

AFTER one of the battles of Ngangati, a warrior named Tangaka, belonging to the long since extinct tribe of Kanae, took refuge in the rocks of Veitatei. He contrived to subsist by stealing food from the interior on moonless nights, and by digging for wild roots. Contrary to the custom of exiles, instead of worshipping, he *ate* the frugivorous bat, which, paralyzed by cold, is easily struck down with a stick at daybreak.

It was a period of incessant warfare. Luckily for Tangaka, the battles of Ngangati were fought at no great distance from his hiding-place. From all these battle-fields he reaped a rich harvest of spoil. Those who had relatives amongst the slain, as soon as the fighting was over, sought out and removed them. The rest were left to rot where they had fallen, for dogs were then unknown. At nightfall, Tangaka, with a sharp bamboo-knife, cut off the legs and arms of the dead, as being the most delicious bits, and, tying them together, carried them off to his cave. The cannibal grew quite dainty amid such abundance.

His grim abode, still called the Cave of Tangaka, was not more than half a mile distant, so that he could easily make two or three trips in a night. It was known that some one had dismembered the slain for the purpose of eating, but no one cared to inquire what had become of the bodies of their foes.

The Cave of Tangaka is very difficult of access. The surrounding scenery is pleasing. The cave itself is a hole, a little over forty feet in depth, about midway in a perpendicular rock of more than a hundred feet, overhung with trees and bushes. This lair is well concealed by an enormous splinter of the solid rock. After climbing up a natural pathway of loose stones, covered with beautiful creepers, the guide said, ' This is the way to the Cave of Tangaka.' In a few moments he climbed up the almost perpendicular rock by dexterously inserting his toes in the small crevices, and clinging with his hands to projecting ledges. I declined to follow, as it would be impossible for any one with shoes to do so with safety.

Upon a second visit we discovered a second entrance to this cave. A short *détour* through the bush brought us to the foot of a huge stone. A pandanus-tree, growing above it, completely hid from view this side-entrance. Carefully avoiding the serrated edges of the thick-growing pandanus leaves, we entered the narrowest part of the rent. At first it seemed impossible to get in, but, following a native lad, I contrived to squeeze in sideways. In the middle of this narrow, gloomy passage are several rope-like roots of the banyan-tree, which have found their way down from the distant top, and lodge in the scanty soil at the bottom.

After a time the narrow passage widened considerably, and we found ourselves right under the cave once inhabited by the cannibal. It was comparatively easy now to climb on a ledge of rocks, and thence to pass, by means of a plank, into what had once been the home of Tangaka. The dividing chasm is nine feet wide. From this point I made a rough sketch of the natural rent in the rock; but no pencil can give an adequate idea of the wildness and solitude of the spot. Ferns of exquisite delicacy grow out of the rock. Far above was a tiny patch of blue sky, bounded by the giant branches of ancient ironwood trees. This secret entrance was used by Tangaka when broad daylight rendered it inexpedient to use the direct one which I first visited. He was wont to bring his prey to the direct entrance at night. To a native it is nothing to climb the almost perpendicular rock, and then to haul up the heaviest burden by means of stout sennit cords. He was too crafty to cook his disgusting food in the cave, where the smoke and fire might attract the notice of his foes. A natural round hollow at the bottom of the deep chasm, in its widest part, was his oven; and a better one for his purpose could not be imagined.

About a mile distant from this stronghold was another resort of this cannibal. One of the main routes from the interior to the beach, named Raurau, passes over a small cavity of the rock. A person inside can distinctly see any one climbing the rugged pathway, but cannot himself be seen. Here Tangaka used to lie in wait for his victims. The cave was one day occupied by Tiaio,[1] who was fed by his sister Koua. As Koua had married into the victorious tribe, she could easily do this.

As soon as Tangaka discovered his victim, he went in, pretending friendship for the fugitive from a later battle-field. As Tiaio was ignorant of Tangaka's cannibal propensities, he was off his guard, and in a moment the fatal slip-noose was passed over his head. After a brief struggle, Tangaka succeeded in carrying off the dead body of Tiaio to his usual haunt. Early next morning Koua

---

[1] So named after the god Tiaio.

came as usual to bring food to her brother, but he could not be found. On carefully examining the earthen floor of the little cave, she discovered traces of the death-struggle and drops of blood. At this distance of time the family name of Tiaio is still kept up in remembrance of their unfortunate ancestor.

As soon as this supply of food was exhausted, Tangaka returned to this little cave to watch for a new victim. The names of several of his unhappy victims are still remembered. A favourite occupation of his was to watch for travellers along the pleasant hill-range opposite to his eyrie. It was easy for him to intercept any solitary woman or child on descending to the lower lands covered with bush.

A party of young girls started early one morning from Keia to collect chestnuts, which had fallen in the night. The clump of trees they visited was within a short distance of the hiding-place of the cannibal. With great glee he watched the party descend towards the chestnut trees, and soon passed out by his secret path to hide in the tall reeds for a victim.

The girls soon filled their baskets and returned home. But one of their number, less expert than her friends, lingered behind, securing her basket with hibiscus bark. A sharp turn in the narrow pathway hid her companions from view. At this moment Tangaka emerged from his hiding-place, and, creeping stealthily behind the poor girl, threw the fatal cord around her neck and strangled her. He speedily dragged the body and the basket behind some stones, until nightfall should enable him to bear both to his lair.

The companions of the murdered girl waited long for her on the hilltop; finding that no response was given to their loud calls, fear naturally took possession of their minds, and they hastened back to relate the mysterious disappearance of the poor girl. Raupo, the father of the missing young woman, went that same day with his friends to seek for her, but in vain.

The paramount chief, Ngangati, with the priest Mautara, then a youth, called a meeting of all the principal men to endeavour to find out what had become of Raupo's daughter. Manini stated what was known only to himself, that Tangaka was yet living, and that doubtless he had eaten the poor girl. In fact, Manini was related to the cannibal, and occasionally supplied him with food, but now gave him up to destruction, because he had eaten the daughter of his friend. Manini headed the avenging party, and led them by a rough and circuitous way to the farther end of the chasm opposite to that by which we laboriously entered. Then, noiselessly clambering over the masses of fallen stone, they hid themselves under the shelving rocks close to the entrance of the cave. The spears provided for the occasion were about twelve feet in length ; these were firmly planted in the rocky soil.

Meanwhile Raupo, unarmed, to avoid suspicion, went up the direct pathway, and looked across the chasm, and saw the ferocious Tangaka, his own near kinsman, fast asleep, it being midday. He could not get across, and probably did not wish to, as the narrow plank had been withdrawn by the wily cannibal. Raupo called him by name, and Tangaka started up with a grunt of displeasure at the unexpected intrusion. So long had the cannibal lived in the rocks, that he did not know that the girl he had murdered was his own cousin ; still less did he suspect that it was to avenge her death that Raupo had tracked him to his very den.

Raupo blandly assured his relative Tangaka that he had come to fetch him to live with him in the interior. Tangaka smiled, but asked in what part of the island their future home should be. Raupo said, ' I will give you a fine taro plantation in Veitatei. You shall eat the firm small taro for which it is famous.'

Tangaka shook his head at this proposal. Did he think it inconveniently near to the scene of his many crimes?

Raupo next proposed that they should both go to Tevaenga, and there 'eat the yellow soft taro for which that district is noted.' It was quite true that Raupo's lands were in that part of the island. Tangaka caught at this, and expressed his entire willingness to give up his solitary life in the rocks and thickets. Raupo said, ' We will go at once. The drum of peace has beaten ; you have nothing to fear.' The cannibal now got the plank and laid it across the chasm. The moment Tangaka stepped upon it, Raupo kicked the plank with his foot, thus precipitating the monster down headlong to a depth of thirty-six feet. His brains were not dashed out on the rock, for Manini and the rest were on the watch, and as he fell firmly held the spears they had planted upright in the soil, and thus transfixed the cannibal. Many were the spear-wounds in his body. After extinguishing the last remains of life, the battered corpse was righteously left to moulder in the very hollow where he had been accustomed to cook his victims. One could not help sitting a few minutes on the edge of this oven, ruminating on the striking contrast between the past reign of cruelty and 'the gentle reign of Jesus.'

Raupo soon discovered several packages in leaves hidden away in a recess of the cave—the remains of his poor daughter. It is said that the head enabled the sorrow-stricken parent to identify the remains. The cord, knife (of bamboo), and club were all there. There is, therefore, no little propriety in the constantly-recurring allusions in native preaching and praying to 'Satan going about, *like Tangaka*, seeking whom he may devour.'

CHAPTER XVI

A FATAL ROLL

CIRCA A.D. 1688

ONE day having occasion to visit the opposite side of the island, and the morning being cool, I crossed over the hills on foot, accompanied by an intelligent young man as a guide. We were halfway on our road when my companion proposed that we should diverge slightly from the narrow track in order 'to see where Vivi rolled himself down.' I gladly assented. A few minutes' walk along a narrow hill-ridge through the crisp fern which we crunched under our feet, brought us to a conical eminence, up which we climbed. On either side was a deep valley with precipitous sides. It might be just possible for a barefooted native to get down alive by holding on to the tufts of fern and branches of trees which here and there shoot out of the clayey soil. A false step, or the snapping of a bough, would precipitate him to the bottom—a depth of some six hundred feet. 'Down there,' said my guide, 'rolled poor Vivi.' We rested a few minutes in the shade of some graceful ironwood trees (*Casuarina equisetifolia*), the wiry leaves of which closely resemble the stems of fine grass. In the distance was the blue ocean, scarcely distinguishable from the azure sky. Nearer rose that impregnable rocky defence against the violence of old ocean which encircles the island, and is itself covered with dense forest. Between it and where we sat it was pleasant to trace out the hills and valleys of Veitatei. The plaintive murmur of the wind through the numerous clumps of ironwood-trees seemed like the distant music of the waves.

The following is the story of Vivi then related to me :

The tribe of Teipe, once very numerous, was devoted to the furnishing of sacrifices to Rongo from an early period. During the former part of Ngauta's supremacy they enjoyed exemption from this terrible fate. But when that great warrior turned his hand against them their doom was sealed. Repeated defeats in battle reduced the clan of Teipe to a mere fragment; as, however, their sisters and daughters were in many instances married into the winning tribes, a few of the males were sheltered and fed. But even they lived as it were by sufferance, and might be killed at pleasure. At the period referred to Tuanui was paramount chief of Mangaia ; Mautara, who at that time lived at the mouth of the valley at our feet, was inferior only to Tuanui in importance. Hearing that his distant relatives, Vivi and Tito, were yet living in the forest near the sea, he sent a trusty messenger inviting them to come by night into the interior and secrete themselves in this lonely valley, where he could easily supply them with food. Very joyfully, but in the end unfortunately, they left the few surviving members of their tribe to shift as they could upon wild roots and fruits, whilst they looked forward to happier days under the protecting care of the priest of Motoro. Vivi and Tito hid themselves in the dense thickets which at that time covered the bottom of the valley, which is very narrow. Rarely did any one pass this way, as it lies out of the ordinary track, and the sides are for the most part inaccessible. Here, if anywhere, they seemed secure under the secret patronage of Mautara, whose son Kakakina brought them food out of the abundance which was supplied to the supposed 'mouthpiece of the god' by the chiefs.

The principal warriors took up their abode near this famous priest, partly in order to learn the commands of their god, and partly in order to assist Mautara in disposing of his food. Amongst this number was the bold and unscrupulous Tamangoru, who, having noticed that the food brought day by day from all parts of the island disappeared with a rapidity not warranted by the small family of the priest, set a watch to discover what became of it. At last he found that Mautara was guilty of succouring these forlorn creatures, Vivi and Tito. Without giving a hint to his priest, on the following morning Tamangoru collected a number of his friends to hunt the fugitives. As soon as the poor fellows discovered their danger they ran up to the head of the valley, in the hope of gaining the crest of the hill where we were sitting, and of so being able easily to balk their pursuers by hiding in another valley. Vivi, being swifter of foot, gained the top of the hill, whilst his younger brother, Tito, was yet only at the base. The ascent must have been an arduous task, but fear works wonders.

Now Tamangoru had foreseen this movement, and from the first setting out had left the body of his followers in order to run up the parallel valley, and so intercept his victims. Hence it happened that Vivi and Tamangoru met face to face on the spot where we were resting. But poor Vivi was unarmed, and, indeed, had he been armed, he would have been no match for his fierce antagonist, who was regarded as the best warrior of his day. Standing in Vivi's path with his uplifted club, Tamangoru uttered the words which have since passed into a proverb, 'Run where thou wilt, thou shalt not escape.' The unhappy fugitive, seeing that there was no hope, at once threw himself down the hill which he had just climbed. He rolled heavily to the very bottom, repeatedly striking against projecting stones, sharp roots, and branches of trees.

Tamangoru, disappointed at the sudden disappearance of Vivi, dashed down into the valley by a circuitous but safe pathway at a little distance. Once at the bottom of the gorge, he ran at full speed, lest any of his friends should deprive him of the honour of slaying his victim. With his own hand he clubbed the battered, insensible, but still breathing form of one who had never injured him.

Tamangoru now searched everywhere for Tito, who was hiding in some thick brushwood. Tamangoru is said to have split his skull with a single stroke of his wooden sword.

Meanwhile Kakakina, in utter ignorance of what was going on, was carrying a large bunch of bananas for the unfortunate fugitives. Thus to befriend two members of the devoted tribe was a mortal sin in the estimation of Tamangoru. The boy was murdered and his body hidden in the fern, but was subsequently discovered by his brave elder brothers and buried. Over that grave were uttered threats of vengeance against the ancient ruling tribe to which the wanton murderer belonged. In the battle-field of Māueue, which took place about two years afterwards, all engaged in these murders were slain, with the exception of Tamangoru, who was reserved by a retributive Providence for a more ignominious end.

A single family, consisting of three brothers, alone

survives out of the once numerous tribe of Teipe. A long line of ancestors were all slain, and for the most part laid on the altar of Great Rongo, the relentless god of war. These survivors are members of the Church. Nothing but Christianity could have saved their lives. Females were offered in sacrifice as well as males, although less often. One of the three survivors has lived many years in our family. Occasionally his countrymen chaff him about his having narrowly escaped the fate of his ancestors; but although said in joke—and nothing can prevent these islanders from joking on all kinds of subjects—I have invariably seen him turn ghastly pale as the fearful vision rose up before his mind.

A 'CRYING' SONG FOR VIVI AND TITO; BY KOROA.

Pertaining to the 'Death-talk' of Puvai.—*Circa* A.D. 1795.

Solo.

Tiō ra Vivi oki nga tokorua
   A Tepeipei.

Solo.

Sing we of Tivi and his brother—
   Devoted Teipe.

Chorus.

   Ua kimikimi Ngariki ē !
Na ivi taito ia Tito te vi para ē !

Chorus.

Ngariki was bent on their destruction.
Shortlived was the shelter afforded to
   Tito !

PAPA.

Solo.

Tei utā Tito ē ī !

FOUNDATION.

Solo.

Ah, Tito was hiding in yon valley.

Chorus.

Tei utā Tito i te vao mangarua,
Po rua oki au e pokia io.

Chorus.

Yes, Tito was hidden in a secluded
   valley.
'Twas but the second day when he
   was caught.

Solo.

Pokia io i te kaivī i te karava,
Ua amanga te rima o te tamaki.

Solo.

Caught on the very crest of the hill,
The hands of his foes were upon him.

Chorus.

I uta i Teauiti i te vao ē !

Chorus.

In the vale of Teauiti (he perished) !

UNUUNU TAI.
Solo.

Vivi ē tueruia ra ē !

Chorus.

Vivi e tueruia, ua atava nga tapuae
O te Tuma nengaia Tepei ī.
Tei miri Tito i Tetanga a teuanuku,
To are rau naū kopiopiotā.
Eiaa te ao i toe ai ē !

Solo.

Tio ra, etc.

UNUUNU RUA.
Solo.

Tipia i nunga e taka i raro !

Chorus

Tipia i nunga e taka i raro :
E taka i raro i te nii taparere
I te aiaia i te tataingo o Vaiariki.
   Oai te puta ia uta?
Mautara koi i te kiko o Tane.
Eiaa te ao i toe ai ū !

Solo.

Tio ra, etc.

FIRST OFFSHOOT.
Solo.

Poor Vivi was hunted to death.

Chorus.

Alas ! Vivi was hunted to death, by
The relentless foes of his tribe.
Tito vainly hoped to escape,—
Hiding in a fern-leaved hut.
(Said Tamangoru :) Not one of the
   vanquished shall live.

Solo.

Sing we, etc.

SECOND OFFSHOOT.
Solo.

The victim rolled down from the
   hill-top.

Chorus.

Ah ! he rolled down from the crest
   of the hill :
From that dizzy height he rolled and
   lay,
A scarcely-breathing mass at the
   bottom.
   Who invited him to the interior ?
Mautara, the saviour of Tanè.
(Said Tamangoru :) Not one of the
   vanquished shall live.

Solo.

Sing we, etc.

A LAMENT FOR VIVO AND TITO. A *TIAU*, OR PARTIAL WEEPING. BY KOROA.

Circa A.D. 1795.

TUMU.

Pukiekїe e kore rai Tokoano ai.
   E oro ei Vivi ē !
   Mei uta i te vao !
Tai puku kakengata, e korua ē !

PAPA.

Kimiia koe i Tepikoiti i te makatea,
Te are ao na Mautara,
Te kino nei a uta e taeakekore
I Tito i te tamaki, e Ano ē !

INTRODUCTION.

Helpless, entirely helpless, were the
   sons of Tokoano.
   Hence the flight of Vivi
   From the deep valley
To the steep hill where both perished !

FOUNDATION.

Ye were sought out of the deepest
   recesses,
To become vassals of Mautara.
Even there the jealous foe tracked
And slew the well-beloved Tito !

Unuunu Tai.

Pukiekie kore, e korē, tei Avaavata-
    kina,—
      Tei Avaavatakina.
Ko te ua marire e piri ai e oo te vere-
    vere,
E verevere aere i Tuanaki.
Kua tika paa ia Rongo ia Tumakatea.
    Kua au te tira ia Veri.
      Mei uta ia te vao !
Tai puku kakengata, e korua ē !

First Offshoot.

Utterly friendless, they first hid near
    the ocean—
      Near the ocean.
They subsisted on wild berries and
    fruits
Found in the depths of the rocks—
Favoured by Rongo and the forest
    gods.
Did they not worship the centipede ? [1]
    (They ran) from the deep valley
To the steep hill where both perished !

Unuunu Rua.

'Oro atu koe, ei iaku Teua,—
    Ei iaku Teua !'
    Kua topa koe i te io,
Kua taka aere, taka io Vivi nei.
Kua tangi te rau o te tuanue ;
O te vaevae oki o te tamaki,
Koputureia e Tamangoru.
    Mei uta i te vao !
Tai puku kakengata, e korua ē !

Second Offshoot.

(At the words) ' Run where thou wilt,
    thou shalt not escape—
      Thou shalt not escape,'
    Thy heart sank within thee !
Thou didst roll down ! Vivi rolled
    down, down ;
The dry fern-leaves cracked beneath
The feet of those who cruelly hunted
    thee ;
Tamangoru himself leaped on thy
    body.
    (They ran) from the deep valley
To the steep hill where both perished !

Unuunu Toru.

Eketia i raro i Teaumoko,—
    E i Teaumoko.
Tei Takimivera oki te punanga,—
    Punanga i te ao ē !
E kai eki ua, te mikorau ra.
Kua pipi vaitorea, ta te ao manga ia,
Ko te ua i mapura ia no Ukuroi ē,
    E i atoro i te rangatira.
    Mei uta i te vao !
Tai puku kakengata, e korua ē !

Third Offshoot.

Once thou wert hidden in a narrow
    valley—
      In a narrow valley.
Impervious thickets were the fit home
    Of the conquered in war.
Thy food was seeds, and the drupe
    of the pandanus ;
A drink at the stream was oft thy
    only solace ;
The tender shoots of wild taro on the
    banks
    Were claimed by the victors.
    (They ran) from the deep valley
To the steep hill where both perished !

Unuunu A.

Tikina i tai ē, tei Motuvera ?
    E tei Motuvera.
Tera roa tei rotopu i te rāei.
Tei Tetuokura ; i kake ake na Pei toe
I o pikimato, anau atu i te kainga.

Fourth Offshoot.

Why were ye fetched from the cave
    near the sea—
      Near the sea ?
From the very bosom of the black
    rocks ?

The god of Vivi and Tito was the centipede.

Mei uta i te vao !
Tai puku kakengata, e korua ē !

From the mossy couches of the tribe
  of Teipe,
Amidst fantastic crags, weeping for
  lost homes !
    (They ran) from the deep valley
To the steep hill where both perished !

UNUUNU RIMA.

Taura tukua ē i te taeva ē !
  I te taeva !
I te tai paku, tei Ronaki,
Tei putaranunga.   Kua au te are
I Avaavaotao, araviki o te ara,
Na uta, no tai, akaea Teipe manua.
  Mei uta i te vao !
Tai puku kakengata, e korua ē ?

FIFTH OFFSHOOT.

A rope[1] was let down yon dreary
  chasm—
    That gloomy chasm—
The wretched abode of the fugitives,
Wandering hither and thither
Through the most inaccessible places.
Teipe[2] is as a defenceless bird, flying
  hither and thither,
    (They ran) from the deep valley
To the steep hill where both perished !

AKAREINGA.

Ai e ruaoo ē !   E rangai ē !

FINALE.

Ai e ruaoo ē !   E rangai ē !

---

[1] This 'rope' was the promise of protection given by Mautara. This their last hope failed them.

[2] The tribe is beautifully personified. As the bird seeks the wildest place for its home, so does this doomed race.

This song is part of the 'death-talk about Puvai,' who was a member of the Teipe tribe, and who died a natural death upwards of a century later.

CHAPTER XVII

THE INGLORIOUS END OF TAMANGORU

CIRCA A.D. 1691

PREVIOUS to his defeat at Māueue, Tamangoru was chief of Butoa, the district in which the battle took place. By a just retribution, the murderer of Vivi and Tito became himself a homeless fugitive, his lands passing into the hands of his foes. Had he not been fleet of foot, he would have fallen at the hands of the brave brothers of Kakakina.

Rori was a dependant of the chief Tamangoru. He sought to hide himself in the inaccessible rocks near the sea, whilst Tamangoru, his former lord, preferred to hover about in the bush of the district once his own. He would sometimes by night enter the narrow valleys of the interior to slake his thirst. He would hide himself for days and weeks together in one of these lonely hollows, stealing food at night, and sleeping by day in the hibiscus thickets or in the gigantic fern. He had no friend to seek him out and to supply his wants.

These little valleys — favourite hiding-places of the conquered—were in those times entirely in a state of nature, but are now everywhere well cultivated. The nicest taro, although inferior in size, grows in these sequestered spots.

In the larger valleys, to obtain possession of which so much blood was shed from generation to generation, families would build their huts close together for the sake of mutual protection.

That misfortune had not softened the heart of Tamangoru towards the feeble is clear from an anecdote which belongs to this period of his history.

Kurapeau, mother of Mautara, was inconsolable for the loss of her husband Akunukunu, who had been put to death by her relatives (the Tongan clan). She had often assured him that her own tribe would be sure to protect him. In a state of distracted grief she wandered alone over the island ; nothing could induce her to stay with her son and his family. One day she fell in with Tamangoru in one of these secluded valleys, and was by him immediately speared to death. The attenuated body was not eaten, but hidden in a neighbouring taro-patch. Eight days afterwards it was discovered and buried by her relatives.

But Tamangoru was not always so particular ; stragglers were sometimes cut off and eaten by this solitary cannibal. He is said to have been a powerful man ; so that, though often seen, nobody cared to attack him. His career after the battle of Māueue was brief, and his end very inglorious.

Under cover of night he crossed the island, taking up his abode in the rocks and thickets on the western shore, where he was but little known. He had no companion but his enormous club, and experienced great difficulty in satisfying his hunger from day to day. Early one morning, soon after his arrival on the western shore, he saw smoke ascending at no great distance. Cautiously approaching it, he discovered two boys roasting a number of rats over a fire—a joyful sight for a famishing Mangaian.

In those days—ere the cat had been introduced—rats were very plentiful. Rat-hunting was the grave employment of bearded men, the flesh being regarded as most delicious.

The rat, though but slightly larger than the English mouse, was the only quadruped on the island.

Oromanarangi and Oromananuku were brothers, the former about fifteen years of age, the younger about thirteen. They were themselves fugitives and orphans, and subsisted chiefly by rat-catching, in which they were adepts. The place selected for their operations was a wild, out-of-the-way spot. Jagged rocks cropped out of the thin soil in every direction, and were covered with a variety of creepers, the most beautiful of which—*Coix lachryma*—yields a profusion of vermilion berries, which furnish necklaces in abundance for the young folks. A dense growth of timber shut out the little open space from observation.

On the previous evening the boys dug a deep hole in the earth and covered the bottom of it with candlenuts, of which rats are excessively fond. A narrow pathway was made on either side for the rats to get down to eat. The lads lay in wait at a little distance, until they thought the hole must be pretty full. Each lad carried a lighted torch in one hand, and a stout iron-wood stick in the other. They quickly killed a large number of rats.

The boys now made a fire to roast the spoil. They then thrust long green reeds (previously prepared) through the rats, eight on each reed, and grilled them over the fire. There were four skewers or reeds of rats, *i.e.* thirty-two in all.

Whilst thus pleasantly engaged in preparing their savoury breakfast, to their great discomfiture the formidable Tamangoru made his appearance. Oromanarangi whispered in his brother's ear, 'If anything should happen, do *you* look after his *feet*; *I* will take care of his *head*.'

Tamangoru seated himself quietly on some dry leaves,

and, eyeing the boys very attentively, ambiguously remarked, 'Cooked *rats* are capital eating.' The word 'rats' thus used might apply to the lads as well as to the little quadrupeds. A cooked boy would be indifferently called a 'fish' or a 'rat.' Oromanarangi and Oromananuku at once caught at the double sense intended, and so prepared for the worst. When the rats were done, the elder took two reeds of rats (sixteen) to Tamangoru. Cautiously, however, avoiding the front of his adversary, he approached him on the side farthest from the dreaded ironwood sword, sharply eyeing Tamangoru's hands as he carried the cooked rats. The famished man greedily devoured them. Tamangoru now called for the remaining two reeds. Oromanarangi, without uttering a word of complaint, carried them by the same circuitous route to Tamangoru. Approaching him from behind, he put them over his right shoulder. In Tamangoru's left hand was the wooden sword ; the right hand was at this moment engaged in taking the cooked rats from the boy, who felt certain that the cruel enemy would slay both him and his brother as soon as the rats were demolished. The choice lay between killing him or being killed by him.

At this critical moment, when both hands were engaged, the elder lad seized hold of his flowing hair with both hands. It was a death-grip. His feet were firmly planted in the girdle of his powerful adversary. Tamangoru was unprepared for this, not deeming it possible that mere boys should attack one who had been greatly feared by their parents. He was almost helpless, as his head was pulled far back by the strong lad. Recollecting, however, a large Barringtonia-tree, growing just by, he walked backwards towards it, of course carrying the adventurous boy with him, purposing to drive his whole force against the tree, so as to kill Oromanarangi. But Tamangoru had found his match, for as he was just about to crush the lad his dexterous foe wriggled on one side, but without relaxing his hold upon the head or withdrawing his feet from the girdle. Tamangoru was much shaken by the heavy blow received against his bare back. Again and again the trick was played by Tamangoru with a similar result, until he at length stood still, considerably exhausted.

This was the precise moment that little Oromananuku was waiting for. Taking up a large irregular stone, he dashed it with all his might against the legs of his huge foe. One leg was quite broken by the well-directed missile, so that Tamangoru fell heavily on the ground. The elder brother cleverly slipped off the back of the doomed man as he fell. Tamangoru, feeling himself to be indeed in an evil case, earnestly begged the boys to spare his life. Little pity could he deserve who had never in his life shown pity to others. The head was now free, but only because he was no longer capable of defending himself. The boys beat out his brains with stones. The body of Tamangoru was left to rot where he so ingloriously fell. But the brave lads were ever after celebrated amongst their countrymen as the punishers of this fierce marauder. The spot where he fell is known as the Pounding of Tamangoru, being marked by a rock four feet and a half high. Boys delight to beat it with stones, on account of the musical sound it gives forth.

LAMENT FOR KURAPEAU.

By her son Mautara. *Circa* 1691.

Tumu.	Introduction.
Ko Te-moe-au tei Torekaro	(Thy mother) 'The-gentle-sleeper'[1] lies buried

---

[1] 'The-gentle-sleeper' was the daughter of Ivi, priest of Turanga. As this tribe, from Tonga, was the most powerful of its time, she is represented as *condescending* to marry Akunukunu, priest of Motoro.

Ei raupoto i Aremangeo,
Akatupu koe i te verevere.
Ka ano ē, kimi tane ē !
Tekura tei rangatira reira ē !

At Aumoana[1] amongst her relatives—
She who succoured the perishing.
Thou the prosperous Kurapeau[2] didst choose
The unfortunate Akunukunu for thy husband.

PAPA.

Mautara kai ngakau ē !
Kimi atu koe i to metua ;
Tei uta ē, i te vao roa,
I te poo i Vaiaua.
Kua pa oki te karanga ē,
Akunukunu e vai ra, e Tekura ē !

FOUNDATION.

Mautara, the wisest of sons,
Sought everywhere for his mother.
He found the corpse in a lonely glen,
In the deep recesses of Vaiaua.
How deep thy grief at the sad news, that
Thy Akunukunu had been slain, O Kurapeau.

UNUUNU TAI.

Te-moe-au, ē, tei Torekaro ē,
Tei Torekaro i te āū o Atakura,
'Tei Nukumau te kino,
Tei Nukumau te kino ai.
Ko te kiko i oongo mai ana ;
Kave atu tanumia,
I oro mai ia Tipou.
Ka ano ē, kimi tane ē !
Tekura tei rangatira reira ū !

FIRST OFFSHOOT.

(Thy mother) ' The-gentle-sleeper ' lies buried
At Aumoana, the resting-place of her tribe.
 'Twas *her* tribe that was angry—
 That caused us this sore trouble,
Piercing our very hearts with sorrow.
 Bury the dead out of sight,
 And return to thy home.
Thou the prosperous Kurapeau didst choose
The unfortunate Akunukunu for thy husband.

UNUUNU RUA.

Te upoko i mua ē, ia Mautara,
Ko Teuanuku ko te vae tapeka,
 Kai te tai i Pokara.
Ko te upoko tikitiki o Ngati Vara nei,
 Kua kavea i Tangikura.

SECOND OFFSHOOT.

Mother of great men !   Mautara first of all ;
Thy grandson Teuanuku, the brave,
Who avenged the wrongs of his ancestors.
The children of Vara[3] can ne'er forgive
The ancient slaughter at Tangikura.[4]

---

[1] Aumoana (' ocean current ') is the name of their *marae*, where the lizard was worshipped.

[2] Kurapeau is shortened into Kura. The definite article is (as is often done) prefixed, giving Tekura throughout this song.

[3] Vara was the second priest of Motoro in order of succession, and an ancestor of Mautara.

[4] The slaughter of the Aitu, or ' god tribe,' at Tangikura in the second battle that occurred on Mangaia.

Ka ano au ē, kimi tane ē!
Tekura tei rangatira reira ē!

Thou the prosperous Kurapeau didst
choose
The unfortunate Akunukunu for thy
husband.

UNUUNU TORU.

Koai, koai te piritanga ē?
  Piritanga ia Tekura?
Ko te anau a Tevaki—
Ko Ngati Vairanga, ko Ngati Vai-
ranga' i.
Aore au e tau, e Akunukunu.
Ko te amo ia Terua i paeke ei.
  Ka ano ē, kimi tane ē!
Tekura tei rangatira reira ē!

THIRD OFFSHOOT.

Who—ah! who—afforded succour?
Who pitied poor Kurapeau?
  Save the children of Tevaki,
Descended from Vairanga — that
ancient stock!
'My case is hopeless,' exclaimed
Akunukunu:
' I cannot escape from my foes.'
Thou the prosperous Kurapeau didst
choose
The unfortunate Akunukunu for thy
husband.

UNUUNU A.

Mangere ikona ē, tei Ruaiva ē,
Tei Kukupunua, ē Tekura,
  I te akamate aere,
  I te akamate aere ei,
Taku moe ngauta iaku,
  Ei tiki ia Tetipi,
Tekura te ranga ia Paeke.
  Ka ano ē, kimi tane ē;
Tekura tei rangatira reira ē!

FOURTH OFFSHOOT.

  ' Leave me here to die,
I will wander over the hills,' said she.
  ' I care not for my life—
  I long to die.
My dreams are of the dead.
I will join my deceased ancestors.
The death of Kurapeau shall avenge
Paeke.'
Thou the prosperous Kurapeau didst
choose
The unfortunate Akunukunu for thy
husband.

UNUUNU RIMA.

Ka peke i nunga ē!
Tei Putoa ē, kua ungā Mautara.
  Ko Tevaki te rave ake;
  Tei Putuputukiau,
  Tei Tekaeruaie!
  Ka ano ē, kimi tane ē!
Tekura tei rangatira reira ē!

FIFTH OFFSHOOT.

  Mautara took flight,
And for awhile was hidden at Putoa,
  Tevaki was his only solace;
  Amidst thickets and bushes
  They both found shelter.
Thou the once prosperous Kurapeau
didst choose
The unfortunate Akunukunu for thy
husband!

AKAREINGA.

Ai e ruaoo ē|! E rangai ē !

FINALE.

Ai e ruaoo ē! E rangai ē!

CHAPTER XVIII

THE EXILES

In two famous instances whole families were driven off the island, to take their chance on the ocean for life or death.

Tauai and Tekaraka, with their respective families and adherents, were exiled by the chief Aeru, of that division of the tribe Ngariki bearing the name Vaeruarangi. The dominant clan wished to kill them on account of an abortive attempt to seize the supreme chieftainship of the island. Packe, priest of Motoro, speaking oracularly, said, 'Exile them.' Two double canoes of the largest size were prepared, and provisions (coco-nuts) laid in for their long and uncertain voyage. These double canoes were connected with each other by means of stout iron-wood poles lashed with strong sennit. A deck was now laid across, a mast set up, and the extempore ship furnished with sails of stout native cloth, mats being unknown on Mangaia in those times.

On the appointed day Aeru ordered these two great double canoes to be launched, and the exiles to embark. Tauai commanded one canoe, Tekaraka the other. Nearly opposite to the mission premises at Tamarua is an indentation in the reef called Aeru, commemorating the exact point of departure. At that period the famous Ngauta was but a child; but in manhood he took ample revenge upon the ancient dominant clan for the expulsion of his relatives, Tauai and Tekaraka. The first exiles must have left the island upwards of two hundred and seventy years ago.

In Christian times the fate of these early voyagers has become a matter of great interest. It is believed that they reached the northern island of New Zealand in safety—that the Tekaraka referred to is the veritable Tekaraka who figures in Maori story. It may be a corroboration of this that the New Zealanders at once fraternize with the Hervey Islanders, and address them as their *ai tuakana*, or 'elder brethren.' Besides, there is a remarkable correspondence between various Maori names and the names of places on the south of Mangaia—Mangonui, Waikato, Waitangi, Waitotara; only in the Hervey Group dialect we print V for the W. The pronunciation of these names is identical. The distance to the nearest part of New Zealand would not be much more than that sorrowfully traversed by Elikana in 1862, in his involuntary voyage from Manihiki to Nukuraerae.

The expulsion of Iro is of a comparatively late date, about two hundred and twenty-three years ago. Like the former band of exiles, Iro and his friends belonged to the ever-restless Tongan tribe, whose headquarters were at Tamarua. The valuable *miro* tree (*Thespesia populnea*) grows spontaneously only on the rugged shore where their ancestors originally landed, bringing (it is averred) the seeds with them.

Ngauta had perished, and with him the overshadowing influence of the Tongan clan. But Iro and Tuavera, wishing to restore the ancient fame of their tribe, plotted the destruction of the leading chiefs of the day. Tuanui was supreme 'lord of Mangaia,' and Mautara priest of Motoro. The plot was revealed by Tia; consequently the ambuscade of the Tongans failed, and the exile of those concerned in the attack was decreed in the name of the god Motoro. The alleged motive for not permitting these Tongans to be slain was, 'that the sacred clothing of the gods might not be defiled with human blood,' and so draw down vengeance upon the ruling race. Pati, priest of the exiled tribe, was the sole depositary or maker of the superior paper-mulberry cloth, as thick as cardboard, used exclusively for clothing the gods, great chiefs, and priests. This 'lordly clothing' was actually worshipped by the tribe that manufactured it, under the name of *te tikoru mataiapo*.

As soon as the decree of Motoro was made known, Iro and his friends mournfully prepared for their enforced departure. As in the former instance, two large double canoes were built in a district called Tuavera, in memory of the event, on the northern part of the island. The timber used was that of the noble *Barringtonia speciosa*, whose large handsome flowers open at sunrise, but fade and fall to the ground at sunset. As the canoes of these exiles were sixty feet long, several of these magnificent trees were required. Like those of Tauai and Tekaraka, these canoes were decked and supplied with masts and sails. A thatched covering or awning was set up in each double canoe, in order to protect the women and children from the sun and rain.

All the valuable movable property of the exiles was taken on board, with a good supply of food and water. Several months were occupied in these preparations, during which time they suffered no molestation.

When no further excuse for delay could be invented, Tuanui gave the command to depart, and led the sorrowful band to the usual place of departure on the west side of the island. A farewell feast made for them by their friends occupied the morning. The sun was low in the horizon when, amid loud lamentations and many tears, they started, with a steady trade wind, on their uncertain voyage. Iro and Tuavera commanded one double canoe, Akaina and Pati the other.

The last words of Iro to his nephew, Arekare, were never to rest until he had avenged their expulsion by splitting up into hostile factions the tribe which ruled the island. They parted to meet no more. Would the exiles perish in the unknown waste of waters towards the setting sun, or would they reach some friendly shore, and there revive the fallen fortunes of their race? As the little 'ships' pressed towards the edge of the golden sky, and darkness came on, it is said that the distant glimmer of the torches lighted by the voyagers to cheer them on their way was the last ever seen here of Iro and his companions.

Some 155 years rolled on without tidings of these exiles, so that no one doubted that the entire party, upwards of forty, had perished in the deep. Not that the event was forgotten, as may be seen in an interesting song composed in memory of their departure.

LAMENT FOR IRO THE EXILE.

By Koroa; recited at 'the Death-talk of Vaiaa.'—*Circa* A.D. 1791.

TUMU.	INTRODUCTION.

Taiku io, e Iro e, ia Arekare—
   Naau ake ia Ngariki.
	Thy last charge, O Iro, to Arekare was—
	   Split up the clan of Ngariki.

E tae koe i te kao nu momoke	Fell the fair palm soaring above all others
I Araata; te ē o Tetipi ka eva ē !	At Araata;[1] now the tribe of Tetipi mourns.[2]

[1] The *marae* of Motoro was named Araata, where only the dominant tribe of Ngariki might worship. This tribe, hostile to the exiles, is compared to a lofty palm growing at Araata, and looking disdainfully down upon all other trees. This was doubtless suggested by the circumstance of a single coco-nut-tree of a rare yellow kind growing in the idol grove. On account of the supposed sanctity of the place it was never climbed, nor was the fruit tasted.

[2] Tetipi, one of the founders of the Tongan clan.

PAPA.	FOUNDATION.

Tuku atu tei te moana, e Iro;
Tei ia Pati te vaka i Tuavera.
Ko Akaina, te rā torikiriki tatou ē!

Start now on thy voyage, O Iro;
Pati has furnished Tuavera with a craft.
Alas, Akaina! our sun disappears in the horizon!

UNUUNU TAI.   FIRST OFFSHOOT.

Taiku io ē ia Arekare—
    Ia Arekare,
E momotu koe i te ivi roa,
    Ei oo paa nooku,
Ka rua vaka o Tetipi;—
E no Tauai tei neē atu,
    Ponakava in Aeru.
E tae koe i te kao nu momoke
I Araata; te ē o Tetipi ka eva ē!

Thy last charge to Arekare—
To thy friend Arekare, was—
End their long-continued sway.
This is the solace I crave.
Twice our tribe has been expelled;
Long since Tauai was driven away
Through the malice of Aeru.
Fell the fair palm soaring above all others
At Araata; now the tribe of Tetipi mourns.

UNUUNU RUA.   SECOND OFFSHOOT.

Oioi ake i te motuone—
    I te motuone,
Tei Vaipia, kua ata paa
I te tikoru i runga ia Pati,
    Kua panaia e Motoro;
Kua tamutu oki Tamangaro ē,
    Kua aaki na e Tia ē!
E tae koe i te kao nu momoke
I Araata; te ē o Tetipi ka eva ē!

The ambush was well laid
    And planned.
The sacred garments of Pati
Scared our hereditary foes.
'Tis Motoro that exiles us.
The attack of Tamangaro failed
Through the treachery of Tia.
Fell the fair palm soaring above all others
At Araata; now the tribe of Tetipi mourns.

UNUUNU TORU.   THIRD OFFSHOOT.

Rangakauria ē i te maroro ē,
    I te māroro ē!
E vaka kura no Tuavera.
    Kua pau Teaaki!
Kua tauna te matakeinga o Tetipi
Poroara io ia Ngariki.
E tae koe i te kao nu momoke
I Araata; te ē o Tetipi ka eva ē!

Our noble canoes are completed;
    What models are they!
Ornamented with red feathers by Tuavera.
    The tribe Teaaki[1] is gone!
The descendants of Tetipi have disappeared,
Driven away by merciless Ngariki!
Fell the fair palm soaring above all others
At Araata; now the tribe of Tetipi mourns.

UNUUNU A.   FOURTH OFFSHOOT.

Kua iti te rā ē kumekume tika—
Kumekume tika kia māro.

Ah! the sun shines brightly. Shine on;
For once hasten not to set.

---

[1] Teaaki, a branch of the once-powerful Tongan tribe.

Kia rou te rua i te matangi.
Na koao o te vaka, mei tatakina.
　Kua aae, kua ueue—
I te ara kaa i te tovere.
　Kua viri Iro i tai enua !
E tae koe i te kao nu momoke
I Araata ; te ē o Tetipi ka eva ē !

Let the wind blow favourably,
The ships sail gallantly o'er the ocean.
The sennit strains, the seams open ;
Yet the fragile barks hold on their way.
Perchance Iro will reach some other isle.
Fell the fair palm soaring above all others
At Araata ; now the tribe of Tetipi mourns.

UNUUNU RIMA.

Opuopu te uru ē no Mangaia ē !
　No Mangaia !
Kua pueke te ai ki vaenga moana,
　Ki te ata kurakura.
　E kaoa te kare i te taoa,
Oromia io Rauaika Nui,
I te papatua e muna ē !
E tae koe i te kao nu momoke
I Araata ; te ē o Tetipi ka eva ē !

FIFTH OFFSHOOT.

The hills of Mangaia are lost to sight.
　Alas for Mangaia !
Torches light our pathway o'er the sea
Where the ruddy sun went down.
The cruel waves attack our ships,
Hoping to sink them in mid-ocean,
And bury them for ever in its depths.
Fell the fair palm soaring above all others
At Araata ; now the tribe of Tetipi mourns.

AKAREINGA.

Ai e ruaoo ē !　E rangai ē !

FINALE.

Ai e ruaoo ē !　E rangai ē !

A few years after the introduction of Christianity into the Hervey Group, about 1826, a young Rarotongan accompanied the Rev. John Williams to Mangaia, and astonished the men of that day by stating that one of those double canoes commended by Iro and Tuavera reached Ngatangiia in safety. Kainuku, the chief of that part of Rarotonga, gave the exiles a kind reception, allotting to them an entire district at Titikaveka, which occupies relatively the same position at Rarotonga which Tamarua, the original home of Iro, does with respect to Mangaia. Like other heathens of Polynesia, the Rarotongans were always fighting. The valour of these exiles assisted materially in after years in raising the tribe with which they were incorporated to the proud position which it enjoyed in 1823, the date of the discovery of Rarotonga by Mr. Williams. ' In proof of this,' said Terei, the acknowledged head of this little colony, 'we alone are permitted to eat turtle and other royal fish when caught by ourselves.'

A block of sandstone in the harbour at Ngatangiia marks the spot where Iro first landed in his new home. At Titikaveka a vast quantity of sandstone (*kea*) is on the beach, and is found on no other part of Rarotonga. It came to be believed that this sandstone foundation of their new home actually accompanied Iro in his flight, and complaisantly settled down in its present position! The foundation of this wild fancy is the circumstance that pieces of 'sacred sandstone' were put on board their canoes as charms to insure the safety of the voyagers.

Terei was a worthy man, and made a consistent profession of Christianity for many years. The old man said that the story of their origin had never been forgotten by the exiles. For himself, he had a strong desire to visit the land of his ancestors (Mangaia), but his duties as chief forbade him to indulge his wish. His name refers to the fading outline of the rocky shore of his ancestral home.

A young man named Taora was left behind, detained by his uncle, Manini, who little recked what his fate would be. Tuanui, ' lord of Mangaia,' wished to offer a sacrifice to the sanguinary Rongo ; none would be so acceptable in *his* eyes as the friendless Taora. It happened that a grand dance was to come off by torchlight; the intended victim would be present as a matter of course. Tuanui resolved to take this opportunity of killing Taora with his own hand, and for this purpose, under his gay *tiputa*, or loose upper garment, concealed a small stone adze.

Just before the torches were lighted, and the dance was

about to lead off, it was whispered in Taora's ear, ' Run for your life ; you will be slain to-night.' But Taora well knew that if the chiefs were resolved to slay him he could not escape. He therefore refused to run, but dressed himself with unusual care, and even had the audacity to steal the beautiful shells which hung around the neck of the god Motoro. Taora now took his place in the dance, admired of all for his gay trappings and his energetic participation in all the required evolutions. Merrily the dance went on, few suspecting the bloody tragedy to be enacted in the name of Great Rongo.

About midnight, when half the songs had been recited, the supreme chief of Mangaia quietly stepped up in front of Taora, who knew that his last moment had arrived, and by one well-aimed blow closed the career of the ill-fated dancer. The blood of the victim besmeared the sacred necklace of Motoro, as the wearer intended. The dance was thus rudely brought to a close, but the required sacrifice was that night laid on the altar of the god of war, and peace was again proclaimed. Happier far if Taora had accompanied the exile Iro to Rarotonga !

The last words of Iro sunk deep into the mind of Arekare = ' House-on-the-Waves '—a new and sad memorial name. The one object of his life now was to foment quarrels amongst the principal men of the day, with a view to war. Several years of unquiet rule under Tuanui had passed away when Arekare collected a number of his friends and made a successful night attack upon those chiefly concerned in the expulsion of Iro. The murder of Vivi and Tito by Tamangoru a short time previously was thought little of at the time, as they were friendless. But now the case was quite different, and immediate preparations were made for a battle that took place at

Māueue, on the east of the island.   In that fight, Tuanui, Arekare, the father of Rori, and many others were slain. Iro's wish was gratified, as in this fight for the first time the original ruling tribe was split into adverse factions, brother fighting against brother, thus preparing the way for their final overthrow some years later at the hands of their oracle, Mautara.

The man who wrought all this dire confusion—' House-on-the-Waves '—had a presentiment of defeat and death. The night previous to the battle of Māueue, Arekare went with his ten wives to catch fish on the reef for a final feast.   It was an invariable custom to enjoy a feast before going to battle, as one might not survive to eat again. Amongst the many wives of Arekare, Eiau, the beauty of her day, was his favourite.   They returned by torchlight to the encampment, each wife carrying her own basket of fish, whilst their joint husband held in his hand a spear. The descent to the interior is still difficult ; by night it is dangerous—a single false step might precipitate one to the bottom.   All had gone down but Eiau and Arekare. The favourite was about to descend, when her loving husband pushed her over the precipice !   Eiau was much injured by her fall, particularly her pretty face.   Covered with blood, she demanded of Arekare, who seemed quite unconcerned, why he thus treated her.   ' It was only an accident,' remarked her husband.   Eiau easily divined the truth ; it was the clear presentiment in his mind that he would be slain to-morrow, and then the lovely Eiau would belong to one of his mortal foes.   Arekare's grief was that she was not killed outright.   She lived many years afterwards, much disfigured by this ' accident,' a slave in the household of Mautara.

ANOTHER LAMENT FOR THE EXILE IRO; BY KOROA.

Recited on the same occasion.

TUMU.

Solo.

Mātua moana ia Iro,
E eke ua i Karanganui,
Ka ana 'tu au kimi kouru matangi.

Chorus.

Ki te iku anau e erara ē !

PAPA.

Solo.

Oki mai Iro i te tumu e reirē !
Tau akatere i te atianga,
Ua rori aere i Teumi,
O te akama nui ē !

Chorus.

Ko Iro i tei ungaia ē !

UNUUNU TAI.

Solo.

Mātua moana ē teia Iro ē !
E eke ua i Anaporea,
E ngakinga apinga'i i ano ai ;
E ngakinga apinga'i i ano ai.
Pāii atu na o te kuonga,
Kautaka aere i Araoa,
Te teka nei i te urutonga
Ka ana 'tu au kimi kouru matangi.

Chorus.

Ki te iku anau e arara ē !

PAPA.

Solo.

Oki mai Iro i te tumu e reirē !
Tau akatere i te atianga.
Ua rori aere i Teumi,
O te akama nui ē !

Chorus.

Ko Iro i tei ungaia ē !

UNUUNU RUA.

Solo.

Taku ara paia ē i te eketinga ē !
I te eketinga ia Poatutokere ē !

INTRODUCTION.

Solo.

Hail, Iro, expertest of voyagers,
Descending (to the beach) at Karanganui,
Awaiting a favouring breeze.

Chorus.

List to the south-west wind awaking.

FOUNDATION.

Solo.

Return, Iro, to thy natal soil.
He is pressing through the breakers,
After crossing the pointed rocks.
Alas, the greatness of thy shame !

Chorus.

Alas, Iro, thou art exiled !

FIRST OFFSHOOT.

Solo.

Hail, Iro, expertest of voyagers,
Frequent at the wave-washed cave
Whenever a feast was preparing—
Yes, whenever a feast was preparing.
Thou didst follow the still waters of
the reef
Plying thine art at Araoa.
Ha ! the wind has veered to the south ;
I am awaiting a favourable breeze.

Chorus.

List to the south-west wind awaking !

FOUNDATION.

Solo.

Return, Iro, to thy natal soil.
He is pressing through the breakers,
After crossing the pointed rocks.
Alas, the greatness of thy shame !

Chorus.

Alas, Iro, thou art exiled !

SECOND OFFSHOOT.

Solo.

Thy way down to the beach is interrupted—
The descent at Poatutokere ;

I te eketinga ia Poatutokere'i !
O Terei[1] e tu mai, ua iria
Te manava, ua iria te manava'i.
Na reo taiku auta mai te anau.
E eke ua i Karanganui.
Ka ana 'tu au kimi kouru matangi.

Yes, the descent at Poatutokere.
Yonder stands Terei oppressed with grief,
With intense sorrow, and the nephew
Treasures up the last charge of his uncle,
As he descends (to the beach) at Karanganui.
I am awaiting a favourable breeze.

Chorus.

Ki te iku anau e arara ē.

Chorus.

List to the south-west wind awaking !

PAPA.

Solo.

Oki mai Iro i te Tumu e reirē !
Tau akatere i te atianga.
Ua rori aere i Teumi,
O te akama nui ē !

FOUNDATION.

Solo.

Return, Iro, to thy natal soil.
He is pressing through the breakers,
After crossing the pointed rocks.
Alas, the greatness of thy shame !

Chorus.

Ko Iro i tei ungaia ē !

Chorus.

Alas, Iro, thou art exiled !

UNUUNU TORU.

Solo.

Tiroia i nunga ē i te rango nei ē !
I te rango nei, te vaa maira i Teanaroa.
Tei Pariki tetai kopunga vaine,
Tei Pariki tetai kopunga vaine'i,
Te tara nei i te rāui, na Iro atu na i tamaka.
Ka ana 'tu au kimi kouru matangi.

THIRD OFFSHOOT.

Solo.

Gaze once more on the sea-shore !
Voices sound from the cave Teanaroa.
It is the hum of women at Pariki,
Yes, the murmur of women at Pariki,
Discussing thy ejection. Iro is girding on his sandals.
I am awaiting a favourable breeze.

Chorus.

Ki te iku anau e arara ē !

PAPA.

Solo.

Oki mai Iro i te tumu e reirē !
Tau akatere i te atianga.
Ua rori aere i Teumi,
O te akama nui ē !

Chorus.

List to the south-west wind awaking !

FOUNDATION.

Solo.

Return, Iro, to thy natal soil.
He is pressing through the breakers,
After crossing the pointed rocks.
Alas, the greatness of thy shame !

---

[1] *I.e.* the sister of Iro, and mother of Arekare by her husband Tuanui, temporal lord of Mangaia. It was the hate of Tuanui that led to the expulsion of Iro and his party. The last charge is that referred to in the ' Introduction ' of the preceding ' Lament,' and which subsequently occasioned so much bloodshedding. Ngangaru, the father of Iro and Terei, was offered in sacrifice to the god Rongo.

This song is given exactly as it was chanted, with all the repetitions, by way of showing how the other dirges in this book were actually performed.

Chorus.

Ko Iro i tei ungaia ē!

UNUUNU A.

Solo.

Itiki Mu ē i tona tai ē!
I tona tai ia Karanganui.
Aore paa e taea ua atu te rāui.
Ua tu te rāui, e tangata metua
E mareva aere i te moana.
Kautaka aere i Araoa.
Ka ana 'tu au kimi kouru matangi.

Chorus.

Ki te iku anau e arara ē !

PAPA.

Solo.

Oki mai Iro i te tumu e reirē !
Tau akatere i te atianga.
Ua rori aere i Teumi,
O te akama nui ē !

Chorus.

Ko Iro i tei ungaia ē !

UNUUNU RIMA.

Solo.

Karanga i uta ē oki maira ē!
Oki maira, ka ano koe kiia ?
Ua tapu oki te tai, ua tapu oki te tai.
Ua tioi te tua'i, ua taeke,
Ua romiromi te oe, i aro ai.
Ka ana 'tu au kimi kouru matangi.

Chorus.

Ki te iku anau e arara ē !

AKAREINGA.

Chorus.

Ai e ruaoo !   E rangai ē !

Chorus.

Alas, Iro, thou art exiled !

FOURTH OFFSHOOT.

Solo.

Mu has tabooed the sea—
His sea at Karanganui.
It is vain to go, for the *rāui* is set up ;
Yes, the *rāui* is set up, and that aged
  man (*i.e.* Iro)
Is now an exile on the ocean.
Let us go together to Araoa.
I am awaiting a favourable breeze.

Chorus.

List to the south-west wind awaking !

FOUNDATION.

Solo.

Return, Iro, to thy natal soil.
He is pressing through the breakers,
After crossing the pointed rocks.
Alas, the greatness of thy shame !

Chorus.

Alas, Iro, thou art exiled !

FIFTH OFFSHOOT.

Solo.

A voice from shore is calling, ' Come
  back !
Come back !   Whither   art   thou
  fleeing ?
The sea is sacred ; yes, the sea is
  sacred.'
Ha ! he is getting into his canoe, he
  starts,
He seizes his paddle and faces the
  horizon !
I am awaiting a favourable breeze.

Chorus.

List to the south-west wind awaking !

FINALE.

Chorus.

Ai e ruaoo !   E rangai ē !

In this song the daily avocation of the fisherman and

the final sad departure of Iro are dexterously intermingled. Hence the references to places which Iro was accustomed to frequent. When a great feast was in preparation, the custom was (and still is) for fishermen not to return to their dwellings at night, but to sleep in some cave, or under some overhanging cliff near the sea.

CHAPTER XIX

A POISONED BOWL

ON the south of Mangaia, on the margin of a little lake, once lived the famous priest Tangiia, guardian of the *marae*, and greatly feared on account of his supposed supernatural powers. The worshippers carried to the priest bowls of intoxicating drink—the nectar of Polynesian gods—in the hope of securing a favourable response to their petitions. Cooked taro and fish were given with the *kava* (*Piper mythisticum*), as without the addition of solid food the narcotic effects of this detestable drink would not be evoked.

But this priest, affecting to speak in the name of his god Tangiia, required *human flesh* as a relish. From time to time he demanded of his infatuated followers that they should furnish him with a young child 'to eat with the *kava*.' Such was the terror which this wretch inspired that his cruel demands were invariably complied with. Receiving from the hands of the worshippers the frothy bowl, Tangiia eagerly quaffed its contents, and (it is expressly said) with his own hands slew the little victim and devoured the quivering flesh. In the haggard, bloodshot-eyed priest was recognized, not the man, but their own fierce god, the supposed arbiter of life and death.

One day Tangiia declared to Marere, a member of the royal Akatauira clan, that he required from him the accustomed bowl of *kava and his little son!* The father knew that the wily old priest had long cherished an ill feeling towards him. Maddened by his demand, which he dared not openly refuse, Marere rose superior to the superstition of his day, and resolved to put an end to the tricks of Tangiia. Luckily for his purpose he had discovered the three sorts of vegetable poisons used to kill fish, and still associated with his name. He resolved to try them upon the hated Tangiia. He accordingly expressed into a small bowl a strong decoction of all three. To test its strength he now threw into it a small salt-water fish and a fresh-water fish, both of which instantly died. The drink was now prepared in the usual disgusting way, by first chewing pieces of the root and then discharging the contents of the mouth into a bowl kept for the purpose. When about three parts full the poison was poured into the stupefying drink instead of water. The whole was now well stirred together and strained off for drinking.

All being ready, Marere led his little boy with one hand and with the other carried the fatal mixture into the presence of the priest, who was delighted to see an unusually large quantity of his favourite drink. Upon taking the bowl, Tangiia looked at its contents and remarked, *Kua tuke te tu* = 'It looks strange.' Yet, as the little victim was brought with every outward mark of deference, he thought it must be a mere fancy, and drunk off the whole. The priest was at once affected by the deadly potion. His face became red ; the eyeballs seemed ready to start out of their sockets as he splutteringly said to Marere, 'Give me the boy.' Reeling about like a drunken man, he advanced a few steps in order to clutch the child, who with his father slowly retreated.

In fact the poison was rapidly taking effect. But Tangiia was not easily to be cheated of his victim. On and on came the drunken priest ; his voice became thicker, and his footsteps more uncertain, as with great difficulty he pursued father and son. Soon the old cannibal stumbled and fell heavily on the ground. It was now evident to all that Tangiia was dying and Marere's boy saved !

The body of the old priest remained where it fell eight days ; until at length, the stench becoming unendurable, it was dragged away into the bush, where it was left to be devoured by rats. In memory of this, the spot is still called Paepaeauau = 'disgusting offal.'

Hence the common saying, 'Beware of the poisoned bowl of Marere.'

In a later age the great warrior-chief Ngangati, descended from this Marere, took up his abode in this neighbourhood. A fragment of the once-powerful clan of Tangiia still lived there. Now Ngangati inherited all the hate of his ancestor Marere against the fallen descendants of Tangiia. He accordingly ordered a grand drinking-bout. The intoxicating root had been chewed, and the feast prepared, when Tangikaara, the head man amongst the devoted race, was invited by his companion, Ngangati, to drink. He declined to do so, and by that refusal saved his life, for every other male member of that unhappy tribe found his head seized by his boon companion, and was clubbed to death.

Tangikaara was of almost gigantic proportions. As soon as he felt his hair grasped by his foe Ngangati, he wisely ran to the lake, with his foe on his back, intending to drown him.   But just as the desperate Tangikaara was about to leap into the deep black waters, Ngangati wisely gave up his hold, slipped off his back, and, much chagrined at his failure, returned to his more successful companions.

Tangikaara long remained hidden in the rocks. Eventually, however, the drum of peace enabled him to make his appearance in the interior.   Unable to wreak his vengeance upon his brave old foe, Ngangati bequeathed to his relative Manini his legacy of hate.   To carry this out, Manini sedulously cultivated the friendship of Tangikaara. Early one morning they went together to the *marae* of Rongo to hear the king offer prayers.   On their way back Manini walked in front, carrying, according to the wont of aged men, a short spear as a walking-stick.   Pretending to have dropped something, he desired his companion to go on.   In another moment he came up with Tangikaara, and dealt him a death-blow on the back of the head. The body, still warm, was taken back to Rongo's *marae*, which he had left about half an hour before.   Manini had accomplished two good things at once ; he had avenged the famous Ngangati, and had provided the god of the invisible world with a bleeding sacrifice.   So much for the natural conscience of the heathen.

The children of Tangikaara lived on for future sacrificial use.   Said the narrator, ' I am a direct lineal descendant of the priest Tangiia and of Tangikaara, and but for Christianity should unquestionably myself have been laid on the altar.'

THE DESTRUCTION OF THE TANGIIA CLAN, AND THE ESCAPE OF KEUKEU.

A 'crying-song' (*tangi*) pertaining to the 'Death-talk' of Arokapiti. Composed by Koroa, *circa* 1817.

TUMU.

Solo.

Tiŭ rā Keukeu tupuna i ora ;
E tangi atu rai ki te pāre.[2]

Chorus.

Ka tua ra tai kopu o Kanaě !

PAPA.

Solo.

Aere mai kotou ě !

Chorus.

Aere mairā Tangikaara i te vāinga kava,
Ia te arutoa o ; na Rongo i ngau ra.
U'a etu !

Solo.

Ei tupa ia Tangiia ia kai ake nga atiaporo ě !

Chorus.

Kapitipitia ě i pau nga pāre e !

UNUUNU TAI.

Solo.

Keukeu tupuna i ora mai !

Chorus.

Keukeu tupuna i ora mai na.
Tuairiaki tangata metua ia koti
I raua Kanae i te ta ta rikiriki.
I tokiā Kaara, o Tetupu, o Tepōia-rongo,
O Vaikakau, na taomarau i te umu kokarakara.
Te ranga aina ia Motoro i Tepatiki ě !

INTRODUCTION.

Solo.

Sing we of Keukeu,[1] our ancestress, who escaped ;
Weep we for the sad fate of her tribe.

Chorus.

'Twas resolved that the Kanae should be slain.

FOUNDATION.

Solo.

Come on, friends ! (said they).

Chorus.

The brave Tangikaara came to the assembly
Of drinkers : but murder was in their hearts.
The fatal signal was given !

Solo.

'Twas planned for the extinction of Tangiia.

Chorus.

Again and again was our tribe slain !

FIRST OFFSHOOT.

Solo.

Yet Keukeu, our ancestress, escaped.

Chorus.

Yes, Keukeu, our ancestress, narrowly escaped ;
Her father and grandfather all perished.
A stone adze clave the skulls of Kaara,
Of Tetupu, of Tepōiarongo, and of Vaikakau,
Firstfruits of that harvest (literally *oven*) of death !
In honour of the god Motoro were they slain.

---

[1] Keukeu narrowly escaped the hands of the cannibal Ngako ; her children, half of the present tribe of Tanè, never tire of praising her adroitness.

[2] For *apare* = clan.

Solo.

Erā Keukeu tupuna i ora ;
E tangi atu rai ki te pāre.

Chorus.

Ka tua ra tai kopu o Kanaē !

UNUUNU RUA.
Solo.

Tangata reua i Ariki ra ē !

Chorus.

Tangata reua i Ariki.
Teia te uri a Marere
E ōra kava ia Tangiia.
Ka rere roa i Paepaeauau.
O te rangi piri na uu-pae-ngaru,
Na ngarumotuia, ua atea i te ara
O te eiva i pakoko i Maraepāpā ra.
Te ranga aina ia Motoro i Tepatiki ē !

Solo.

Erā Keukeu tupuna i ora ;
E tangi atu rai ki te pāre.

Chorus.

Ka tua ra tai kopu o Kanaē !

Solo.

Rejoice we at the escape of our ancestress Keukeu ;
Weep we for the sad fate of her tribe.

Chorus.

'Twas resolved that the Kanae should be slain.

SECOND OFFSHOOT.
Solo.

Alas, that murdered throng at Ariki ![1]

Chorus.

That great company at Ariki fell
By the hand of a descendant of Marere,
Who skilfully poisoned the priest Tangiia ;
The carcase lies at Paepaeauau.
Like fish in the billows at the reef,
They fell under the sharp pointed spear ;
Yet he himself barely escaped with life.
In honour of the god Motoro were they slain.

Solo.

Rejoice we at the escape of our ancestress Keukeu ;
Weep we for the sad fate of her tribe.

Chorus.

'Twas resolved that the Kanae should be slain.

---

[1] Ariki is the general name of the district where the famed Ngangati slew his multitudinous victims.

CHAPTER XX

THE STORY OF NAMU

AT Rarotonga it was customary for fishermen and voyagers to take with them in their canoes pieces of wood carved roughly into the human form, as charms. At Rakaanga and Manihiki, islands lying 700 miles N.N.W. of Rarotonga, if a king, priest, or distinguished fisherman died, the body, after lying three days in the grave, was exhumed, and the head cut off. A coco-nut was planted in the grave in lieu of the head, the fruit of which was eaten by strangers. The head was deposited in a finely-woven coco-nut-leaf basket, and placed in the fore-part of the canoe as a sea-god. When overtaken by unfavourable winds on a voyage, or drenched with heavy tropical rains, the head would be taken out of the basket and held aloft by the hair whilst prayers were offered to it for favourable weather. The hands and feet of defunct chiefs, priests, and fishermen were used for the same purpose by people of inferior rank. Upon the introduction of Christianity into those islands in 1850, these ghastly objects of worship were buried.

In heathenism no canoe ever ventured over the reef at Mangaia to fish without first fastening to its bows the fisherman's god. This consisted merely of the extremity of a coco-nut frond secured with fine-plaited sennit tied into a bow.[1] This Mokoiro, as it was called, was supposed to be all-powerful in regard to the winds and waves. The family of Namu were priests of Mokoiro; it was their hereditary office to equip each canoe in the fishing-season (from September to December) with this little protector. No other hand than theirs might perform this sacred office.

The aged king of Mangaia informed me that in those days a fleet of, say, two hundred small canoes—carrying only one man apiece—would assemble in front of the site of the present village of Oneroa at the beginning of the fishing-season. The little leaf-gods would be got ready against the appointed night, which was indicated by the recurrence of the phase of the moon favourable for catching certain kinds of fish. It was for Namu to give the word, and then the entire fleet of canoes would start off. The first night's fishing was in honour of the elder sons, who would eat part and give part to their respective gods. The second night's fishing was in honour of the elder girls, who likewise ate part and gave part to their respective gods. After this the *tapu* was removed; men, women, and children now ate freely, always, however, giving a fish—often the worst—to one of their supposed ocean divinities.

The family of Namu was specially obnoxious to the clan of Tongaiti, or 'little [2] Tongans,' who are believed to have reached Mangaia at an early period from Tonga, a distance of about one thousand miles. These Tongan settlers were very warlike; they provoked a battle on their first landing on the south of the island. In this engagement they were worsted by the primitive tribe of

---

[1] I have deposited one of these charms in the British Museum.
[2] So named ('little') as being an offshoot or colony of the parent stock.

Ngariki, from whom Namu was descended. The chief ground of hatred was the fact that from the date of their disastrous defeat at Teruanonianga the entire Tongan clan was devoted to the furnishing of the oft-required human sacrifices to Rongo, god of war. At least three other tribes were afterwards set apart for the same vile use; the choice lying with the warrior-chief and the king of the day as to the individual who should be slain and offered on each particular occasion.

One night the boy Namu was sleeping with his father, the priest Motau, in their own reed hut in a sequestered spot named Pakia. Their slumbers were disturbed by the sudden hum of angry voices from a number of armed men, who violently pushed aside the sliding door of the hut, and felt all round in the dark for the obnoxious offerer of human sacrifices. The father was discovered and slain; but Namu, taking advantage of the door being for a moment left unguarded, slipped out unperceived, and escaped.

When Namu had grown to man's estate he took part in several engagements fought at that especially turbulent period on the southern part of the island, not far from the cave of the cannibal Tangaka, who, unknown to the combatants, from his lofty hiding-place witnessed these conflicts with grim satisfaction, knowing that, whichever party might win, *he* at least was sure of a feast.

In the second of these encounters, at a place called Teaupapa, it is said that eighty persons fell on the side to which Namu belonged, amongst whom were most of his own male relatives. Being, however, fleet of foot, he succeeded in saving his life. At length, gaining the highest ridge of the interior range of hills, he paused to look back at his pursuers, when he saw Pautu and his party exultingly perform the war-dance ere proceeding to occupy the lands and homes of the unfortunate Namu and his slaughtered friends.

The fugitive, under the friendly shelter of night, crossed the island to Ivirua, and hid himself in the thickets and rocks at no great distance from the utterly desolate spot immortalized by the long residence of Rori. Yet Namu and Rori never met until afterwards, in times of peace, when both lived in the interior, under the protection of Mautara and Manaune. Namu spent seven weary months in hiding at Ivirua, occasionally supplied with food by his faithful wife Tetui, whose pretext for going to their appointed meeting-place was the necessity for collecting candlenuts (*Aleurites triloba*) for evening lights. The candlenut-tree grows very plentifully in the neighbourhood of the rocks where Namu secreted himself. The collecting of candlenuts is a grand employment of native women. When obtained, they are slightly baked; the remarkably hard shells then easily crack and fall off, leaving the oily kernel entire. These kernels are skewered together with the midrib of the coco-nut-leaf, not unlike a row of large yellow beads. This curious torch yields a good light, but requires some care, and is attended with a disagreeable smell.

At last it became known that Namu was hiding amongst the gloomy rocks, and that the secret of his wife's exemplary diligence in collecting candlenuts was that she might supply him with food. The hereditary foes of his race resolved to make a careful search through the thickets and rocks until they should find him. One morning Namu happened to be cautiously making his way along a narrow fishing-path, when at a sharp bend he caught sight of his foes advancing towards him. Very wisely, Namu, instead of turning back or running on through the bush (either plan would have insured his destruction), merely turned aside and crouched under a low rock, still pointed out, which was at that time entirely overgrown with wild vines and creepers. In extreme terror he held his breath whilst they passed by—his hiding-place being sufficiently near to the pathway for him to hear his foes breathing out vengeance against him.

Namu now felt that it would never do for him to remain in that part of the island, as his enemies would be sure to resume their search. However, he stirred not from his leafy hiding-place until nightfall, when he made his way into the interior to the dwelling of his faithful wife. He told her of his marvellous escape, and that he must seek a new asylum. Leaving him hidden for a short time in the fern, she ran off to consult her father Keu, priest of the Tongan clan—*i.e.* of those at deadly enmity with him. Keu seems to have been a humane fellow, for he at once offered to secrete his sorely-hunted son-in-law inside the very recess or portion of his dwelling where his god Teipe was kept and worshipped. In the company of this uncouth ironwood god, Namu spent one month in safety, all that time secretly supplied with food by the priest himself, for the presence of a female in that sacred enclosure would be an unpardonable offence. But a servant of Keu, wondering at the greatly increased consumption of food in his master's small family, impiously lifted the sacred curtain and peeped inside. To his disgust he there saw the enemy of his tribe sleeping alongside of the wooden god whom all that section of the Tongan clan adored. It was soon noised abroad that Namu was hidden by their own priest. The enraged tribe assembled to take him out of his father-in-law's hands and put him to death. They did not regard the tears of his wife, although she was one of themselves. Namu had fought against them, and therefore must die. Happily, however, for their intended victim, he caught a glimpse of the killing party in time to force an opening through the reeds of his asylum on the side farthest from his foes. To elude detection the opening was at once carefully closed up by Keu. Namu scampered off to the neighbouring hill, then, as now, covered with tall fern, in which the poor fugitive hid himself. The Tongans had by this time arrived at the house of their priest, who truly averred that the man they were in search of was not there. Disregarding his words, they instituted a strict search, even entering the sacred enclosure itself. This was sacrilege, but they cared not, so that they might kill Namu. Finding, however, that he was not there, they rushed out again in search of their victim. The fern was trampled down in every direction in the hope of discovering him. For an instant the body of the trembling fugitive—who gave himself up for lost— was actually between the legs of one of his pursuers, without, however, being perceived by him. After a long and fruitless search, it was proposed to set fire to the fern, a perilous trick, but at the same time a certain means of driving a poor wretch out of the only covert the bare hills of Mangaia afford. At this critical juncture one of their number came upon two nests of wild ducks. The fortunate finder shouted, ‘Here is a lot of duck-eggs!’ That shout saved Namu's life, as several were approaching very close to him at the moment. Several of the party now made a rush for the eggs. Hervey Islanders will not taste a raw egg. The cooking and eating effectually diverted their thoughts for the time.

Whilst they were thus engaged, one of the killing

party, gazing down upon the main valley so lately dotted with huts, but now utterly desolate, said, *Kua tiraa a Ivirua vaine,* 'There sleeps Ivirua, like a bride forsaken.' These words at once passed into a proverb. At dusk Namu descended into the neighbouring valley to slake his burning thirst. He determined to make his way to Veitatei, whither his wife had fled to escape the anger of her tribe for so persistently sheltering Namu. Had he taken the ordinary road—a distance of nearly four miles—he would certainly have been captured. He wisely resolved to cross the nine deep but narrow valleys which lie between. This is no slight undertaking on a dark night; yet he succeeded in making his way to the house where Tetui was. Resting awhile on the brow of the hill, he was greatly pleased to see a light shining through the reeds of the dwelling. A pebble thrown lightly on the thatch drew the attention of Tetui, who, guessing that her husband had thrown it, went outside. They wept together as Namu told her what had befallen him. He said that he must leave his old haunts altogether, and would henceforth hide himself in the most inaccessible rocks of the district where they had happily met again. They parted; and ere daylight dawned Namu had reached his proposed hiding-place. For another weary period of seven months did this fugitive conceal himself amongst the thickets and vine-clad crags of Veitatei. Still, this was a paradise compared with the inexpressibly desolate home of Rori, who had not a single friend left to care for him; whereas Namu was regularly, although secretly, fed by his devoted wife.

Namu subsisted partly on wild roots and fruits. It does not appear that he manufactured anything during his sojourn in the rocks; for he was not a craftsman, but the mouthpiece of the gods in regard to fishing and feast-making—quite enough, in the estimation of that day, for any one man.

Tetui's friends at length got into great straits themselves. As the only chance for life, she threw herself upon the protection of Mautara, who had recently worsted her own clan in battle. Despite this severe reverse of fortune, she contrived, slave though she had become, occasionally to convey food to Namu. To her great joy, the all-powerful Mautara one day asked his slave whether her husband was yet alive. She answered, 'Yes.' 'Go, then, and fetch him to aid me in performing the religious ceremonies preliminary to peace.' Raumea, the brother of Teuanuku, who a few months later fell in battle, was appointed his protector. Three entire districts (*tapere*) were bestowed upon Namu as the price of his services, of which, however (such are the rapid changes of savage life), only one remains in the hands of his descendants. Namu was now at the height of prosperity, for he lived on good terms with Mautara to the end of that great priest-chief's days. Tetui was thus abundantly recompensed for her singular attachment to her husband, who now in his turn succoured *her* near relatives Kaiara and Tavero, who found a secure asylum in his home.

The sway of Teuanuku was brief. The murder of that young chief in his own dwelling at Ivirua led to the battle of Auā, where a decisive victory was gained by Mautara over the murderers of his son. Under the rule of the priest-chief the island was cultivated, and great abundance prevailed. It is said that chestnut-trees were covered with nuts even to their very trunks. Long did the wise old man rule, until 'his teeth dropped out, of sheer old age :' certainly a remarkable event with a Polynesian, many of whom retain their teeth in soundness to the age of eighty.

The death of Mautara was the signal for new wars. In one engagement it was asserted that Namu was riddled through with a spear, and was left for dead by his enemies. But life was not quite extinct; and eventually through the care of friends he recovered. This circumstance led his foes to believe that a supernatural power resided in him.

Some years after the visit of Captain Cook, Potai (nephew to Namu) feigned mortal sickness, and sent a special messenger to fetch his uncle and his cousin Manini. Not suspecting mischief, they paid a visit to the crafty fellow, whose couch was spread at a place called Rautauri —a wild spot, under vast overhanging rocks. The couch consisted of dry grass, covered with fine native cloth; his head resting on a pillow of stone (still pointed out), neatly covered over with folds of *tapa*. At his head sat his wife, weeping at the seemingly near dissolution of her husband. Potai had purposely kept himself awake several nights, so that his eyes were red and swollen. It was late in the afternoon when Namu arrived unarmed, so as to spend the night with his dying (?) nephew. According to invariable native custom, he wept long and loudly after he had deposited by the side of the sick man the farewell present. Uncle and nephew slept together that night. Lofty forest trees kindly intercepted the fall of dew. Early on the following morning, as they sat chatting together, Manini made his appearance, also unarmed. When the new-comer was close to Potai, and about to 'kiss' him, by a previous secret arrangement the Tongan clan rushed out of their hiding-place, and slew Manini. At the same moment, Potai, hitherto supposed to be dying, seized his uncle Namu's flowing hair, and held him firmly until his ancient foes had put an end to his existence. The limbs of Namu were severed one by one from the trunk, and buried in different parts of the island, lest by some supernatural agency he should live again !

Namu was an old man at the time of his death. Potai would on no account slay him with his own hands, save on the field of battle. But he had no scruple whatever about holding his uncle's head while the body was repeatedly speared through.[1] A son of Manini happily escaped over the rocks by a narrow pathway left unguarded.

It was not until Namu's peaceful residence in the interior that Tetui bare him a son. 'So that,' remarked Rouvi, who told me the preceding story, 'if Namu had perished in the rocks, you would never have seen me, his grandson. I had the honour to be one of those who set fire to the idol-groves of Mangaia upwards of forty years ago. The heathen party said that I should speedily die for my sacrilege. I am now aged, but healthy, and have long outlived all those who engaged in idolatrous rites.'

LAMENT FOR NAMU.
By Potiki, *circa* A.D. 1790.

TUMU.	INTRODUCTION.
Taia Namu i Tevaenga,	Slain was Namu at Tevaenga.[2]
Kua motu koe ia Potai,	Thy death was planned by Potai.
I te puputa motu no te metua	The garment of the uncle was rent by
A ngaro ai Namu.	the nephew.[3]
O te anau tupu ua te ta ē !	Namu is gone for ever—
	Smitten by the nearest of kin.

PAPA.	FOUNDATION.
E piri ake Namu i te rau puka ;	Once Namu wandered in the forest ;
Noo mai paa i te makitea.	His home was in the rocks.

---

[1] A number of similar atrocities has made the name of Potai in Christian times almost synonymous with Satan.

[2] Tevaenga is the name of the district where Namu fell.

[3] 'The garment of the uncle' is a figurative way of saying that the claims of kindred were disregarded by Potai. The garment represents the entire clan, which is now split up by the murder of Namu.

Eiea ra tau ai ē?
Raumea oki te rave
I te tarangaora i noo ei !

Who then succoured him ?
'Twas Raumea that pitied him ;
His life was secure in *his* hands.

Unuunu Mua.

E pa tikoru i Tekorokoro
Tetai ora anga ia Namu.
O Teipe oki te toko.
Auraka e taū are rau i maru ei !

First Offshoot.

In a shrine by the mountain-side
Was Namu once hidden.
Teipe was his guardian.
My wife became a tower of safety.

Unuunu Rua.

Mauria Namu tei Pakia ē !
Tei Pakia, a tai ora anga ia Namu.
Kua motu koe. Tai ataai
Na Teipe ia Namu. Kua ora koe.
O Teipe oki te toko.
Auraka e taū are rau e maru ei ?

Second Offshoot.

At Pakia was Namu captured.
Very narrowly did he escape.
Thou wast doomed. Yet friendly aid
Was afforded to Namu by Teipe.
Teipe was thy guardian divinity.
My wife became a tower of safety.

Unuunu Toru.

Reureu te po e tei paporo e,
    Tei paporo.
Kua ka te ai i Tutapa.
Ko te roimata o Teaputa,
Kua pou te pare i Ariki.
Kua tangi au i te tava ē !
Auraka e taū are rau e maru ei !

Third Offshoot.

In the dark night he was on the hill-
    top—
        On the hill-top.
The light was burning in the dwelling.[1]
Plenteous tears were shed by Teaputa
    (*i.e.* Namu),
For his tribe slain in battle.
He wept o'er their loss.
My wife became a tower of safety.

Unuunu A.

Punipuni aere i Teauiti ē !
    I Teauiti.
Kite ake au i reira ki te ao taka nunga.
Te vai nei te ponga ia Tetuma.
Ee koto na Pautu. Kua piri oki tau
    mata.
Kua kapitiia, e matara koe i te rima ē !
Kua kave i te riri ra e ora.
Auraka e taū are rau e maru ei !

Fourth Offshoot.

He hid himself in the valley—
    In the valley.[2]
Then did he taste the bitterness of a
    fugitive's lot.
Ah ! the undying hate towards our
    clan ;
The shouts of Pautu in chase of me !
Trembling lest I should be o'ertaken
I ran swiftly to save dear life.
My wife became a tower of safety.

Akareinga.

Ai e ruaoo ē !   E rangai ē !

Finale.

Ai e ruaoo !   E rangai ē !

---

[1] The light in the house occupied by his wife upon his final flight to the rocks of Veitatei.

[2] I have translated Teauiti by 'valley;' it is in reality the name of a particular valley. But Namu traversed nine valleys in all on that memorable night, although only one is named. The order of events in the song is not strictly correct ; the chronological order is that observed in the narrative.

CHAPTER XXI

THE BANDAGED FOOT

CIRCA A.D. 1718

ALL existing families attribute their preservation to the favour and powerful protection of one man, Mautara, priest of Motoro. For more than a hundred years that family ruled the island. Their two ancestral districts (*tapere*) are the only ones that have never changed hands.

With the rise of this priestly caste the modern history of Mangaia may be said to commence.

Ngauta, 'eight times lord of Mangaia,' was slain by Ngangati, who assumed the supreme temporal sovereignty. Of Ngangati it is said that, emulating the fame of his predecessor, he became 'five times lord of Mangaia.' But one evening, when training his yam-vines over some low bushes, he was in turn slain by his nephew, Akatara, who declared himself supreme chief by the will of the gods.

The head-quarters of the new chief were on the eastern side of the island, at Ivirua. The constant wars of that period had hitherto made but little difference to 'the mouthpiece of the god Motoro,' who was perfectly safe amid all the bloodshed. A change now came over the scene. The bosom friend and confidential adviser of the new temporal sovereign was Aro, who recommended Akatara to root out the priestly family of Mautara, as the surest way of perpetuating his own authority.

A great feast was to come off at Ivirua for the formal installation of Akatara. The principal people of the island would attend it. An armed party were to hide themselves in the long grass to await the arrival of Mautara and his two famous sons. At a preconcerted signal they were to surround and slay all three. Success seemed certain, as no man ever went armed to a feast.

The plot was arranged by Akatara and Aro at midnight, when all were wrapped in slumber. A few yards from the conspirators slept their cousin Kārua, who, roused by a low murmur of voices, drank in every word with intense interest. She inwardly resolved at all risks to save her brother-in-law Raumea, second son of Mautara.

On the following evening the women went on a grand fishing excursion, on account of the approaching feast. Kārua met with considerable success. Arrived within a mile of Raumea's residence, she contrived to lag behind the throng of women; and, quenching her torch, hid the basket and scoop-net, having first taken out of it a large fish. Kārua now ran as for her life along a narrow pathway to the interior. The rough road, winding between frowning jagged rocks, is not very agreeable even by broad daylight. Arrived at the house of her brother-in-law, she hastily opened the sliding door, and in so doing aroused Raumea. Kārua gave him the fish, and said, ' This is yours ; it may be your last, for your.death is resolved upon if you attend the feast. Only let it not be known that I warned you.'

She had accomplished her purpose. Away she sped through total darkness by the road she had come. Upon reaching the sea again, she relit her torch, took up her basket and net, and hurried after her companions. To do this she had to walk several miles, fishing all the way, until she found them at a certain spot supping on part of the spoil. Her collected manner, as she referred to her having fished alone through the night with remarkable success, disarmed suspicion. Being expert at torch-fishing,, it was easy for her to fill her basket, whilst the others were almost empty.

Night after night torch-fishing for the approaching feast went on whenever wind and surf favoured. As soon as the finny spoil was brought home, it was wrapped in *ti*[1] leaves and cooked, being re-warmed each day until the feast came off. No other plan was possible for people ignorant of the use of salt.

When every precaution had been completed, Aro, in person, made the circuit of the island, delivering a formal invitation to all the chiefs and landowners. Mautara and Teuanuku at once agreed to go ; but Raumea declined, on account of the agony he was enduring from a heel scooped by an *ungakoa*, or *serpula*. Everywhere on the reef the coral is pierced in a myriad holes by this animal, which often attains the length of several yards. At the top the creature is protected against attacks by a dense shield, whilst the circular edge of the cavity is as keen as the edge of a razor. This animal grows with the bed of coral, the long cavity becoming increasingly large. Young *ungakoa*, like young oysters, are easily detached from the coral by means of a hammer. Children eat them raw, not forgetting a supply of cooked taro out of their tiny baskets.

Hence the necessity of using sandals for the protection of the feet. Occasionally the sandals get loose ; woe betide

---

[1] *Cordyline terminalis.*

the luckless wight who should then tread with his entire weight upon one of these 'cobblers' awls!' Round pieces of flesh are in this way scooped out of the foot. The thing most dreaded is when a bit of it breaks off, remaining behind. Months may elapse ere it works out by suppuration.

Aro pressed Raumea to attend the inaugural feast; the assembly would not be complete without so great a man. As a landed proprietor it was incumbent on him to be present. But Raumea, to the evident chagrin of Aro, declared such a thing impossible, for an *ungakoa* had broken off in his foot, and he was in great pain. Aro asked to see the foot, to which Raumea at once assented. The entire foot was covered up with a series of bandages. These were removed one after the other, with much seeming pain, all saturated with blood. And yet the wound itself was not reached! Raumea now assured his visitor that it was impossible for him to proceed further on account of excessive pain. Aro was by this time convinced that Raumea was effectually incapacitated from attending the feast. He at once returned to Ivirua and told Akatara of his ill success. Yet the feast must come off.

How little did they suspect that the bandaged foot was only a ruse, and the abundance of fresh blood which saturated the wrappings had been obtained from *rats!*

On the day appointed, nearly the whole population was present at the feast. There was abundance of such good things as the island could afford. As soon as the sun rose the guests began to arrive; in a short time all had come save Raumea; and perhaps after all he would contrive to be present. As a last resource Akatara received the visitors with every outward mark of respect, but proposed to defer the eating of the feast until Raumea should come. Akatara correctly reasoned that it would be of little use to kill Mautara and Teuanuku if the valiant Raumea survived to avenge their deaths. All three must die together or none.

Hour after hour passed wearily, the guests becoming excessively hungry. Still no Raumea made his appearance. Late in the afternoon this strange feast was disposed of, the invariable custom being to divide out and eat as soon after daylight as practicable.

After the lapse of two or three months a return feast by Mautara and his sons was to come off on the west of the island. A large number of fugitives who had survived the frequent battles of those days agreed to come out of their hiding-places on the appointed day, and, concealed in the neighbouring bushes, engaged to do the bidding of Teuanuku and Raumea. Of these armed fugitives the most brave was Tokoau, ever afterwards associated with his cousin Mautara.

In the centre of the sacred districts of Keia, a spot perfectly level is pointed out as the feasting-place. It is known by the name of Tapati. It was carefully weeded for the occasion; broad banana-leaves and green coco-nut fronds were thickly strewed over the ground. On this natural tablecloth was piled abundance of food for the expected guests; but underneath the leaves and food were hidden spears and wooden swords for a deadly fray!

At length the procession of chiefs connected with Akatara arrived, each carrying a fan of enormous proportions,[1] in token of profound peace. The guests found the feast-makers busy over a preparation of scraped coco-nut and taro, called *poke*. In compliance with ancient etiquette, each visitor seated himself opposite to one of

[1] About four feet in length.

his friends, and vigorously began to grate raw taro on madrepore coral.

Raumea wished to save one of these doomed men. To this end he seated himself by his side, and, getting into conversation, obligingly offered to clear his head of vermin—a proposition most acceptable to Polynesians of the olden times, on account of the great length of their hair, and the circumstance that combs were unknown. Ere the task was completed there was a mighty shout, 'There comes the lord of Mangaia!' Akatara came alone, some half-hour after his friends, indicating his rank by not deigning to come with the inferior chiefs. On his way to the feast he had been stopped by his relative Tuakura, who advised him to retrace his steps. But Akatara scoffed at the idea of danger. Was not the island in a state of peace?

As this great chief came near, Teuanuku rose to his feet, as if to do the honours of the occasion. Wiping his hands, he enigmatically remarked to those about him, *Era te pipi ra e mou, i.e.* 'Let each seize a mussel-shell.' Advancing to meet Akatara, he saluted him in the now famous words, 'Ah, brother-in-law, how well your new dignity suits you!' They now pressed each other's nose, as in token of affection. Every eye was fixed upon Teuanuku, who instantly seized his adversary by his flowing hair. Almost at the same moment each of the Mautara clan did the same with his astonished neighbour sitting opposite to him. But Raumea, instead of seizing the head he had been cleansing, suddenly grasped another, and forced the unwilling neck under his immense thigh, waiting to see what the other would do. At that moment Raumea saw him stoop to pick up a spear in order to cleave his skull. By a quick movement Raumea caught him, too, by the hair, and dragged him to the ground. And now, with his right hand in the hair of the first victim, his left in the hair of the second, he literally ground his foes to death on the earth by sheer strength! A similar feat of horror was performed that day by King Kanune. Both these warriors are said to have been possessed of wonderful strength, and were the terror of their contemporaries. Those in ambush did their share of that bloody morning's work, in the hope of sharing the lands of the slain. Of the entire party of Akatara, only one escaped to tell the tale. As the solitary fugitive ran past the dwelling of Tuakura, loudly lamenting the unhappy fate of his murdered friends, the only comfort he received was, 'May your ears be cooked![1] Did I not forewarn you all?'

The feast was untasted, for it was bespattered with the blood of the guests. Early next morning Mautara and his two famous sons marched a little army over the hills to Ivirua, to do battle with the now dispirited tribe of Ngariki, of which Akatara had been the leader. Ruanae now assumed the command. In point of numbers they had a decided advantage, standing 'thick as the eaves of thatch.' By this I understand that they were eight deep— double the usual number. As the clan of Mautara came in sight, the war-dance of Ngariki 'caused the earth (seemingly) to tremble under their feet.' The old priest exhorted his clan to do their best, saying, 'If we fail, we shall certainly be cooked and eaten.'

Williams correctly remarks, in the *Enterprises,* 'Contrary to the usual practice in the islands, the people of Mangaia do not practise bush-fighting, but meet in an open plain, from which every shelter is removed.'

---

[1] A native curse.

The great clan of Ruanae awaited the onset of their foes drawn up in a line at the base of the hills. Mautara and his clan descended the hills in a single column ; but, on account of the disparity of numbers, declined to conform to the usual custom of ranging themselves in a line parallel with their foes. A sudden rush was made at the centre of Ruanae's army, cutting it at once in two. After a well-contested battle, Ruanae and his clan were compelled to seek refuge in a gloomy stronghold known as Te Ana o Kākāia, 'The Cave of the Tern.'

Tradition expressly declares that Mautara himself did not fight ; that he only carried his enormous fan. To the doomed clan of Ngariki he was the visible embodiment of their god Motoro. To get rid of him the hand of some unscrupulous atheist must be employed.

Mautara remained simply priest of Motoro ; the supreme chieftainship was reserved for his eldest son, Tcuanuku. On account of the considerable numbers of Ruanae's unreconciled clan, the pleasant drum of peace could not sound, and human life was still insecure.

CHAPTER XXII

THE UNFORGIVING AND THE UNFORTUNATE LOVERS; OR, INCIDENTS CONNECTED WITH THE CLAN OF RUANAE

AN ill-looking but brave warrior of the cannibal tribe of Ruanae, named Vete, fell violently in love with a pretty girl called Tanuau, who repelled his advances and foolishly reviled him for his ugliness. His only thought now was to be revenged for this unpardonable insult. He could not kill her, as she wisely kept close to the encampment of Mautara.

After some months Tanuau sickened and died. The corpse was conveyed across the island to be let down the chasm of Raupa, the usual burying-place of her tribe. There are two openings to this gloomy abode of the dead— a large one for those slain in battle (*te vaa noa*), a small one for those who die a natural death (*te vaa tapu*). The corpse was to be let down the smaller hole by means of immense rope-like lianas obtained from the forest, and sometimes attaining the length of one hundred and fifty feet. These *kākā* ropes are of great strength when green. In general the friends of the deceased were content, after the corpse had descended about halfway, far out of sight, to allow it to fall into the dark waters beneath. Two demons were supposed to inhabit this chasm—a lizard of gigantic proportions, and an enormous fresh-water eel. This eel-god was believed to be ever on the watch for the descent of a corpse, in order that it might feed on human flesh.

But these *dii inferi* were disappointed of their prey on this occasion. Vete, hearing of Tanuau's death, guessed that her body would be carried to the ancestral burying-place. Now was the time to be revenged. With nine companions he left the Cave of the Tern ere dawn of day, and hurried to Raupa at Tamarua. On their way they provided themselves with ropes of Nature's own manu-facture. Arrived at the mouth of the chasm, Vete and two others were let down about halfway, where a ledge permitted them to take their station in almost total darkness. The rest of the cannibals now drew up the ropes, and secreted themselves in the forest to await the arrival of the burying party.

The sun was high in the heavens when the body of the poor girl was brought and let gently down the gloomy hole, the friends little thinking that three men below were awaiting its arrival. As soon as the body came within reach they drew it on to the ledge and hastily untied the ropes. According to custom, the ropes were thrown after the corpse, and splashed in the unseen waters far below these resurrectionists. At brief intervals came one by one opened coco-nuts and other food offerings to the dead.

As soon as the friends of the deceased girl had disappeared the seven cannibals came out of ambush and let down their ropes again. In a few seconds the body of Tanuau was drawn up, and shortly afterwards Vete and his two companions gladly emerged from their cold and gloomy subterranean prison.

The corpse was quietly carried near the sea to a natural hollow, shrouded from observation by a dense growth of lemon hibiscus. It was found to be impossible to eat the decomposed body. It was, however, cut in pieces, and at sunset burnt to ashes. At midnight, finding that a few bones remained, a new fire was made, so that by morning light no trace whatever remained of this poor creature.

A month or two subsequently Vete and his friends met with the due reward of their numerous misdeeds at Pukuotoi, within a short distance of the scene of this barbarous burning.

'The burning-place of Tanuau' is included in the mission premises at Tamarua. During our residence there I had the forest in the neighbourhood of Raupa cleared for the first time, and the rocky soil planted with coco-nut-trees.

It is owing to numerous incidents of this sort that the natives are absurdly sensitive to threats of *burning* anything belonging to themselves. There is no surer way of drawing down their anger than to hint at such a thing as the *burning* of a canoe, a hut, or even a garment. To *chop the property* of another is regarded as symbolical of an intention to *chop his person*, even as the corpse of Tanuau was cut to pieces.

Among those who escaped at the fatal surprise of Ruanae's clan at Pukuotoi was a young man named Oimara. At the back of the mission premises at Tamarua a curious hollow rock stands out by itself like a round tower. It is eleven feet high, and will comfortably admit one person. The hardened coral surface is so rugged that it is an easy matter for a native to climb in or out.

By day Oimara hid in the savage recesses of the

primæval forest, behind vast blocks of stone, or inside one of the thousand natural grottoes. At nightfall he invariably returned to his stone fortress, which is still associated with his name. The starry heavens were the only roof. Ere dawn the fugitive again retired to the forest.

The reason for this strange procedure was that Oimara had a sweetheart, who, though a member of the victorious clan, did not forget her lover. By some means or other, shortly after the battle she became aware that he was still alive. It was agreed upon that he should hide in this curious rock, which was close to the principal path to the beach, so that she might easily supply him with food.

This loved one, whose name is not preserved, at dusk of every evening hastily thrust through a small aperture, most conveniently situated, a small package of food. Sometimes on her return from fishing she would linger behind her dusky companions in order to throw in a fish. Scarcely a word could be exchanged under such circumstances, lest her delay should excite suspicion.

Things went on prosperously with Oimara for some time ; but, unhappily for the fugitive, one of her companions resolved to ascertain why this girl was generally a little behind. One evening this curious one hid herself near the narrow turn in his pathway where her friend had so often loitered. Unseen by the lovers, she overheard their brief conversation, and saw the food-packet put through the little hole. This was told to the parents of this over-curious girl.

That very night a party of armed men surrounded the hiding-place of Oimara. Their cruel shouts as they scaled the sides aroused him from sleep. Escape was impossible, as the only means of egress was the very opening by which his enemies were attacking him.   He threw himself in his despair on his face on the earthen floor.   He was quickly stoned to death, and his body found a grave where he had often peacefully slept under the azure canopy of heaven. Many and loud were the lamentations of his beloved one over his untimely end.

CHAPTER XXIII

CAVE OF THE TERN; OR, THE MISDEEDS OF RUANAE

In the face of a perpendicular cliff at Ivirua, overlooking a picturesque valley cut up into innumerable taro-patches, is an opening to which access can only be gained by a long ladder planted on a projecting point of rock. A party of us contrived to extemporize a ladder out of the tapering stems of two papao-apple (*Carica papaya*) trees, and so gained an entrance to the famous cavern which is known as Te Ana o Kākāia, 'the Cave of the Tern.' Here for many a long day were the headquarters of Ruanae and his clan. The cavern is extensive, and abounds in beautiful stalactites. A deep natural recess in the side nearest to the sleeping-place of the fierce chieftain was the repository of the weapons of the clan. On each club and long spear was a private mark, so that each warrior might know his own weapon.

Outside, at the entrance to the cave, is the spot where the cannibal feasting was held. It is in reference to this that it still bears the significant name of Ruokai, 'Feasting Hollow.'[1] Here we picked up one or two large rounded stones, designed to crack the skulls of any who might be foolhardy enough to attack those who kept watch outside. A fearful chasm runs across the interior of the cave.

[1] For Ruakai.

Great stones hurled down by some of us splashed heavily in the unseen waters far below.

The clan of Ruanae used to cross this abyss on a bridge of long logs. Not having this advantage, we had to descend our ladder and make a considerable circuit. Our worthy guide Rouvi, about seventy-five years old, with the clan of Vaeruarangi, once occupied this cave. He showed us the secret entrance to this stronghold through a thick grove of plantains. Near the entrance the roof is very low, but soon becomes loftier. The cave eventually opens up into a noble cathedral-like nave. The arched roof, as well as the walls and flooring, being composed of stalactites, sparkled and glittered magnificently in the light of our torches. Right and left branched off aisles all richly ornamented with a wondrous fretwork of Nature's own moulding. After proceeding a considerable distance, we found ourselves on the brink of the same chasm we had previously approached from the opposite side. The united light of our torches in no degree lessened the gloom of this fearful abyss. Yet Ruanae and his warlike followers were accustomed by torchlight to cross this ill-omened spot daily when bent on a secret descent upon the persons or lands of their foes. The water they drank was drawn up from this deep natural reservoir, which abounds in large eels and shrimps. Under the prevalence of Christianity, and the consequent feeling of security, this impregnable fortress was constantly used by the natives of the eastern part of the island. Rouvi assured us that in those days, lighted by the glare of torches above, he often descended, holding on crag by crag, to fish in these unpromising waters.

Hard by, and connected with this stronghold, is a sort of chapel, small but most exquisite in structure. Column rises upon column of seeming alabaster. No torch is needed to display its beauties, sufficient light coming through the entrance to illumine it. All around and beneath sparkle a myriad gems, walking over which were a desecration. This fairy place is known as Te Koatu Kurukuru o Angita, *i.e.* 'the Cave of Beautifully Carved Stones.' The exit is over moss-grown crumbling stones, as if the remains of an ancient flight of steps !

The signal defeat of Ruanae at Arera made the sons of Mautara lords of the island. The entrance to the Cave of the Tern, the hiding-place of the beaten tribe, who were still formidable in point of numbers, is so difficult that to force an entrance would be impossible. Hunger, however, occasionally compelled the men to go on foraging expeditions. On such occasions they generally picked up some stray members of the victorious party of Mautara, whose encampment was on the opposite side of the island. These unfortunates were invariably cooked and eaten. It is asserted that the first person deliberately eaten by Ruanae was Itieve, over whose body was registered the unholy vow to spare neither sex nor age whenever a victim should fall into their hands.

Teange was one morning fishing on the reef about a mile from the present mission premises at Oneroa, when to his dismay he found his retreat cut off by a sudden descent of Ruanae and his cannibal warriors from the neighbouring rocks and bush. Under cover of a dark night they had crossed the island and hid themselves at a convenient spot, where a never-failing spring of fresh water gushes up amidst stones and sand. Delighted to see Teange, a man of no ordinary size and prowess, carrying only a scoop-net and utterly unconscious of danger, they rushed out upon him. The only possible

means of escape was to swim out to sea ; which Teange
did without hesitation, knowing that at a short distance
is a block of coral rising up from the ocean depths. At
high water it is covered ; but even then a man sitting on
it would have no fear of drowning. On came the clan
of Ruanae like a number of hungry sharks to devour their
victim ; but they were astonished that he did not attempt
to run in the direction of the camp, but coolly swam out
to sea and succeeded in gaining the rock referred to.
Teange climbed on it and defied his foes. Many were the
stones thrown at him, but at that distance he found it
comparatively easy to avoid them. Tired of this, some
of the disappointed cannibals swam out to the coral rock
on which the brave Teange stood pouring abuse and
curses ; but when they got uncomfortably near he wisely
swam out to sea. Being an excellent swimmer, he quietly
watched his foes until they returned to the reef, when he
returned to his old standing-place.

In their joy at the prospect of securing their victim,
the cannibal tribe did not notice a little boy sitting in the
bush near the pebbly beach, awaiting the return of his
father from fishing. At the beginning of the attack the
little fellow ran as fast as his legs could carry him through
the bush and over the hill towards the encampment—a
full mile. In a few seconds more the entire body of
warriors, led by Teuanuku and Raumea, the brave sons
of Mautara, were in motion, eager for fight, hoping to
crush for ever the adverse tribe. On descending the hill
which overlooked the scene of conflict they were seen by
the scouts of Ruanae. A prolonged shout caused the
entire troop of cowardly cannibals to take to their heels.
The pursuers strained every nerve to cut off the retreat of
Ruanae, and thus terminate the contest which had dragged

on slowly for many months. Ruanae, however, succeeded in gaining the sharp-pointed rocks, where it were vain to follow him. The coral rock on which the fearless swimmer rested is still known as Te Turanga o Teange, 'the Standing-place of Teange.'

A few weeks after this, three women went one evening from the encampment of Mautara to the lake in Veitatei, to catch shrimps and delicate *kokopu* fish, which are obtained at night by the aid of torches. The shrimps are easily caught with coarse coco-nut-leaf baskets.

Now these women had been very successful, and at dawn cooked the fish, for convenience' sake, and to appease the cravings of hunger. The romantic little spot chosen for the oven is in a dense thicket under the shadow of a mass of rock about a hundred feet high, where, if anywhere, they might hope to be unnoticed.

Little did they imagine that Ruanae and his clan were on a foraging expedition in their immediate neighbourhood. They slept in the rocks overlooking the lake, without noticing the women. Early in the morning, when about to march back, their attention was attracted by the smoke of the oven. Finding that it was a party of defenceless women, the cowards descended as quietly as possible by a rough pathway, still used, called Raurau. At the first sight of their cannibal foes, Mapi rushed off as fast as she could in the direction of her home. Her path lay underneath those frowning lofty rocks which form an imperishable defence against the advance of the ocean. In a short time she came to a narrow pass, occasioned apparently by the severance and fall of a vast block of rock, overgrown with dwarfed banyan-trees shooting out of the crevices of the stone. The long roots hang like ropes of immense strength from the summit to the ground.

Mapi in her flight recollected that at the distance of ten feet from the earth, and overhanging the narrow path, is a round fissure, opening up into a narrow chamber capable of containing three persons. In a twinkling, with the aid of fingers and toes, sailor-like, she climbed by means of this natural rope into this curious hiding-place, and lay flat to elude notice. Had she been seen, escape would have been impossible, as there is only one way of entrance and exit. Hardly had she lain down on the flooring of her strange retreat when her foes rushed past close underneath, little suspecting that Mapi was hidden there. On, on they pressed at full speed, not thinking it possible that she should escape. At length they stopped and resolved to return, and carefully to examine every bush that could possibly afford shelter to a fugitive, their long spears being thrust repeatedly through the bush without a trace of their intended victim. In passing again under the overhanging rock, in the very heart of which Mapi still lay, they little thought that every threat of vengeance was distinctly heard by her.

In this rocky chamber, on the side nearest to the lake, is a small hole, through which she ventured a glance at her retreating foes, and with inexpressible relief saw them disappear in the distance. When all was quiet she cautiously descended from her hiding-place, and descended to the ground. Very warily she made her way through the tall tufts of reeds and clumps of pandanus-trees to the mountain-ridge, whence it was easy for her to gain the distant encampment, *minus*, however, her fish.

The fate of the two other women, who were sisters, was diverse. Koua, the elder, and Anauaukura, the younger, in their affright took different paths. Koua ran into the neighbouring thickets, and thence made her way to the rocks and so escaped, ascribing her safety to the friendly aid of Matarau, the lizard-god, the guardian of all rocks and caves. Her ill-fated sister, after running a short distance in the open country, was caught, her hands tied behind her, and led back to the smoking oven which she and her two more fortunate companions had just left. The savoury contents of shrimps and *kokopu* were speedily demolished by the famished cannibals. But for their haste to enjoy this unexpected feast, it is very probable that the search for the missing woman might have been successful.

As soon as this meal was despatched, Ruanae hurried off his people, through fear of a sudden attack from their foes. They started off in single file across the fern-clad hills of the interior to their gloomy stronghold at the Cave of the Tern, at Ivirua. Anauaukura, with her hands tied behind and well guarded, walked in the centre, *in order to save the labour of carrying her dead body !*

At the top of the first eminence she looked back, and for the last time caught sight of the lake where so lately she had been disporting with her companions. Just beyond was the sad scene of her capture. It is said that she travelled on in silence under a midday sun until they reached the taro-patches of Ivirua, where the cannibals felt themselves safe, as in the event of a sudden alarm they could easily betake themselves to their stone fortress. The hands of the victim were now untied, and by a refinement of cruelty she was compelled to collect a quantity of dry firewood and to break off a lot of banana leaves to wrap her own body in. Near the entrance to the cave, and in full view of the women and children, was the large oven used by Ruanae's party in cooking their victims. Anauaukura was directed to heat this oven, which she did. As soon as the stones were sufficiently hot, the poor unoffending woman was clubbed to death and cooked in the very oven her hands had lighted. The body was carefully divided out and devoured by these horrid cave-dwellers.

Upon another occasion a number of women and girls engaged at lobster-fishing at Tuaate were surprised and slain by Ruanae. Eight poor women were cut off by daylight when digging for wild yams. Four females collecting chestnuts were slain early one morning, and, skewered on long spears, were borne with fiendish shouts of joy to the great oven at the foot of the ladder.

Now a man named Matautu was appointed by Ruanae to keep the chiefs supplied with shrimps and eels. He alone lived in the middle of the valley, and unceasingly plied his avocation. On the morning of the capture of the chestnut-gatherers he was horrified to see his own aunt cooked and devoured. Burning for revenge, he sent word to Teuanuku, who, with the victorious clan, ventured by night close to the cave where Akapautua was keeping watch, his long spear resting on the earth. The spear was quietly stolen. The clan slept on, all unconscious of danger. A beautiful daughter of Ruanae named Kimiatu, descending at dawn of day to bathe in the neighbouring stream, was at once pounced upon, her hands tied, and led weeping and calling for help to a well-known spot in the centre of the taro-patches, in full sight of her distressed relatives in the Cave of the Tern. Dry coco-nut fronds were collected and piled up round this unhappy girl, and the whole lighted. It is said that her arms, now released by fire, were stretched out towards her father in the cave, imploring succour. But Ruanae well knew that any effort to rescue his daughter would ensure the immediate destruction of himself and his tribe.

Thus it is that the heathen corrupt themselves from generation to generation, 'hateful and hating one another.' Only a power from above can arrest the downward progress, and transform savages into human beings with kindly affections one towards another.

We have seen that the elder sister Koua escaped. One of her direct descendants is Turoua, the present worthy chief of Tevaenga, one of the six principal governors of Mangaia, a man of marked character, who has long made a consistent profession of attachment to Christ.

THE OVERTHROW OF RUANAE.

Composed by Potiki, *circa* 1791, for the 'Death-talk of Vaiaa.'

TUMU.	INTRODUCTION.
Solo.	*Solo.*
Kua pau te vaka o Ruanae ! Ana mai nei kua tuā tei Atea, Te viri nei i te ara ē ?	The tribe of Ruanae has perished ! As the reef covered [1] with dead fish Is the ground where they fought.
Chorus.	*Chorus.*
E vaio ïa ngaere i reira ē !	Let the dead rot there !
PAPA.	FOUNDATION.
Solo.	*Solo.*
Tipoki te aro o Ruanae, Pakia io ia mou ei, Kia riro te papa iaia. Akapautua i mamao atu, Oi mai koe ia piri ē ! Kia kapitia i te mate.	Ruanae lies low in the dust, Where he rushed on to his fate In the vain hope of victory. Akapautua pressed behind (saying) 'Come on, stand shoulder to shoulder, That we may die together.'
Chorus.	*Chorus.*
Kia vai reka raua katoa ē !	Both warriors lie in one place !
UNUUNU TAI.	FIRST OFFSHOOT.
Solo.	*Solo.*
Kua pau te vaka ē ! No Ruanae ē !	The tribe of Ruanae Has perished !

[1] At times the reef is almost dry, and the small fish die by hundreds, on account of the excessive heat of the sun.

Chorus.

Tei Vaitangi na taukarokaro anga.
Tei Vaitangi na taukarokaro anga' i.

Solo.

Me ē te ē ia taua,
Me kite atu i te rangatira,
Ka ati te ati Tangaroa.
Ana mai nei kua tuā tei Atea,
Te viri nei i te ara ē !

Chorus.

E vaio ïa ngaere i reira ē !

UNUUNU RUA.
Solo.

Tatari aere
I te vaka nei ē !
I te vaka nei !

Chorus.

Kua kake i te maunga,
  Noo atu i reira,
Kua taumate aere—

Solo.

Kua taumata aere ei.
Te tara nei i tena atua,
E ui paa i te ānū e te kouo.
Ana mai nei kua tuā tei Atea,
  Te viri nei i te ara ē !

Chorus.

E vaio ïa ngaere i reira ē !

UNUUNU TORU.
Solo.

Kimiia te ara ra ē,

Chorus.

By the purling brook the fight took
  place,
Ay, by yon purling brook the fight
  took place.

Solo.

(The chiefs said): ‘Should the worst
  come to the worst,
Should we be overpowered by our
  foes,
Our bodies shall lie on the field of
  battle.’
As the reef covered with dead fish
Is the ground where they fought.

Chorus.

Let the dead rot there !

SECOND OFFSHOOT.
Solo.

Waiting for a sign
Of advancing foes—
Of any advancing foe.

Chorus.

(Ngako) climbed the mountain top,
  And long watched there
To get notice of their approach—

Solo.

Ay, for the faintest token of their
  approach.
The priest-leader gave the fatal
  command,
‘Climb the trees and bare them of
  their fruit.’
As the reef covered with dead fish
Is the ground where they fought.

Chorus.

Let the dead rot there !

THIRD OFFSHOOT.
Solo.

The only thought was

Chorus.

—— e marere ai ē !
E marere ai !
E na tai atu i Teone ē,
E na Paeru, na veiveitamaki—

Solo.

Na veiveitamaki ai ?
Na veroinga i te io,
Na ookainga i te korero.
Ana mai nei kua tuā tei Atea,
Te viri nei i te ara ē !

Chorus.

E vaio ïa ngaere i reira ē !

UNUUNU A.

Solo.

I uiia te ara ra ē,

Chorus.

—— e aere ai ē,
E aere ai !
Tei Arakino Ruanae,
Tei te utu tutai,

Solo.

—— tei te utu tutai ai.
Te pao nei i te ara,
Te kai nei i te ua nono i te rāei,
Aore e tumu ia uta.
Ana mai nei kua tuā tei Atea.
Tei viri nei i te ara ē !

Chorus.

E vaio ïa ngaere i reira ē !

AKAREINGA.

Ai e ruaoo !   E rangai ē !¹

Chorus.

—— now of flight—
Of mere flight !
Shall it be by Teone, the path to the sea ?
Or by the hill Paeru, overlooking the battle-field—

Solo.

Ay, overlooking the battle-field ?
Dare thy utmost to live ;
'Tis hard to escape.
As the reef covered with dead fish
Is the ground where they fought.

Chorus.

Let the dead rot there !

FOURTH OFFSHOOT.

Solo.

Ask the road

Chorus.

—— by which to fly—
To fly for one's life !
Ruanae's home had been in the rocks,
Where a solitary Barringtonia grows—

Solo.

Yes, where a solitary Barringtonia grows.
He subsisted on pandanus berries,
And the sour fruits found in the wilds.
For none befriended him !
As the reef covered with dead fish
Is the ground where they fought.

Chorus.

Let the dead rot there !

FINALE.

Ai e ruaoo !   E rangai ē !

¹ This song is printed as actually chanted.

CHAPTER XXIV

THE STORY OF KAIARA

AFTER the defeat at Arera, a family of three girls, whose parents had been slain, fled to the rocks at Mataorongo, not far from the hiding-place of Rori. Most of the beaten party took shelter in the Cave of the Tern; but these young girls were sure that they would be singled out for destruction on account of the murder of Packe, 'mouth-piece' of Motoro, by their father Arekava some years before.

One afternoon an armed party, headed by the cruel Ngako, issued from the stronghold of Ruanae in quest of victims. On reaching the crest of a hill on the east, they turned aside to inspect the old battle-field of Māueue, which marked the rise of the priestly clan of Mautara, and the downfall of their own. In those days the slain were rarely buried, so that some had become mummy-like, dried up in the sun; others were reduced by the rats to skeletons. The fern had everywhere grown about the dead, many of whom were the near relatives of these cannibal visitors.

A thin distant curl of smoke caught the sharp eye of Ngako. It came from the rocks, and must indicate the presence of fugitives. Very willingly they left the unburied bodies of their ancestors on the slope of the hill, and made for the distant fire in the rocks. Upon leaving the open country they became very careful not to give their victims any intimation of their approach. The three girls were cooking *nono*[1] apples over a fire for their supper, when the quick ear of Kaiara, the eldest of the party, caught the sound of advancing footsteps. She at once ran to hide herself in the deepest recesses of the forest; but her poor sisters were both caught, and led over the distant hill to the lair of Ruanae. That same night they were cooked and eaten by their own tribe! The passion for human flesh had grown so strong, since the destruction of Itieve, that it must be gratified at any cost.

Now the crafty Ngako correctly concluded that Kaiara, whose presence had been thoughtlessly revealed by her sisters, would after a time come back to get some cooked *nono* apples, in order to satisfy the cravings of hunger. Instead, therefore, of following the rest of his party leading the captive girls, he laid himself down by the fire to await the return of his expected victim, of course solacing himself with the roasted apples. At last she came; but, on espying the huge form of the cannibal, she again ran for her life. Ngako gave chase, calling her to come back and be his wife. He espied the trembling girl crouching down under a ledge of rocks, and put down his long spear to enable her to climb up to him, secretly resolving to club her as soon as she should be fairly in his power.

Kaiara feigned compliance, but perceiving over her head a narrow opening on the side farthest from her foe, she at once availed herself of it. That she had disappeared was clear, but how Ngako could not make out. The cannibal drove his long spear (twenty-five feet in length)

[1] *Morinda citrifolia.*

in various directions, but with no good result. He now got round the chasm and gave chase. The poor girl again hid herself in a hollow, hoping that the increasing darkness of evening would effectually conceal her from her relentless foe.

Ngako came up to the spot, and thrust down his spear several times at a venture, once narrowly missing the body of Kaiara, who now gave up all hope of escape. But the cannibal, not dreaming that, after all this riddling with his famous spear, his much-desired morsel lay quietly at the bottom, her head hidden by a mass of magnificent bird's-nest[1] fern (*rau kotaa*), went on his way chagrined. He would not return to the cave of Ruanae without his victim, to become the laughing-stock of his friends. He therefore slept in the rocks, hoping to catch this 'little fish' in the morning.

But again he was doomed to be outwitted, for Kaiara, after a short, but much-needed sleep, rose at midnight, and tremblingly climbed up out of her hollow, and pursued her painful way over the sharp rocks. She had no sandals to protect her feet, which became much lacerated. Fortunately Ngako was at some little distance sound asleep, so that, when the first streak of dawn admonished her to hide herself from observation, she had gained the 'wild rocks' where Rori, all unconscious of her presence, was at that time hidden. The probable reason why they did not meet is that Kaiara kept as near as possible to the interior, whilst Rori lived in the very heart of the *raei*. Besides, Kaiara was on her way to Ivirua, where most of her time was passed in the solitudes beyond the region frequented by Rori, and close to the site of the present village.

<hr>

[1] *Asplenium Nidus.*

Very slowly did Kaiara traverse this rugged part of the island, grieved at the loss of her young sisters. She subsisted exclusively on what could be obtained in the rocks, without daring to descend to the open country of the interior. Her greatest difficulty was to obtain water; however, she contrived to slake her thirst at the various hollows where rain had collected. In the midst of the rocks she discovered a spacious cave, where she took up her abode and cooked what food she could collect. One night, as she slept, her rest was disturbed by what she regarded as supernatural voices reproaching her with having desecrated a cave sacred to the god Tanè by cooking food. As most of the larger caves have long winding passages leading towards the sea, it is easy to understand how the winds would whistle and howl most ominously in the ears of a terrified solitary woman.

After occupying this cave, named by her Tevarovaro, 'the Whistler,' for fifteen days, she again started on her travels. One day she suddenly came upon a wasted woman pounding pandanus seeds to eat. Seeing she was alone, Kaiara spoke to her. The astonished fugitive looked up—it was her near relative, Tavero, who had lately fled for life to the rocks. They cried heartily over each other, and rehearsed the sad story of their escape. Henceforth they would keep together, come what might. They took up their residence at the rocks of Ivirua, having somehow discovered that Ruanae's cannibal clan no longer occupied the Cave of the Tern. Month after month passed in comparative security, for the cannibal tribe had perished whilst Kaiara was hiding in the Whistling Cave; and Ngako, though alive, prowled over the southern part of the island, having now his head-quarters with Vaiaa at Marotangiia.

Meeting with no molestation from day to day, the two half-starved women grew imprudent. One evening at dusk they carried a lot of bitter yams (*oe*) to a stream rushing under the rocks, in order to make them eatable. The children of a man named Mauiki saw them and gave the alarm. In a few minutes, Mauiki himself and his friends overtook the wretched women and drove them to his house, in order to slay and eat them, in revenge for injuries received from the now extinct tribe of Ruanae. Thus too late the captive women learned that the drum of peace had not yet been beaten.

Firewood was collected, and leaves piled up for a grand feast in the morning. To prevent the escape of Kaiara and Tavero, they were tied up to the two principal posts of the house. The doors were made fast with the strong bark of the paper-mulberry. All hands were to keep awake that night. What so sweet to a savage as revenge? The wretched captives listened with deep interest to their conversation, from which they learned the downfall of their own wicked tribe ; that the island was, for a second time, declared subject to Teuanuku, the eldest son of the priest-chief Mautara, and that their cousin Tetui was wife to Namu, the spiritual chief or king of the island.

At midnight the entire household was hushed in deep sleep. Kaiara too slept of sheer grief, not thinking escape possible this time. Tavero was wakeful, and resolved to attempt a rescue. By repeated contractions of the muscles, the cords which bound her to the post slipped down. A dexterous use of her teeth freed her hands. Softly approaching her relative, she whispered in her ear, untied her hands, and set her at liberty. Untying the fastening, and withdrawing the door as gently as possible (in Mangaia doors are opened by sliding in a groove), both women got out without any one inside being aware of their escape. At this critical moment Tavero recollected a calabash full of water, which would be invaluable in their flight. She coolly re-entered the house, felt about for it, and succeeded in getting out again without being discovered.

Off they ran now at full speed for the rocks and bush. In a few minutes the cool air through the open door roused some of the sleepers, whose first thought was, 'Are the victims safe?' As soon as their exit was discovered, the entire household started off in hot pursuit. The fleeing women could distinguish their cries and threats as they entered the thick bush, and speedily gained the summit of the first ledge of rocks. Every inch of the difficult path was familiar to these starved fugitives, who were soon beyond pursuit. The path they took is well known, but such as only women in extreme peril could dare to follow. Their feet were bare ; but then their forms were extremely light and agile, and they had the great advantage of moonlight to guide them on their way. Daylight found them in an extremely wild place, overgrown with pandanus-trees laden with fruit. They resolved if possible to make their way to their cousin, wife of the spiritual sovereign, in the hope of obtaining shelter and protection.

It was many days before they reached Tamarua, where their cousin lived, a journey which might well be made now by the direct interior road in a couple of hours. Opposite to the king's residence was a small cave called Ruaanau, where they hid themselves till sunset. The children of the chief first discovered them, and ran to tell their mother that two starved ill-looking women were hiding in the cave. Tetui went to see whether the report was true, and was not a little moved to find her long-lost relatives. The children were strictly enjoined to be quiet about this pleasing discovery until the king Namu should come home from the ceremonies connected with the beating of the drum of peace.

Taro[1] was hastily taken up to feast their new-found relatives. What a treat for the starved women! They wished to help their cousin in her labours, but Tetui would not hear of such a thing. Ere the taro was done, Namu came and heard the story from the lips of his wife. He pledged himself to protect them *as slaves*. That night they told the story of their perils and wonderful escapes. At daylight it became known that Kaiara and Tavero had come out of the 'wild black rocks,' and were under the protection of Namu, who remained at home, spear in hand, to protect them.

Mauiki heard with infinite mortification of their safety. He had hoped that they would die miserably of hunger in the rocks. Mautara recollected that his grandfather had been slain by the father of Kaiara, and thirsted for the daughter's blood. As 'mouthpiece of Motoro,' *i.e.* high priest of the god worshipped by Namu, he declared that the two young maidens should be killed and eaten by Mautara. Three times did armed men come to fetch them 'by order of the god Motoro.' Three times did Namu nobly refuse to 'put his wife in mourning' for her young relatives; for Tetui had threatened to commit suicide if he gave them up to be eaten.

It seems strange that the great priest should have been so persistent in his endeavours to get possession of these girls; but the ceremonies connected with the drum-beating were not yet completed. Besides, the sacred duty of revenge was never forgotten in heathenism. Only Christianity can originate the true spirit of forgiveness.

[1] *Caladium petiolatum.*

The devouring of a poor wretch like Kaiara could be a matter of no consequence whatever in those days.

Namu prevailed ; and the young women lived. Great must have been the disgust of Tokoau, the unscrupulous factotum of the high priest, who too closely imitated the evil practices of the slain Ruanae, of infamous memory.

Kaiara was resident in the rocks and woods for about two years. This woman and Tavero became slaves to Tetui, and secondary wives to the king. A numerous progeny exists to this day, possessed of a good share of lands. The various places where these poor girls lived in the rocks have given rise to family names. Two individuals are called after the Whistling Cave ; but all modern inquiries to discover it have failed. Of course the entrance has been blocked up.

A set of songs once existed in reference to Kaiara ; but they are forgotten for the most part. The technical name for the set is Te Kakai ia Namu, or 'The Death-Talk about Namu.' Here is a fragment :—

SONG OF KAIARA FOR HER SON TENIO.

TUMU.

Tenio pi i te po ē !
Kua keukeu takoto.
Kua ara i roto ia metua' i,
Ka eke ai Motoro ē !
I te riu i Ivirua' i tara mai—
O te meringa kai ra i topa ē !

INTRODUCTION.

Dear little son Tenio, by night
Painfully tossing from side to side
On the lap of thy sleepless mother,
'Tis the anger of Motoro
Admonishing his erring worship-
    pers,—
'You omitted my accustomed offer-
    ing !'

PAPA.

Te vā nei i Vaitepongi,
Te maru nei e tapautu ;
O te eketumu ta Kaiara
O Tavero e o metua oki
Mau ki te tama e teia ē !

FOUNDATION.

Ah ! my home was once in the
    desolate rocks,
Hidden in the densest thickets ;
Death stared Kaiara in the face.
Thy aunt Tavero was my companion ;
Here (with Namu) we found shelter
    and plenty !

It is curious that after the lapse of so many (184) years the spot where these poor women were tied up by Mauiki for death is in the possession of one of their descendants.

Kaiara died about the year 1777, from the fall of a green coco-nut. The offending tree was immediately cut down.

CHAPTER XXV

MANAUNE'S FORTUNATE ADOPTION

IN the olden time, if a man wished to marry he must select a wife from another tribe. To marry into one's own tribe was usually regarded as a heavy offence against the gods. Each clan had its separate gods, customs, traditions, and songs—constituting but one great family, with a single head, and pledged to defend each other to the death. These tribes were almost always at war with each other, so that a man was often compelled to fight against his wife's nearest relatives. In general the boys went with the paternal tribe.

One of the most memorable instances of adoption into a hostile tribe was that of Manaune.

We have seen that the vanquished tribe of Ruanae, after the battle of Arera, took refuge in the Cave of the Tern, at Ivirua. This cave is very difficult of access; inside is a fearful chasm, down which it were easy to hurl an intruder. Amongst them lived Teora, whose husband and all her sons but one had fallen in successive battles with Mautara's victorious clan. Teora's great anxiety was to save her remaining boy. Night after night she dreamt that she saw her warlike nephew, the priest Mautara, alone on the distant spur of a mountain opposite to their stronghold, slaying some invisible foe. This seemed to the anxious mother a sure intimation that all those in the cavern were doomed to destruction. She resolved therefore to go secretly to her nephew and beg him to adopt the orphan Manaune into the winning tribe. She whispered to her boy her design, and directed him to watch through the ensuing night until the morning star should rise, and then stealthily descend the perilous pathway from the cave and meet her at a certain spot a little way off. The reason for this arrangement was that at midnight Ruanae was in the habit of going round with a lighted torch and counting his sleeping clan, so as to detect any who might attempt to go over to his foes. Now Ruanae and his whole tribe were cannibals, but the victims were usually stray members of Mautara's clan, caught at a disadvantage. Deserters and suspected parties belonging to his own tribe shared the same horrible fate if caught.

As soon as the bright herald of day made its appearance Manaune left the cave and met his mother at the appointed place. The fugitives luckily reached the summit of the interior mountain-ridge without being pursued, and now ran with all possible speed along the narrow path through the fern and ironwood-trees. By daylight they were beyond the reach of the terrible Ruanae ; and whilst it was yet early morning they reached the encampment of Mautara, on the west of the island.

Meanwhile Teko, the wife of Mautara, was quietly cooking her oven for the early morning meal. According to the ancient but now obsolete custom of native women, as soon as the taro was covered up in the oven with leaves she sat upon it to make it retain the heat. If inconveniently hot in one place, she would move herself to another part of the oven until the food was properly done. She had fallen asleep over her oven when she was heard by her husband muttering to herself, 'My boys are fighting at Tamarua.' Mautara roused her by asking what she had been talking about. She replied, 'Nothing: it is only a dream.' But the sagacious Mautara felt sure it was her god Tanè Ngakiau addressing him through his wife, and that a great crisis was at hand.

Whilst the priest-chief was pondering over the words, his aunt Teora suddenly entered the back door of his hut, the other and principal entrance being *tapu*—unlawful to her as a woman. Teora kissed the feet of her nephew in token of profound respect. It was usual in this and many other ways to honour the first-born and future head of the family; besides, Mautara was the greatest man on the island at the time.

The priest-chief inquired the object of his aunt's visit. She frankly confessed that she wished to put under his protection her beloved son, Manaune. At that moment the lad came out of his hiding-place, was 'kissed' and kindly greeted by Mautara. It was forthwith arranged that Manaune should stay in the victorious encampment and be adopted into Mautara's clan, but Teora should return to the Cave of the Tern for their property.

The oven of taro was now opened, and Teora once more partook of a nutritious meal. In a few minutes more the now happy mother, having succeeded in her purpose, set off towards Ivirua. Mautara and the lad accompanied her some distance along the hillside, and finally, at a spot named from the circumstance, took a farewell with tears. Would Teora's share in the transaction of that day be discovered and punished with death? Three times she turned back to get a last look of her son, but Mautara waved his hand for her to be gone.

The cousins made their way back to the place where the warriors were encamped. They had heard that some one was to be formally adopted into the tribe, without knowing whom. For so important an occasion they put on their war head-dresses and covered their persons with many folds of twisted native cloth. With spears poised, as if for an immediate attack, they stood in file awaiting the new arrival. As the two relatives came in sight from the hill at the back of the encampment (Mautara shouting to them with all his might), they were immediately enclosed between the ranks, and a mimic fight began. As soon as this was concluded Manaune was led to a sacred stream to wash off the taint of his old antagonistic associations, and his person became 'sacred' in the eyes of his new companions.

Teora's return to the cave excited no remark from the women and children left in charge, for the males had that day started to Tevaenga in quest of food. They obtained plenty, but were particularly jubilant because they had caught Patea in a lofty tree collecting Brazilian plums. They ate the plums *and the poor man who had gathered them.* Fortunately, the wife, Piriau, escaped through being at a little distance gathering candlenuts. Thus amid the excitements of the day Manaune's escape did not attract notice.

That evening Teuanuku, eldest son of Mautara, led his victorious clan to Tamarua, in hope of intercepting the flight of Ruanae's force, who marched from Tevaenga to Tamarua in order to collect coco-nuts. Mautara's clan hid in the bushes until daylight revealed the precise whereabouts of their foes, who, not suspecting danger, were scattered in all directions, climbing after nuts. Unhappily for themselves their spears were all piled up against a large chestnut-tree still standing. To their dismay Teuanuku and his little army suddenly came in sight, and stood between them and their weapons. Two or three of the attacking party got their skulls cracked by green nuts dexterously thrown by men in the trees. Others, by main force, wrenched off branches of the coco-nut, and belaboured their adversaries. The struggle was brief and disastrous to the cannibals, who all perished, save a few who at the beginning of the conflict ran to the rocks for shelter.

Young Manaune evinced his bravery that day at the expense of his deceased father's nearest kin. Many were laid low by his spear. As a punishment, he was long afflicted with insanity, until he had made atonement to the gods. The reward of his bravery was a *tapere* on the east side of the island. A *tapere* is literally 'a slice' (as of a cake) from the outer reef to the central hill of Mangaia. He married, and lived with his mother on his lands, where to this day lofty coco-nut-trees bear the name of Manaune. Here he succoured Rori, who lived under his protection in after years.

Many were the battles which he afterwards fought side by side with the sons of Mautara. The lordship of Mangaia twice devolved upon Teuanuku—first, after the battle of Arira; and, secondly, after the surprise at Pukuotoi, just described. Now, for the first time, the drum of peace was beaten, and human life was for a while respected.

Thus originated, in process of time, one of the principal warrior tribes of Mangaia, named after the founder Manaune, and possessing now about half the soil of the island. When the Rev. J. Williams, in 1823, vainly endeavoured to locate teachers, a grandson of Manaune, named

Pangemiro, was temporal chief for the second time.
Pangemiro did not live to embrace Christianity; but his
son, Simeona, became the first deacon, and in connection
with Barima laid the foundation of Christian society by
sanctioning the destruction of idolatry, the establishment
of law, and the protection of the early native evangelists.

CHAPTER XXVI

SCARCELY SAVED; OR, THE STORY OF VAIAA

AMONGST the few of the cannibal clan of Ruanae who survived the disastrous surprise at Pukuotoi were Vaiaa and his sister Mangaia, who ran across the island and hid themselves in the rocks and caves of Marotangiia, on the west. The motive for selecting this hiding-place was the abundance of wild food in that neighbourhood. Here they subsisted on crabs, rats, frugivorous bats, and berries, nutritious roots, and cooked herbs. Occasionally they made their way to the reef and caught a few fish, without attracting notice.

One day, to their dismay, Ngako came upon them well armed. His character for ferocity was too well known to them to make his company desirable. They were both young and unarmed, whilst Ngako had been one of the chief warriors of Ruanae, and was particularly addicted to cannibalism. On the fatal day of Pukuotoi he was scout, and, finding that there was no chance for victory in fight, rushed to the rocks, and actually subsisted on the stray fugitives belonging to his own unfortunate clan. Twice Kaiara narrowly escaped his ruthless hands. On one occasion Keukeu with difficulty got away from this noted cannibal—a circumstance which her numerous descendants have not failed to celebrate in song. Month after month passed in this ignoble employment, when Ngako resolved to change the scene of his infamous exploits, and made his way to the western part of the island, where, as we have said, he fell in with the children of Akapautua, the chief next to Ruanae in point of dignity. Ngako proposed that they should all live together; of course, pledging himself to protect the children of his fallen chief. To this the brother and sister assented with as good grace as was possible, seeing they were in his power. The fierce old cannibal went from time to time in quest of human victims, and rarely did he return without one. Especially did he look out for children wandering about the rocks in search of berries wherewith to satisfy the cravings of hunger. The cooking fell to the lot of Mangaia and her brother. Nearly two years had been spent by them in the rocks, when it became evident that they must in their turn be eaten, for victims had become very scarce. More than once Ngako had returned without anything, with an ominous scowl upon his face. The last man living amongst the rocks was caught, and his body brought home to the brother and sister to be cooked as usual by night, lest the smoke should lead to their detection and death. Ngako greedily devoured his own portion; but Vaiaa and Mangaia hid their share for their dreaded companion. On the following day the old wretch again ate, and then started off in search of another victim. At nightfall he returned in no good temper, but was pacified with the reserved portions of food. Next morning he again ate, and went off in quest of a victim. At noon Ngako came back cross and hungry. There was still a bit left; it was speedily devoured by their grim 'protector.'

During the absence of Ngako that morning Vaiaa and

Mangaia held an important consultation. Should he again come back without a victim, it was evident that the brother would be killed and eaten, and afterwards the sister. They must lull Ngako to sleep, and then run for their lives.

After his meal the old cannibal became cheerful and chatty; so that Vaiaa ventured to propose that he should lay his head upon his lap and allow him to hunt for disagreeable insects. The ruse succeeded, and it was not long before Ngako gave signs of feeling drowsy under this agreeable operation. A significant elevation of eyebrows to his sister caused her to rise and cautiously remove to a safe distance, when she took to her heels and ran by a well-known path towards the interior, never stopping to get breath until she had reached the summit of the hill Aretoa, overlooking the beautiful and fertile valley of Keia. This was about a mile from their old hiding-place at Marotangiia.

At last Ngako went off into a sound sleep, and his head was gently laid on some leaves collected for the purpose in the morning. Vaiaa felt sorely tempted to take up the cannibal's spear and drive it through one of his eyes into the brain. But he was so weak and attenuated, from want of food, that he judged it best to leave the muscular form of the old warrior alone and betake himself to flight.

Vaiaa ran a short distance; but, thinking it possible that Ngako might wake up and give chase, he stepped aside from the path and hid himself in the rocks. Ere long his fears were realized, for he heard Ngako running past and grunting, 'My little fish have escaped.' Vaiaa dared scarcely breathe, for fear of detection. After awhile Ngako returned without having caught his victims. With infinite satisfaction Vaiaa saw his huge form and long spear take the narrow path leading to the sea, in the vain expectation of falling in with his old companions.

Vaiaa felt it to be now best to venture out of his hiding-place, and run by the direct path to the hill where his sister lay hid. This he safely accomplished. Brother and sister wept for joy that they were at last safe from the evil designs of the dreaded Ngako, who durst not venture into the open country. But, if safe from their old foe, they knew not what their reception might be upon their discovery by the winning tribe occupying the fertile valleys of the interior.

Having slaked their thirst at a small spring—but without tasting a morsel of food—they slept in the crisp fern. On the day following they could distinctly see the huts studding the valley, but durst not approach. At dusk they made for a picturesque wide valley known as Tongarei ; the lights in the various houses became distinctly visible. A second night was spent in the fern. Ere daylight of the third day they reached a very solitary place where a clump of bread-fruit trees grew. Under the rule of Teuanuku the entire island had become fruitful again. Vaiaa got up into the best of the bread-fruit trees and gathered the fruit, throwing it to his sister below.

Not far off happened to be a woman collecting chestnuts which had fallen in the night. Espying a strange-looking fellow in the bread-fruit tree, she left off her work and ran back to the main valley to give the alarm. In a short time the tree was surrounded, and brother and sister were made prisoners. It was resolved to cook and eat both, in revenge for the many who had fallen at the hands of their cannibal clan. Dry firewood and the largest banana-leaves were at once collected for this purpose.

By this time the mother of Teuanuku heard that her relatives, supposed long since to be dead, were caught, and in a few minutes would be in the oven. She said to her son, *Tera ake taū kiko*—'There goes my own flesh.' Teuanuku took the hint, and ran towards the place where the prisoners were said to be. Fearing lest he should be too late to save them, he shouted, as only a chief can shout, *Oi, e kiko no Teko !*—'Spare the relatives of Teko !'

This timely shout saved their lives. The crowd, disappointed in their hope of getting a taste of human flesh that day, fell back. The captives were led to the feet of Teuanuku ; a coral-tree marks the spot where they met. In a few minutes they reached the home of Teuanuku. Hard by was that occupied by the priest-chief Mautara and his wife Teko. Tears of joy were freely shed, that auspicious day, at their narrow escape. Vaiaa remarked to his sister, *Kua tatara te enga, i.e.* 'The fear of death has passed away'—words which have passed into a proverb.

Vaiaa possessed medical[1] knowledge derived from his father : this was one reason for his life being spared. Lands were bestowed upon him at Tamarua, the ancient home of the Tongan tribe. Vaiaa married, and became the father of a number of sons and daughters.

Not long after their happy deliverance, Vaiaa and a number of his protectors made an expedition to the rocks in quest of Ngako, with a view of punishing him for his many cruelties. They found him starved to death in the old domicile occupied by Vaiaa and his sister. They left the corpse to the tender mercies of the rats which infest that wild district.

Mangaia became a dependant of Teuanuku. Whenever she went on the reef for the purpose of torch-fishing she

---

[1] *Ta pito.*

took *two* baskets, whereas it is customary to carry but one. The best fish she put into the basket reserved for her protector Teuanuku; all the inferior sort went into the other. On returning to the interior her invariable practice was to present each person she met, whether man, woman or child, with the best in her *second* basket. If anything remained at the bottom it would be hers; if not, she would be quite content, for was not her life secure? When asked why she alone of all women in Mangaia carried a second basket, she would say, 'Who can tell but that in some future hour of peril one of those to whom I have given fish may save my life?' Hence the proverb, *E takinga ta Mangaia*, 'Good-natured as Mangaia.'

She was eventually married to Maruata, who was offered in sacrifice to Rongo when the drum of peace was beaten for Kirikovi, in whose brief reign of five or six years Captain Cook came. She had the misfortune to see some of her children laid on the altar.

Rori obtained some of her beautiful hair to adorn the then newly carved image of Motoro. At the period of the surrender of the idols to Mr. Williams the hair of this woman was still on it. She was aunt to Rori the Hermit.

Mangaia lived to a very advanced age.

The identical bread-fruit tree in which Vaiaa was caught was blown down in the dreadful cyclone of March, 1846. A sucker from one of its decayed roots has grown into a noble tree. Standing on the interesting spot, I heard the story in all its particulars. I once heard a native pastor run through the outline of the story in illustration of a greater salvation.

At the commencement of Potiki's reign a set of songs were prepared in honour of Vaiaa, who had just died, and whose son, Nguare, had rendered important service to the ruling tribe in a recent battle. These are known as *Te Kakai ia Vaiaa*, or, 'The Death-talk about Vaiaa.' The sister is not referred to in these songs, marking the low estimation in which the sex was held.

THE CAPTURE OF VAIAA: 'A DEATH-TALK.'

Composed by Temaru, *circa* A.D. 1791.

TUMU.

Tongarei te kuru i kake ei Vaiaa.
  Kitea i Maruia,
Kua ngara i te mate ra aia !

INTRODUCTION.

In Tongarei is the bread-fruit Vaiaa climbed.
    Found in a shady vale,
He thought his last hour had come !

PAPA.

Kitea mai Vaiaa mei uta i Tongarei,
  Kua rongo koe i te pati e,
Tetai mama ia Vaiaa.
Kua rave a Teuanuku.
Te kou rauaika topa ē !

FOUNDATION.

Found was Vaiaa in the valley of Tongarei.
    He heard each one asking
    For a bit of Vaiaa.
    It was Teuanuku that saved him.
So the leaves for cooking thee were useless !

UNUUNU TAI.

Tongarei te kuru i kake ei—
Tei kakea, kapi oki a raro !
Kua kapi oki a raro ē !
  Te kete kuru mania,
Te matapa, no uta i Tongarei.
  Kitea i Maruia,
Kua ngara i te mate ra aia !

FIRST OFFSHOOT.

In Tongarei is the bread-fruit he climbed.
The ground was covered with foes—
    Covered, alas ! with foes.
Oh, the baskets of choice bread-fruits—
The fine fruits that grow in the vale of Tongarei.
    Found in a shady vale,
He thought his last hour had come !

UNUUNU RUA.

  Nooia ra te Kātara—
  Te Kātara, tei Tutama te ai !
Tei Tutama te ai, tei motu ii karoa ē !
I ui mai te vaine, Vaiaa oki teia.
  Kitea i Maruia,
Kua ngara i te mate ra aia !

SECOND OFFSHOOT.

    Thou didst tarry on the hill-top,
On the hill-top where thou didst see the lights,
Near the grove of tall chestnut-trees.
A woman asked and found it was Vaiaa.
    Found in a shady vale,
He thought his last hour had come !

UNUUNU TORU.

Ka akapiri i te ara ē !
  Na Katongi ïa.

THIRD OFFSHOOT.

The crowd led thee by the narrow path
    Through the valley—

Na Katongi tei Kāpuue,
Tei Kāpuue te ara nui,
Te vao roa koe i Tongarei.
  Kitea i Maruia,
Kua ngara i te mate ra aia !

Through the dell and past the water-
  fall,
Until they gained the main road
From the long valley of Tongarei.
  Found in a shady vale,
He thought his last hour had come !

UNUUNU A.

Tapiri i roto, ei te pu meika,
I te pu meika, kua nānā te mata ē !
  Eaa ta tatou ika ē !
  Aore au e pa atu ;
  E kiko oki no Teko.
  Kitea i Maruia,
Kua ngara i te mate ra aia !

FOURTH OFFSHOOT.

  Hidden in a banana grove,
On peering through the leaves (they
  exclaimed),
   ' Here is our sweet morsel.'
(A shout was heard :) ' Slay him not !
  He is the kinsman of Teko ! '
  Found in a shady vale,
He thought his last hour had come !

Ai e ruaoo !   E rangai ē !

Ai e ruaoo !   E rangai ē !

THE WANDERINGS OF VAIAA: 'A DEATH-TALK.'
Composed by Temaru, A.D. 1791.

TUMU.

Akapautua tei poro io ia Vaiaa,
Ei Ivirua te ora ake ia tatou,
  Reviri ake i reira.
Kua maru te rakau o te ao ē !

INTRODUCTION.

Akapautua's last words to Vaiaa were,
' Let the survivors fly to Ivirua,
And take refuge in the rocks.'
The shade of the forest is the home
  of the conquered.

PAPA.

Noo mai Vaiaa i te makitea,
E tai paa, tei ora ake ia tatou ;
Taumata io i te uru mato.
E roimata te manga ē !
E marere mai nga rau aoa ē !

FOUNDATION.

Vaiaa's shelter in the rocky heights
Near the sea. From a distance we
Wistfully gaze at our old homes,
Tears being now our constant food,
Sere banyan leaves falling all around !

UNUUNU TAI.

Akapautua ē, tei poro io ē,
  Tei poro ia Vaiaa,
  E tatari ra, e roa e,
Kua pau akarere, kua pau akarere ai,
  Te vai ra i Pukuotoi,
E tauna kapitia io e te puruki.
Ei Ivirua tei ora ake ia tatou,
  Reviri ake i reira ē !
Kua maru te rakau o te ao ē !

FIRST OFFSHOOT.

  Akapautua's last charge,
His parting words to Vaiaa, were,
  ' Watch the event of the fight :
Should we be utterly worsted,
And our bodies cover Pukuotoi,[1]
Slain and mangled by our foes,
Let the survivors fly to Ivirua,
And take refuge in the rocks.'
The shade of the forest is the home
  of the conquered.

---

[1] Pukuotoi is the spot where the surprise took place. This ' death-talk '
was gone through within a stone's-throw of the fatal battle-field.

UNUUNU RUA.

E ū te ara aerenga ē,
I te aerenga i te raei i Teua ē !
Kua tairo aere ē, tairo atu Vaiaa ē,
    Te peu toa i Rangimotia,
    Te pa puku i tu maunga,
I te karava i Kotikoti tei Pangorua.
Ei Ivirua tei ora ake ia tatou,
    Reviri ake i reira ē !
Kua maru te rakau o te ao ē !

SECOND OFFSHOOT.

'Tis difficult to discover the path—
The track o'er rocks and sharp stones.
Carefully note, Vaiaa, each turn of
    the road.
Yonder are the ironwood-trees of the
    interior,
And the gently-sloping hills
We have so often gazed upon.
' Let the survivors fly to Ivirua,
And take refuge in the rocks.'
The shade of the forest is the home
    of the conquered.

UNUUNU TORU.

Ka ka ano au ka kimi e,
    Kimi ra i Tomoariki ;
    Te reira te uinga ao,
    Mai te uinga ao.
E kimi i to ara e, e umi to inangaro,
E naea ra Vaiaa, e na tai aina?
E eke i raro atu, mei eke atu ki raro,
    I raro i te tapa utu,
Kua akarongo aere i te varara rakau.
Kua ariu ki miri, e tamaki aina?
Kua ēanga, meanga aere atu.
    Te mua paa to mate,'
    Te tangi nei te atua.
Akatapā Vaiaa ko Temakavetai ē !
Mei Temakavetai ra, e naea taua ē ?
E naea taua ē ?   Ei tai ngai atu.
Kua meamea i te nooinga,
Kia kite te mata i te enua ;
    Mai kite atu Vaiaa !
E te tangi nei ia Akapautua.

THIRD OFFSHOOT.

They will hunt about for thee
E'en as far as Tomoariki,[1]
The usual haunts of the conquered,
Where they meet together.
Seek out thy path ; take heed to each
    step.
How, where shall Vaiaa now go?
Descend to the beach, hide there
    awhile
Amongst groves of Barringtonia-trees.
Start not at the rustling of the leaves.
Lookest thou behind thee for a lurking
    foe ?
Ah ! how timidly thou turnest round !
Perhaps a deadly foe is at hand.
Hark to the cry of a guardian bird !
Call, Vaiaa, upon the god Temaka-
    vetai,[2]
' O guardian spirit, go with me ;
How shall I proceed? How can I
    escape ?
I weary of this desolate place.'
Oh, to set foot again in the interior !
How would the heart of Vaiaa then
    rejoice,
Who now grieves for his father,
    Akapautua !

Ei Ivirua tei ora ake ia tatou,
    Reviri ake i reira ē !
Kua maru te rakau o te ao ē !

' Let the survivors fly to Ivirua,
And take refuge in the rocks.'
The shade of the forest is the home
    of the conquered.

---

[1] Tomoariki is the designation of a very desolate tract of rocks where Vaiaa once took refuge.

[2] Temakavetai—' Single Ringlet '—was the supposed guardian of all ' black-wild-rocks.' Temaru, the composer of these songs, in his youth, *ate his female slave*, Rongo-ika-eke !

Unuunu A.

E kitea koe ra ē, i te nooinga e,
   I te nooinga i te vao ē,
   Mei raro i Tongarei,
   Mei raro i Tongarei,
Te ui nei i te kotu ma te katitaa ;
Karangaia ia eke, teia te mate iaau.
Ei Ivirua tei ora ake ia tatou,
   Reviri ake i reira.
Kuà maru te rakau o te ao ē !

Akareinga.

Ai e ruaoo ! E rangai ē !

Fourth Offshoot.

Thou wast captured in a tree,
   When at ease in a shady valley,
   In the vale of Tongarei—
   Ay, it was in the vale of Tongarei,
Thou wast plucking young bread-
   fruits,
When they shouted, ' Descend to die !'
   'Let the survivors fly to Ivirua,
   And take refuge in the rocks.'
The shade of the forest is the home
   of the conquered.

Finale.

Ai e ruaoo ! E rangai ē !

CHAPTER XXVII

SIN AND ITS PUNISHMENT

CIRCA 1727 (POSSIBLY 1730)

ONE day, as Rāei, a chief of secondary rank, was playing at quoits, he noticed the stately figure of Teuanuku gliding towards his hut in the sequestered hollow of Rupetau. Coincident with this, the monotonous music of his wife's cloth-beating hammer ceased. Ere the day closed she confessed her guilt, and Rāei had laid his plans for revenge. The seducer being, like himself, a worshipper of Motoro, he dared not take satisfaction with his own hand; but this did not, in heathen morality, render it improper in Rāei to arrange with Kikau and his Tongan tribe for the murder of 'the lord of Mangaia' as soon as the affair should apparently blow off, and the intended victim be put off his guard.

Day after day Rāei, like one demented, defiled the sacred district of Keia—the home of the gods—by wearing a *scarlet* hibiscus flower in each ear, a sin which, in a previous generation, had sealed the fate of Tiaio. The sagacious old priest inquired of Teuanuku the possible reason for this extraordinary conduct, and discovering the truth, passed over the insult to his god.

The just anger of the husband at length seemingly cooled down, and nothing further was dreaded. Teuanuku therefore cheerfully went back to his home at Ivirua. But that night he was slain by Kikau and the Tongans.

The younger brother, Raumea—a man of giant strength —had fallen in the battle of Pukuotoi, about two years previously, when the cannibal clan of Ruanae was exterminated. The exulting force led by Kikau collected most of the men of the northern half of the island, and encamped in great force at Keia, with the declared intention of crushing the remaining adherents of Mautara, and of conferring the supreme chieftainship upon Rāei. Luckily for the hitherto unconscious followers of Mautara, a swift messenger warned them of the near approach of their foes. In a short time the sorrowful old priest, with as many of his family and retainers as lived in the neighbourhood, crossed the hills to Ivirua to secure the corpse of the murdered chief. At the entrance to his hut lay the disfigured body, guarded by his weeping widow. Restraining his feelings until he had taken revenge, Mautara hastily wrapped up the corpse, and hid it in the tall fern on the hillside. He now beat up for recruits; but it was not until he had reached the ancestral seat of his tribe in Veitatei that he met with much success.

Night came on, but sleep was out of the question. Would he be able to cope with his foes and avenge the murder of his first-born? One-half of his extemporized army consisted of raw youths and *women*, most of the acknowledged warriors being ranged on the opposite side.

In a corner of Rāei's camp that same night a secret conference was held by Namu, the royal husband of the famous Kaiara; Manini, husband to the only two daughters of Mautara; and Pārae, priest of the Tongan tribe which had slaughtered Teuanuku. Said Manini to Namu, 'Whom should we pity?' Namu unhesitatingly replied, 'Our god [represented by his priest Mautara] alone deserves our pity'—words which afterwards became famous. The three resolved to save Mautara at all risks, and deputed Pārae, under cover of darkness, to go off to his camp and divulge to him their plans. Mautara's force was to take a hasty meal, and make a sudden attack upon Rāei's hungry army, when the three conspirators with their friends should attack them in the rear.

Pārae's visit did not transpire. Upon his return to Keia he ordered a grand feast requiring several hours to prepare—a feast that he well knew would never be tasted. In the midst of their cookery, to their dismay, the brave little army of Mautara appeared on a hill overlooking the camp. Each warrior rushed inside the enclosure for a spear or a club, and hastily put on his war gear.

Meantime Mautara was preparing to descend by a short narrow path, where half a dozen brave men could easily keep an army at bay. Pārae saw at a glance that Mautara's cause was lost if he trod that narrow causeway. Taking advantage of the desperate confusion which momentarily prevailed in the camp, and under pretence of washing his hands in the running stream (his face towards Rāei's camp), he most energetically beckoned Mautara to a circuitous side-path. Mautara at once understood the signal, and, making a slight *détour*, crossed the taro-patches in the rear of the hostile encampment. The fight now took place in right earnest, and on more equal terms, as the nature of the ground prevented a considerable portion of Rāei's army from engaging at all.

Namu, Manini, and Pārae had stationed their friends in the rear. In the heat of the battle they mercilessly attacked their former comrades, so that, hemmed in between the two, there was no chance whatever of escape. The slaughter was great. Amongst the slain was Rāei, but Kikau was taken alive.

When the fight was over, this wretched man, bound hand and foot, was conducted to Mautara. His fingers and toes, hands and arms, feet and legs, were cut off joint by joint with flint knives. As each limb was severed, the writhing victim was asked, ' Why did you not spare our brother ? ' The unvarying reply of the unhappy Kikau was, *Kua ē ia Ra* (Rāei)—' I was misled by Rāei '—now a proverb. The sufferings of the victim were terminated by his stomach being ripped up, and his intestines entwined on the trees shading the dwelling of Mautara.

That same day Teā was laid upon the alter of Rongo ; but Mautara deferred the ceremonies connected with beating the drum of peace until he had buried Teuanuku in the ancestral *marae*. In the re-division of lands which followed, the three arch-conspirators received ample shares. Mautara was declared temporal sovereign—the first since the days of Tiaio, but not the last instance in which a priest was invested with a dignity strictly pertaining only to warriors.

Mautara's reign of twenty-five years is the longest on record. Unbroken peace prevailed. Few vanquished warriors survived ; but their little orphan children grew up to maturity ' under the shadow of Mautara,' and the island again became populous. Ikoke, the third son of the priest-chief, had six wives ; his slave Terimu boasted as many—widows of those they had slain.

The sway of Mautara is looked upon as the model one of historical antiquity ; for no blood was shed, and no one of note died, during the entire period. At his death he must have been over fourscore.

In that wondrously long interval of peace the enormous fan and ornamented staff took the place of the spear and the club. The old priest-chief was ever chanting to himself the well-known words—

<table>
<tr><td>Ua purukia e au tamariki,
E maraerae io Mangaia ō !
Ka aere ua ra to raua metua.</td><td>My boys have won many a victory ;
Have crushed every foe in Mangaia,
That their old father might rest in peace.</td></tr>
</table>

As soon as death closed his eyes, the new generation thought the time had come to avenge the slaughter of their sires. A battle was fought at Tuopapa, where Ikoke fell. His slave Terimu, having abandoned him, was afterwards, despite his grey hairs, selected for sacrifice, when the drum of peace declared Uarau sovereign. A short reign of two years was terminated by the last surviving son of Mautara seizing upon the reins of power.

Ngarā, like his father priest and chief, slew and laid upon the altar the woman Ike. After a peaceful reign of fifteen years, the priest-chief died. Under the shadow of that romantic pile of rocks called the Cave of Terau, a battle was fought, which conferred the supreme power upon a grandson of Mautara, known as Kirikovi, Maruata being the victim for the altar. In this reign (1777) arrived the famous Captain Cook. It was not until the year 1814 that the supreme temporal power passed into other families, and the Mautara clan could henceforth boast only their ancient prowess in arms, and the richest collection of traditionary songs in the Hervey Group.

Koroa sung thus, *circa* 1815 :—

<table>
<tr><td>Kavake te au o Mautara ra teaore ē !
  E rima tau aitu.
Na nu roa o te Amama ē !</td><td>Long and peaceful was the rule of Mautara,
  Enduring five sacred lustrums.
Like a tall palm was the priestly sway.</td></tr>
<tr><td> No Kavainga [1]
No Ngarā nga tau ra e toru ē !
  Ie tiria i raro,
Unuia e Rongo te aratoko e tu i vaengapu.</td><td> His descendants, Potiki
And Ngarā reigned three lustrums apiece ;
  Then Rongo willed
That those who had been chiefs should be slaves.</td></tr>
</table>

---

[1] Kavainga is better known as Potiki. In point of time, Ngarā's title should precede Potiki's by many a long year.

CHAPTER XXVIII

RORI, THE HERMIT

ETIQUETTE in the South Seas, as at home, requires an express invitation to a great feast. One morning a nephew of the chief at Tamarua entered the mission premises, walked up to the door of my study, and inserted the extremity of a coco-nut frond in the thatch. Without uttering a word he departed, to act similarly at the houses of all the parties expected to attend—*i.e.* the king and six principal chiefs, beside the three native pastors. There was a peculiarity in this silent invitation—the separate leaves amounted to fifteen, the meaning being that the entire household should go. Two or three leaves would be but a poor compliment.

Not wishing to be deficient in courtesy, on the following morning at break of day I rode over to the village of Tamarua, and rested awhile at the native minister's house. At length a messenger announced that all was ready. Accompanied by the valued native pastor, I proceeded to the feasting-ground, which is a level spot in the centre of the settlement, covered with long grass and neatly enclosed. Huge heaps of food were arranged in two long rows opposite to each other, one for the guests, the other for the entertainers themselves. At eight o'clock silence was called for, hats of all descriptions were taken off, and a blessing was asked. The chief of Tamarua then called out the names of the guests over the respective piles of food, beginning with the missionary and the three native pastors, to evince their respect for the Word of God. Then came the king and six great chiefs, whose names were announced in a certain order handed down from time immemorial. Curiously enough, these chiefs at once said to the subordinate landowners, ' Divide our food ; ' and when that was done the chiefs got no more than their people. But they alone had the honour of their names being called out before the assembly ; so that in reality the food became their gift to those who according to ancient feudal usage followed them.

My heap consisted of sixty baskets of taro, large bunches of ripe bananas, cooked fish, which no European would care to eat, and a large quantity of the coco-nut *poi* for which Mangaia is famous. This concoction, which is sour and disagreeable to foreign palates, is made of scraped coco-nut, allowed to ferment, and afterwards mixed with cooked taro. It is regarded as a great treat by the natives ; no great feast is complete without some. Each basket of raw taro had a lot of this *poi*, well packed in broad fern-leaves, on the top.

Surmounting the whole heap were several joints of pork, an entire pig half-cooked, and—rare treat !—a joint of raw beef. The pile was also garnished with young coco-nuts intended for immediate use.

The problem now was, how one solitary mortal could dispose of a heap of food nearly as high as himself. This was quickly decided by dividing the whole amongst our servants, students, gratuitous doorkeepers of our church at Oneroa, and some Rarotongans on a visit to their friends. In this way the whole pile of taro, *poi*, fish, and pork disappeared in the course of a few minutes. I reserved for ourselves merely the piece of beef.

The guests quickly disappeared; their friends and retainers bearing away huge baskets of food, cooked and uncooked. To leave anything behind were an insult.

Three valuable fish-nets had just been made at Tamarua, their united value being nearly £20. The entire pecuniary value of the food disposed of would be about eight or ten times the worth of the nets. But then it is ever considered a mean and disgraceful thing for a chief to make and use such nets without inviting all the magnates of the island to a feast. The waste of food is only in appearance; for at certain seasons it is necessary to replant the taro patches by planting the tops of the old taro.

A VISIT TO THE RĀEI.

Desirous of a little change, I now expressed my wish to the native pastor to visit the *rāei kere*—'wild black rocks,' so famous in Mangaian story. Notwithstanding a long residence in the island, I had never been there. It was agreed that we should start at once. Three young men from Oneroa got an inkling of my intention, and followed us. After a walk under the shadow of the continuous belt of rocks which, like a second reef upraised by some mighty subterraneous agency, surrounds the island, we reached the nearest pathway to the *rāei*.

At first the ascent over the stones was tolerably easy; but the atmosphere was stifling, on account of the extreme luxuriance of tropical vegetation, often literally growing out of the very rocks without an inch of soil. At length it became needful to wear native sandals, made of the twisted bark of the lemon hibiscus, and secured by thongs of the same material wound round the toes and ankles. As I had on a stout pair of boots reserved for the occasion, there was some difficulty in fastening them on. This happily accomplished, there was little danger of slipping, a misfortune inevitable to a visitor with only European shoes on.

We soon emerged upon a perfect wilderness, where no leaf of any description was to be seen. This was the *rāei kere*—'black rocks,' of which I have heard so much from old warriors! In every direction, save that we had just left, spread out before us an unvarying succession of black pointed rocks, over which it was difficult to believe that a human being could pass. Our party preferred keeping strictly to what the natives satirically call a pathway, which in truth was only a faint track over the rocks. Off that track only a native could venture : at each step the pointed stones cracked ominously. Yet native boys, well-sandalled, run races over the more tolerable parts. Our guide walked on in front. Each step had to be taken with the utmost caution. In one hand I held a long pole ; a native lad held my other hand.

There are in all eight ridges, each bearing a distinct name. Midway we found a rock recently levelled by a sledge-hammer to form a comfortable standing-place, although not larger than a table. An excellent view of this Land of Desolation was obtained from this spot. The *rāei kere* extended on every side, being about three miles in length and two in width. The low mountains of the interior were here lost to view. Before us rolled the vast, blue Pacific. About a mile from our resting-place was the spot where of old Rori hid himself from his relentless foes. Looked upon from a distance, the *rāei* closely resembled a map of the moon ; the hollows appearing as mysterious black spots enclosed by strangely-contorted ridges. We resolved to press on to the sea. But as the sun was nearly vertical, and there was no tree or even a low bush to afford shade—we could not even see one—we suffered greatly from thirst. I inquired for the water-holes where Rori used to slake his thirst; but the search of our guide was unavailing. The walk across occupied two hours. On reaching the beach we rested awhile, despite the burning thirst, on the sandy floor of a cave.

Anxious not to return by this rough path, we now endeavoured to skirt the shore, as the water was high on the reef. For some time we persevered, but eventually found it impossible to go on. A small yellow creeper had so completely covered the many fissures and holes in our course that more than once our party nearly disappeared from sight in these natural pitfalls. With great difficulty we made our way back to the old resting-place in the cave by the sea, and prepared to wade along the reef as best we could. Sometimes the water was up to our chins; at times as low as our waists. The force of the current made it difficult at times to maintain one's footing. Occasionally we were compelled to swim, clothes and all.

On first wading on the reef, the feeling was one of delicious coolness, allaying our thirst in no small degree. But before long the weight of water in our clothes became intolerably fatiguing. Midway we espied a little cavern, hollowed out of the overhanging rocks by the ceaseless beating of the waves, and known as the Cave of Uanukutea. Here we rested for a few seconds, and listened to the

STORY OF UANUKUTEA.

In the days of Tiki a woman from the island of Mauke, named Uanukutea, took up her solitary abode here. The reason of her being exiled was that on more than one occasion she was caught by her father, Uanukutaketea, eating human flesh and drinking human blood. Without hesitation he drove her away from her pretty island-home. Sent to sea alone in a small canoe with a mat sail, and a scanty supply of coco-nuts to serve for food and drink, she reached Mangaia, a distance of one hundred miles. Landing unobserved on this wild part of the coast, she sent the canoe adrift and took shelter in the cave that bears her name. Uncertain what her fate might be, she did not wish her arrival to be known.

She had lived some months on the island, when Matariki, priest of Tané, third in order of succession, met her in the dusk of evening prowling about the adjacent rocks. Learning the name of the stranger woman, he inquired, 'What are you *crunching*, Uanukutea?' Her reply was, 'Only *the legs of a god*'—words which have since passed into a proverb. Matariki's impression was that she referred to the legs of land-crabs, which abound in that neighbourhood. In reality Uanukutea was picking a human bone. To this incorrigible female cannibal nothing was so delicious as human flesh: she never wearied of it. It is asserted that her habit was to waylay any solitary young person who might lag behind the bevies of women and girls engaged in torch-fishing on the reef whenever the tide was favourable. In the utter darkness of moonless nights the stranger woman might easily escape notice, or, if seen by the distant glare of the torches, be mistaken for one of their number. Uanukutea used an ironwood dagger, two feet long, called a *tui* or 'needle.' A stab in the naked back whilst her victim was intent on picking up a drowsy fish or chasing a lobster would be sufficient for her purpose. The body was of course borne to the little cave which bears her name, to be devoured at leisure.

An inquiry was set on foot respecting the fate of several young persons who had mysteriously disappeared. Matariki advised that a visit be paid to the lair of a stranger woman from Mauke whom he had accidentally met and conversed with. A new sense was given to her famous words. The suggestion was at once complied with, and abundant evidence of her guilt was discovered. Uanukutea was forthwith speared to death. The name of this monster in human form is indelibly associated with this little cave, which now forms a pleasant resting-place for the wearied traveller, despite the cold drops of purest water which occasionally fall from the stone roof upon his head.

So runs the ancient story. That a stranger woman so named once met her fate there is doubtless true. The story of her crimes may have been a mere excuse for the murder committed by these islanders, who looked with an evil eye upon all visitors.

Vaipo in his *fête* song (*circa* 1819) refers to this woman :—

[Call for dance to begin.]

Uanukutea te vaine ē !
Ka aere i te piaki roa i Mataorongo ē !
Kua taia koe.

Solo.

Taipo ē !

Chorus.

Noo maira i te rua roa tei tai ē !
Tei tai te rua roa o Uanukutea.
Te ara e kai tangata ua ē !
Te raro aturā Uanukutea ē !
Te raro atu Uanukutea i te papa
I te moana.   O Tanè-aiai, e vari
  Tautiti ē !

[Call for dance to begin.]

Ah, Uanukutea !
That wanderedst by the shore of
  Mataorongo,
    Thou hast met thy deserts.

Solo.

Go on !

Chorus.

There once dwelt in a cave by the sea,
Far away from the dwellings of men,
A she-cannibal, a stranger, named
  Uanukutea.
Her home, scarcely noticeable, was
Where the white breakers ever foam.
Tanè,[1] the evening-star god, revealed
  her ;

---

[1] Tanè is put for Matariki, priest of Tanè. The evening-star was 'the eye of Tanè.'

Kua kitea, e kitea mai ana,	He who presides over the merry dance.
Te kai maira te kai o te Atua :	She was devouring the food [1] of the gods ;
Turinga, turinga mou ai rai.	Utterly addicted to eating human flesh.

Again we pressed on our way ; perpendicular rocks at our back threatening us with certain destruction should the sea suddenly rise, this being the weather-side of the island, where the trades unceasingly blow in all their mighty strength. After an hour's wading we happily reached the well-known Big Cave, which has a tragic history of its own. Here was the path by which we thankfully made our way back to the interior, dripping as we were with sea-water, through a thick growth of candle-nut and other trees. At last we emerged upon a cultivated spot, where grows a clump of low coco-nut-trees. Here we soon enjoyed most refreshing draughts of coco-nut water. Overheated as we were, we knew that we might drink without fear of evil consequences : a striking instance of the Divine Wisdom which adapts food and drink to the climate.

We now returned to the village of Tamarua, weary and footsore. Forthwith mounting my horse, I rode home, much gratified with my brief adventure. But to my surprise I found that I had suddenly become famous ; for it had got wind that 'the missionary had gone to see the *rāei*,' which very few on the west side have ever visited. Many were the kind congratulations, as I rode along in my tattered garments, that I had returned from so famous and so rugged a spot without accident.

There were several points of interest connected with this trip, of which the principal is

[1] The dead were regarded as food for the gods, which she was impiously devouring.

Rori's grandfather, Una, arrived on the eastern coast of Mangaia in a drift canoe from Iti, the only name by which Tahiti was formerly known here. By a Mangaian wife he became the father of Rongoariki. Now, father and son were famed for their skill in all manner of carpentry and fine sennit work. Una died; but these well-guarded secrets were faithfully transmitted in the third generation to Rori, the only son of Rongoariki.

When Rori was a lad of say eighteen years, the decisive battle of Māucue was fought on a pleasant hillside within a stone's throw from the home of these artisans. The immediate occasion of that fight was anger at the expulsion of a section of the Tongan clan, who were imagined to have been swallowed up in the ocean, but in reality had found a comfortable home on the southern part of Rarotonga.

Sixty fell on the losing side, to which Rori and his father belonged. The old man fought as a warrior in the ranks; behind him stood his son, spear in hand, ready to occupy his father's place should he fall.

Their party being utterly routed, they both ran for shelter to their hut. But seeing the victors in hot pursuit, the old man urged his children to leave him to die, and take refuge in the *rāei kere*—'wild black rocks' on the east of Mangaia. Rori and his two sisters willingly obeyed, and ran in the direction indicated.

During the few minutes wasted by the attacking party in killing the father and disposing of the valuable articles which his skill enabled him to produce, Rori succeeded in gaining the summit of the cliffs not far from his future home; but from that inaccessible height witnessed the unhappy fate of his sister Amio, and a younger one, whose name is forgotten. To kill women was contrary to the ordinary usage of war here. So swift were the brother's movements that his pursuers gave up the chase as fruitless.

Finding himself no longer an object of pursuit, Rori looked carefully about for a place of refuge in the very bosom of the 'wild black rocks.' He deliberately made his home in the very worst spot in all Mangaia, because it was impossible that any one approaching his hiding-place, however cautiously, should escape his observation.

The spot selected by the young exile as his head-quarters was a hollow about thirty feet square, towards the interior effectually sheltered from observation by a rock. Here he resolved to settle down as in an utterly unknown or forsaken land. He worked hard night by night to level the sharp-pointed rock, until at last he succeeded in making it tolerably smooth. The only hammers used by him in breaking off the tops of these rocks were large pieces of basalt, stolen by him in his nocturnal visits to the interior. Thus in the midst of this fearful scene of desolation he had gained an unsuspected hiding-place, just midway between the ocean and the fertile interior, where dwelt his foes.

Tradition asserts that, after he had thus levelled the surface of this hollow, the place was still rough and uncomfortable. Rori found amusement in chipping sharp stones into the appearance of sea-worn pebbles, such as are invariably used to adorn the dwellings of Polynesians. In the course of time the irregular surface of Rori's Hollow was neatly covered with artificial pebbles.

The heavy dews and rains of the tropics admonished the solitary fugitive to build a house. Abundance of suitable wood could be procured for this purpose at night from the dense forest skirting his barren domain.   But he had no adze wherewith to cut down a single branch. Nothing daunted, Rori set to work to make a set of stone adzes out of pieces of basalt stolen from the interior under cover of darkness.   These adzes are made by ceaselessly chipping with sharp fragments of red quartz.   A mountain of red quartz exists on the north-east of the island, which, tradition says, travelled all night of its own accord from Rarotonga, and at daylight settled down where it now is ! Natives go from all parts of the island to this spot, appropriately called Maana, the Rarotongan word for ' hot,' for supplies of quartz, which they use as flint, and which are obtained by roasting the rock.

Handles must be sought for these adzes.   Sennit must be plaited to fasten them on the top of the wooden handles. In all this Rori was an adept : it was to perpetuate this invaluable knowledge that the father begged his boy to leave him to his fate.   But the fugitive dared not venture so near to human habitations as would be needful to obtain the materials for making sennit.   In those times coco-nut-trees were only planted in the immediate neighbourhood of the dwellings of the proprietors, who kept constant watch, spear in hand.   A substitute was hit upon in the bark of the banyan-tree, which here grows best on the rocks skirting the barren kingdom of Rori.

The set of adzes was finished.   A few dark nights enabled Rori to obtain from the forest the wood required. Two small houses were now built—one for a workshop and for sleeping ; a second for storing and cooking food.   The ordinary pandanus thatch was unattainable to a man in his circumstances.   Rori therefore had recourse to a beautiful broad-leafed fern[1] (*rau kotaa*) which abounds in

---

[1] Bird's-nest fern.

the moist recesses of the rocks outside this desolate domain, and which is well adapted for temporary dwellings, being perfectly impervious to rain. But there was one serious drawback to this sort of thatch—it must be renewed every fifteen or twenty days. At the present time, if a party of natives felling timber in the forest are overtaken by darkness or by rain, they extemporize a house of this kind for the night. A couple of men with sharp Sheffield axes can run up a house of this sort in half an hour—a labour of many weeks to Rori, with his clumsy tools.

The fear that his solitary home would eventually be discovered, and that he would be surprised and slain, led to his seeking an additional hiding-place. At no great distance was a cave admirably suited for this end. Here was carefully hidden his treasure of red feathers and stone adzes not in use. When a strong sense of danger crept upon him, here, too, he would sleep in safety during the day—the period when most liable to be discovered. After the death of Rori the entrance to this cave was carefully built up with stones by his sons, so that it might prove to them a refuge, as it had been to their father, if needed. This famous little cave has of late years been sought for in vain—so completely have the stones closing its mouth assumed the blackened, mossy appearance of the rocks around them.

Water exists in the crannies of the rocks sufficient to sustain life, although a superficial seeker like our guide could find none. The Well of Rori, in the midst of this waste, is a natural hollow, to which the ingenious fugitive adapted a stone cover. In a second visit to this romantic spot we found it, and tasted its water. The purport of the cover was to hide the water from sight, and to keep it free from insects.

Rori subsisted on a sour wild fruit, known as the *nono* (*Morinda citrifolia*), a species of wild yam, candle-nuts, and pandanus drupes, which have a pleasant flavour. To obtain these necessaries of life he made frequent expeditions to the neighbouring woods. His main support during the early months of the new year was the fruit of the chestnut-tree (*Inocarpus edulis*). A single nut, divested of its thick husk, is usually four inches long, three wide, and one thick. Not far from the *rāei* in the interior of the island there grew at that time a noble grove of seven of these valuable trees. Three of the seven still stand, and bear the name of Rori's Chestnuts.[1] Though they have weathered the storm of centuries, they are still magnificent trees.

At dusk Rori approached as near as was safe : as soon as it was pitch-dark he boldly left the rocks and made for the well-known trees. If there was nothing to excite suspicion, he ventured farther into the interior to a second clump of trees, to collect worm-eaten chestnuts, which he easily distinguished from the good by their lightness. Rori's basket being full of these worthless nuts, he would return to the grove which bears his name, and feel about the ground for good chestnuts. For every good nut he picked up he substituted a worm-eaten one, in order to avoid suspicion. Nobody would imagine that a fugitive would venture to the distant clump of chestnuts ; but the frequent disappearance of the fruit of the trees so near the rocks could not but eventually lead to his destruction. So cleverly did Rori manage matters that his existence was for a long time unsuspected.

The sandals of Rori—so necessary to his safety—were made of prepared banyan-tree bark, the best possible for

---

[1] Often designated Rori's Delight.

this purpose. It was needful to beat the bark out on a log of wood, after being steeped in water. The same sort of bark yielded him a coarse coverlet (*tiputa*) and the never-forgotten girdle. The paper-mulberry tree (*aute*) is invariably used for these purposes; but Rori was an outcast and a fugitive. The all-important point with him was to have a good supply of sandals, to enable him fearlessly to run over these spear-pointed rocks; a single pair lasting him only two or three days. Throughout the Polynesian islands cloth-beating is a female employment. To dull the sound of his cloth-beating he half-buried his log (*tutunga*) in the ground, taking care to beat out the bark very gently. The cloth made under such disadvantageous circumstances was of the coarsest description.

Rori usually slept soundly during the early part of the day, after the toil of the night in providing and cooking. His favourite employment in the after part of the day was the manufacture of stone adzes, articles of the greatest value in these islands before the introduction of iron. His unwearying industry is attested by the abundant chips of basalt and red quartz which may yet be seen in his solitary home in the very bosom of the *rāei*, which is simply hardened coral. These stones are never found there unless taken by some clever fugitive from the interior in order to beguile the weariness of his exile. These stone adzes require continual sharpening on hones, obtained from softer portions of the mountain of red quartz. A hone of this sort was hidden in the garden where he had once lived in peace. He tremblingly ventured there one night, and, finding the place entirely deserted, succeeded in carrying away his treasure. That hone, much worn by use and broken, was long in my possession.[1]

[1] It is now deposited in the British Museum.

Close to the hiding-place of this industrious fellow is a small quarry of the finest stalagmite, used in making valuable pestles (*reru*) for preparing food. It is said that he made numbers of these useful articles during his long exile in the *rāei*. A beautiful specimen was presented to me lately by the native pastor, saying, 'It is the best stone; it came from the quarry of Rori.'

A favourite employment of Rori was to tame wild birds, which at that time were numerous. The gun and the wild cat of the white man have effectually thinned them out. Some species are entirely extinct. Having with some difficulty succeeded in taming one or two young tropic birds (*tavaki*), he fed them on a rock near his home, taking care to secure one foot by a string. By means of snares he caught numbers of the birds, in order to get the beautiful red feathers (two only) found in the tail. These feathers are still prized by the natives, but were then of much higher value for head-dresses. Other birds yielded to him black and blue and golden feathers, without, however, preventing his winged companions from seeking their own livelihood. The dark feathers were in those days used to decorate their dances in time of peace, and their long spears on the battle-field.

However short of food he might be, he never killed these birds, as they were in his estimation his special guardians in time of peril. Two species were sacred to the god Tanè; the rest to Tamakavetai, the spirit of the 'wild black rocks.' If, when on his nocturnal marauding expedition, one of these birds would cross his path and cry over his head, Rori devoutly believed this to be a hint from these divinities that he had better hide himself from impending danger, or fly for his life.

To facilitate his movements, he built a rough pathway,

half a mile in length. The stones were so fixed that whilst capable of bearing the weight of Rori they would rattle; so that, if discovered and pursued in his strange asylum, he would thereby get timely notice of danger. In running away at his wondrous speed from danger, he was careful to take a direction contrary to his home, lest his retreat should be discovered. The stone pathway referred to approaches the sea route which our party so painfully traversed. A practised eye is required to see that it was made by human hands at all, as time and weather have made all the stones equally black.

Seasons came and went; years rolled on in this monotonous way with Rori, whose existence was unknown, and whose name was all but forgotten. It was known that he had taken refuge in the rocks after the fatal battle of Māueue, but it was believed that he had long since starved to death. One or two individuals professed to have seen an ill-looking, cadaverous fellow flying like the wind over the most inaccessible rocks; surely this must be Rori. But this was regarded as a wild imagination. Such was Rori's wonderful fleetness of foot, when once sandalled, that it was hopeless to chase him. Upon one occasion he ventured on the reef to fish for sea-eels. He had caught several, and, for once, unwisely cooked and ate on the sandy beach. Meanwhile a number of armed men, themselves exiles from a later battle-field, but who eventually all perished of hunger, caught sight of Rori. These fugitives were in quest of human flesh, and stealthily approached so near to their intended victim that escape seemed impossible. Rori, perceiving their shadow on the white sand, raised his head, and to his dismay saw his foes preparing to spear him from an overhanging crag. With the wonderful instinct of a native, he instantly caught up a cooked fish in one hand and his sandals in the other, and, making a desperate leap, happily succeeded in gaining a projecting point of rock on the side farthest from his pursuers. Running a short distance with his naked feet, he deliberately stopped to fasten on a single sandal; then, holding the other in his hand, he advised his foes to go back, as they would only cut up their feet (they were without sandals) in pursuit of Rori, without catching him. They gave chase, but to no purpose. Rori purposely led them over the worst places, and disappeared from his foes like an apparition.

Seven pitched battles had been fought during the long years of Rori's first exile in the *raei*. Five times had the brave Ngangati been declared 'temporal lord of Mangaia,' and at length fell by the hand of the rival chief Akatara, who thus succeeded to the chieftainship. The priestly tribe of Mautara had avenged the death of Ngangati by the well-arranged daylight murder of Akatara. In the battle of Arira that followed, the great tribe of Teipe, of which Akatara had been head, was worsted ; the remnant, still powerful in numbers, taking refuge in the Cave of the Tern, at Ivirua.

The present chief of this unfortunate clan was Ruanae, who had introduced cannibalism, in order to strike terror into the hearts of his victorious enemies. Numerous instances of cannibalism are remembered of solitary hungry fugitives, but Ruanae was the first chief to practise it openly in the presence of his entire tribe.

The chief adviser of Ruanae was old Butai, a near relative of Rori, the only one living who remembered and cared for him. Now, Butai had incurred the hatred of Ruanae by foolishly boasting that, ' let worst come to worst, *he* should be safe at the hands of their foes.' From that day his fate was sealed, although well known to be 'the wise man' of the tribe.

Now, Rori, in his nightly peregrinations, had become increasingly daring; he ventured once as far as the neighbourhood of the Cave of the Tern, and overheard the gossip of some stragglers. Learning from these unwitting informants that Butai still lived, he made himself known to his relative, and consented to share the waning fortunes of the clan. Although living with Butai in the cave, he wisely forbore to give information of his old hiding-place, as he might have occasion yet to return. It does not appear that Rori had any definite purpose of leaving his old haunts; but upon hearing that Butai, his near relative, was living close by where he had chanced to wander, an irresistible yearning for human society and sympathy induced him at once to join the cannibal clan, although himself not a cannibal.

It so happened that on the day afterwards the entire body of well-armed men left the cave in search of food, leaving the women and children to the care of Butai. About a mile distant, in a sequestered hollow, was a grove of wide-spreading Brazilian plum-trees (*Spondias dulcis*) covered with fruit, so that it must have been the month of February. On account of his lithe and wiry form, Rori was chosen one of the fruit-gatherers. A very large quantity of fruit was obtained and packed in baskets, to be cooked inside the stronghold. Said Ruanae to his cousin Akapautua, 'As soon as we get back we will eat that prating old fool Butai, and the new-comer, his relative Rori; for one victim would not be a taste all round.' Little did these intending victims imagine that their bodies were to be the relish for these half-ripe plums.

But Akapautua in his heart pitied the unoffending

Rori. Without being seen by Ruanae, he contrived, whilst washing his hands at a brook, to give a hint to Rori. As soon as the tribe had arrived at the foot of the long ladder leading to the cave, Rori deposited his basket of fruit on the ground, and saying to those about him he must collect some dry sticks for the great oven of the clan, disappeared in the bush. Thought Ruanae, 'Those sticks will serve nicely for the cooking of Rori himself.' But so it was not to be; for Rori darted through the bush as fast as his legs could carry him. The wind bore to the ears of the fugitive the death-wail of old Butai, *Aue tou e! Ka mate au e?* ('Alas! alas! Must I, too, die?')

Congratulating himself on his narrow escape, Rori did not stop his flight until he knew that he was beyond pursuit. Embittered at heart at this brief sojourn amongst mankind, he once more made his home in his old quarters in the desolate *rāei*, where he could live comparatively without fear, for it was difficult to take him by surprise.

One good resulted from his short residence with Ruanae's clan in the stronghold—he became acquainted with Manaune, at that time a mere youth.

It was after this narrow escape of Rori that Manaune was adopted into the winning tribe of the priest Mautara, and so rose to power and fame.

To Rori's apprehension every human face was that of a foe bent on his destruction, and doubtless intending to cook and eat him. He resolved to end his days where he had so long lived, in the 'wild black rocks.' Years passed on during this second flight to the *raei;* two more pitched battles were fought, of which our hero was happily ignorant. The cannibal tribe of Ruanae had been swept utterly out of existence. Again had the chieftainship of the island changed hands, while Rori lived on in his wild home. Only once before during these long years had the drum of peace been beaten, making it safe for a poor fugitive like him to enter the interior of the island by daylight, and yet live. Altogether Rori could not have spent less than thirty years in his solitary residence among the rocks ; and when eventually he returned to the interior he had not a single relative living !

Teuanuku and Raumea were dead. Their clever father, the priest Mautara, now held undisputed sway over the island. Peace reigned ; consequently food became plentiful again. But Rori was still in the old place in the rocks, ignorant of this, and dreading every human being.

He had, however, grown less careful of himself. One evening, as he approached the outskirts of his barren domain, he saw a number of women going to fish by torchlight on the reef. He hid himself near the beach until they returned, and had, according to custom, cooked and eaten part of their fish, and then returned to the interior. As soon as the women had disappeared, he went to pick up the morsels of fish and ends of taro—food untasted by him for many a long year. Whilst thus engaged, two men—one of whom was the Manaune he had become acquainted with in the Cave of the Tern— passed along the reef with scoop-nets in their hands. They caught sight of a wild-looking elderly fellow entirely absorbed in consuming his dainty meal of odds and ends. They advanced in perfect silence towards him, and when tolerably near ran to catch Rori, who started to his feet, and with his ancient agility leaped on the rocks. He could now easily escape, as he had no equal in the art of running. Manaune now saw that this bird of the desert was his old acquaintance Rori, who was supposed to have perished with the scattered remnants of Ruanae's cannibal clan. Knowing that he possessed the invaluable secret of working in wood and stone and sennit, he earnestly called out to him, ' Rori, come back and carve my god for me.' The fugitive, astounded at the mention of his name and craft, stood a second to inquire who was lord of Mangaia, and whether the drum of peace had been beaten. Finding that Mautara was chief, and that perfect peace prevailed, he altered his purpose of flight, and descending from the cliff gave himself up to Manaune.

Fishing was out of the question now. All three made their way to the beautiful valley of Ivirua, where the lands of the chief Manaune were situated. The pathway from the sea was that by which the writer gained the interior, after his expedition to the home of Rori in the 'wild black rocks.' The welkin rang with merry shouts of *Kua tau mai Rori!* ('Rori is found!') The news spread all over the island the same day, so that crowds came to see this poor fellow. And a miserable skeleton he was, his skin almost black through continual exposure. A feast was made for him by the people of Ivirua, but he scarcely tasted the unaccustomed food. He was then led in procession round the island by his protector and others ; the crowning point was for him to bathe in Rongo's Sacred Fountain, in token of his being cleansed from a state of bondage and fear, and being allowed to participate freely in all the good things of the dominant tribe.

A day or two afterwards he went back to his old haunts in the rocks, to say farewell to the guardian deities of the *raei*, to look after his old feathery friends, and to bring away as much as he could of the treasures he had accumulated during his long residence there. Many subsequent visits did he pay, until all his stone adzes, pestles, and feathers were removed—a fortune in those days.

When he first took up his abode in the rocky wilderness, he could not well have been more than eighteen years old. He came back with a large sprinkling of grey hairs.

A granddaughter of Mautara, named Motia, was given to Rori as his wife. By her he had several children. The spot where his house stood is still pointed out ; and a number of ancient coco-nut trees, planted by Manaune a little before his discovery and adoption, are still growing. These palms, about 106 feet in height, are the oldest on the island.

His employment was now to instruct the young men of the time in the art of carving, plaiting sennit, the manufacture of adzes, and the building of houses. He not only carved Tiaio, the god of his friend Manaune, but all (excepting Teipe) the other gods of Mangaia, once kept in the idol-house of the king, but about sixty-three years since removed by the Rev. J. Williams to the museum of the London Missionary Society. During Rori's residence in the rocks, the former rudely-carved idols had all been destroyed by fire—a significant hint that, being thus unable unitedly to take care of themselves, they could still less succour those who trusted in them.

Beautiful red parrakeet feathers, brought to this island by his grandfather, and concealed with Rori's other treasures in the *rāei*, were used by him to adorn Motoro, to the great admiration of the men of that day. His last great work was to build a temple to Tanè, supported by a single post. This temple had just been completed at the time of Captain Cook's visit in 1777. Rori lived happily with his family in the district generously assigned to him by Manaune, and died at a very advanced age.

Some years afterwards his sons resolved to celebrate the sufferings and happy escape of their father in *e tara kakai*, or 'death-talk.' The food was planted for the feast, and most of the songs got ready, when war again broke out. In the battle of Akaoro, which followed, three grown-up sons were slain. Contrary to a promise to their mother, they took up arms against her clan. Hence it is said that when Motia heard of their death, she refused to weep, and cursed their memory!

The intended 'death-talk' *in memoriam* never came off, and most of the songs[1] were forgotten ; but the story of Rori will never be forgotten, so long as there exists a native of Mangaia.

Two younger sons of Rori did not go to battle, and consequently were allowed to live as slaves to the victors. There is now (1874) living a venerable man, Vainekavoro, about ninety-five years of age, who was born just after the said battle. It is certain, therefore, that the three sons of Rori fell about 1780. The heirlooms of the family were hidden in a cave, to which the only means of access was by holding on to the roots of a banyan-tree which, like a strong cable, ran over the precipice to the soil below in a deep fertile gorge. A lad, hunting for bats to eat, saw a number hanging from a tree, paralyzed with the cold of early morning, and, in climbing, discovered grand head-dresses, wooden drums, adzes, and sennit. These were the property of the slain sons of the hermit of the *raei*.

The most popular of the songs about Rori is the following :—

RORI HIDING IN THE ROCKS.

TUMU.	INTRODUCTION.
Māueue te taua ē,	Māueue was the battle-field,
E taua puruki na Arekare,	The fighting-ground of Arekare,

---

[1] The two accompanying songs were composed for this intended 'death-talk' of Rori.

I ao ei Rori i te makatea,
  Kua oki au ki miri :
Kua piri atu ki te rau puka ē !

When the fugitive Rori fled to the rocks,
  Everything was lost ;
My home was where the laurel-trees grow.

PAPA.

Akatu koe i toou are, e Rori ē,
Te are rau kotaa e !
Noo mai koe i te rāei i Mataorongo.
Kua tupu te mato ia Maurangi ē !
Aere, akatu are i nunga i te rāei ē !

FOUNDATION.

Thou buildedst thy house, O Rori,
Thatched with broad fern-leaves ;
Thy home was in the rocks of Mataorongo until
The *very stones grew* in the presence of the Rockite,[1]
So long was thy home in the *rāei* !

UNUUNU TAI.

Māueue ra te taua nei ē,
Te taua e puruki mataati,
E paeke to vaevae, paeke to vaevae,
  e Rori ;
Kave atu te riri i Akatangiateriro,
Kia kite atu i tau metua.
  Kua oki au ki miri,
Kua piri atu ki te rau puka ē !

FIRST OFFSHOOT.

Māueue was the battle-field—
That unfortunate battle-field,
When Rori became a fugitive, a poor fugitive.
Thou didst thy best on the hill-slope,
Once more to see thy father,
  Everything was lost ;
My home was where the laurel-trees grow.

UNUUNU RUA.

Kukupa te manu ra e tangi nei ē,
E tangi nei i nunga i tau tukiavake—
  Tau tukiavake !
Ko te vāi pare koe e karanga nei.
Tai ataai na Temakavetai ia Maurangi ;
  Kua oki au ki miri,
Kua piri atu ki te rau puka ē !

SECOND OFFSHOOT.

The cooing of doves was thy only music,
Sounding warnings over thy head—
  Over thy devoted head !
In pity they called to thee ;—
Sent by Temakavetai to save the Rockite.
  Everything was lost ;
My home was where the laurel-trees grow.

UNUUNU TORU.

U, kua tu ei to are,
Are raukapakapa kotaa ē !
  Kua kapitia e te ua,

THIRD OFFSHOOT.

Ah ! such a miserable hut—
A single side covered with fern !
  Oft wast thou drenched ;

---

[1] Rori was originally named Barapu—' West.' Whilst yet living peacefully in his father's house, a little sister died through eating a poisonous *rori* (*bêche de mer*). To evince his grief at her loss, he thenceforth assumed the name of the poisonous fish *Rori* (all *roris* are not poisonous ; the poison arises from the sort of food they have been devouring). After his return to the interior he was nicknamed ' The Rockite' (Maurangi) in allusion to his long residence in the rocks. In his death-lament only the latter names occur.

Kapitia Rori e te ua nui i te rāei ē!
E aoa te tamaka e aere ei i te rangi
    piri ē!
   Kua oki au ki miri,
Kua piri atu ki te rau puka ē!

Often was Rori drenched with heavy
    showers.
Rori's sandals were of banyan bark
    for the hour of peril.
   Everything was lost;
My home was where the laurel-trees
    grow.

Unuunu A.

Kapara te ii e, te piaki ē,
I te piaki koi aere atu i te kapara o
    te ii,
   Koi aere atu a Maurangi e,
E i te ngai tapureu atu i reira,
   Kua kapitia e ta ao.
   Kua oki au ki miri,
Kua piri atu ki te rau puka ē!

Fourth Offshoot.

Ripe chestnuts covered the vale;
In that vale thou didst gather the
    ripe nuts:
Laboriously were they gathered by
    the Rockite;
And ofttimes ere they were cooked
Grey dawn surprised thee.
   Everything was lost;
My home was where the laurel-trees
    grow.

Unuunu Rima.

Kakea i nunga i te rāei ē!
I te rāei i Mataorongo,
I nunga i te tau are o Ue na,
Te reira nga vairanga i te kura ē!
   Kua oki au ki miri,
Kua piri atu ki te rau puka ē!

Fifth Offshoot.

Thou didst roam o'er the sharp-
    pointed rocks,
The sharp-pointed rocks of Matao-
    rongo,[1]
Near the ancient home of Ue.
'Twas there thou didst hide thy
    treasures.
   Everything was lost;
My home was where the laurel-trees
    grow.

Akareinga.

Ai e ruaoo ē!   E rangai ē!

Finale.

Ai e ruaoo ē!   E rangai ē!

The companion song of the foregoing is not destitute of
interest :—

RORI PROSPEROUS IN THE INTERIOR.

Tumu.

Akatauria i te tura,
I te kainga ia Manaune,

Introduction.

Kindly succoured by a friend,
On the lands of Manaune,

---

[1] Mata-o-Rongo is a general name for the east of Mangaia; it means
literally 'the-face-of-the-god-Rongo,' because originally his *marae* and sandstone image were there, face towards the sun-rising; but were subsequently
removed to the west. The reason alleged for the change was that the afternoon's sun burnt his back.

The present generation have taken such an interest in the adventures of
Rori that scores have visited the lonely *rāei*, hunting after memorials of the
fugitive. Not content with surveying the interesting spot, they have pulled up
the neatly-built flooring, in the vain hope of finding some of his famous stone
axes; as if he would have left such precious property behind him, having
now a secure home in the interior in the midst of plenty! Bits of red quartz
used as flint and basalt left by him are plentiful enough.

Kua anau te tama.
Tai piritanga i maru ai au ē !

Rori reared up a family.
Oh for a rock [1] under whose shadow
I might rest !

PAPA.

Tai tuamata i kite ia Ruanae,
O te rangi piri tei ia Aro.
Kau mai Rori i te uru enua
Ia Mangaia : kua ngara ua i te mate.
Ka piri i te rau puka i tangi ē !

FOUNDATION.

A curse upon thee, Ruanae !
And on all thy warrior friends ;
Rori has again set foot in the
interior
Of Mangaia : he who once seemed
doomed to die,
A fugitive hiding in the rustling
forest.

UNUUNU TAI.

Akatauria i te tura, i te tura ē !
I te kainga ia Manaune,
Kua anau te tama, kua anau te tama.
Ko Amio i te atu e Rori
Naai e rave ake ?
Tai piritanga i maru ai au ē !

FIRST OFFSHOOT.

Kindly succoured by a friend—
such a friend,
On the lands of Manaune,
Rori reared up a numerous family ;
Yet still laments for his sister Amio,
On whom none took pity.
Oh for a rock under whose shadow I
might rest !

UNUUNU RUA.

Kauanga kore, tavare onge,
Kua noo Rori i te toko pe
Ia Maruata : naai e rave ake ?
Tai piritanga i maru ai au ē !

SECOND OFFSHOOT.

Utterly friendless and starving—
Thy god, Rori, proved but a rotten
stick,[2]
E'en as Maruata's, who left *him* to die.
Oh for a rock under whose shadow I
might rest !

UNUUNU TORU.

Moemoe rango ē, i te ana roa ē !
I te ana roa i Turu-atua.
Kua tae to eka, kua puapua to ina,
I te ruaine metua—
I te ruaine metua noou, e Barapu
Tai piritanga i maru ai au ē !

THIRD OFFSHOOT.

Thy bed was at the entrance of a deep
cave,
A cave hard to discover in the rocks ;
Thou wast wearied out with thy long
residence,
Grey hairs had made their appearance;
Old age was fast creeping upon thee,
Barapu.
Oh for a rock under whose shadow I
might rest !

AKAREINGA.

Ai e ruaoo ē !   E rangai ē !

FINALE

Ai e ruaoo ē !   E rangai ē !

---

[1] The 'rock' so long wished for was Manaune, under whose 'shadow'
Rori lived happily in later years.

[2] A *god* was usually designated a 'stick,' or support, on which the
worshippers were accustomed to lean. The unknown poet considers that
Rori's own god Teipe had left him in the lurch, almost as badly as Maruata,
and in his descendants, who generation after generation were offered in sacrifice
to Rongo. As the god's name, Teipe, means 'the rotten one,' it almost reads
like a pun : I think this was the design of the poet.

The worshippers of Tanè Ngakiau, Teipe, Turanga, Utakea, were all
devoted to Rongo, the lord of Hades, in sacrifice. In each generation a few
were spared, to perpetuate the race for future altar use.

CHAPTER XXIX

SELF-SACRIFICE

A YEAR or two previously to Captain Cook's visit to this island, a canoe, with half a dozen men on board, sailed from Aitutaki to Manuae (Hervey's Island), a distance of fifty-five miles, in order to collect red parrakeet feathers. Having succeeded in their object, after a brief stay on Manuae, they started upon their return voyage, but were driven out of their course by strong contrary winds. After a few days, food and water began to fail, and a miserable death stared them in the face.

Routu, the commander of the canoe, now addressed his companions : 'I see why we are thus driven about over the ocean by unfavourable winds. We have sinned in taking away the sacred red parrakeet feathers. A costly sacrifice is demanded by the angry gods. Throw me into the sea, and you will yet safely reach home.'

Very sadly the voyagers, as their last chance for life, complied with this request, and Routu speedily disappeared in the unknown depth of the ocean.

The question now arose, Who should be captain? Tamaeu, son of the drowned Routu, said, 'I will be captain. My father taught me the course by the stars.' The others looked upon this as a piece of presumption on the part of so young a man ; but Tamaeu persisted, and they yielded out of respect to the memory of Routu.

That same night the anxious captain roused his sleeping companions with the remarkable words, 'Wake up, friends ; we have reached Mangaia-Nui-Neneva!' The canoe had happily drifted to the southern side of Mangaia. A number of women engaged in torch-fishing on the reef at once fled to the interior at the sight of strangers, fearing they might be slain.

Tamaeu and his companions, having hauled up the canoe, followed the retreating lights, but missed the true path. To aid their painful progress over the extremely rugged rocks on that part of the island, the visitors built up part of the road. Through the livelong night, notwithstanding the moon had risen, they succeeded in travelling but half a mile.

On the following morning the islanders came down in search of the intruders, intending to exterminate them. They were found fast asleep on the rocks, with their priceless parrakeet feathers concealed in calabashes between their legs. For the first time in the modern history of these islanders, they pitied their defenceless visitors, hoping to share their treasures. This was doubtless owing to their inconsiderable numbers.

These Aitutakians remained some months on the island, and built a *marae*, on which human sacrifices were sub-sequently offered. It is said that Tamaeu first called this island by its present name, Mangaia - Nui - Neneva—'Mangaia Monstrously Great,' which suited the fancy of the men of that day, and almost supplanted its original designation Auau.

The path which the Aitutakians traversed that night bears the appropriate name, Arakino, 'Bad Road'; the part built up by them is known as *koro o te mánuiri*, 'the work of the visitors.'   Eventually, Tamaeu and his companions safely got back to their own pretty island-home, thus realizing the prediction of Routu.

The beautiful red feathers presented to those who had so kindly entertained them were collected and put on their god Motoro.   When that idol was given up to Mr. Williams these identical red feathers adorned it.

It is to this Tamaeu that reference is made in the song of Captain Cook.

CHAPTER XXX

CAPTAIN COOK'S VISIT TO MANGAIA

WHILE conversing with one of my native teachers (a very intelligent man) and another native of this island respecting Captain Cook's visit to Mangaia in 1777, I showed them a picture (from Cook's *Voyages*) of Mourooa,[1] the only Mangaian who ventured on board his ship. Mourooa is a fierce-looking fellow, with a knife stuck in his right ear, and wearing a beard. They said, what I had often heard before, that they had never heard of Mourooa's going on board Tute's (Cook's) ship; but that everybody on the island knows that Kavoro was the bold fellow who ventured on board the first ship that ever touched at Mangaia. They stated that this Kavoro received from Captain Cook an axe, a knife, some large beads and nails, and a few yards of print. At the date of our first landing, in 1852, the axe and knife were in existence. The blue beads were especially valued; they were buried, as a mark of great distinction, with a woman named Rimarima.

I have remarked above that, beside the teacher, another native of this island was present. That other native is a grandson of Kavoro, who went on board the Resolution,

---

[1] The natives of Mangaia were much surprised that I possessed a minute printed account of the transactions of March 29 and 30, 1777, and still more to find that there exists a portrait of their savage countryman Mourua.

March 29, 1777.   I asked him to relate the native tradition
of Cook's visit to this island.   The tradition coincided
with the printed account in the *Voyages*, with but few
variations.   For example, only one ship is mentioned in
the tradition ; whereas the Resolution and the Discovery
visited Mangaia.   I find, too, that the native of Raiatea
(Ulietea in the *Voyages*), called Omai in Captain Cook's
account, who was the medium of communication with
these islanders, is in the tradition called Mā-i.   Mā-i, in
the Hervey Group dialect, is written without a break—
Maki—and signifies 'sick,' a very common name indeed
throughout these islands ; I dare say we have a dozen or
two of that name on this island alone.   The O is simply
a prefix to a proper name, not by any means a part of it.
Thus Otaheite is now more correctly written Tahiti.   The
only remaining difference between the native tradition and
the printed account is that the man who went on board
the Resolution is named by Cook Mourooa ; whereas the
natives of Mangaia insist that his name was Kavoro.
Feeling sure that, like most of his living countrymen, he
had two or more names, I inquired whether Kavoro might
not have been also named Mour*oo*a or Mour*u*a.   Kavoro's
grandson now recollected an old lament about this man,
beginning thus :—

> Mourua, burning star of heaven, how pleasant in life !
> Grief fills thy widow as she turns (on her pillow).

The natives now found that Mourooa and Kavoro were
identical, and that their missionary had a veritable likeness
of this celebrated native.   The news brought great numbers
from all parts of the island, eager to get a sight of Mourua
(or Mourooa) and his distinguished friend Captain Cook.
Some old men remarked that the peculiar short twist of

his hair was an invention of Mourua to prevent his being caught by the head when fighting, and so put to death.

Captain Cook mentions a scar on the forehead of this native (which does not, however, appear in the portrait lying before me). Mourua got it by fighting—not with invaders from another island, but with a tribe of his own countrymen living at Tamarua. These hostile natives had been cutting down wood for a canoe in one of the valleys. Mourua and his companion Kirikovi were walking along the ridge of hill above, unconscious of danger. So good an opportunity of destroying a foe was not to be lost. Overpowered by numbers, they were left for dead ; but their loud cries ere they fell brought help. On coming up with Mourua and Kirikovi, their people found them insensible, with terrible gashes on the forehead. The father of one of them pulled out by the roots the hair on the great toes. A slight vibration of the foot assured him that life was not extinct. Both ultimately recovered ; and the spot, which I have visited, is known as the Fighting-ground of Kirikovi. This Kirikovi afterwards became 'lord (or great chief) of Mangaia.'

Mourua took his new name—the name by which everybody on Mangaia knows him—Kavoro—*i.e.* 'skin and bones'—on account of the death of his mother, who wasted away to a skeleton. To the great English navigator he appeared to be a very docile, agreeable fellow. His real character will appear by the following anecdote : Mourua had a sister named Teāo, who married Moenga, a member of the very tribe who handled him so roughly on the mountain ridge. The head-quarters of that tribe were at the Cave of Tautua. Mourua went to the mouth of the cave professedly to pay his brother-in-law a friendly visit. They met. Mourua told his relative that if he would meet him the following evening at dusk at a certain place he would give him a valuable stone axe. The bait took. At the appointed hour Mourua met his sister and her husband. Moenga was delighted with his beautiful stone adze; but whilst bending over it found his flowing raven hair seized by his powerful and pitiless brother-in-law. The poor fellow struggled hard for dear life, but in vain. Teāo, horrified at this tragedy, rushed in obedience to her husband's dying word to the cave, to seek protection from her husband's relatives from the cruelty of her own brother Mourua, who afterwards confessed that he intended to murder both that fearful night. That his sister Teāo had married one of the hated tribe who attacked him many years before on the mountains was with him sufficient reason why she should die : she happily escaped.

Mourua had a very pretty daughter, named Kurakaau. Tradition says that the crafty parent was very anxious to get Captain Cook to come on shore and become his son-in-law. Through this projected splendid alliance he hoped to become all-powerful among his countrymen. However, the great navigator declined the proposal. He sent a few yards of print to furnish Kurakaau with a decent dress.

Mourua was after his fashion very devout. Captain Cook correctly guessed that he had invoked the protection of his idol god ere he ventured to take hold of the line thrown to him from the stern of the Resolution. That idol, named Motoro, is a rude representation of the human form, carved in ironwood.

My own impression is that the captain would never have got off alive again had he taken Mourua's advice in coming ashore. There being no boat harbour, he must have trusted himself entirely to the tender mercies of the heathen, and they are cruel.

After a life of bloodshed, Mourua was murdered on a sandy beach, about one hundred yards from our island residence. He was one of a party of five who had been fishing. They had returned, and were asleep when their foes surrounded the house. Only one escaped, by creeping through the legs of the attacking party. Three were speedily despatched, but still Mourua struggled hard with his cruel foes. Whilst some were vainly endeavouring to twist a cord round his neck to strangle him, another chopped his legs with a large stone adze. This sealed his fate, for he fell. A single blow on the head closed this sad episode of a warrior's life. Mourua perished about two or three years after Captain Cook's visit.

It is not unworthy of remark that the full name of this island (but little known now) is given by Captain Cook with but a slight deviation from the true spelling. This full name, as a native would write it, is Mangaia Nui Neneva, which may be translated 'Mangaia, Monstrously Great.' This is pretty well for a little island about twenty-five miles in circuit. We had lived amongst these people more than fourteen years before I learnt the full name from the lips of an old man, who was reciting to me a scrap of an ancient song in which the name occurs. This is a striking proof of the general correctness of the observations made by the illustrious Cook.

On arriving at Atiu, the natives asked where he had come from. He told them 'From Mangaia.' The Atiuans called it by the queer-looking designation of Owhavarouah, which, being so dissimilar from Mangaia, Cook conjectured (very naturally) to be the name of another island contiguous to Mangaia. Such, however, is not the case—it is only an ancient name of this island. It should be written Auau, the O being merely the prefix to *all* proper names preceding the verb. I may remark in passing that Auau means 'terraced.' Mangaia signifies '*peace.*'

I asked one of our teachers who had laboured long and usefully in the Loyalty Islands, where the natives of those islands got their pigs from. The reply was, 'From Tute (Cook), the first white man they ever saw.' Tute's name is preserved, amid a vast variety of dialects, in these Southern Seas, as the material benefactor of the natives. A dog was the only animal that he left in the Hervey Group.

A LAMENT FOR MOURUA.

Pertaining to 'the Death-talk of Vaepae,' in the reign of Kirikovi, *circa* A.D. 1774.

TUMU.

Mourua ! te etu ka i te rangi ē !
Ua reka te taa ora.
Ua tangi rai to vaine e uri mai ei !

INTRODUCTION.

Mourua, burning star of heaven,
How pleasant in life !
Grief fills thy widow as she turns (on her pillow).

PAPA.

Ko te atiu mua na Vaepae ē !
Ua riro te au iaia ;
Ua mou paa i te mouranga,
I Auau no Motoro.
Ua ta ē ! Te rā i mou ki tau rima ē !

FOUNDATION.

Beloved son of Vaepae,
Victorious in battle,
Hold firmly thy own,
Won in Auau through Motoro.
Thou hast slain, in the day of thy strength.

INUINU MUA.

I tangi, i tangi atu ki te tama ē !
Tama ā Vaepae. Ua punipuni aere ē !
*Kia punipuni aere kia ngaro paa raua.
Tei Aramoi te rua i te piritanga ē !
Ko te piritanga akera ē !
Ua tangi rai to vaine e uri mai ei !

FIRST OFFSHOOT.

Weep, weep for the eldest son !
Son of Vaepae, hiding himself—
*Hiding himself, perchance with his father,
In Aramui, the unknown cave.
Yonder is that cave.
Grief fills thy window as she turns (on her pillow).

INUINU RUA.

Ii rare i te karanga ē !
Karanga'i i Bukamaru—
Ua taiku. E autaa ē !

SECOND OFFSHOOT.

How they startle at the call,
The call from Bukamaru—
The shout. Yonder ones !

*E ano rai i reira.
E ano rai i reira. Aca'i?
Apopo taua e ana atu, ana mai.
Ana mai. E rua ē!
Ua tangi rai to vaine e uri mai ei!

*Thither let us go (*i.e.* to take food),
Thither let us go. Ah, when indeed!
To-morrow we will go and return.—
Come back, my husband, come back.
Grief fills thy widow as she turns (on her pillow).

Inuinu Toru.

Eke e, eke atura ki tai ē!
Te tai i te kavakava ē!
Ua mana ia Rongo
Ua mana koe i te koatu Ovaiomaao.
Ei ara paa no tana—
E aere ei ki te rau puka.
Ua ao eera ē!
Ua tangi rai to vaine e uri mai ei!

Third Offshoot.

Go, go to the shore,
The shore by the valley.
Mighty art thou by the power of Rongo,
Mighty by the stone (idol) Ovaio-maao—
The protector of us both,
As we walk where the laurel-trees grow.
Daylight dawns.
Grief fills thy widow as she turns (on her pillow).

Inuinu A.

Aengara te ata ē!
Ata ka mārama
E tu ra e tama ē!
Ua ao ē! Ua iterere i te moe.
Iterere ake Kavoro nei i tana moe.
Ua mou te tamaka e!
Te mua oki te mate,
Ua tangi rai ki tona tama, e uri mai ei!

Fourth Offshoot.

The shadows of night are breaking!
Light is increasing.
Rise, eldest son,
It is day. He has risen from sleep.
Kavoro has risen from sleep.
His feet are sandalled.
But death is at hand.
Grieves for her eldest son as she turns (on her pillow).

Akareinga.

Ai e ruaoo ē! E rangai ē!

Finale.

Ai e ruaoo ē! E rangai ē!

This lament refers to a disastrous period of his life, when Mourua was a fugitive hiding in a cavern. It may seem strange for a wife to address her deceased husband as 'the eldest son' (*e tama e*); but it is common, and is a mark of respect. In the lament two parties would be engaged. The song would be recited slowly, in a plaintive voice. At two points (marked by me with asterisks) both companies—*i.e.* the men and the women—would wail loudly in unison. Although a lament for the dead, there is no reference to the future; for the obvious reason, it was altogether too gloomy and uncertain a topic for a heathen to dwell upon. 'Without hope in the world!'

After the lapse of some ninety-eight[1] years this song is for the first time written. In quoting from it, a native would give not only the words, but the stanza in which the words occur. In some such way as this all the remains of extreme antiquity (as the Homeric poems) must have been handed down from generation to generation.

[1] This was written in 1872.

CHAPTER XXXI

THE DRAMA OF COOK

THE following song is a pantomimic description of Captain Cook's visit to Mangaia. For several years after that event constant wars prevented the more agreeable employment of song-making. But when peace had at length been secured, and plenty reigned in consequence, a chief named Poito resolved to give a grand feast, with the indispensable accompaniment of dancing and music. A level spot was selected for the festival and carefully weeded. From one end to the other, a spacious canopy of plaited green coco-nut-leaves protected the many hundreds present from the heavy dews of night—as such entertainments never took place by day. Men only, or women only, not men *and* women, might take part in the dance and song. Sometimes men danced, and women held the flambeaux. At other times women danced, and men held the torches. Poito's dance was for men, numbering, it is said, nearly two hundred; the entire remaining population being present as spectators and as flambeaux-holders. Twenty songs were required for one *fête:* these songs were usually encored. At sunset the performance began, and continued till midnight, when refreshment was taken, and once more the entertainment proceeded. As soon as the day-star appeared, the last song (reserved for the purpose) and the last dance were gone through, and the whole concluded. Six artists were usually employed to compose the songs, and to arrange the whole proceedings.

The words were slowly chanted in a pleasing though monotonous tone; sometimes by the master of the ceremonies only, who stood on an elevated platform, and sometimes by all the performers. In what is termed 'the introduction,' no musical instruments were employed, and consequently the dancing, which was to keep time with the music, had not commenced. The musical accompaniment consisted of a *kaara*,[1] or large wooden drum hollowed out of *miro* (*Thespesia populnea*)—a beautiful dark-red wood. It was prettily carved all over, and was suspended from the neck with strong cords, being beaten, not as with us, on the *end*, but in the *centre*, the long slit emitting a considerable volume of sound.

Another sort of drum, called the *pañ*, was used on such occasions. A round piece of *Thespesia* was dug out at one end, and the aperture covered over with a tight-fitting piece of shark's-skin. It was designed to stand upright. The drum-sticks were the tips of the musician's fingers.

A subsidiary musical instrument was the *riro*, a sort of harmonicon, consisting of two pieces of dry hibiscus wood, supported at each end by banana-stalks, and lightly tapped with ironwood sticks.

The great wooden drum used for Poito's dance is still preserved, and is used by the police in drumming their prisoners to court. The *pañ* has entirely disappeared. The *riro* now gives amusement only to idle boys. But the dance itself was invariably connected with very serious

---

[1] For *akaara* = 'the awakener.'

evils ;[1] so that upon the establishment of Christianity it was entirely abolished.

This dramatic song was composed by a warrior named Tioi, who was afterwards slain in battle. It is complete, and is now written for the first time—an interesting proof of the power of memory in thus retaining a song during a period of three generations. It begins with a reference to Tamaeu, who drifted here in his canoe from Hervey's Island a year or two before Captain Cook's visit in 1777.

A year was required for getting up one such entertainment, so that the number of such festive occasions served to chronicle the duration of peace. This long interval was required, first, for the making of the songs and the rehearsal of the performers ; secondly, for the growth of taro, etc., etc., requisite for the grand feasting, which is a necessary sequel to any assembly in the mind of a Polynesian ; and, thirdly, for the very important purpose of blanching the complexions and fattening the persons of those who were to take part on the occasion. The point of honour was to be the fairest and fattest of any present.

Each such entertainment was in honour of the gods. Thus, if the originator were a worshipper of Motoro, all those devoted to the service of that idol would feel bound to take part. In the present instance, the dance was in honour of Tiaio (the shark-god) and Tanè conjointly ; consequently the entire body of worshippers of those gods were performers. This inherent idolatrous tendency was one reason for the suppression of these dramatic efforts.

The fate of Poito, who got up this exhibition, is an instructive picture of heathen life. In his old age a battle took place, in which some of his sons fought with the

---

[1] The chiefs, whether married or not, often wore phallic ear-ornaments. Two of them may be seen in the British Museum.

father, and some on the other side. In the hour of conflict, it was Poito's unhappy fate to find himself opposite to his second son Pakuunga. As there was no retreat, the old man made a faint thrust at his boy; whereat Pakuunga gave his father a lunge, which at once terminated the old man's career! This occurred a few years previous to the landing of the first teachers.

The reader will bear in mind that Captain Cook never set foot on the soil of Mangaia, although very desirous to do so, so forbidding was the aspect of the armed natives.

<table>
<tr><td>

PE'E MANUIRI.
</td><td>

THE VISITOR'S SONG.
</td></tr>
</table>

PE'E MANUIRI.	THE VISITOR'S SONG.
TUMU.	INTRODUCTION.
Chorus.	*Chorus.*
Koaniia e Tu ma Tangaroa Ei tia i te ara oa a Tamaeu. E kutu i te rangi.	Great Tangaroa [1] and Tu assist In caulking the canoe of Tamaeu. Oh! the deafening noise (of the workmen)!
Solo.	*Solo.*
Nga utu ake utu.	Caulk [2] the seams.
Chorus.	*Chorus.*
Ngu! Ngu!	Ay! Ay!
Solo.	*Solo.*
Nga puru ake puru.	Here is plenty of fibre.
Chorus.	*Chorus.*
Ngu! Ngu!	Ay! Ay!
Chorus.	*Chorus.*
Unuia, e Tumatangirua, I te varo kia rauorooro, Tamaua i Avarua, Kia peka te iku i te matangi.	Grant, O thou ruler of the winds, That the weather may be propitious, Surfless be the reef of Avarua, [3] Compel thy slave to obey.

---

[1] Tangaroa was not worshipped on Mangaia; but, as the god of some other islands, it was supposed that he had led the voyagers to the island.

[2] The individual who uttered the words 'Caulk,' etc., held in one hand a wooden mallet, and in the other a stone chisel, which he struck vigorously, as if instructing his workmen in the art of caulking canoes with coco-nut fibre. Upon this signal the entire body of performers, uttering simultaneously the cry 'Ay, ay,' drove stone chisels brought for the purpose into logs of soft wood for the occasion, and extending from one end of the dancing-ground to the other. Canoes were 'caulked' from time immemorial. This scene was twice enacted.

[3] Avarua is the name of the spot where Cook wished to land.

'Nako! Nako!'
'Iko! Iko!'

Solo.

Tokonga kumi o Avarua ē.
Tukua maira tai ori i te vaka.

Chorus in falsetto.

'E Bere![2] E Bere!'

'Maīo! Maīo!'

Chorus.

Ikā! Kua rau; kua rau
Te toa, te toa. Kua ta, kua ta,
Kua ta Mangaia, kua ta te pai!

TE KARANGA MUA.

Solo.

No Tangaroa te vaka:
Kua tere i te aka i te rangi ē!

Chorus in falsetto.

'This way![1] this way!'
'No; that way, that way!'

Solo.

O that vast ship off Avarua!
Launch speedily a canoe.

Chorus in falsetto.

(They say:) 'We are Britons. We
are Britons.'

'Maī, Maī.'

Chorus.

We come; hundreds on hundreds
Of warriors to fight;[3]—yes, to fight!
The Mangaians will attack and destroy
the ship.

THE FIRST CALL[4] (for the dance to
lead off).

Solo.

Tangaroa has sent a ship,
Which has burst through the solid
blue vault.

---

[1] 'This way,' etc., grotesquely describes the contradictory directions given to Captain Cook by the natives as to where he should land. The 'falsetto' throughout is an absurd mimicry of the language of the visitors.

[2] Bere is a shortened form of Beretane, for the sake of rhythm; just as Captain Cook's usual designation, 'Tute,' is for a similar reason abbreviated to Tu. Maī is of course the Omai of the *Voyages*, to whom the captain naturally appealed from time to time.

[3] Their aspect was very warlike; but they wisely abstained from hostilities. The heathen of Mangaia looked upon all strangers as mortal foes, to be opposed and slain, if possible. The only exceptions recorded by tradition are those referred to in this song. Tamaeu and his friends escaped because they carried a priceless treasure—red parrakeet feathers for adorning the gods. When Mourua found that the foreigners were after all men like himself, he slapped his thighs, and shouted with all his might—

A mate! A mate!! A mate!!!
Kia mou! Kia mou!! Kia mou!!!
Let them die! Let them die!! Let them die!!!
Seize them! Seize them!! Seize them!!!

It appears, however, that his courage afterwards evaporated.

At the stanza, 'We come, hundreds on hundreds,' etc., a mimic attack was made with real spears upon imaginary invaders.

[4] Hitherto no drum had been beaten, nor any dancing performed. Hence

Solo.

No Maīo tai manuiri ē !

Chorus.

No Tu te tere i tau ē !

Solo.

Koai ma ē ?

Chorus.

Tei tai te vaka manuiri a tae,
Ouaraurauae !

Solo.

Nai ua rau te vaka ē !
E manuiri.   Maīo no tai enua ē !

Solo.

Veroīa !

Chorus.

Veroīa, e Tu, te rua i te matangi,
Tirangoa te moana ia tiai,

Solo.

Terō !

Chorus.

Tero.   Tero.

Solo.

Tero !

Solo.

Here is a stranger, Maī.

Chorus.

'Tis Cook, who has paid us a visit.

Solo.

Who has come ?

Chorus.

A boat full of guests is here.
What gibberish they talk !

Solo.

Numberless are the boats
They are foreigners.   Maī from some
other land.

Solo.

Blow softly !

Chorus.

Blow softly, ye winds, from your
holes,[1]
That the ocean may be smooth.

Solo.

Where are they ?

Chorus.

Yonder, yonder.

Solo.

Ay, there they are.

'the call' now is for dancing and music, beginning with the words 'which has burst through,' etc., and pausing awhile at the word 'Britons.' After a moment's rest the master of the ceremonies gives the 'second call' in a very soft and plaintive voice : on again pronouncing the words, 'which has burst,' the whole two hundred performers were on their feet once more, chanting and performing the remarkable evolutions which they term a *kapa*, or dance. On again uttering the word 'Britons,' a slight pause occurred ere 'the finale' was gone through.

[1] At the edge of the horizon are supposed to be a set of holes, through which the god of the winds amuses himself by blowing away with all his might, often much to the discomfort of mariners. It is hoped that he will be propitious on this occasion.

Chorus.

Aere mai ! Aere mai, e Beretane !

TE KARANGA RUA.

Solo.

No Tangaroa te vaka ;
Kua tere i te aka i te rangi ē !

Solo.

No Maīo tai manuiri ē !

Chorus.

No Tu te tere i tau ē !

Solo.

Koai ma ē ?

Chorus.

Tei tai te vaka manuiri a tae.
Ouaraurauae !

Solo.

Nai ua rau te vaka ē !
E manuiri. Maīo no tai enua ē !

Solo.

Kiritia !

Chorus.

Kirikiritia atu tai ua manu,
E Tu, kia pārai i te tua o te manuiri.

Solo.

Kua ta te rā e !

Chorus.

Kua ta ! Kua ta !

Solo.

Kua ta te rā e !

Chorus in falsetto.

O murenga oa. O murenga oa, e Beretane !

Chorus.

Come on, come on, ye Britons.

THE SECOND CALL (for the dance to lead off).

Solo.

Tangaroa has sent a ship,
Which has burst through the solid blue vault.

Solo.

Here is a stranger, Maī.

Chorus.

'Tis Cook, who has paid us a visit.

Solo.

Who has come ?

Chorus.

A boat full of guests is here.
What gibberish they talk !

Solo.

Numberless are the boats,
They are foreigners. Maī from some land.

Solo.

Lord of the winds !

Chorus.

Lead forth some bird to settle down
Upon the shoulders of these guests (*i.e.* to detain them).

Solo.

Splash [1] go the oars !

Chorus.

Ay, splash, splash.

Solo.

Splash go the oars !

Chorus in falsetto.

They are white-faced—they are white-faced men and Britons.[2]

---

[1] 'Splash go the oars.' At this stage of the entertainment, a mimic rowing takes place with the arms. The way in which Europeans handled oars was a very wonderful thing in the eyes of the men of that day.

[2] It is interesting to find that the name Beretane, or Britain, was enshrined in the native dialect long before the first preachers of the Gospel had set foot on any of these islands.

R

MAUTU.

Chorus.

E pai parere i tau mai
No tai tuamotu e !

Solo.

E pai kua aa teia ?

Chorus.

A ! e atua mataku oki.

Solo.

E pai kua aa teia ?

Chorus.

Taau ariki o Avarua.
No Tu oki e Mai te rā e !

Solo.

E pai kua aa teia ?

Chorus.

E pai omurenga !
Auere toa.

CONCLUSION.

Chorus.

A people of a strange tongue have
    arrived
From some distant land.

Solo.

Of what sort are they ?

Chorus.

Oh ! they are a godlike race.

Solo.

Of what sort are they ?

Chorus.

A great chief is off Avarua.
The ship belongs to Cook and Mai.

Solo.

Of what sort are they ?

Chorus.

A people with white faces.
Unheard-of event !

CHAPTER XXXII

CAPTAIN COOK'S VISIT TO ATIU

THE island of Atiu, called Wateeoo by Cook, lies a hundred and twenty miles north of Mangaia. These are the twin islands of the Hervey Group, being nearly alike in height, shape, extent, geological formation, and products. It is remarkable that the great navigator, in sailing from New Zealand, should discover in succession Mangaia, Atiu, Takutea (spelt Otakootaia in the *Voyages*), Manuae, or Hervey's Island, and, lastly, Palmerston's Island, and yet miss the only two rich and fertile islands of the group (Rarotonga and Aitutaki), possessed of harbours and capable of furnishing all the supplies urgently needed by the Resolution and Discovery. During a visit to Atiu I inquired of some aged men what their fathers, who had seen Captain Cook, had told them of the first visit of white men to their rugged coral shores. Their verbal account agreed well with the printed narrative, with a few additional particulars.

Atiu was sighted March 31, 1777. On the following day Lieutenant Gore, of the Discovery, landed on the southern shore at an indenture in the reef called Orovaru, which the natives pointed out to me. Thence the visitors were conducted to the interior by a passable road, and all honour shown to them. That the people would have forcibly detained their wondrously fair-skinned friends but for the extravagant statements given by Maī (Omai, the interpreter) of the prowess of Europeans, and the effect of firearms, is certain.

The natives of Atiu pretended to be greatly surprised at the question whether they ever ate human flesh. Many now living have confessed to me that they had often gorged themselves therewith. A native of the neighbouring island of Mauke told me that in 1819 most of his countrymen were slain and devoured by the victorious Atiuans. The people of Mitiaro were similarly treated by the 'meek-faced Atiuans,' as they amusingly nickname themselves.

Originally there was but one chief on Atiu. At the period of Cook's visit there were two possessed of equal authority—viz. Tiaputa and Tangapatolo.

Captain Cook did not go ashore himself. On Lieutenant Gore's landing, the chiefs asked him, amongst other things, ' Are you one of the glorious sons of Tetumu ? Are you a son of the Great Root or Cause, whose children are half divine, half human ? ' According to their mythology, Tetumu[1] (= Root, Origin, or Cause) was the father of gods and men, and the maker of all things. The white complexion of the visitors, their wonderful clothing and weapons, all indicated, in their opinion, a divine origin. To these inquiries no reply was given ; in all probability they were unintelligible to Maī as well as to Lieutenant Gore.

On that memorable day the strangers were the guests of Tiaputa, who ordered the dances and other amusements in honour of the occasion. The *kava*-drinking, the nectar of the Polynesian gods, and the feasting were extravagant.

---

[1] *Te*, the first syllable, is merely the definite article = The Root, etc.

Forty pigs, mostly small, were cooked and presented to their visitors, who were led to the *marae*, where a sort of worship was paid to them as the favoured children of Tetumu.

The Atiuans maintain that the ships were four days off their island, whereas the *Voyages* seemingly give an account of the transactions of a single day. But if we recollect that the uninhabited islet of Takutea (where Cook took in a supply of coco-nuts, etc.) is regarded by the Atiuans as an integral portion of their own territory, only separated from the main island by a narrow channel of fourteen miles, the discrepancy vanishes. Atiu was sighted March 31, and sail was finally made from Takutea April 3, proving the correctness of the native tradition.

A curious heathen prophecy[1] was known to these islanders previous to the discovery of Atiu by Captain Cook. A god named Tanè-mei-tai—'Tanè-out-of-the ocean'—would some day visit their shores. This new divinity would speak a strange language, would introduce strange articles and customs, and would ill-treat the natives. This oracle was at once applied to their illustrious visitors, so that no little distrust and fear mingled with the pleasure of seeing Tute. Tanè was regarded as one of the 'glorious sons of Tetumu.' Hence the appropriateness of the question proposed to Lieutenant Gore upon his arrival.

For the first time they now became acquainted with the existence of a race entirely different from their own. Many were the gifts bestowed upon these islanders in return for their hospitality, such as beads, iron nails,

---

[1] The old men of Rarotonga invariably apply to Christianity the following ancient oracle : ' Yonder are the children of God, floating over the ocean like birds on drift coco-nut fronds—some are in advance, and others are following ! '

knives, strips of cloth, and several iron axes, exactly corresponding with that given to Kirikovi, the warrior chief of Mangaia, a few days before. The crowning present of all was Mai's dog, the first ever seen in the Hervey Group.

Captain Cook expresses his astonishment at their 'incredible ignorance' in making the 'strange mistake' of calling the sheep and goats on board the Resolution 'birds.' The word actually used by them was *manu*, which means any living thing moving on the earth or through the air. The term is frequently applied to human beings, so that the Atiuans were strictly correct.

It is much to be regretted that the great navigator and his officers never gave them a hint as to the existence of the One living and true God. It was not until forty-six years after that the Gospel was introduced to Atiu by the martyr of Eromanga. The idols so long cherished and worshipped, as visible representations of the invisible and glorious sons of the unworshipped Tetumu, were speedily given up. Some were burnt ; others are now, and long have been, in the museum of the London Missionary Society. Amongst the latter is the famous Terongo, to whose *marae* the guests were taken.

Atiu is said to be the name of the first man on the island. A singular myth is related in reference to this Adam of Atiu. A pigeon, the pet bird of Tangaroa, sped hither from spirit land, and rested awhile in a grotto still known as the Pigeon's Fountain. Big drops of water kept falling from the stony roof, producing little eddies in the transparent water beneath. As the pigeon was refreshing itself by sipping the cool liquid, it noticed a female shadow of great beauty in the fountain. Now the pigeon of Tangaroa was in reality one of the gods, and therefore readily embraced the lovely shadow, and then returned to its home in nether-land. The child thus originated was named Atiu—'First-fruit,' or 'Eldest-born'—and from him the island derives its name. It was on this account that 'they dignified their island with the appellation of "A Land of Gods," esteeming themselves a sort of divinities, and possessed with the spirit of the gods.'

The double canoes of Atiu are usually fifty feet in length, provided with a mast and mat sails. The cordage is made of the bark of the lemon hibiscus. As many as a hundred and fifty men, women, and children are often accommodated on board one of these primitive vessels. In launching them, one may still hear the following song, referring to Captain Cook's visit to Atiu. It was composed somewhere about the year 1780 :—

ATIUAN CANOE SONG.

Solo.	*Solo.*
Tuku ake au e Tahiti Nui,	I sail to Great [1] Tahiti ;
O ariua, O Tu-papa, O Tangaroa,	O ye divine Tu and Tangaroa,
Mea ō, kua oti.	Be propitious, and I am off.

Chorus.	*Chorus.*
Reti ē !	Tug away.

Solo.	*Solo.*
E te tupu ō, kua oti	Friends, 'tis done.

Chorus.	*Chorus.*
Reti ē !	Tug away.

Solo.	*Solo.*
Tangi mai te pupui, te pupui,	Hark ! the guns, the guns are firing.
Te pupui iea ?	What are these ' puffers ' ?
Te pupui i teimaa ē !	Terrible weapons.
I teimaa iea ?	Whom do they terrify ?
I te teimaa i nga tamariki.	The whole of the people, calling
Tuoro mai i te pai o Tute ra ē !	That Cook's vessels have arrived.
Ritana.	Tug away.

[1] To the native mind there are two Tahitis, the Greater and the Lesser, united by a narrow isthmus. The latter is now commonly known as Taiarabu.

Chorus.	*Chorus.*
Ae, ritana, ritana !	Ay ; tug, tug away.

Solo.	*Solo.*
Tuoro, tuoro atu ica ?	To whom do these guns speak ?
Tuoro atura i te kiato mua ia Otu,	To the offspring of divine Tu,
Tangi mai i te tangotango,	Startling even the spirit-world.
Taku rakau mei apitia ;	Ah ! the sleepers are slipping ;
Mei ia tauae te vaka ē !	The canoe is upsetting !
Tavai te ruē !	Right her.

Chorus.	*Chorus.*
Tavai te ruē !	Right her !

Solo.	*Solo.*
Tavai te ruē i te rakau, ko mea ra	Steady her—all of you,
Ko vaka, o taurekareka, o pai taia	Our noble ship is afloat.

Chorus.	*Chorus.*
Aea, e pai ē !	Bravo, ship !

In examining the best charts of the Pacific, it is puzzling to the novice to find that in very many instances two, three, or even four positions are given for a single island or reef, owing to the unskilfulness of observers. But it is no slight praise to our great navigator, Cook, that the positions of islands laid down by him remain unaltered to this day.

CHAPTER XXXIII

THE STORY OF AN AXE

ONE day an old man came to me bringing in his hand a bit of old iron. I was surprised that he should set store by such rubbish, and desired him to take it away. The old man then said, 'You have been inquiring about Tute's (Cook's) visit here. This axe[1] came from Tute; it is the first foreign axe ever seen here. I give it to you as a countryman of his.' Feeling interested, I made careful inquiries, and learnt that whilst Captain Cook was in his boat, on March 29, 1777, looking about for a landing-place, several natives swam off to him. To the most influential man amongst them, named Kirikovi (commonly known by his nickname, Tiāci, or 'Beardy'), the near relative of Mourua, and the then 'lord of Mangaia,' this axe was given. It is of a very peculiar shape, and of course is much worn with constant use. It is, in fact, merely a bit of iron: doubtless it was beaten out on the ship's anvil to please the natives. It has one excellence—it is easily fastened on a wooden handle with sennit.

I was not previously aware that anything was left on this island by Captain Cook on the occasion of its discovery in 1777 but what was given to Mourua, who alone of his countrymen had courage to venture on board the 'big

---

[1] It is now in the British Museum.

canoe.' Yet, in the *Voyages*, after referring to the 'beads and nails' given to Mourua, Captain Cook speaks of taking with him in the boat 'such articles to give the natives as might serve to gain their goodwill.' Tradition says that strips of cloth were freely distributed by him among his visitors, who seem to have been very unceremonious, according to the great navigator's account. These bits of cloth, instead of being applied to their legitimate purpose, were wrapped round the head as ornaments and as marks of distinction from the vulgar crowd.

The strips of cloth would quickly perish; but this bit of iron, unquestionably the first ever seen on this island, must have been a wonderful object in the eyes of the men of that generation. The native adze was with great labour chipped with pieces of flint out of bits of basalt. Some of these adzes are beautifully finished off, and constituted the gold and silver of former days. A present of two or three was usually sufficient to insure protection to one of the vanquished.

Kirikovi at once understood the value and use of the present he received from Captain Cook. A suitable handle was prepared for it, and the axe secured by strong sennit of the finest quality. When not in use, it was kept wrapped round and round with many folds of *tapa*. The old man who gave it to me had had possession of it for nearly fifty years. It was almost forgotten, as it had become useless on account of the numerous American and Sheffield steel axes on the island at the present time.

The axe was in constant requisition amongst the chief people of the island for preparing smooth blocks of wood, on which their wives and daughters beat out the bark of the paper-mulberry for cloth; also for the finishing off of the wooden troughs which, in native life, answer to our tubs, buckets, and basins. The beautiful finish of some of the existing *tamanu*, or native mahogany troughs, is said to be owing to Tute's famous iron adze. It is to be regretted that the first Tahitian teachers caused these mahogany trees [1]—the growth of centuries—to be burnt, on account of their supposed connection with idolatry

Another use to which it was applied was the making of long spears and wooden swords for battle. To a Mangaian heathen the one object of life was to fight, and, as he thought, gain an imperishable name in the traditions of his countrymen. From the date of Captain Cook's visit here (1777) to the year of grace 1823, when the gospel of peace was first brought, no less than six general pitched battles were fought, involving in every case a total or partial redistribution of lands. More than one powerful tribe at the date of the captain's visit has long since disappeared. For each battle this iron axe, with numerous stone auxiliaries, was put into requisition in preparing weapons. The old man who gave me this unattractive-looking curiosity was himself in four of these battles. But times have happily changed, and he has changed with them.

A painful point of interest in regard to this relic of Captain Cook is, that it was used in slaying human sacrifices for Rongo, who was supposed to feed exclusively on human flesh. His chief representative was a triton shell (Rongo means ' The Resounder '). A large block of stone, rudely shaped like a man, was also regarded as an inferior representation of this Polynesian Mars. Many years ago, when these people embraced Christianity, this huge stone idol was utterly defaced, and the fragments form part of the stonework of the church at the principal village.

About the year 1810, Ngakauvarea, a leading warrior

---

[1] *Callophyllum inophyllum.*

of the now almost extinct tribe of Tongaiti, was appointed
to guard the entrance to the cave of Tautua, where they
took refuge after having been defeated in battle. Unluckily
for themselves, they had resolved on a midnight attack
upon their victorious adversaries. This plot was revealed
by a woman, and consequently failed. The dominant
party, greatly incensed at this discovery, doomed the
entire tribe of Tongaiti to destruction. But it was no easy
thing to carry out this cruel design. The cave in which
they had taken refuge is large and very difficult of access.
Underneath the vast pile of hardened coral rock there
passes on towards the ocean a stream of water from the
valleys in that part of the island. There were two
entrances, a 'sacred entrance' for warriors, guarded by
Ngakauvarea; the other entrance was for women and
children employed in collecting food, where, Robinson
Crusoe fashion, a ladder was placed, to be drawn up when
not required. At the top another armed man kept guard.
The interior of the cave is spacious, with a level earthen
floor, at that time covered with dry grass, on which the
poor refugees huddled together as best they could, and
where in the earlier days of the siege they amused
themselves with dancing. Beyond is a dreadful chasm,
over which a single plank was laid, to enable the entire
party to gain the other side, should the entrance be forced.
The grand difficulty was how to get food. It was only
possible to get supplies at night under cover of darkness.

On a given night it was resolved to attack these
cave-dwellers. The leaders of the attack were anxious to
ascertain the will of the gods in reference to their intended
expedition.[1] A number of centipedes, green lizards, and

---

[1] Sometimes the will of the gods was supposed to be made known by the
success of a fish hunt. Three or four large fish of a certain species would be

dragon-flies were collected, and at the same instant thrown into a folded leaf of the gigantic taro plant,[1] filled with water—a single leaf will easily hold half a bucket of water. Only one insect perished out of the entire number; therefore it was sagely concluded that the gods had decreed that only one person should that night die at their hands.

That very evening, as Ngakauvarea (or 'Deceived Heart') was sleeping at his post, with his spear by his side, a foe named Terake (or 'There-he-is') climbed up the almost perpendicular rock with his hands and feet, and succeeded in gaining the sacred entrance unobserved. Had Ngakauvarea been awake and given the alarm, nothing would have been easier than to have hurled down the daring climber on the sharp-pointed rocks below, a depth of thirty feet. In the moonlight, Terake plainly discerned the form of his unconscious victim, and with a single blow of Captain Cook's axe clove the skull of the sleeping warrior. The body was hastily thrown to those below. The noisy formula for killing sacrifices—*Taumaa, Rongo, toou ika, i.e.* 'Rongo, slay thy fish'—roused those within, so that the attacking party were glad to retire with a bruise or two from a shower of stones, bearing away, however, their bleeding victim in triumph. The supposed command of the god Rongo had been obeyed—at any rate, their malice was gratified.

The slaughter of the devoted tribe had thus favourably

seen enjoying themselves in the shallow waters of the reef. It was known beforehand that these fish, if chased, will not return to the ocean, else the chase were vain. They invariably make for the shore, or for some hiding-place in the reef. A most exciting chase now takes place : the fish are literally hunted to death. Sometimes one will escape the utmost efforts of the hunters by rushing past them and taking refuge in some large hole in the coral too deep to permit a human hand to reach the coveted prize within. The number of fish caught was believed to prefigure the number of the doomed.

[1] *Alocasia indica* (Seeman).

commenced. A most vigilant watch was kept on the starving wretches who tremblingly crept out at nightfall in search of food. Relatives from the attacking tribe still visited their starving friends inside the cave, but were carefully searched, lest a bit of taro or coco-nut should perchance be hidden in their long hair or within the girdle. Scarcely a day passed without some of them being caught and killed. All the dead bodies were collected and laid in rows on a rising ground, where in after years a church for the worship of the living and true God was erected. About fifty in all, when sufficiently dried in the sun, were borne across the island to the *marae* or idol-grove of Rongo, ' to feed him and his mother Papa,' according to their mythology. At length it was resolved that the drum of peace should be beaten, and that Marokore should, in the name of the gods, be declared 'lord of Mangaia.' To accomplish this, another bleeding victim must be expressly slain and offered to this insatiable Rongo.

Few men were by this time left in the cave, and they were reduced almost to skeletons. Nevertheless, they kept watch as well as they could. Ngutukū was the guardian of the common entrance, where the ladder was occasionally let down. One morning, by broad daylight, the grand-father of one of my deacons, being on the watch, observed from a distance that Ngutukū had laid himself down to sleep. Axe in hand, the murderer crept around stealthily to the foot of the ladder, and, finding that his approach had not been observed, he boldly mounted it and slew Ngutukū. No attempt at rescuing the body was made by the poor dispirited creatures within. The body was at once carried off to the *marae* in the sacred district of Keia as an offering to the gods. To show the thorough change which has passed over these people, I may mention that this very spot was many years afterwards presented by the chief of that district to the missionary, my esteemed predecessor, as a pen for his cows! After being exposed there for some days, the body was taken to Orongo=O (definite article) Rongo—where the great stone idol Rongo once stood—and was eventually thrown into the bush, *not* buried. The gods thus appeased, the drum of peace was beaten, and the few half-starved wretches yet living in the cave were permitted to crawl out and show their faces once more in the light of day without fear of being clubbed.

So much for the history of this old axe. About the same time the aged king gave me two beads, the size of large marbles, which had recently come to light when digging a foundation for a new house. A string of these beads was tied with some nails to a piece of wood and thrown by Captain Cook to Mourua and Makatu, in the hope of establishing a friendly intercourse with these islanders. The beads, the first ever seen here, were greatly admired. As their blue colour corresponded to that of the supposed 'solid stone vault above,' they were named 'sky pebbles,' as if veritable chips of the azure arch which encloses earth and sea. To this day all beads are designated 'sky pebbles,' although their earthly origin is well known. A solitary nail is yet preserved as a relic— not of the giver, Captain Cook, but of his dusky friend, who alone of his countrymen ventured on board the moving monster. A neat ironwood handle was made for this nail. It was long used as a bradawl for boring holes, so as to secure the different portions of canoes with strong sennit.

TUMEA'S LAMENT FOR HER FATHER NGAKAUVAREA.

Circa A.D. 1810.

1.

Na metua-noo-rua e ketu i te metua.
Teiia rā Ngakauvarea?
Tei te ana o Tautua, vai ake i reira.

A daughter is seeking for her cave-
    dwelling father.
Where, oh, where is Ngakauvarea?
He who guarded the cave of Tautua.

2.

Vai ake i reira, tiki na te rima,
Retia mai, mauia ē
Paria ra i te toki pai ē !

Asleep there, his hands were stealthily
    grasped :
Cruelly seized and dragged was he,
And slain with the white man's axe !

3.

Toki pai ē noou ua rava
Te tokotoko i raka atu.
O te toa ua te tua iaau !

It was the white man's axe that slew
    thee—
So utterly unlike all others !
Why did not the wooden spear lay
    thee low ?

4.

Toki pai ē, aue koe i o teina,
Aue Uruata e, aue te tamaki ē,
Aue ka mate, ka mate ei au !

Oh, that white man's axe ! Alas for
    thy brother,
Alas for Uruata ! Oh, that cruel
    stratagem !
That fearful blow ! Oh, that I too
    had died !

5.

Kounuunu ia Kaarau.
Kāku oki te metua, e tama,
E Ngakauvarea ; kavea ra i raro

Kaarau saved his own skin.
Was not Kāku his father ? But *thou*,
Ngakauvarea, wast pitilessly hurled
    to those below.

6.

Kavea ra i raro, koai te tarava i to
    vaka e rava'i ?
E rave ua ake i o matou tokotoru ua ē,
Kua rai oki te tara, akairia ake koe
    ra !

Pitilessly hurled down ! Who now
    will fill up the ranks ?
Would that these three (warriors) had
    been saved !
Why did the babblers oppose thy
    wish (to fight) ?

7.

Akairia koe ra ; kopunga i raro,
Naoe ra te karanga e, Aere mai a
    puruki.
Ariana ia karo ake ia te ao e !
Kua mataku oki Avaiki.

They opposed thy wish. The foes
    beneath
Kept shouting, ' Come out and fight.'
' Wait, that we may for awhile gaze
    at the light of day,'
Said his death-fearing friends.

8.	8.
Avaiki e ! a reru ra te tāki, a kave ra te kura, Ei tiki ki te rua e, te aa maira te tara i te rua ? Aore, te noo ua, ka mate rava i reira.	Death ! Dance the war-dance : send a message of defiance. Fight the cave-dwellers. Will they venture out ? No, they will not. *There* they are doomed to perish.

9.	9.
A mate rava i reira. Kua ruma te aiai, Tuatu, ka aere tatou. Kua tangi i te metua i te vairanga ua.	Ay, doomed to perish ! The sun is setting. Come, let us go and greet our father In his miserable abode.

10.	10.
I te vairanga ua e, Oro i Butoa, tao mai I te paka raurangi.	Alas, that wretched abode ! Let us go to Butoa to collect and cook His repast of wild leaves.

11.	11.
Te paka raurangi, e tatari i te metua. Aore e taia e vero, E tiaki na te ara.	Yes, a repast of cooked leaves was ready for our father. He was not killed by hunger. Our approach (to the cave) was prevented.

12.	12.
E tiaki na te ara, kua pa te rongo Kua pou te puruki, kua ingā Ngakau-varea Te vai rai i Tamarua.	Our approach was prevented. We heard a report, 'The fight is over ; Ngakauvarea is slain.' His corpse lies exposed at Tamarua.

13.	13.
Te vai ra i Tamarua : vairanga kino ē ! Vairanga taurere ē ! E taeake ē ! E Tuturi i rave ake ai.	Lies exposed at Tamarua : sad resting-place ! Exposed on a rock ! Ah, my brother, O Tuturi, why didst thou not save him ?

14.	14.
E rave ake ai ra, tiki na, retia ē ! Te aronga ē tangi i te tuaine ē ! Kurakaau i vai ake ai.	Why was he not saved ? He was dragged and slain. Such was your pity for your sister ! Kurakaau is left utterly desolate.

This is a specimen of the ballad poetry of olden times. In general, each stanza catches up the last words of that preceding, and carries forward the train of thought. This mournful ballad was composed by a daughter of Ngakauvarea. The Kurakaau referred to in the last verse was the pretty daughter of Mourua, whom the father wished to marry to Captain Cook. As the great English navigator declined this kind offer, she afterwards became the wife of the ill-fated 'Deceived-Heart,' but did not, however, share her husband's fate.

All their weapons of warfare were made of ironwood. Ngakauvarea (third stanza) fell by a weapon previously unknown. Their own adzes were of stone.

Kaarau (verse 5) was a near relative of the three warriors (verse 6) slain in the cave—namely, Ngakauvarea, Uruata, and Ngutukū. It seems that through his wife, who was nearly related to the attacking party, Kaarau received more than once a hint about an intended attack, and retired into the interior of the cave, thus 'saving his own skin.' In verse 7 the idea is that, seeing death was inevitable, Ngakauvarea proposed that the unhapy tribe should give battle, and so perish honourably; and not be cut off one by one. The starving cave-dwellers would not fight against such fearful odds—one to four or five.

Butoa (verse 10) is a wild but pleasing spot not far from the cave, where the daughter is represented on the evening of his death as going to collect leaves—the only food obtainable—for her parent's supper. She had married into the attacking party in happier days ; but persisted in going by stealth to take a little food to her father.

In this ballad style of composition the verses are invariably designated *knots*, in reference to an ancient method of counting by making knots in a piece of cord.

A son of Ngakauvarea who was spared was ever afterwards known by the name of Wild-Leaves, in memory of the wretched food on which the old man subsisted in the cave.

Thank God that the grandchildren of the murderers and the murdered meet in Christian friendship now at the table of the Lord Jesus ; ' for *He* is our peace.'

CHAPTER XXXIV

A STONE THROWN IN THE DARK

CIRCA A.D. 1781-1789

THREE or four years after the discovery of the island by
Captain Cook, an elderly chief named Paī—brother to
Kirikovi, supreme warrior-chief of Mangaia—was sitting
one evening warming himself at the oven his wife was
preparing. The reverie of Paī was rudely interrupted by
a smart blow on his bare breast from a stone thrown out of
the darkness. The incensed chief rushed into the bush, in
the vain hope of catching the unknown offender. Finding
it impossible to overtake him, he solemnly charged his
grown-up son Paoa never to rest until the stone-thrower
should be discovered and slain.

Some months after, Toē, belonging to the unhappy
tribe of Teipe, confessed to his friend Paoa that he had,
from sheer wantonness, thrown the stone on the night
referred to. On learning the name of the offender, Paī
greatly wished to club him, but out of respect to his
brother, the paramount chief at the time, restrained his
feelings. He commanded his son Paoa never to consent
to any intermarriage between the two families, lest such
an alliance should prove a hindrance to revenge at a future
day.

About this time Paoa married and set up a separate

establishment in a neighbouring district, a sister living with them. One day Paī was astonished by hearing that Paoa had been stupid enough to give that sister to Toē to wife, notwithstanding the pledge solemnly given to his father. Toē and his wife started off to the opposite side of the island, to avoid the anger of the old chief.

Upon hearing of the marriage, Paī hurried off to see his son. High words ensued. Paoa excused himself as well as he could ; but the proud father, growing wild with anger, ordered his disobedient son to quit the island for ever ! Paī returned home. That same night Paoa went fishing, and secured a great cavally. In the morning he called together a few friends to announce his resolve to take his chance on the ocean. The remonstrances of his friends were without effect ; so they moodily feasted together for the last time. Paoa afterwards went to the *marae* to take a farewell of the gods, by playing on his famous wooden drum, with the tips of his fingers, his best tunes in their honour, for he was an excellent musician.

Next day Paoa went to the edge of the reef and launched his little canoe all alone, for he desired no companion on his ill-starred voyage. The entreaties and tears of his wife, who, with their two infants, accompanied him to the top of the hill overlooking the point of departure, were unavailing, and Paoa started on his unhappy expedition.

By this time it had got wind that Paoa had gone. Several near relatives, not in the secret, ran as fast as they could to the beach, but did not arrive in time to detain him. Determined to save him, they launched a number of small canoes, paddling with might and main after the runaway, who madly hurried on far out of the lee of the island to escape their importunities to return.

Meantime the sky became overcast, and the wind, which had been blowing steadily from the east, veered round to the north and blew with considerable violence. The friends assembled on the reef, watching the chase after the fugitive, could only discern tiny specks on the boisterous inky waves. Darkness came on, but no canoe returned. Numerous torches were now lighted ; but the chiefs, fearing that they could not be seen at so great a distance, ordered the hills to be set on fire ! The dry fern and reeds quickly spread the fire over the interior, consuming all the ironwood and pandanus trees on the hills, and numerous coco-nut trees in the valleys.

Guided by this magnificent beacon-light, several canoes got back about midnight, with the sad news that the foremost canoes, containing the King Tcivirau and his brothers, when within hail of the runaway, whom they entreated to return, were suddenly engulfed by a mighty wave, which at the same time drowned the infatuated Paoa. The remaining canoes escaped by being nearer shore, out of the track of the pitiless billows.

Thus the folly of this wilful youth cost him his own life and the lives of four relatives, one of them the grandfather of Numangatini, the present (1872) King of Mangaia. An essential emblem of Tcivirau's dignity was a triton shell, used to summon chiefs and leading men to council whenever he thought fit. This shell, bearing the name of Ororakiau, or 'The Royal Messenger,' is in my possession.[1]

But where was Paī? After his memorable quarrel with his son he remained in his own dwelling, nursing his anger, not dreaming of the fate of Paoa. But when the news came that his unhappy boy and four others—all men

---

[1] Formerly used by 'the shore-king' Vaerua-rau, ancestor of Numangatini. Deposited by me in the British Museum.

of mark in their day—were lost, he became as frantic with grief as he had a short time before been with anger. He sought out his cousin Mourua, the friend of Captain Cook, who was always ready to shed blood, and arranged a plan of revenge. Toē, his hated son-in-law, must perish, as the prime author of all these troubles.

On a starless night these worthies set out for the other side of the island to murder Toē and his aged father Aretere. As father and son occupied different houses, it was arranged that Paī should club Aretere, whilst Mourua should despatch Toē—the old chief not liking to kill his son-in-law in the very presence of his wife. Mourua, however, was never troubled with scruples of any sort when his services were required. He sat in the dark before the open door of the unsuspecting inmates. The wife was busy weaving a coco-nut-leaf basket, by the light of a candle-nut torch, whilst the doomed husband lay asleep at her side on the dry grass strewed over the hut. For some seconds Mourua watched his cousin's work without being himself observed ; but at length growing impatient, he rushed through the open doorway past the astonished wife, and transfixed the sleeping Toē ! The spear with which the victim was thus pinned to the earth was left standing upright, whilst Mourua, without uttering a word to his cousin, so lately wedded but now a widow, strode out of the dwelling to rejoin Paī, who had about the same time despatched the father of Toē.

But this was only the beginning of years of bloodshed and anarchy. The charm of peace was broken ; Paī and Mourua and their retainers went about killing people day by day. The entire population had resort to arms ; a pitched battle was fought at a place known as Taukuera, in which Kirikovi was worsted by his brother Paī and

Mourua, and the proud Paī was declared 'lord of Mangaia' instead of his brother.

But ere the ceremonies preparatory to the beating of the drum of peace could be completed, war again broke out. Kirikovi, aided by his friends, one dark night surrounded the house on the rocky beach where Mourua and several others were resting after a fishing expedition. Of the sleepers but one escaped. The struggle with Mourua was protracted, by his immense strength, long after his companions lay dead at his side. His brave wife stripped off her clothing to enable her the better to ward off the blows intended for her husband; her left arm, was broken in the contest. Forced to retire from his side, Mourua received the fatal blow which he had long since richly deserved.

All this resulted from a stone wantonly thrown in the dark by one heathen at another.

It is pleasant to be able to add that a grandson of this irritable old chief Paī, and nephew to the foolish Paoa, named Taata, was for many years a valuable deacon of the Church.

Throughout the preceding narrative I have called the proud chief by his later name of Paī—'Canoe.' In point of fact, however, his proper name was Kaiau. When his son perished miserably at sea, according to their national custom, he adopted the new name of 'Canoe,' to evince his grief at the loss of his foolish boy. It is by this later designation that he is invariably called by his countrymen.

A LAMENT FOR THE KING TEIVIRAU.

By Potiki, *circa* 1790, for the 'Death-talk' of the drowned King.

TUMU.	INTRODUCTION.
Tangi te maunga, e Teivirau.	Weep for the mountains, O Teivirau !
Koai a uta ia tatou, ko Temokomoko !	For friends left behind in the land.
Ko te karava i reira,	Oh, those pleasant hills,—
Ko te kaivi maunga i roa ē !	The long range of mountains at home.

Papa.

Ka pura te ai i te uru kare, e
    Teivi e !
      Ei akatere ia tatou.
      Oe atu koe i te tai roa.
Kua maru te maru i tuitui nunga
    Kua reu te reu po.
Kua meaki te kare nga tama ē !

Unuunu Tai.

Ka tangi te puku ē tei te maunga ē !
Tei te maunga, kua kapu i raro,
Kua kapua ei i raro ki te tapa rakau,
Ki te tapa rakau Pouekakeariki,
    I te taata roa i Angara,
    Ko te oroki i te nu tanu.
      Ko te karava i reira,
Ko te kaivi maunga i roa ē !

Unuunu Rua.

Maunga i uta ē kua teitei ē !
Kua teitei, kua aaura i runga,
    Kua atura i runga 'i.
Tau tangi e i te poo i Tongarei,
    Ko te taparere i raro ē !
      Ko te karava i Teroto
Ko te kaivi maunga ra i roa ē !

Unuunu Toru.

Ka vero te ai tei te maunga :
Tei te maunga ; kua tui ki te moana
    Kaa tui ki te moana.
Kua ka te vera i Poue.
Kua tungia Mangaia ē !
    Ko te karava Uira,
Ko te kaivi maunga ra i roa ē

Unuunu A.

Kau mai Taa ē i te poiri ē !

Foundation.

Lights are seen by Teivi[1] o'er the
    white-crested waves,
      Intended for thy guidance.
      Why venture so far out to sea ?
The island is lessening in the distance.
      Darkness o'erspreads the ocean.
The king is lost to sight in the waves !

First Offshoot.

Weep for the well-known mountain
    tops,
Now hidden by the swelling waves :—
Though hidden they are covered with
    verdure,
Pouekakeariki[2] is lost to view ;
Stretching towards the *east*,
With a smooth summit and coco-nut-
    tree.
      Oh, those pleasant hills,
The long range of mountains at home !

Second Offshoot.

How lofty[3] those distant hills,
Lying piled one above another !
    How vast are they !
Weep for the sight of Tongarei,[4]
    And its precipitous sides.
Oh, those pleasant hills on the *west*,
The long range of mountains at home !

Third Offshoot.

Smoke is rising from the hills ;
The mountain ranges are on fire !
The fierce heat is felt on the ocean ;
The blaze is extending all around :
All Mangaia is on flames !
Oh, those pleasant hills on the *south*,
The long range of mountains at home !

Fourth Offshoot.

Taa[5] has gained the shore in the
    dark.

---

[1] For Teivirau. In the last line of this verse he is termed 'eldest son : '
all kings were so called out of respect. I have simply rendered it 'king.'

[2] A prominent hill, serving as a landmark to those on the ocean.

[3] This is amusing, considering the highest hill of Mangaia is about 500 feet
above the level of the sea !

[4] Another prominent hill.

[5] Taa was one of those who got back alive. Of course it was Taa and his
more fortunate companions who saw the lights ashore on the edge of the reef,

Ite poiri tatango ; kua noo tona io—
Kua noo tona io 'i, ko Tiaio rangi ē !
O kereteki : kua mataku te ika i noo
reva ē !
Uru mai koe i te tauirangiapa.
Ko te kaivi akau ra i roa ē !

In the starless night he was preserved.
The ' shark-god ' was his protector,
And Kereteki too, to save him from
All monsters of the deep, and to
bring him to shore.
Oh, the far-extending *reef* at our
home !

AKAREINGA.

Ai e ruaoo ē !   E rangai ē !

FINALE.

Ai e ruaoo ē !   E rangai ē !

LAMENT FOR PAOA.

A song pertaining to the ' Death-talk of Teivirau.'   By his repentant father, *circa* 1790.

TUMU.

Tumatuma te pau i Itikau na Paoa.
Oro mai ana, e tau ariki, kia ongi ake
taua ē !
To poū kino i oro ei !

INTRODUCTION.

At Itikau [1] Paoa beat softly his drum.
Come, beloved son,[2] let us once more
kiss each other.
Why this ill-omened flight ?

PAPA.

Tamaki na te medua i ara 'i Paoa ē !
Auraka kia akamoū, kua erueru i te
one.
E tangi ai Moeau i te takanga.
Ei kona korua e, ka aere ē !

FOUNDATION.

The angry words of the father exiled
Paoa.
Yet bear not malice.   The mother, in
grief
For her lost son, scratches the dried
grass.[3]
Alas (those words)!   ' Farewell ! I
leave you for ever ! '

UNUUNU TAI.

Tumatuma te pau ē, tei Itikau ē,
Tei Itikau na Paoa ;—
Ko te uinga ïa o te karioi.
Kua akarongo mai nei au taeake
I te pau tangi reka :
Tangi reka te pau a Paoa !
Oro mai ana, e tau ariki, kia ongi ake
taua ē !
To poū kino i oro ei !

FIRST OFFSHOOT.

Softly sounds the drum at Itikau,
The famed drum of Paoa.
It is the gathering of young men.
Entranced by the music of their
friend.
Oh, that sweetly-sounding drum !
The incomparable touch of Paoa.
Come, beloved son, let us once more
kiss each other.
Why this ill-omened flight ?

---

the prominent hills, and that awful spectacle, an island on fire.   Hence the
pleasing change in the chorus, intimating the course taken by the returning
canoes, until they joyfully set their feet on ' the far-extending reef at home.'

[1] Itikau is the name of a place close to Paoa's dwelling.

[2] ' Beloved son.'   In the native it is ' my king,' a common appellation for
a beloved *elder* son.

[3] The custom still obtains of scratching the grass or earth where the
deceased last sat, in token of excessive grief.

Unuunu Rua.

O Mumuu te are ra e moe ai ē !
   E moe ai i te avatea.
  Kua akapiripiri Paoa ē
    Na nunga i Aparai,
Ka kitea mai au e Moenoa !
Oro mai ana, e tau ariki, kia ongi ake
  taua ē !
    To poū kino i oro ei !

Second Offshoot.

Sequestered was the dwelling
Where he slept when the sun was
  high.
Paoa loved to saunter about
The shady hillside Aparai
In company with the lovely Moenoa.
Come, beloved son, let us once more
  kiss each other.
    Why this ill-omened flight ?

Unuunu Toru.

Te umea te maro ē, ka napea ē,
Ka napea to maro i Vairotokava,
Kua pou ai to angai urua.
   Aere tu tei tai ē !
Tu mai koe i Arataa !
Oro mai ana, e tau ariki, kia ongi ake
  taua ē !
    To poū kino i ore ei !

Third Offshoot.

Thy girdle is adjusted and well
  secured (for flight),
'Twas done in desperation at Vairo-
  tokava,
After feasting on a great cavally.
Ere starting on that fatal voyage
Thou didst take a last lingering look.
Come, beloved son, let us once more
  kiss each other.
    Why this ill-omened flight ?

Akareinga.

Ai e ruaoo ē !   E rangai ē !

Finale.

Ai e ruaoo ē !   E rangai ē !

CHAPTER XXXV

A STORMY NIGHT IMPROVED

SOMEWHERE about A.D. 1785 nearly a hundred persons took refuge in the cave Touri,[1] and double that number in the great cave Eruc, about three miles distant. Both companies owned the authority of the clever but unscrupulous Potai. Unfortunately for the smaller party, a hostile chief named Poito, with a number of warriors, took up his quarters under Touri, and laid siege to this natural fortress. The long ladder, which hitherto had enabled the fugitives to collect supplies from their old plantations, was at once destroyed. The secret subterranean passage conducting to the forest on the hillside was so difficult to traverse as to be of little use. It became evident that, unless Potai came to the rescue, the whole party inside the cave must die of starvation.

By the secret path a message was sent to Potai acquainting him with their critical state. They were promised assistance on the first stormy night.

Potai was afraid to attack Poito, as he had already had painful experience of his bravery. The women and children could not hope to escape by means of the perilous secret subterranean path. The only feasible mode of rescuing these despairing fugitives was to draw them out

---

[1] For a romantic story connected with this cave, see Chap. II., 'A Dress of Feathers.'

of the cave with ropes. The main force of Potai at Erue was unwatched, and enjoyed plenty. Four-stranded ropes, of great length and strength, were twisted, sticks being inserted at one end, to enable the poor creatures to *sit* whilst being drawn up.

Potai now watched with great anxiety the appearance of the heavens. It so happened that on the first moonless night a tremendous storm burst forth. Those who have not seen a tropical storm can form no adequate conception of its terrific grandeur. Poito and his warriors took refuge inside a neighbouring cave, which still bears his name. In fine weather he delighted to seat himself at the entrance and play the harmonicon—a rough sort of music, set to the war-songs of his tribe.

Potai and his well-laden followers arrived on the crest of the overhanging rocks by the forest path in the early evening, before the tempest had reached its height. The starving and expectant creatures inside the cave soon perceived, by the flashes of lightning, a number of ropes dangling in the air, but far out of reach, opposite the entrance to their rocky asylum. In a few seconds the ropes were brought near by means of long fishing-rods with hooks fastened to the extremities. Those above—a distance of some eighty-eight feet—feeling, by the weight, that some of their friends were perched on the cross-trees below, joyfully hauled them up. A father would clasp his child in his arms whilst being pulled up. Women with their infants in this way escaped a miserable death ; of the entire number not one lost his life that night ; but when Taaki, the last to ascend, arrived at the top, it was discovered that two of the four strands of the rope by which he had been pulled up had been cut through by the sharp projecting rock !

All this time Poito and his besieging force were fast asleep. So near were they that any of those drawn up could easily have thrown a stone amongst the slumberers. The time chosen for hoisting up the fugitives was when the thunder was the most terrific, and the rain the heaviest. The strife of elements went on through the livelong night ; by dawn the poor creatures had all reached the magnificent stalactite home of Potai at Eruc, to the utter chagrin of their foes beneath.

This famous relief of Touri long remained an enigma. But many years after, when Poito was dead, it was whispered that *one* of the sleeping guards beneath was aware that the fugitives would that night be rescued. That individual was the clever harmonicon-player, himself chief watcher! As a last resource the crafty Potai selected the prettiest girl in his tribe and sent her stealthily to Poito, who, heathen-like, readily fell into the snare. This woman acquired such influence over Poito that he yielded to her entreaties and tears to permit the escape of her perishing tribe. On the night of the storm he told the guards that they might as well sleep, as he himself would keep watch. He felt sure that on such a dreadful night no foe would venture out. When the exit of the fugitives was discovered on the following day, Poito apologetically said that he supposed he must have fallen asleep! Poito would gladly have made this girl his wife, but by so doing would have betrayed his secret and disgraced himself in the eyes of his own people.

CHAPTER XXXVI

MAIKAI'S CHESTNUT-TREE

CIRCA A.D. 1787

ONE of the noblest trees in the Pacific is the chestnut (*Inocarpus edulis*), which almost rivals the coco-nut in height, and for shade has no equal. The timber, however, is worthless. At the beginning of the year it puts forth innumerable tiny white blossoms, filling the air with fragrance. The fruit is a staple article of diet, not of luxury ; it lasts from the middle of February to the end of June. This tree attains to a great age, far exceeding that of the coco-nut. The oldest coco-nut-trees now standing on Mangaia were planted at the commencement of Mautara's chieftainship, *i.e.* about one hundred and seventy years ago ;[1] whilst certain chestnut-trees at Tamarua are believed to have been planted by Amau, about four hundred and twenty years ago. The age of the chestnut is, however, exceeded by the banyan, which is almost imperishable.

A striking peculiarity of the chestnut is the circumstance that the trunk of the full-grown tree throws out five or six lateral supports, each above an inch thick, and running out some distance into the soil. A fall from one of the lofty

---

[1] Mr. Ellis, in his *Polynesian Researches*, thinks the coco-nut-tree may attain the age of fifty or sixty years, or even more. I have no hesitation whatever in doubling this estimate.

branches of this tree on one of these plank-like buttresses would be certain death. The skull would be cleft in two. I have known several fatal accidents to occur in this way. The larger trees, if beaten with a stick, give forth a very pleasant sound, which can be heard at the distance of a mile. In former times it was usual to select the most musical for beating, in order to assemble the population of an entire district for dancing, reed-throwing matches, etc.

Not long since I went to see a particular chestnut-tree which has become historical. With some difficulty we climbed up its ancient trunk, and there I listened (not for the first time) to the following incident :—

About one hundred and eleven years ago, Maikai, wife of Tetonga, went with a number of other women to a distant plantation to obtain food for her family. They did not know that their foes, under Moerangi's guidance, had that morning left their stronghold in the rocks for the same spot in quest of plunder. A year or two previously, in the time of peace, one of Moerangi's clan had been abused in no measured terms by Maikai for lurking about their premises after nightfall. Upon relating to his tribe the indignity he had undergone, it was resolved to murder Maikai, if ever she should be in their power. It is a point of honour with a heathen *never* to forgive.

On the day referred to they were delighted to see amongst the women the very one they wished to wreak their vengeance upon. They therefore gave chase to Maikai, allowing the rest to escape. Maikai ran for her life, well knowing their cruel intentions. She wisely left her friends, who ran by the accustomed path through the open country, where she must have been overtaken and slain. She chose for her hiding-place a narrow valley where a number of fine chestnut-trees grew. She recollected that in the largest of these trees was a hollow occasioned by the limbs of the chestnut shooting out of the stem at the same distance from the ground. Maikai made for this clump of chestnuts. Running to the side of the tree farthest from her foes, in a second she climbed the tree and completely secreted herself in the natural hollow, which was just big enough to admit her.

Now it fortunately happened that one of the pursuing party, named Raimanga, was greatly in advance of the rest. He caught a glimpse of Maikai making for this large tree, and at once divined her purpose. But, being secretly anxious to save her, he ran at full speed a good distance up the valley, and threw some large stones into the sluggish stream to make it muddy, and pretended to be looking everywhere for the fugitive. When the rest of the pursuers came up with him and saw how turbid the water was, they concluded that Maikai had taken to the bed of the stream. On and on they rushed up the valley, in the vain hope of overtaking their victim. After a long and fruitless search for Maikai, they returned by the same path to the very tree in the top of which she lay hid. Tired with their chase, they piled up their spears against the trunk of this chestnut, and sat down under its grateful shade to refresh themselves. They slaked their thirst from the stream at their feet, and chatted about Maikai's marvellous disappearance. The majority thought she must have been specially helped by the gods; but Raimanga was sure that it was due to her wonderful fleetness of foot. After awhile Raimanga remarked, 'Let us be off, or our enemies will catch us.' At this the entire party took up their spears and returned to their old haunts.

All this time Maikai lay crouching down in the

hollow of the great chestnut, scarcely daring to breathe, and expecting every moment to be discovered and speared to death. At first she distinctly heard the rush of feet and the voices of eager pursuers on their way up the valley, for the pathway then, as now, ran under the branches of the tree, and then all became quiet for awhile. But again the sound of human feet and human voices was heard. She was conscious that the entire party, hot and angered by their bootless chase, were resting under the chestnut. It is said that not a word of their conversation escaped her. But when they finally departed she could scarcely credit the truth that her life was safe.

At last she ventured to rise from her cramped position, and cautiously peered beneath to see if there were any traces of her foes. Finding there were none, she descended to the ground, and ran as fast as her legs could carry her along the narrow mountain-path to her husband and children, who, on hearing the report of the women who had seen her chased, gave her up for lost. Hence the commemorative name still kept up in their family, Ate-ru ('Trembling Heart'), as descriptive of Maikai's feelings while she lay trembling in the curious recess of this famous chestnut-tree.

Her preserver was called E koinga ta Raimanga ('Raimanga the pitiful'), an epithet that would be appropriate to but few of his heathen countrymen.

The narrator of this story, a deacon of the Church, is grandson of Maikai.

CHAPTER XXXVII

PADDLING FOR LIFE

AN old and respected native of the village of Oneroa gave me the following account of the escape of his maternal uncle Matenga from a miserable death about the year 1810.

During the long and peaceful rule of Potiki, Matenga grew up to manhood, and married the sister of the chief Raoa. The rival factions which eventually overthrew the government of 'the supreme temporal lord' brought sorrow and tears to Matenga and all the Tongan tribe. The crimes of former days were remembered against them, so that they resolved to take refuge in the impregnable natural fortress known as the Cave of Tautua.

Underneath flows on to the ocean a never-failing stream of water; but the difficulty of obtaining food was considerable. At first their wives and children were permitted to collect food to supply the wants of the warriors inside the cave. But at last the then all-powerful tribe of Mautara resolved upon their extermination. For a distance of one hundred yards lofty palisades were firmly planted in the soft soil in front of the cave, in order to prevent all egress. Armed men were appointed to keep constant watch that nothing eatable should be taken into the cave. Any member of the doomed tribe venturing outside was at once clubbed. Persons connected with the winning tribes wishing to visit their starving relatives inside were first rigorously searched, so as to prevent the possible concealment of food in the narrow girdle or flowing hair.

As Matenga's young wife belonged to the dominant party, she went inside to see her husband as often as she pleased. Months of misery passed away, and yet Matenga lived on, though but the shadow of his former self. The fact was that his faithful wife was in the habit of stealthily conveying food by a long and circuitous path to a certain hollow nearly a mile from the carefully guarded entrance. This secret entrance is now shaded by lofty cedars,[1] covered during the summer months with delicate lilac-tinted blossoms. The subterraneous passage is exceedingly tortuous and difficult. A yawning chasm, bridged by a single plank, ran across the cavern. A lighted flambeau was absolutely needful. But the instinct of self-preservation enabled Matenga to find his way to the secret entrance, where his wife awaited his arrival with a small basket of cooked taro.

This could not go on for ever. The leading men of the unhappy tribe had been slain. It was evident that the clan was doomed. In a nook of the cave a sad meeting was held, when the father and brother of Matenga urged him to escape and leave them to die. To make sure of Raoa's favour, a valuable fish-net,[2] called a *nariki*, an heirloom of the family, was given to Matenga. This treasure was conveyed to the secret entrance, and entrusted to his wife

---

[1] Introduced by myself from Australia.
[2] Such a net will now fetch £6 in cash.

to be carried across the island to Raoa the chief. On her way to her brother she fell in with a party of armed men, who at once took possession of the fish-net, as being the property of the cave-dwellers. Raoa was not disposed to relinquish so valuable a net; he therefore made a formal demand for it, and succeeded in recovering it. Thus the price of protection had been paid; but the difficulty now was how to get Matenga across the island in safety to the district where Raoa exercised authority. Intercession with the cave-watchers would be futile. Happily, however, a plan concocted by Raoa and his sister proved successful.

On a given day Matenga met his faithful wife at the unsuspected opening amongst the rocks near the sea. A morsel was eaten; few words were exchanged, for the fugitive had just taken a last farewell of his nearest relatives. Carefully threading their way through the bush and over jagged rocks to the beach, they fortunately found a small canoe with a paddle in it, belonging to one of the watchers and murderers of the unfortunate tribe. In a few minutes the frail bark was on the ocean, and the wife hastening back through the bush to give tidings to her brother Raoa.

The fugitive paddled leisurely towards the west, taking care that the canoe should not be sufficiently near the reef to permit his features to be recognized. Every now and then he made a pretence of dropping his line for fish, and after a time, as if unsuccessful, would take up the tackle and press forward. Had Matenga met any other canoe that day, he would undoubtedly have perished; but, fortunately, he succeeded that afternoon in getting opposite to the boundary-line of the district where his brother-in-law resided. The poor fellow now breathed freely. Being well provided with fish-hooks, he began to angle in right earnest. The fish-hooks of those times were laboriously manufactured with bits of round coral out of the hardest coco-nut shells. Twenty fine *namu* rewarded his exertions. These were intended as a gift to his future protector. Thus the life-work of the serf had commenced.

The sun had set when the fugitive, with his stolen canoe, arrived at the usual landing-place on the west. Though unassisted, he succeeded in shooting his canoe through the breakers at the right moment on to the rugged coral reef, and dragged it through the shallow water to the beach.

Matenga had paddled a distance of five miles. With his face well hidden with native cloth, and lugging his fish, he started for the interior, about a mile away. Once he gave himself up for lost, for one of his foes passed him ; but happily the muffled figure moving in the dark was not recognized.

My friend Kirimaniania, referred to at the commencement of this story, was that day engaged with his father Raoa in digging a new taro-patch. Though a tall youth at the time, he was not entrusted with the secret of Matenga's escape, lest it should be betrayed to some of his bloodthirsty foes. As the evening shadows from the neighbouring hills fell upon their romantic home, the lad observed that Raoa frequently paused in his work and glanced uneasily at the Rat's Pathway, the only road thereabouts to the sea. At last a figure hurried over the brow of the hill to the spot where they stood. It was Matenga, with his load of fish.

To avoid a surprise, he was at once concealed in a tiny hut built on long poles as a sort of watch-tower. His companions were his nephew and his wife, who had also been on the watch, whilst Raoa went to his principal neighbours to induce them to promise their assistance in saving the poor fugitive.

Only one refused—Tavare, who had already imbrued his hands in the blood of the Tongans. Apprehensive that Tavare would some day slay his brother-in-law, a small cave near at hand was selected as the temporary home of Matenga. It was well strewed with dried grass. His constant companion was his nephew, whose duty it would be to give the alarm at the first appearance of danger. Tavare again and again asked permission to dispose of 'the bird in the hole,' but was invariably refused.

For many months this little 'bird' durst not leave its nest in the rocks. Matenga was well supplied with food by his wife. But when at length Ngutukū had been offered in sacrifice to Rongo, arbiter of peace and war, and the drum of peace had been beaten all round the island, the fugitive left his hiding-place and ventured to walk about in open daylight, taking care, however, to keep to Raoa's district.

Matenga lived to see the first native evangelists land on Mangaia, and witnessed the earlier triumphs of Christianity. But he would have nothing to do with the new religion, because his kind protectors were at that time averse to the new order of things. Raoa fell in battle two years prior to the landing of Papehia and Haavi. A son of Matenga was a truly pious man, and after leaving a most cheering testimony to the truth of the Gospel, passed away to the better land.

The real cause of the extinction of the Tongan tribe was their excessively warlike propensities. The clan was familiarly called Tumu o Miro, *i.e.* 'The Root of all Bloodshedding.' The common saying in reference to this tribe was, *E kuru i tai vaa koatu ei ako ia Tonga-iti, i.e.* 'Carve out a *stone mouth* that will never weary of admonishing the Tongans.'

CHAPTER XXXVIII

A BRAVE WIFE

WE have seen that the priestly tribe of Mautara retained absolute sway over the island of Mangaia for about a century. They claimed descent from Papaaunuku, who came as a vassal in the train of Rangi from Avaiki. In successive battles the descendants of Rangi and his brothers were almost exterminated. The vassals became lords, the ancient masters being fearfully massacred and often literally devoured.

In 1814 this once all-powerful clan lost their power and most of their lands, as the inevitable result of several years of bitter dissension and constant fighting amongst themselves.

About A.D. 1811 one of the factions into which the tribe was split, led by Kaunio, made a raid upon Ata-toa, chief of Keia, and his aged father Tukua, because they were firmly attached to the opposite party. This was but a prelude to the battle of Rangiura, the last fatal victory of the shattered clan.

Taking a sorrowful farewell of their families, Ata-toa, Tukua, and several others awaited the onset under the shadow of the romantic overhanging rocks of Okio. I have stood with Ata-iti, the present chief of the district, whilst he pointed out to me the stone on which Tukua's brains were pounded by his foes, and, a little higher up, the place where Ata-toa fell with a ghastly spear-thrust in the neck.   Several others fell in that unequal fight.

The heroic wife of Ata-toa fought bravely by the side of her husband.   To save him from the fate of Tukua, as soon as he fell she picked up the still breathing body and succeeded in carrying it off to some distance, where she laid him on the grass.   Finding their enemies on their track, she again took up her living burden, and carried Ata-toa to a large cave, hoping to be able to staunch the wound. Again they were pursued : again the noble-hearted Kie refused to leave her husband to his fate.   Eventually she secreted him in a cavern, named Teakautu, near the sea. Here she tended him for seven days and nights, till the unfortunate man died.   Their little children brought food by stealth every evening.

Now Ata-toa had a grown son, Muraai, who afterwards became chief of Keia.   By a singular arrangement he and his brothers were adopted into the maternal[1] tribe, at the tearful solicitation of Kie.   Hence it was that during the fight they were sitting secure in their house listening to the distant clashing of spears.

The present (1870) chief, Ata-iti, whose name frequently occurs in the songs, well remembers the sad events of that day—the farewell, the fight, the stealthy visit by the sea, and finally the well-wrapped-up body gently let down the gloomy chasm with long cords, without a ray of light regarding a future life.

Kie, then a grandmother, lived several years after the introduction of the Gospel to Mangaia.   When old and decrepit, it was a great pleasure to her to attend all the services of the sanctuary.   It must have been a significant

---

[1] Exactly like Manaune in a preceding generation.

fact to her mind that the spot on which the church is built is where she once hid her husband from the cruel vengeance of his foes. The singular love and tender care of this poor heathen woman was commemorated in the songs of the clan.

KOROA'S LAMENT FOR HIS FRIEND ATA.

Pertaining to the 'Death-talk' of Arokapiti.—*Circa* A.D. 1817.

TUMU.

Kua maru te rā i Okio ē !
Kua tangi atu Muraai ki te roronga,
No Ata koia te mate, te metua tatari
　　roa ē !

INTRODUCTION.

The shades of evening rest on the rocks of Okio.
Muraai is disconsolate and wretched,
For Ata-the-Elder, who perished so miserably.

PAPA.

Kaitanga, e Kie,
Ia Makitaka no ta iaku.
Na tika ra ka maru au ia korua,
Kua noo au i te vao ;
E Tamarua karotonga e Mariki.

FOUNDATION.

Distressed indeed was Kie
With the priests who slew Ata : said he,
'Had ye befriended me,
I had still dwelt in prosperity,
And my children would not be in tears.'

UNUUNU MUA.

Kua maru te rā ē tei Okio ē !
Tei Okio ! Ariu te mata i Auroa, e Metuaiviivi !
Te noo ua maira tau mokopuna,
O Ata-iti, kua anau e Taora nei.
Ei ara veu i Rautetiki ka arara.
No Ata koia te mate, te metua tatari
　　roa ē !

FIRST OFFSHOOT.

The shades of evening rest on the rocks at Okio.
From Okio I glance fondly towards our dwelling.
Yonder lives my beloved grandson,
'Ata-the-Little,' he whom Taora bare. Her children
Are like the many-rooted pandanus on the mountain-side.
Alas for Ata-the-Elder, who perished so miserably !

UNUUNU RUA.

Mata mai oki ē i mamao ra e !
I mamao ra. Te noo maira
I te utu ruru na ngati Mautara ;—
Ka ano paa ka koke e, ia Keia.
Mei vai te aka o Muraai ka arara.
No Ata koia te mate, te metua tatari
　　roa ē !

SECOND OFFSHOOT.

Yet glance again towards me—now far away,
Ay, far indeed ! Bitter as fish poison
Is the tribe of Mautara against me.
Perchance they will utterly root up my family,
Lest one of its branches avenge my death !
Alas for Ata-the-Elder, who perished so miserably !

AKAREINGA.

Ai e ruaroo ē ! E rangai ē !

FINALE.

Ai e ruaoo ē ! E rangai ē !

TUKA'S LAMENT FOR HIS FRIEND ATA.

Recited on the same occasion.

TUMU.

Kua mou te piro ia Kie.
Runaio i te putiki.
Ka ano paa, ka rave i te tane.
Aurā koe e vāvao e, kia uuna atu i te
mata ra i te metua ē!

INTRODUCTION.

Kie has girdled on her war-
petticoat;
A gay yellow band well secures it.
She fights to-day to save her husband.
Forget not the day when thy father's
face was hidden (*i.e.* in death).

PAPA.

I ikaio, e Kie, i to tane;
E apai atu i te ana-roa, i te ana-iti,
Akarongo ake, e Mariki e,
I te koumu e, 'Apai atu i te ao:
I Auraka tanukere ai rai ē!'

FOUNDATION.

Tenderly wrap up thy husband, Kie,
And carry him from cave to cave;
For did not thy daughter overhear
The cruel words, 'Take away the
wretch!
Throw him down the gloomy depths
of Auraka'?

UNUUNU TAI.

Kua mou te piri ē, i te popongi ē,
I te popongi no Kie ē, no tera vaine,
No tera vaine! Naai ra e ranga?
Na Tamarua, na Meduaiviivi,
Na tama vaine ia Tanè ē! E Muraai,
Aurā koe e vāvao, e, kia uuna atu i te
mata ra i te metua ē!

FIRST OFFSHOOT.

At dawn she girded on her war-
petticoat.
Thus did that brave woman Kie—
That heroic woman—equip herself.
Will not Tamarua and Muraai avenge
thee?
Are they not adopted into the tribe of
Tanè?
Forget not the day when thy father's
face was hidden.

UNUUNU RUA.

Pikiio e i te putiki ē, i te putiki o
Mariki,
Tau kata Takinga e to tama akarongo,
To tama akarongo ei, to anau, e Kie.
E titiri atu ia maua kia mate ua atu,
I taua matenga i Okio, e Ata,
Aurā koe e vāvao kia uuna atu i te
mata ra i te metua ē!

SECOND OFFSHOOT.

Tenderly wrap him up in thy gay
yellow cloth.
Ah, beloved Takinga, and thou first-
born,
Ever-obedient children of Kie—fare-
well!
Grieve not, little Ata, at our fate,
Slain on the jagged rocks of Okio!
Forget not the day when thy father's
face was hidden.

UNUUNU TORU.

Tikitikie, e Kie e, i to upoko e, i to
upoko, ka mate ē!
Kua pou to manava, kua pou to
manava, e Kie e!
Na tika ra ka maru e kia tamuru ia
Itirere,

THIRD OFFSHOOT.

Shave off thy locks, thy raven hair;
For thy heart is breaking for sore
grief, O Kie!
Oh that those had helped who *could*
have helped

Ei kokou i to upoko, e Ata-iti ē !	To shield thy head, little Ata !
Aurā koe e vāvao kia uuna atu i te mata ra i te metua ē !	Forget not the day when thy father's face was hidden.

AKAREINGA.	FINALE.
Ai e ruaoo ē ! E rangai ē !	Ai e ruaoo ē ! E rangai ē !

How strikingly does the repeated call for vengeance ('Forget not the day,' etc.) contrast with our Saviour's dying words, 'Father, forgive them!' Here lies the essential moral antipodes between the religions of the world and the religion of Christ.

ANOTHER LAMENT FOR ATA; BY KOROA.

For the same 'Death-talk.'

TUMU.	INTRODUCTION.
Purunga ra o Mariki ē !	Thy aged mother-in-law, Mariki,
Akanooia e Kie ra—	Cherish fondly, my Kie ;—
Te tauinu para o Marua,	Thou fair-leaved *tauinu* [1] of Marua,
Kua pipiri tane āna ē !	So tenderly faithful to thy husband !

PAPA.	FOUNDATION.
Papaio i te parai o rireio o Ata ē !	Piles of cloth were heaped around thee, O Ata,
Ki te akaunoanga rai, na Maikai oki rai.	On that joyful day when Maikai's wish was realized.
Kua kaka e ariki tiare rautonga ra na Kie.	Kie had gained a princely husband. [2]

UNUUNU TAI.	FIRST OFFSHOOT.
Purunga oki ra ko Mariki nei ē !	Yonder sits thy aged mother-in-law.
O Mariki nei : kua pipi te vai o Marua,	Poor Mariki ! sprinkle on her the sacred water
Ei enua taurere, ei enua taurere,	Against her day of departure, of sad death.
Tei Poiria te are i Motuariri ra.	Her hut is at Poiria, near to Motuariri ;

---

[1] The beautiful leaf of the *tauinu* (Tournefortia) tree is almost white, and is poetically supposed to grow at the sacred fount Marua, where Kie (who is said to have been exceedingly fair) lived.

[2] Literally 'a flower to wear in her ear,' alluding to the ancient custom of wearing a single flower of the beautiful and fragrant gardenia in the pierced ear. Hence a husband is designated 'a precious ear-ornament' by the wife. A similarly endearing phrase is used by the husband towards a beloved wife,

Kua karanga ia Kie e,
  I te tauinu para o Marua,
  Kua pipiri tane āna ē !

UNUUNU RUA.

Tiaretiare rautonga ē rautonga ē,
No tai matavaka no Motuaaercroa.
No Motuaaereroa 'i ; tena, e kua kakau
I te tititai : kua rere nui mai e,
  Te moe atura i Teakautu.
  I te tauinu para o Marua,
  Kua pipiri tane āna ē !

UNUUNU TORU.

  E taua tamaine, e tamaine,
  E Tamarua, e Mariki ra,
Kua reuiui reui atu nga taokete ;
Muraai oki tei mavae ia maua,
Kua akarongo i te tara tu,
  I te tauinu para o Marua,
  Kua pipiri tane āna ē !

AKAREINGA.

Ai e ruaoo ē ! E rangai ē !

She delights to address thee, Kie, as
  ' The fair-leaved *tauinu* of Marua,
  So tenderly faithful to thy husband.'

SECOND OFFSHOOT.

Thy loved husband, thy chosen companion,
Travels slowly and painfully along
The rocky shore ; clothed with seaweeds
And wild creepers, he eventually gains
His last hiding-place, the cave Teakautu.
Thou fair-leaved *tauinu* of Marua,
So tenderly faithful to thy husband !

THIRD OFFSHOOT.

My beloved daughters,
  Tamarua and Mariki,[1]
How pleasantly we once all lived together !
Muraai now is separated from me,
Protected by his mother's clan.
Thou fair-leaved *tauinu* of Marua,
So tenderly faithful to thy husband !

FINALE.

Ai e ruaoo ē ! E rangai ē !

TAUAPEPE'S LAMENT FOR ATA.

. **For the same occasion.**

TUMU.

Ka tuku ra nga tama, e Ki, te te metua.
Ei rave ake, e Tegonga e ; akameeria te ivi
To tama kai kino ra, e Ata ē !

PAPA.

Me ka maara rua ē, ei metua tangiia !
Mei e tangi atu, e Ata e, ceuria i te ruru,
Kia karo atu i te metua ka aere ;
  Vai ake te tama urunga ē !

INTRODUCTION.

Go, my sons, to your new parent.
Adopt them, Tetonga. Take to thy bosom
This poor orphan grandson, 'little Ata.'

FOUNDATION.

Cease to grieve for your father, so well beloved.
Yet once more, 'little Ata,' untie the bandages,
And take a last look of love at thy grandfather,
  Ere thou turn homeward in peace.

---

[1] The Mariki in the Introduction was the grandmother of this one ; the former being the mother of Ata-toa, the latter his daughter.

UNUUNU TAI.

Kua tuku i te tama ei te metua, i to
  metua,
Akaurunga reka i te tama ka aere,
E nga tama tangi ei, nga tama tangi ei.
E takipu te manava ē ! Kua tae mai
  te ta rai.
Tena Rongo tatā ē ! Ia taua tipoki
  atu to mata.
Akamoeria te ivi to tama kai kino ra,
  e Ata ē !

FIRST OFFSHOOT.

Go, my sons, to your new parent.
I leave you in safety, beloved children.
Beloved ones, my heart yearns for you
  all.
Terror seizes me ; the slayer is at hand.
Pitiless Rongo approaches to close
  for ever my eyes.
Take to thy bosom this poor orphan
  child, ' little Ata.'

UNUUNU RUA.

Ka urunga te tara vacakauta ia taua.
  Ei kona ra, e tau ariki !
Ka aere koe kimi metua ke atu,
Ei kona ra, e Aro, e Muraai !
Auā e anau ki te metua, e karo atu te
  mata.
E riu ke atu taua, to tama kai kino
  ra, e Ata ē !

SECOND OFFSHOOT.

Rest in the pledge so solemnly given.
  Farewell, dearest child !
  Go seek another parent.
Farewell, Arokapiti and Muraai !
Leave me to my fate. Gaze not on
  my face.
Turn away, my poor orphan grand-
  son, ' little Ata.'

UNUUNU TORU.

Ka unui te o ē i te aerenga,
I te aerenga i te puruki Takinga ē !
  O Ata tangi i te anau ;
Mei tangi i te anau tokoitu rai i te ao,
Nga tama ra e aere ki te titirimoe,
I te akaaraara e ara. Na Rongo-toi-
  maui,
Na Rongo i toi tamaki tamauria i Ma-
  raeara.
Te tama aia e ko te vaaranginui.
Na Takinga akera ko Ata ra i mamao
Ia uti tane au, e Kie, te aroa tangi atu.
  Mei tangi akera, e Mura,
Kua autaa te reo i te tara taiku,
E to ai tuaine Takiakaumu-i-te-vai-ta-
  maki.
E kua tokatua aere te metua.
Ka ngongoro te anau tangata.
Ka ngongoro ana, e Kie, te anau,
Kua pingoi koe ra, e Ata,
E riu ke atu taua, to tama kai kino, e
  Ata ē !

THIRD OFFSHOOT.

Hold on firmly to thy god on thy
  journey—
The journey to the battle, O thou
  father of Takinga !
  Ata weeps for his children—
His seven children living yonder—
As he goes sadly to his last sleep,
He marches forth to meet Rongo,
The war-god Rongo worshipped in
  yon grove,
Ever imperious, the arbiter of destiny.
Takinga and ' little Ata ' are far
  away,
Whilst Kie lovingly bears along her
  husband.
  Grieve not for me, Muraai :
Remember my last solemn charge—
To protect thy sister who watched
  the fight,
And ministered to her outcast father.
Ah ! the children must weep.
Yes, Kie, even thy loved ones will
  weep,
And ' little Ata,' too, will bitterly
  grieve.
Turn away, my poor orphan grandson,
  ' little Ata.'

UNUUNU A.

Ka tuku te tama e vaekauta ia taua.
Naau ake, e Aro, a Muraai, te tama,
   Mei maru ake te tama e aroa,
E tutakiria ia Takinga o Metuaere to
  teina akaui.
Na Rongo-aroa-kai, ko Ata te tuku i
  runga,
Ko Ata te tuku i raro, taumaa atu ia
  Naupata,
Papaaere, Enguengu to tuaine, O
  Mariki ra.
Kua kokou, kua reva te tama korikori,
   Tuku ua mai, e Ata,
E mei roto i te itiki i te akeke,
E aitu tatakina, o Rongo-tatakina-te-
  toa ;
   Tatakina te uru tupu ariki.
Te rangi tuku ki raro. Tei Tukua mai
  Ata ē.
Ei maringi te vai ki Avaiki ; maringi
  mai te vai i Avaiki.
Te tangi nei Takingi ē i tongi paā
  Tokotoko,
Kua rikarika nga tama i te tainga—
   I te metua titiri, e Ata ē !

FOURTH OFFSHOOT.

Go, my son, and rest in the pledge
  so solemnly given.
O Arokapiti, be a parent to Muraai,
  my first-born :
   Lovingly shelter my children,
Remember Takinga, and Matuaere,
  his brother.
Yonder is Rongo-giver-of-food. Ata
  will be hunted
From crag to crag. The father of
  Naupata must die.
Alas for Papaaere, and their sisters
  Enguengu and Mariki !
Who lie huddled up and cling together
  in terror,
   Whilst their father Ata is driven
   out
   Of his strong enclosure,
To become a disfigured corpse, to
  please pitiless Rongo,
   Amid deafening shouts (of
   triumph).
Tukua and Ata, once so great, have
  fallen.
Their blood like water is poured out
  on the ground.
Takinga is weeping, and Tokotoko
  too.
They shudder, my 'little Ata,' to see
The slaughter of their forsaken father !

UNUUNU RIMA.

Vairanga kino ē, tei Okio ē, tei Okio.
Kia pange to metua te vairanga otai ;
E uui paa to toa i te komata toto,
Ei ta paa ia Tukua i te riu koatu,
Kia kapiti i te tama. Ka acre taua i te
  puokia—
Te puku : kake atura i runga i te mau-
  nga tauri.
Kua taparere Tukua ; kua motu te ivi i
  Avaiki.
Motuia ra kia motu. Tatari atu taua.
Taua tei rongo—ko te puipui matangi
Te' kave kura i tai—Auenei, apopo,
  ooku rā,
E tau ariki, e kare ei i te ao,
Karo ake paa, e Mariki e, i te tangi
  paa a te tokotoko,

FIFTH OFFSHOOT.

Sad scene of blood at Okio ; yes, at
  Okio !
Fell father and son in one place,
And thirsty spears drank in their
  life-blood.
In a romantic pile of rocks fell
  Tukua ;
By the side of his brave son was he
  slain,
Death o'ertook both on that mountain
  of safety.
The death of Tukua will ever divide
  the tribe.
Now rend it to fragments. Await
  events.
I hear something—a faint breath of
  wind,
A whisper—To-day or to-morrow.

<table>
<tr><td>

Kua rikarika paa nga tama e,
I te tainga ki te metua titiri, e
Ata ē !

</td><td>

Pet grandson, I cease to gaze on the light of day.
Gaze, Mariki, on the clashing of spears.
Well may the poor children shudder, my 'little Ata,'
At the slaughter of their forsaken father !

</td></tr>
<tr><td>

AKAREINGA.
Ai e ruaoo ē.   E rangai ē !

</td><td>

FINALE.
Ai e ruaoo ē !   E rangai ē !

</td></tr>
</table>

'Little Ata' lived to see better days. When the Gospel was first introduced in 1823 he was a young man. In 1840 Muraai died, and 'little Ata'—then about forty years of age, and father of a family—became chief of Keia. In rank he came next to the king, and for many years acted as chief judge. Ata was of a remarkably humble and gentle disposition, and yet he could be firm as a rock when duty dictated. I never knew him to be guilty of a mean or a wrong action; indeed, he was always scrupulously careful not to bring the faintest slur upon his Christian profession.

CHAPTER XXXIX

A DIRGE FOR TUKUA AND ATA-TOA

(Accompanied by the harmonicon and drums)

By Tangataroa, son of Ata-toa, *circa* A.D. 1817

Tera !—	Now !—
Tutangoria ïa kopu ka aere ē !	Go root up this family—
Kuriki ē ! kuriki ē !	Utterly, ay, utterly !
Te pakupaku a miri,	(List to) the trampling of feet—
Te pakupaku a miri, a miri !	To the trampling of feet yonder.
O Ata e, apopo a titiri.	To-morrow, Ata, thou must die !
Mokopuna te amo i te aitu.	Mokopuna bears the corpse.
Ka ia ruru apopo ?	How many more to-morrow ?
Tai kura tu no korua.	'Twas no fair open fight.
Kua ta Kaunio, kua ta tai vaka.	Kaunio smote and crushed his foes.
Oi Avaiki teia Rongo ē !	Rongo has come up out of Avaiki.
Kua tu i miri.	(Ata) makes a brave stand ;
Tu e tu ka aere ē !	Though brave, he must die.
Te ui mai na Rongo ē,	Rongo demands of each
Tai okiri, tai korare,	A spear and a club,
Tai okiri, tai korare ;	A spear and a club ;
Tai naau peiaa ē,	An army longing to fight,
Tai naau peiaa ē !	An army longing to fight.
Tai okiri oki ē,	Each now wields a spear.
Ka tu ē ka puruki.	Lead on to the attack.
E tu, e Rongo, e tukatakata ;	O Rongo, arise, laugh heartily !
E tu, e Rongo, e tukatakata.	O Rongo, arise, laugh heartily !
Taūna aea tai o tukatakata na.	This work of slaughter is thy delight.
Tingiri—ringiri.	
Rangara—rangara rā takiri.	} Harmonicons and drums only.
Rangirira tatangaa.	
E popo ta i miri ;	A wooden sword for the battle ;
E popo ta i te tangata.	A wooden sword to slay warriors ;

U

Popo taia atu na ;
Kauariki i te toē.

 A sword that has often been proved ;
 To transfix the foe.

Anangirira tatangaa.

 Harmonicons and drums only.

Kutu mai te ta i miri ē !
Kutu mai te ta i miri ē !
Kutu mai te ta.
I karuru te ruru i tiria,
Pururu atu na i raro ē !
Ei papa one i au ei.

 War weapons are clashing.
 War weapons are clashing.
 'Tis the crash of battle.
 Bind up the slain for burial—
 To be hurled down some deep chasm,
 To rot and mingle with the soil.

Tikiriki, etc.

 Harmonicons and drums only.

Titiara kokopu e, maua e,
Kikaoa a tua te utu i Rangiue,
Kua riri koe nei, e Rongo,
Vāvaiia te upoko ē !
E kutu ana Tane ē !
E kutu ana, e reru ana,
E tu ana i te aiti puruki aere.
Kua pau maira i te mate,
Viri ake te kiore,
Ina kokopu e, Ina ō ![2]
Te ngurengure kiore ;
Te ngurengure kiore.

 We are like the fish on the hook ;
 Cut down like a stately *utu*[1] at Rangiue.
 Art thou very wroth, O Rongo ?
 Split open yon skulls.
 Fight bravely, O tribe of Tanè !
 Fight on ; beat them down.
 In that narrow space fight it out,
 Until the last be destroyed,
 Like rats in a snare,
 As Ina's fish in a net.
 The rats (*i.e.* men) are squeaking,
 The rats (*i.e.* men) are dying.

Tingiri—ringiri.
Rangara—rangara rā takiri,
Anangirira tatangaa.

 Harmonicons and drums only.

Ana taia ora Tukua.
Taia ora Tukua,
Aitoa koe ia mate,
Ia tiria i te rua nui no Akaotu,[3]
I te rua nui no Akaotu,
Oa tangi to upoko,
Kutu i te rangi a ta ē !
Viri ake te ina i raro ;—
Viri ake te ina i raro.

 Scatter the brains of Tukua,
 Spare not the aged Tukua.
 Ha ! thou must die—
 Must be thrown down the terrible chasm—
 That dark chasm, the grave of the slain.
 The club resounds against thy skull,
 Like thunder. He falls !
 Thy white locks are scattered about ;
 Ay, thy white locks are scattered about.

---

[1] The *utu* is the *Barringtonia speciosa*. This is a covert reference to the extinction of the Tekama clan at Rangiue some centuries ago.

[2] An allusion to the pretty myth of Ina. See *Myths and Songs,* Chapter VI.

[3] Akaotu = 'Terrible,' a name applied to Auraka, one of the grand repositories of the dead.

<table>
<tr><td>

O na tai atu i Tuakiva.
Te ngaoro, te ngaoro.
Tu ka aere e miri ē !
Mau takitai ua i te araa,
Ei tautipitipi na Arepee
I te tāei a titi ē !
Kua ora paa Nguare ;
Kua ora paa Nguare.

</td><td>

(Ata-toa) was borne over the cliffs
To a level grassy spot ;—
But still hunted by his foes,
Each armed with a war-club,
To smite him like Arepee (of old) ;
Or like a defenceless bird (= *titi* [1]).
Yet one escaped the fight ;—
'Twas Nguare [2] who escaped.

</td></tr>
<tr><td>

Tikirangiti—ngitingiti.

</td><td>

Harmonicons and drums only.

</td></tr>
</table>

This species of song is called an *eke* = 'descent ;' because it refers to the descent of friends to the spirit-world, and of their bodies to the grave. Despite this, they believed that the spirits of the slain eventually attained to the warriors' paradise above.

The alliterative sounds produced at intervals by the harmonicons and drums are, though very remarkable, destitute of meaning. The object evidently is to make the instruments 'speak.' Thus *takiri* must not be taken for the word meaning 'entirely ;' although the coincidence of sound is singular. The fascination for the native ear is great. Our own 'Fal, lal, lah' is meaningless.

---

[1] The particular bird in the native is the *titi*, which is easily deceived by an imitation of its cry, and is then caught by the hand.

[2] Nguare was a relative of Ata who escaped at the battle of Akaoro. This was intended as a compliment to that branch of the family who were present at the performance of this dirge.

CHAPTER XL.

A COMPLETE LIST OF BATTLES FOUGHT ON MANGAIA.

Place where fought.	Victor and consequent real 'Lord of Mangaia."	Tribe defeated.	Priests of Motoro in Order of Succession.	Remarks.	Recognized 'Lord of Mangaia.'
1. Teruanonianga, in Keia	Rangi	Tongan colony	Papaaunuku	...	Rangi.
2 Tangikura, in Veitatei	Rangi and Tamatapu	Tribe of Tanè	,,	Touriitepitokura fled to the rocks. 140 slain	Teakatauira.
3. Raumatangi, at Tamarua	Mokē	Raratongans under Kateateoru	,,	...	Vaeruarangi.
4. Iotepui, at Tevaenga	Amū	Aitutakians under Toapini and Toarere	Vara	...	Teinaovātea.
5. Ikuruākā, in Keia	Tiaio	Atiuans under Matatia	,,	...	Tiaio.
6. Parainui, at Karanga	Tirango	Tekama tribe	Terau	...	A member of the tribe of Ngariki, name unknown.
7. *First* oven of men at Tutaeuū Putoa	Ungakute	Teaitu, *i.e.* Tanè	,,	...	Ungakute.

8. Rangiue, at Ivirua	Tirango	Tekama tribe	,,	*Circa* A.D. 1570	A member of the tribe of Ngariki, name unknown.
9. Areutu, at Ivirua	,,	,,	,,	Autea offends his lord	,,
10. *Second* oven of men at Angaitu, in Tevaenga	Kaveutu	Teaitu, *i.e.* Tane	,,	*Circa* A.D. 1600	Kaveutu.
11. Vaikakau, *i.e.* Ma-ungarua, in Vei-tatei	Ruaika	Tirango and the Tongan tribe	,,	Tirango slain	Tenau.
12. Taaonga, in Veita-tei, at the Tui-tui	One	Ruaika	,,	...	One.
13. Kumekume, in Vei-tatei	One and Panako	Vete and his tribe of Vairuarangi	,,	...	Panako I.
14. Kouramaiti, in Vei-tatei	One	Mokora and Tekama	,,	...	,, II.
15. Tepapa, in Veitatei	One	Kotaa and Tekama	Packe	Tauai and Tekaraka exiled	Panako III.
16. Teruakeretonga, in Karanga	Ngauta	Ruaika	,,	The original Mautara turned cannibal, and fled to the rocks at Ivirua	Ngauta I.
17. Arakoa, in Keia	,,	Tata and Panako	,,	Panako slain	,, II. Taia nominally en-joyed the dignity.
18. Auruia, in Teva-enga	,,	Maruataiti and tribe of Teipe	,,	...	Ngauta III.
19. Iotepui, at Teva-enga	,,	Motuoro and Akata-uira tribe	Akunu-kunu	...	,, IV.
20. Punanga, at Ta-marua	,,	Tiauru and Tuma tribe	,,	Kauate and Reketia fly to the rocks. They fall in with and eat the original Mautara. 100 warriors slain	,, V.
21. Teruanonianga, at Keia	,,	Ngariki	,,	...	,, VI.

A COMPLETE LIST OF BATTLES FOUGHT ON MANGAIA—*continued*.

Place where fought.	Victor and consequent real 'Lord of Mangaia.'	Tribe defeated.	Priests of Motoro in Order of Succession.	Remarks.	Recognized 'Lord of Mangaia.'
22. Ikuari, in Keia	Ngauta	Arepee and tribe of Teipe	Akunu-kunu	*Circa* A.D. 1666	Terea, by consent of Ngauta.
23. Each - slave - slew his - own - master throughout the island, the same night	Ngangati	Ngauta and the flower of the Ton-gan tribe	Mautara	*Circa* A.D. 1670. Iro and his clan expelled	Tuanui, by consent of Ngangati.
24. Māueue, at Ta-marua	Tauii	Arekare and his clan	,,	Rori fled. 60 warriors slain	Tauii.
25. Ariki, in Veitatei (1st)	Ngangati	Namu and his Va-eruarangi	,,	Tangaka feasts on the slain after this battle and the four succeeding engagements	Ngangati I.
26. Ariki, in Veitatei (2nd)	,,	Tribe of Tangiia	,,	This battle was fought on the third day after the preceding one	,, II.
27. Ariki, in Veitatei (3rd)	,,	Tribe of Kanae	,,	...	,, III.
28. Teaupapa (1st)	,,	Kotuku (father of Ngauta) and Ton-gan tribe	,,	...	,, IV.
29. ,, (2nd)	,,	Kaoa and his Vae-ruarangi	,,	Namu fled to the rocks. 80 warriors slain	,, V.
30. Auā, in Keia (mid-night surprise)	Akatara	Ngangati and his tribe	,,	...	Akatara.
31. Tāpātiu (daylight surprise)	Sons of Mautara	Akatara	,,	...	No chief declared.

32. Arirā, at Ivirua	Teuanuku	Tuōkura and Teipe	Mautara	Ruanae, etc., fly to the rocks and turn cannibals. Kaiara flies to the rocks	Teuanuku I. No drum of peace beaten.
33. Pukuotoi, at Tamarua	,,	Ruanae and his cannibal clan	,,	Vaiaa saved. Kaiara and Tavero saved, after spending two years in the rocks	Teuanuku II. Drum of peace beaten.
34. Auā, in Keia	Mautara	Rāei and his clan	,,	Rori saved by Manaune. Namu saved by Mautara	Mautara (25 years).
35. Tuopapa, in Teva-enga	Uarau	Amai clan	Ngarā	...	Uarau first, then Ngarā
36. Teopu, in Karanga	Kirikovi	Tongia and Tongan clan	Tekā	Captain Cook touched at Mangaia in 1777. The woman Ike offered to Rongo in sacrifice	
37. Taukuara, in Keia	Paī	Kirikovi and his divided clan	,,	...	Paī.
38. Akaoro, in Keia	Potiki	Potai slain ; clan Ngariki	,,	*Circa* A.D. 1787	Potiki.
N.B.—Marokore seized the government, after presenting the needful human sacrifice.			Makitaka	...	Marokore.
39. Teatuapai, at Ivirua	Koroa	Marokore slain ; one section of the priestly clan	,,	...	Koroa.
40. Rangiura, in Vei-tatei	Makitaka	Koroa slain ; other section of the priestly clan	,,	Reigned three years	Makitaka.
N.B.—Temporal lordship peaceably transferred to Pangemiro after offering Teata to Rongo as sacrifice.			,,	Reigned seven years	Pangemiro I. A.D. 1814.
41. Araeva, in Keia	Pangemiro	Tukua and Makitaka, *i.e.* the whole priestly clan of Mautara	,,	Second reign of three years	Pangemiro II.
42. Putoa, at Tamarua	Numanga-tini	Tereavai and the heathen	,,	Fought on February, 1828	Numangatini

CHAPTER XLI

THE PRIESTHOOD

SUCCESSION OF THE PRIESTS[1] OF MOTORO (= TE ARA
PIA O NGARIKI).

1. Papaaunuku, from Avaiki.
2. Vara.
3. Terau.
4. Packe; slain by Ngauta at Keia.
5. Akunukunu; slain by Ngautu at Veitatei.
6. Mautara.
7. Ngarā, youngest son[2] of Mautara.
8. Tekā.
9. Makitaka.   Died in 1830: professed Christianity.

SUCCESSION OF THE PRIESTS[3] OF TANE (= TE ARA
PIA O TANÈ).

1. Turuia, from Iti (= Tahiti); slain by Tamatapu.
2. Mouna.

---

[1] All these, except the two indicated, died natural deaths at extreme old
age. Sometimes a tenth priest, Tereavai, is named. But the truth is,
Tereavai was never invested with the priesthood of Motoro, as at the time of
Makitaka's death Christianity was altogether in the ascendant. Tereavai was
the last priest of the shark-god Tiaio. He died in 1865.

[2] The succession was from father to son.

[3] The first five priests were worshippers of that unpopular but feared deity
Tanè-ngaki-au. The last four were priests of Tanè-i-te-ata, *i.e.* Tanè-kio,
regularly descended from Terangai, who came from Iti (= Tahiti).

3. Matariki ; offered in sacrifice to Rongo, at Ariki.

4. Tiora ; offered in sacrifice to Rongo, at Ariki.

5. Tepunga ; offered in sacrifice by Tuanui, at Tamarua.

6. Tevaki ; saved by Mautara, priest of Motoro.

7. Tacimua (*i.e.* Kakari).

8. Vackura.

9. Pangeivi (= Erekaa).   Died in 1830, a Christian.

SUCCESSION OF THE PRIESTS[1] OF TURANGA (= TE ARA PIA O TONGAITI).

1. Teaō, from Tonga : time of Rangi.

2. Tāmakeu : time of Teakatauera.

3. Ivi : time of Mokoiro, *i.e.* Vaeruarangi.

4. Tirango : slain at Angamoa.

5. Tamangaro ; driven, with his friends, off the island.

6. Moa.

7. Ngangaru ; slain by Ngangati at Tamarua.

8. Pārae (whom Potai vainly sought to kill).

9. Teā, *i.e.* Poa.

10. Ivi.

11. Māucue.   Died in 1828, a heathen.

The above is a correct list of the three principal orders of priests on Mangaia, from the date of the first settlement on it until the subversion of idolatry.   There cannot be any material error in the list, as I derived it from the proper depositaries of such knowledge.   The three orders fairly tally, the priests of Motoro ever taking the proud pre-eminence due to their superior rank in heathen society. When Captain Cook visited the island in 1777 Ngarā had been dead some three years.

[1] All descended from Teaō (*i.e.* The Man of the Long String. See *Myths and Songs*, p. 287, note), who came from Tonga. The two last priests, however, were in the *female* line from Teā, eighth priest of Turanga.

LINEAL SUCCESSION OF THE 'RULERS OF FOOD,' FROM AVAIKI DOWN TO 1829 OR 1830 (= TE PA ARIKI NO TE TAPORA KAI).

1. Mokoiro, from Avaiki ; buried at Rangikapua.
2. Mokoiro ; died a natural death, and buried at Karorā.
3. Amū.
4. Maru.
5. Kaoa ; drowned at Teruavaaroa.
6. Namu ; slain by Ngauta, at Te-uma-tuna.
7. Kaoa ; slain by Ngangati, at Teaupapa.
8. Motau.
9. Namu ; the friend of Mautara, slain by Potai.
10. Kaoa ; held office during the sway of Potiki.
11. Metuarangiia.
12. Mauri ;[1] visited by the Rev. J. Williams in 1829, but died soon after without accepting Christianity.

It seems to me that a comparison of this list with the three preceding ones irresistibly leads to the conclusion that the island had been populated only some five or six centuries.[2] The list of kings proper is disputed ; but the most accurate list obtainable contains only twelve names, from the days of Rangi down to the reign of the present worthy king Numangatini (1874).

KINGS OF THE ISLAND OF MANGAIA.

The sign of installation of the kings of Mangaia was to be formally seated by the temporal lord, in the presence of the leading under-chiefs, upon 'the sacred sandstone' (*te kea inamoa*) in Rongo's *marae* (O-Rongo) on the sea-shore

---

[1] The connection in each case was that of father and son. This remarkable list is undisputed, and was given me by Kouvi, the brother of Mauri. Many old men that I knew at Mangaia in 1852 were well acquainted with Kaoa, who lived to a very advanced age.

[2] See in pp. 627–637 of vol. ii. of *Australasian Association for the Advancement of Science*, a paper on this subject by myself.

facing the setting sun. This was *their* equivalent of our coronation in Westminster Abbey. The special duty of a king was by rhythmical prayers[1] to Great Rongo to keep away evil-minded spirits (*pa tuarangi*) that might injure the island. For this end the principal king[2] (*te ariki pa uta*) lived in the interior, in the midst of abundance, in the sacred district of Keia. His prayers were supposed to keep away bad spirits coming from the *east*. On the barren sea-shore, at O-Rongo, lived the secondary king (*te ariki pa tai*), who kept away bad spirits coming from the *west*. Besides this primary ghostly function, many other important duties devolved upon these royal personages.[3]

I derived the following lists many years ago from my late valued friend King Numangatini. They are the most accurate now obtainable ; some points, however, are disputed. The kingly office was hereditary ; nevertheless, the installation rested with ' the lord of Mangaia ' for the time being. Thus a father *might* be set aside in favour of his eldest son, or one brother in favour of another ; still, it must be the same blood divine (as it was believed to be). The *shore* king was not unfrequently a natural son of a great *interior* king. All kings were *ex-officio* high priests of Rongo (*ara pia o Rongo*), tutelar god of Mangaia.

Succession of Kings defending the Interior (= Te au ariki pa uta).

1. Rangi = Sky.
2. Te-akatauira-ariki = The-arrived-king.
3. Te-mata-o-Tangaroa = The-face-of-Tangaroa.
4. Te-upoku-rau = Two-hundred-heads.

[1] Of great antiquity.

[2] Also called ' the praying king ' (*te ariki karakia*). The real authority was vested in him, as he alone could select human sacrifices, appoint feasts, etc., etc.

[3] See *Myths and Songs*, p. 293, etc.

5. Ruaika I. = Fish-hole I.; slain by Ngauta, when for the first time 'lord of Mangaia.'
6. Rau-ue = Gourd-leaf. Son of the shore-king Vae-ruarau. The drum of peace for the last (*i.e.* the seventh) 'lordship' of Ngauta (enjoyed by Terea) was beaten by Rau-ue over the body of Inangaro.
7. Poa-iti = Small-scale (of fish); reigned in the days of Ngangati.
8. Te-ao I. = Day I.; reigned in the days of Mautara.
9. Rua-ika II. = Fish-hole II.
10. Te-tipi = The-cutting, *i.e.* the slaughtering.
11. Te-ao II. = Day II. Died A.D. 1829. Professed Christianity.
12. Nu-manga-tini = Palm-of-many-branches (purely allegorical). Reigned from A.D. 1821 till his lamented death in 1877.
13 and 14. Ioane Terego (son) and Davida-iti (grandson) of Numangatini rule conjointly now, under the protection of the British flag.

SUCCESSION OF KINGS DEFENDING THE SHORE (= TE AU ARIKI PA TAI).

1. Tui = Sew; from Rarotonga.
2. Tama-tapu = Sacred-son; son of preceding. Some say Te-pa = The Defender, born on the 'sacred sandstone.'
3. Vari = Beginning. Vari was sister to Te-pa.
4. Puanga = Budding (a female).
5. Vaeruarau = Two-hundred-spirits; son of preceding. Deified after his violent death. His son Rau-ue appointed principal king of Mangaia.
6. Ito = The-ancient; slain and eaten by his hereditary enemies in Mautara's time.

7. Kaiau-paku = Kingly-office-holder-the-elder ; also called Tuki-rangi = Sky-striker. Son of Ito.
8. Te-nio-pakari = The-strong-toothed. Son of Ito.
9. Kanune. Son of Te-nio-pakari. Lived in the days of Mautara. Slain by Raumea.
10. Te-akatau-ira. Son of Kanune.
11. Teivirau = Two-hundred-bones (*i.e.* relatives) ; drowned at sea when in chase of Paoa.
12. Kaiau II. = Kingly-office-holder II.
13. Numangatini ; appointed by Pangemiro in A.D. 1814. When, in 1821, Teao was deposed, he became sole king of Mangaia. The final word and collective kingly authority were then vested by the conquering chiefs in Numangatini alone.

Even the shore-king, although second to the interior king, when once formally installed at O-Rongo on 'the sacred sandstone,' was so sacred in the eyes of men of past generations that even 'the lord of Mangaia' approached him, after his attendants had deposited his offering, *crawling on all fours!* Yet, strangely enough, when the charm of peace had been destroyed by the shedding of human blood, this sacredness disappeared, and he returned to his ancestral lands in the interior. Some authorities omit the seventh in the list of shore-kings (Kaiau-paku).

May I remind all students of these pages of the *un*-wisdom of laying too great stress upon the meaning of names. In mythology nothing is more important; but in history (which this undoubtedly is) nothing is more misleading.

TABLE OF GENERATIONS FOR THE HERVEY GROUP.

	I. Rarotonga:	II. Mangaia.	III. Aitutaki.	IV. Atiu, Mauke, Mitiaro.
Parent	Metua	Metua	Metua	Metua.
Child	Tamaiti	Tamaiti	Tamaiti	Tamaiti.
Grandchild	Utaro [1]	Mokopuna-mua	Mokopuna	Mokopuna.
Great-grandchild	Mokopuna-mua [2]	Mokopuna-rua	Mokotua-mua	Mokotua-mua.
Great-great-grand-child	Mokopuna-rua	Mokopuna-toru	Mokotua-rua	Mokotua-rua.
Great-great-great-grandchild	Mokopuna-toru	Mokopuna-ā	Mokotua-toru	Mokotua-toru.
etc., etc.	etc., etc.	etc., etc.	etc., etc.	etc., etc.

Reckoning backwards, we have for the entire group simply the following :—

		Literal translation.
Parent	Metua	*i.e.* Parent.
Grandparent	Tupuna mua ; or, simply Tupuna [3]	*i.e.* First ancestor ; or ancestor.
Great-grandparent	Tupuna rua	*i.e.* Second ancestor.
Great-great-grand-parent	Tupuna toru	*i.e.* Third ancestor.
Great-great-great-grandparent	Tupuna ā	*i.e.* Fourth ancestor.
etc., etc.	etc., etc.	etc., etc.

Nothing could be simpler or more accurate than their mode of counting past generations. This table, with the needful dialectic variations, will stand, I believe, for the entire Polynesian race.

[1] At Rarotonga *utaro* is a *real* 'grandchild;' whilst at Aitutaki it is simply an *adopted* child, or literally 'a child whose food is (chewed or beaten) *taro*,' in lieu of its mother's milk. Still there is a real agreement underneath, as almost universally the custom obtains for the grandparents to bring up one or more of their grandchildren as their own. Thus Koroa-iti (my worthy co-pastor) was brought up by his grandparents. *He alone was allowed to eat with the renowned warrior Koroa,* dipping his morsel in the same cup of salt water or rich fish-sauce.

[2] *Mua, rua, toru,* etc., are merely the ordinal numerals, which may be extended indefinitely.

[3] The word *tupuna* comes from *tupu* = 'to grow,' and *ana* (shortened for euphony into *na*) = 'before.'

PART II—LIGHT

HOW CHRISTIANITY WAS INTRODUCED INTO MANGAIA

ISLAND OF MANGAIA.

CHAPTER I

ON the morning of March 29, 1777, the natives of Mangaia were startled by the apparition of a 'mighty canoe,[1] without paddles or outrigger,' but rapidly approaching the southern coast as if possessed of life. By the time it reached the lee of the island, numbers of armed men had made their way to the outer edge of the reef, and gazed at this seeming monster of the deep with admiration and terror. The famous warrior Potai remarked, 'This is unquestionably a visitor from the spirit-world.' Another chief oracularly declared that 'it was the great (god) Motoro himself come up from paying a visit to Vātea.'

After some natural hesitation, Mourua and his friend Makatu, both worshippers of Motoro, launched a canoe and approached the huge visitor that had successfully 'pierced the solid blue vault.' The gift of a string of large blue beads (afterwards shown about as veritable chips off the azure arch), and a few nails (subsequently converted into bradawls), rewarded their daring. The boat of the Resolution rowed along the reef in the vain hope of finding a landing-place. Mourua without hesitation jumped into the boat, and receiving from Captain Cook

---

[1] Only one ship is mentioned in tradition, whereas the Resolution and Discovery visited Mangaia.

a large knife, stuck it in his right ear—the pocket of those days. He was thus sketched by an artist connected with the expedition.

Numbers of natives now took courage, swam off to the boat, and received gifts from the great navigator. To Kirikovi, the then temporal lord of Mangaia, was presented an iron axe, the first ever seen on the island. A general scrimmage now took place ; but Captain Cook, with great forbearance, after permitting these unceremonious fellows to 'possess themselves of all he could spare, returned to the Resolution, accompanied only by Mourua, who deemed himself wonderfully brave in venturing on board. This he would not have done but for the assurances of Mai (the Omai of the *Voyages*) that he would be perfectly safe. Much to his satisfaction, Mourua was eventually brought back to the reef in the ship's boat. He swam ashore, and related to his admiring countrymen the wonders he had seen ; whilst Cook sailed on to Atiu, which lies about one hundred miles north of Mangaia. An important step had thus been taken in civilization : they had become acquainted with the existence of a race different from all that they had hitherto seen or heard of, wiser, stronger, and more benevolent than themselves.

At the beginning of the present century, an English whaling ship, name unknown, touched at Mangaia. Emboldened by the profitable intercourse of their fathers with Captain Cook, several canoes at once pushed off to the ship. A brisk traffic was for some time carried on ; but no native was allowed to board the ship. A chief named Koroa had just concluded a splendid bargain in exchanging a fine octopus for a knife and a tenpenny nail, when a wild fellow called Tairoa paddled up in his canoe, and, watching his opportunity, mortally speared a white man who was

holding on to the ship's iron braces, and amusing himself
with the scene. Highly satisfied with his valour, Tairoa
paddled back to what he considered a safe distance, and
watched the confusion on board the vessel. A long
bamboo (as it appeared to the natives) was pointed at the
aggressor, who did not dream of danger. An unaccountable
light and noise issued from this hitherto unknown weapon,
and Tairoa fell lifeless at the bottom of his canoe.

All now was consternation amongst the natives.
Ngaunui proposed to Koroa to rescue the body of the
slain ; but Koroa wisely refused to interfere, and cursed [1]
Tairoa for having spoiled the traffic. Ngaunui persisted
in attempting to get the corpse, when a few swan shot in
his shoulders induced him to retire with all convenient
speed. A boat was now lowered, the crew of which took
possession of Tairoa's lifeless body and his canoe. All
being drawn upon deck, the captain made haste to leave
this inhospitable island.

A sister of Tairoa commemorated this incident in the
following lines :

Kua kite uā Tairoa ē	Weep for Tairoa, who first fell
I te māro i te tokotoko a to te pai.	By the weapon of the white man.
I aa' i koe, e Tai e,	By what mysterious means
I kakina naia iko roa ia tai ?	Wast thou hit far off on the sea ?
Akaruke atu, e Koroa e !	Thy body was abandoned by Koroa,
Akaruke atu ia Tai e !	Was left in the hands of thy foes.
Vairanga mamao e !	How distant thy resting-place !
Vairanga iko roa e !	Far away on the wild ocean
Vairanga ia Tai.	Is thy grave, O Tairoa !
Akaruke atu oia ua,	Utterly left alone ;—
Kua oro te mataati.	The cowards all fled.
Kua pou te puruki—	The fight was soon over—
E puruki ia tai ē !	The sad contest on the waves
E ta 'i ia Tai ē !	When Tairoa perished !

---

[1] 'May Tairoa's head be cooked for my wife's supper !'

About 1814, when Makitaka was lord of Mangaia, and a terrible famine prevailed over the island, another whaler arrived—the third vessel they had seen. The weather was remarkably fine. The captain, wishing to see something of the island, landed with a companion. The names of the two white men who first landed on Mangaia are unknown. They crossed the reef, and walked in quiet over part of the ground now occupied by the mission premises. Very unwisely one of them displayed a fine pearl oyster shell. A rush was made by the natives to get possession of this wonderful treasure. The fortunate thief was himself chased into the interior by scores of envious countrymen. With this magnificent ornament dangling from his neck, he would be sure to carry the palm at the festive dances. The white men, alarmed for their own safety, fired repeatedly, though without effect, upon the retreating natives. Recollecting the fate of Tairoa, the natives disappeared in the thick bush then growing to the water's edge, whilst their white visitors hastily took their departure.

The next vessel that touched at the island was a schooner, having on board the lamented missionary Williams. This was in 1823. Papehia, Taua, and Haavi, with the wives of the two latter, were landed as the first evangelists of Mangaia. But the very rough treatment they at once experienced induced the five to swim back through the surf to the ship's boat. Their escape in safety was owing to Mr. Williams ordering a charge of powder to be fired from the ship to frighten the heathen, who were plainly intent on killing the men and taking possession of the women. All their property was stolen.

In 1852 good old Haavi revisited Mangaia; and in an address delivered to a most crowded congregation, he touchingly contrasted the savageness and wretchedness of 1823 with the pleasant and Christian aspect of the villagers before him. Many were affected to tears by his remarks, for not a few of their number had taken part in the attack upon these humble servants of God.

Mr. Williams left behind him a valuable souvenir in the shape of a couple of pigs.[1] The boar was named Tauiti, 'Little Pet'; the sow Makave, 'Ringlet.' They were gravely conducted to the *marae* of the war-god as foreign divinities. They were wrapped in sacred white[2] tapa, and the best of food set before them day by day. But the speech of these divinities was a great mystery. From their grunting about the *marae* the Mangaians derive the proverb, *Ua aue nga atua,* 'the gods are crying.' Eventually the filthy habits of these foreign animals made the heathen suspect that they were no gods after all. The finest of the first litter was solemnly offered to Rongo in lieu of a human victim. Great was the indignation of some of the chiefs, in after times, at discovering that a mere *rat* (pig) had been presented to the tutelar god of Mangaia instead of a man !

After the departure of the teachers, their little property and books were used as ornaments for the night dances. Nobody suspected that the printed characters had a signification, the islanders regarding them as ingenious cloth-patterns. But soon after dysentery—hitherto unknown —decimated the population. The heathen very naturally referred this scourge to the anger of the visitors' God on account of the ill-usage His followers had experienced at their hands. A vow was registered that, should He ever

---

[1] Soon after our landing in 1852 a grand feast was held, when upwards of a thousand hogs were killed and eaten.

[2] The gods, and also the priests when on duty, were invariably clothed in white garments (*tikoru*).

deign to send messengers again to their shores, they should be duly protected from insult and injury. The leaves of books, which had been worked up into head-dresses, and strips of calico, once the garments of the teachers and their wives, were carefully collected, and thrown down the deep chasms where they were accustomed to bury their dead, hoping that the scourge would disappear with these things.

On June 15, 1824, their sincerity was put to the test. Two members of the church of Tahaa—Davida and Tiere—were landed on Mangaia by Messrs. Tyerman and Bennet on their voyage to Sydney. With the Tahitian New Testament wrapped up in their shirts, and secured to the top of their heads, these intrepid men leaped into the surf, and swam ashore in the presence of many hundreds of heathen. As Davida's feet touched the reef a long spear was thrust at him by a warrior, who exultingly shouted, 'Thou shalt never catch sharks,' meaning that the new God should never win victories on Mangaia. Providentially, the present king of the island—then a young man—was standing close behind the intending murderer, and at the very moment the lunge was being made arrested the weapon.

These humble evangelists landed on the reef, and were at once *literally* taken by the hand by Numangatini, the king, and conducted to his own sea-side *marae*, dedicated to Rongo, so as to invest their persons with a sacred character. The crowd dared not follow. After a brief rest the king led them to the interior, where his ordinary residence was. All this had been pre-arranged between the king and principal chiefs, as the schooner had been recognized on the previous evening as 'God's ship.' The carrying out of their wishes was entrusted to the king and his warlike friend Maungaati, who showed the strangers great kindness.

A feast was prepared for the teachers. The crowd was surprised that the strangers should close their eyes and pray before eating. On this well-remembered occasion the following colloquy occurred between the heathen and their new teachers :

'What are you doing ? '—'Thanking God for His gifts.'

'Where does your God live ? '—'In heaven.'

'What is His name ? '—' Jehovah.'

'Does your God eat food ? '—'God is a Spirit. He is not like us ; He lives for ever. It was He that made the earth, the sky, the sea, and all things. He made us.'

The people were astounded at these simple truths. After a pause they inquired—

' Has this God a wife ? '—' No.'

'Whence, then, came mankind ? '—'Out of the earth fashioned by God. He breathed into him, and he became a living man such as we are.'

At this the crowd laughed outright, for to their dark minds this account of the creation of man seemed absurd.[1] They loudly exclaimed, ' You are liars ! ' The teachers persisted that they only spoke the truth.

'What was the name of the man who was made ? '—'Adam : we are all his children.'

' Had Adam a wife ? '—' Yes.'

'Who were *her* parents ? '—' She had none.'

'Then how did she come into existence ? '—' She was formed out of Adam ; a rib was taken out of his side, and made by God into a woman.'

The heathen multitude laughed immoderately at this, and wanted to know whether Adam was not much hurt, etc.

[1] The natives mostly claim Divine descent.

They next inquired *why* they came to Mangaia. 'We come to make known to you the true God Jehovah, and His Son Jesus our Saviour.'

Amongst other things Davida remarked that all who believe in Jesus will go to heaven (sky).

The heathen said, 'Are there people there?'[1]—'Yes, good angels and the spirits of the good.'

'Ah! the flames from the oven of Miru will burn them all up.'

A reed house was now built for the use of the teachers; and a rude hut for worship and daily teaching. The site was the enclosure where human sacrifices were first exposed.

Very diligently did Davida and Tiere labour to instruct the younger men in the mysteries of book-learning, and all who would attend in the first principles of Christianity. Nor were their efforts vain, for numbers came from all parts of the island to hear the wonderful words that fell from the lips of these devoted evangelists. After several months two warriors, Metuaarutoa and Rongoinga, came to have their long hair[2] (so much prized by the heathen) cut off, in token of their having renounced the ancient worship. Soon one and another came and submitted to Christianity.

At length Davida found himself strong enough to form a Christian village near the sea, where a good site could easily be obtained for the erection of a larger church and school-house. This had been originally suggested by the Rev. J. Williams. The new village was called 'God's town.' At that period its rocky shore was covered with

---

[1] This was in the spirit of jesting; for *they* believed 'the sky' to be inhabited.

[2] In heathen times the women wore short hair (not parted in front); the men very long hair done up in a knot.

large ironwood and other trees. It was the custom of the early converts, like Nathanael of old, to retire at midday to the seclusion of these trees to pray—each having his own particular tree.

Now, for the first time, husband and wife ate together at meals, and parents tasted food with their firstborn. The oppressive restriction thus broken through had prevailed throughout the South-Sea Islands, although no better reason could be assigned for it than that 'such was the will of the gods.'

In September, 1825, Mr. Bourne, the pastor of Davida and Tiere, visited Mangaia, and was much pleased with the striking change so speedily brought about by the blessing of God. 'The natives laid hold of his hands, and examined curiously to see whether they were verily made of flesh and blood. When, to gratify their curiosity, he turned up his sleeve, they were startled at the whiteness of his skin, and one of them cried out that he must be a great king, or he would never have been of that complexion.'

Not long afterwards—in 1826—Tiere passed away to his rest and reward, so that Davida was left to labour alone for some years. Tiere was a man of amiable disposition and winning manners.

Opposite to the *marae* of Motoro and the altar for human sacrifice was the idol-house, known as 'The-prop-of-the-kingdom' (*Te kaiara*). Inside were the principal gods of Mangaia, which, with the exception of Rongo and Teipe, all consisted of rude representations of the human form carved in ironwood by Rori about one hundred and eighty-five years ago. They were as follows:—

1. RONGO = 'The Resounder.' Tutelar god of Mangaia, dwelling in the shades, and feeding exclusively on mankind. His

chief representative was a triton shell, used only by the king, and deposited at the entrance. It is now preserved in the London Missionary Society case at the British Museum. A block of stone, shaped like a man, and covered with cloth and coarse sacrifice-nets, was set up at his *marae* O-Rongo for the convenience of worship and sacrifice ; where also stood a smaller image named Little Rongo, or ' Rongo-of-the-red-tongue.'

2. *Motoro ;* proudly called *te io ora* = ' living-god,' as his worshippers were *not* eligible for sacrifice. His *marae* was named Araata. Supposed to be enshrined in sennit-work, in the oronga-plant, and in the blackbird (*mo'o*).

3. *Tanè*, i.e. *Tanè-papa-kai* = ' Tanè-giver-of-food.' Greatest of the four Tanès, the other three being in subjection to this, the original Tanè.

4. *Tanè-ngaki-au* = ' Tanè-striving-for-power'; worshipped at Maputū. Supposed to be enshrined in *birds*—the *kaua* and *kerearako*.

5. *Tanè-i-te-utu* = ' Tanè-of-the-Barringtonia-tree '; worshipped at Maraetēva. Supposed to be enshrined in *fish*—sprats.

6. *Tanè-kio* = ' Tanè-the-chirper'; worshipped at Maungaroa. Supposed to be enshrined in *planets*—Venus and Jupiter—and in sennit-work.

7. *Tiaio ;* worshipped at Mārā. Supposed to be incarnate in the eel and the shark.

8 and 9. *Tekuraaki* and *Utakea ;* worshipped at Nuvēe. Supposed to be incarnate in the woodpecker (*tatangaēo*).

10. *Turanga ;* worshipped at Aumoana. Supposed to be incarnate in the white and the black-spotted lizards.[1]

---

[1] The crocodile was regarded as sacred to the god Typho by the Egyptians. Several species of the lizard were worshipped in Polynesia. Whence this worship of a perfectly harmless reptile ? May not the original settlers from Asia have brought with them traditions of crocodile worship? The lizard being the only representative of that order in their new-found homes, may not its worship by the South-Sea Islanders be only a modern adaptation of the old crocodile-worship? It is noticeable that lizard-worship was introduced into the Hervey Group by Tongans. The fear of the lizard was intense. I have seen strong men tremble at the sudden approach of one. A large tree-lizard exists in the forests of Rarotonga. It was formerly regarded as the incarnation of a Tongan deity, devouring solitary travellers. The crocodile is unknown in Polynesia, notwithstanding the assertion of a popular writer that they are found in the noble lagoon of Penrhyn Island.

11. *Teipe :* worshipped at ,Vaiaua. Beautifully carved by Tapaivi.[1] Supposed to be incarnate in the centipede.
12. *Kereteki ;* worshipped at Araata and Tauangaitu. Believed to have no incarnation.
13. *Tangiia ;* worshipped at Rangitaua. Believed to have no incarnation.

The keeper of this Pantheon just before sunset cooked (or rather half-cooked) 'an oven of taro for the use of the gods! The first half-raw taro was thrown into the bush with these words, ' Rongo, here is thy food ; eat.' Next came, ' Motoro, here is thy food ; eat.' After going through the whole thirteen, the keeper threw in the deepening gloom a single taro, saying, ' All ye little divinities, whose names and attributes are unknown to me, here is your food ; eat.' The last was addressed to those inferior gods who had no representatives in the Pantheon, and who might possibly feel angry. To this almost innumerable throng only one taro was given! The essence (*ata*) only was supposed to be eaten by the gods.

The entire family of gods was fed *before* the sun had actually sunk beneath the horizon, as that was the signal for them to go on their travels all over the island. At break of day they were said to rush back with a great noise ' like wind in a coco-nut grove,' ashamed of daylight ![2] Occasionally the idols were sunned, to prevent their fine wrappings from getting mouldy. New white cloth was put on them from time to time.

Some time after the introduction of Christianity it

---

[1] Curiously enough, Rori the Hermit would on no account carve *his own* idol. He therefore asked his friend Tapaivi to carve it.

[2] The constellation of the Pleiades held an important place in the heathen mythology. Its appearance on the horizon at sunset, about the middle of December, determined the commencement of the new year. When at sunset the constellation was invisible, the second half of the year was supposed to have commenced. The reappearance of the Pleiades on the horizon at sunset was in many of the islands a season of extravagant rejoicing, and was welcomed with frantic dances and discordant shell-music.

happened that one of the regal family was taken dangerously
ill.   Whilst the heart was softened by affliction, the parent
was struck with the glaring absurdity of professed adherents
to Christianity keeping up this idol-shrine with its daily
oven of food.   What should be done with the idols?   It
was decided by the king, Parima, Simeona, and the other
leading men of the day, to surrender these dangerous things
to Davida.   To the horror of the heathen, but to the great
joy of the Christian party, the whole thirteen were carried
in triumphal procession to the house of Davida by the sea.
The wrappings were thrown away, and for the first time
since they were carved by Rori they were exposed to the
vulgar gaze.   Soon after Messrs. Williams and Platt paid
an opportune visit to the island ; and they proceeded to
Raiatea laden with these idols, which were eventually
deposited in the museum of the London Missionary
Society, and are now in the British Museum.

The day the idols were removed, the house in which
they had been kept was set on fire ; the *maraes* all over the
island were desecrated, the little houses in which the deity
was supposed to be invisibly present were burnt ; the great
stone idol of Rongo at the sea-side, where human sacrifices
were offered, was smashed to atoms, and (what is much to be
regretted) the magnificent native mahogany (*tamanu*) trees
were set on fire, on account of their supposed connection
with idolatry.   Coco-nuts were planted on the crest of the
marae of Motoro in commemoration of this happy event.
In their wild excitement the war-dance was actually
performed, as if they had gained an important victory !
The heathen everywhere mourned the fate of their gods ;
but no chief was willing to do battle on their behalf.

Another important step was then taken.   The chiefs
had accepted Christianity, but polygamy prevailed.

Davida, who had recently married, represented the incompatibility of this with the New Testament. To the credit of the chiefs be it said, that they heartily acquiesced in the proposition to abolish polygamy. The powerful chief Parima, who had six wives, set the example by putting away five. By divorce these women were not condemned to want, as to each was given a plot of land with fruit-bearing trees on it sufficient for her own subsistence and that of her children.

But a sharp trial was at hand. The heathen could not endure the radical change which had come about. A large tribe of defeated heathen had been living at Butoa, with whom Davida had no influence whatever. A teacher sent to them from the Christian party was ignominiously repulsed : a noble *puka*-tree (species of gigantic laurel) growing on a *marae* was cut down by Davida. Next day a clan blackened their faces, and covered with ill-smelling clothes as a sign of mourning, paraded the island with loud lamentations, and prepared to attack the converts to Christianity. The Christians were decidedly in the minority ; but the upholders of idolatry were so divided amongst themselves that when the battle came off in February, 1828, the numbers on either side were about equal. The heathen were led by Tereavai, priest of Taiao, who, during the actual conflict, was in a thatched hut perched upon a rock engaged in rolling out, with his fine voice, prayers to the shark-god to destroy the worshippers of Jehovah for ever. But his incantations were cut short by the utter discomfiture of the heathen. Arakauae, a brave warrior on the winning side, forbade pursuit of the fugitives,— a noble act, which will never be forgotten.[1]

[1] When twitted afterwards with their ill-success, Tereavai said, ' It was not for want of will on the part of his god, but for lack of power ; because *the Christians' God is the strong God.*'

The terms given to the vanquished were that they should each receive a taro-patch from their conquerors, and for the future live in the Christian village, and give up their heathen practices. During all the years that have since elapsed the peace then made has never been disturbed. Tereavai afterwards became a useful deacon of the church at Tamarua, and an eloquent builder-up of the faith he had striven to destroy. From his own lips I learnt that *he provoked the fight, in order that his name might go down to posterity with glory!* He was the tenth priest in direct succession from Papaaunuku, who followed Rangi and the first settlers to this island. Tereavai died in March, 1865, washed, as I trust, from all guilt in the atoning blood of Jesus.

On one occasion a plot was laid to revive heathenism. The preacher Davida was to be slain and offered to Rongo, although the stone idol had been for some time destroyed. But these were merely the expiring agonies of an effete worship. The Christian body daily grew in numbers and in general intelligence. Scores learnt to write and cipher on slabs of wood covered with sand, the finger being used as a stylus. As the idea of book-learning became inseparably connected with Christianity, those who were friendly to the new order of things were nicknamed 'Book-eaters' (*kai parau*); whilst their opponents, now that idolatry was outwardly given up, were called 'Iron-Rust' (*tutacauri*). And these names have been in use ever since.

In the year 1834 the first church of twelve members was formed at Oneroa, by the Rev. C. Barff, of Huahine. That band consisted of persons who did honour to their profession, but who have all passed away to the church of the Firstborn whose names are written in heaven. On

January 1, 1872, we had in the three churches of Mangaia a total of seven hundred and forty-five members. This wonderful increase may well cause the devout and thankful exclamation, What hath God wrought!

Subsequently to the formation of the church a code of civil laws was adopted by the chiefs of the island for the protection of life and property.

In the year 1839, that noble and apostolic man Maretu, the valued helper of the Rev. C. Pitman, of Rarotonga, was sent over, in the hope of building up the faith of the church; for in truth the knowledge of Davida was not great. Up to this period the island had been connected with the Tahitian Mission; but it was now transferred to the care of the brethren at Rarotonga. Hitherto all religious instruction had been imparted through the medium of the Tahitian dialect, which differs materially from that of the Hervey Group. In the ignorance of a half-enlightened people it was imagined that acceptable worship could only be offered in this almost foreign language. Maretu came amongst them with a strong genial nature, and exclusively used their own dialect— thus at once winning the hearts of all. He applied himself diligently to study their unwritten history and traditions, in order to understand more thoroughly the people amongst whom he was temporarily appointed to labour. What had been but dimly apprehended before, because expressed in a foreign tongue, became clear and attractive in their own. In the Austral Group the original language of the islanders has entirely disappeared. And but for Maretu the same fate would have befallen the language of Mangaia.

The Rev. W. Gill of Rarotonga paid repeated visits to this island—staying for several months at a time. To him the natives attribute their first acquaintance with the use of European tools. In many ways his visits were richly blessed.[1]

In July, 1845, arrived their first resident missionary, the Rev. G. Gill (brother to the preceding), who remained at this station until his removal to Rarotonga in April, 1857. His labours were incessant, and were owned by the Great Master to the ingathering of many to the fold, and in the general enlightenment of the islanders in spiritual truth.

A stone church and a substantial school-house, erected in each of the three villages, testify to his energy. A mission-house of a superior character was built by him at the principal village of Oneroa. Although many years have elapsed since his removal, he still lives in the loving remembrance of the people.

On his arrival it was difficult to travel from one village to another ; before he left an excellent road had been made round the island. Several oppressive laws were cancelled by the king and chiefs at his suggestion.

On July 15, 1851, the writer left England in the missionary barque John Williams, but did not land at Mangaia until March 1, 1852. Not long afterwards the character of the people was put to a severe test by the wreck of two vessels within a few months of each other. Most of the property was saved for the captains. Upon the whole there was every reason to be much pleased with the way the people behaved.

In the year 1853 orange rum was first introduced from Tahiti, and for many years proved very pernicious to the health and morals of the young men of the island. In heathenism the only intoxicating drink known to these

---

[1] The reader is referred to the interesting narrative given in his *Gems from the Coral Islands*.

people was the highly narcotic *Piper mythisticum*, which was used exclusively by aged men. Stringent laws against the manufacture and use of rum were at length enacted by the authorities; and thus eventually the evil was quelled. Had the chiefs been younger and possessed of less firmness of character, the probability is that this terrible evil would still be dominant.

In 1853 a severe hail-storm passed over the island. On the southern part, where we were then stationed, the stones were of the size of pigeons' eggs. One native collected quite a number of these 'sky *seeds*' (as they were called), and placed them carefully in a chest on his Sunday clothes. Next day he unlocked his box in order to have a look at these novel treasures; but they were all gone! He came to me about this clear case of diabolical agency, incidentally remarking that his Sunday clothes were, queerly enough, all wet!

During our absence from the island for twelve months on a prolonged missionary voyage in 1862, the Peruvian slavers first prowled about these seas. One Sabbath afternoon, at the conclusion of the service, a barque exactly corresponding to the well-known John Williams hove in sight. The natives at once concluded that their missionary had come back. Accordingly a canoe with six young men on board was sent off to fetch him ashore. Five climbed the ship's side, and were at once pinioned and carried off, the man in charge of the canoe being left to paddle back alone. Amongst the five was the king's eldest son and intended successor. Through the prompt exertions of the English and French consular residents at Lima, eventually a general delivery of South-Sea Island slaves was made. But, alas! thousands had already perished.

A mournful episode in the business was the fate of three hundred and sixty natives, who were by the terms of agreement to be sent back to their island-homes by the Peruvian Government. A vessel was chartered for the purpose, and sent to Rapa—to which island, however, none of those on board belonged. The poor creatures were dying of smallpox and dysentery at the rate of ten or twelve a day—the latter complaint arising from an insufficient supply of water and food. The natives of Rapa naturally objected to their landing, from fear of infection ; but the captain coolly said that 'he should force the wretched survivors overboard, and let them swim for their lives.' Under these circumstances the Rapa people permitted the surviving sixteen to land —though, as it afterwards proved, at a heavy penalty to 'themselves. Out of that number only one survived to tell the late Captain Williams the tale of woe. A third of the population of Rapa was cut off by the contagion.

The terror of the Hervey Islanders is the cyclone, which may be expected any time during the first three months of the year. In its awful fury it lays low their dwellings, bananas, plantains, coco-nut palms, and other fruit-bearing trees, invariably occasioning famine.

The natives are mercifully forewarned by seeing the strange twists and contortions of the stem of the indigenous banana, and the extraordinarily crinkled appearance of the inner leaves of the *kape*[1] (a gigantic aroid), some weeks previous to the event. The leaf and stem of the indigenous banana are marvellously sensitive to atmospheric changes. At first I laughed at the native proverb referring to this

---

[1] *Alocasia Indica* (Seeman). Its leaves measure from eight to twelve feet in circumference.

natural barometer ; but long observation has completely justified it.

The proverb referred to is this ; *Kua taviriviri te kao o te meika =* ' The stem of the banana is twisted.'

On March 27, 1866, a fearful cyclone devastated the island, unroofing the churches at Oneroa and Tamarua, destroying two hundred and sixty-eight houses, and uprooting two thousand coco-nut trees. The sea rose more than thirty feet above its ordinary level. The people suffered greatly from want of sufficient food afterwards ; and many deaths were accelerated thereby. Yet this cyclone was over in eight hours! For exactly twenty years the island had been happily exempt from such visitations, though heavy floods had on several occasions inflicted severe injury on the island. In the same month of the following year (1867) there was another cyclone, which although of much longer duration did far less damage, as the natives had time to secure their dwellings with wild-vine ropes of immense strength. In March, 1869, a third cyclone occurred; but since then, by the goodness of God the island has been spared.

The group is healthy, but the natives are liable to severe epidemics. Rarely do vessels from colder latitudes (say from New Zealand) touch at these islands without leaving influenza behind them. It is amusingly said by a native when unwell, *Kua pai au =* ' I am shippy,' *i.e.* ' I am suffering from sickness brought by some ship.' Of late years the population of Mangaia has been slightly increasing. The census of January, 1872, gave a total of two thousand two hundred and sixty-six.

Nothing could exceed the whiteness and regularity of the teeth of the islanders at the period of our first acquaintance with them. The natives themselves attribute this to their non-acquaintance at that time with hot stimulative drinks, such as coffee, tea, etc., and especially to their ignorance of ' the fragrant weed.'

In most of the islands generation after generation passed away without ever tasting a warm drink of any kind. The almost universal practice of chewing sugar-cane is unquestionably a great preservative to the teeth, cleansing them and removing the tartar. A dying native over eighty years of age, whom I visited daily, had a perfect set of teeth.

Most of the sons and grandsons of our first converts have served for years on board American whalers and other ships, and thus have contracted a fondness for tobacco, coffee, molasses, etc. The tobacco-plant *now* grows freely in most of the islands. Men *chew*, as well as perpetually smoke tobacco, rising twice or thrice in the night for the purpose. Far worse is the introduction of virulent diseases by the white race, with the violent medicines used for their cure. From all these causes together there can be no question that the teeth of the civilized South Sea Islanders to-day are inferior to those of their heathen ancestors.

Of the men who welcomed the first white missionary in 1845, and myself in 1852, few now survive ; they were men who knew by bitter experience the cruel bondage of heathenism, and who lovingly embraced Christianity. We thank God that these worthies died as they had lived in the faith of the Gospel.

Our converts do not seem to be troubled with the doubts and fears which affect the highly-cultured European. May not this be owing to the childlike nature of their faith—just taking God at His word ?

Amongst the excellent men whose death-beds it has

been my privilege to visit I would refer to Rakoia, chief
of Tamarua, who died in September, 1865, nearly eighty
years of age.   He was emphatically a good man, ready
for every good word and work.   He was never absent
from his place in the adult Bible-class or in church, except
when ill.   During the last two years of his life he became
childish ; yet I could nearly always fix his attention for
a few minutes by referring to the interests of his soul.
The last words I heard from his lips a few days before
his death were, 'I am dying ; but I am in God's hands.
Jesus alone is the Way, the Truth, and the Life ! '

Three months afterwards Tamatangi, chief of Ivirua,
died of inflammation of the lungs.   I had ridden over
twice to administer medicine and to converse with him.
On the first Sabbath of December, 1865, I spent the entire
day at Ivirua.   After the morning service I went to see
him, and at once perceived that the last enemy was near,
although the chief was in full possession of his mental
faculties.   Tamatangi might be seventy years old, and was
reclining on a mat supported by a near relative.   Like
Jacob, he died in the midst of his people ; for perhaps one
hundred natives were in the chamber of death.   His mind
was fixed upon Jesus.   Twice we offered prayer on behalf
of the dying man ; and twice we sung (first a version of
'When I can read my title clear,' and then a version of
'Rock of Ages, cleft for me ').   I held his hand, uttering
such words of comfort as I could think of.   He looked
around upon his wife and relatives, and then fixed his
dying gaze on me.   His last words were an exhortation
to his clan to cleave to the Word of God.   He then said,
' Farewell,' and expired.

Mauapa died in the same year.   He was the oldest
man on the island, and had been a valuable deacon for

many years. In visiting this worthy old Christian, I have often come away refreshed in spirit, beholding what Christianity can do for one who grew up to mature age in heathen darkness. His mind was clear to the last. He passed away without a cloud.

In October, 1866, Paunui, who had been my leading deacon at Oneroa for many years, was called away. His removal was rather sudden. Although by no means faultless—indeed, being possessed of great energy and decision of character, he often occasioned me great anxiety—his death was a brilliant sunset. One Sabbath morning early he sent for me. I was grieved to find him suffering greatly. Gasping for breath, he said, ' My teacher, I am going. Do not detain me by your kind prayers and wishes. Let me go. I want to be with Jesus. There we will meet again.' To me it seemed incredible that such a robust, noble frame should be so near dissolution. I spoke of his possible recovery, and the medicines I had in my pocket. He again said, ' I know I am dying. I wish to go and be with Jesus. Medicines will not avail. Detain me not.' I inquired the ground of his hope. He said that he was trusting in Jesus only. He then commended me and the native pastors to the special care of a chief (his relative) who was by his side. This he did partly from kind personal interest and friendship, and partly as devolving a sacred trust derived from his cousin Parima, the first chief who embraced the Gospel, and who thereby was universally considered to be the special protector and helper of the ' servants of God.' Other chiefs who visited him successively received the same charge, proving how sacredly he regarded the trust committed to him by those who nearly fifty years ago embraced the Christian faith.

I bless God for the many dying testimonies I have

met with among these poor natives to the power of the Gospel to take away the sting of death, and to impart in its place a bright hope of a blissful immortality. It should be remembered that these men were all warriors in heathenism, and had freely shed blood without compunction in those days of darkness. They grew up in the practice of a debasing superstition, and yet cordially embraced the teachings and moral requirements of the Gospel.

CHAPTER II

HOW MANGAIA HAS PROGRESSED UNDER CHRISTIANITY

FOR many years past the contributions from Mangaia to the general funds of the London Missionary Society, after defraying all local expenses, have exceeded £200. During the same period, Rarotonga has contributed a much larger sum; Aitutaki has done nobly; but the other islands of the group collect a much smaller amount.

Throughout the Christianized islands of the Pacific the observance of family worship is almost universal. In some cases it may be an empty form; but even then it is better than entire neglect. In the flying-fish season a fleet of twenty-five or thirty canoes will assemble at dusk at the edge of the reef, whilst a church member in a necessarily stentorian voice commends the entire party to God's care. This is because they cannot reach home till late, so that family worship will have been conducted by the wives with their children before their arrival.

The first edition of the entire Bible in Rarotongan reached the islands in 1852. In two years every one of the five thousand copies was disposed of. The writer will never forget the unbounded enthusiasm with which this priceless boon was received by the islanders. At Mangaia a case of Bibles was taken into the church; after a short thanksgiving service, copies were given to those who had

TEPOU, A RAROTONGAN CHIEF (ONCE AN IDOLATER AND CANNIBAL, BUT AFTERWARDS ONE OF THE EARLIEST CONVERTS TO CHRISTIANITY).

some time previously paid for them. At a Friday exhortation meeting, held at break of day, a venerable native, named Tenio,[1] said that he had secured a copy of the Bible, but could not sleep until he had finished reading the entire Book of Job, which had never before been seen in a Rarotongan dress. Lifting up the sacred volume before the entire congregation, he concluded his address in these memorable words:—'This is my resolve: the dust shall never cover my Bible, the moths shall never eat it, the mildew shall never rot it. My light! my joy!'

Until 1852 the Books of Ezra, Nehemiah, Esther, Job, and the Minor Prophets had never been in the hands of the natives. It was no ordinary privilege to expound to an eager auditory books absolutely new to all present but oneself. The natives seemed never weary of asking the meaning of these novel portions of Scripture.

In 1855 a new edition (of five thousand copies) was called for.

In 1872 the Bible Society issued a third and greatly improved edition of five thousand copies. Marginal references were added, and numberless words of foreign origin exchanged for purely indigenous expressions.

In 1884 I was requested by the Committee of the Bible Society to prepare a standard edition with a view to its being stereotyped. Innumerable printers' errors were corrected; the article (*a*) before all proper names in the nominative when they follow the verb (having, strangely enough, been dropped out in the edition of 1872), was everywhere restored; out of the various renderings given by preceding editors, that which seemed to be the most faithful representation of the original was finally selected;

---

[1] Named after the son of Kaiara, whose pathetic story is related in the earlier part of this volume (see p. 184).

many terms of natural history derived from the English Revised Version have been inserted (in their native form) in the text or side-notes of the Old Testament. In regard to the italics, I have followed the rule laid down by the revisers of the English Bible. It is for others to say whether I have succeeded in a difficult task, conscientiously carried out.

If my work is a success, it is due mainly to the untiring aid of Taunga, who for considerably more than forty years has been a faithful preacher of the Word in the Western Pacific, in Samoa, and latterly in Rarotonga—the land of his birth. Taunga, the pupil and beloved friend of the late Rev. C. Pitman, is acknowledged to be the best living authority on the Rarotongan language. In 1852 I heard the Rev. W. Howe remark that the Tahitian brethren found by experience that no one could beat ‘Noti’ (the Rev. H. Nott’s version). Even so the unexpected result of the several revisions of the Rarotongan Bible has been to prove conclusively that, overlooking the serious blemish of words of foreign origin, the work of the original translators[1] is beyond all praise for idiomatic purity, nervous strength, and beauty. And well it is for the islanders that it is so, as throughout the Eastern Pacific the various dialects are rapidly deteriorating, by admixture from various sources, native and foreign. I subjoin a single illustration of the grip which the early translators possessed of the Rarotongan language. In the edition of 1851, the phrase in Zechariah v. 3, ‘ on the *face* of the whole earth ’ is correctly rendered, *i te tua enua.* The translator is compelled to reverse the figure. It is no longer ‘ the *face*,’ but ‘ the *back*,’ broad and strong, of the earth-parent. A subsequent editor, scandalized at the alteration of the figure, to solve the difficulty, dropped

---

[1] Revs. J. Williams, C. Pitman, and A. Buzacott—chiefly the two latter.

out the clause. Of course the original translation (the only possible one) is now restored.

Having used the Rarotongan Bible for forty-two years, I may be pardoned for saying that I regard it as an admirable rendering of the original. Many of the improvements found in the English Revised Version have been anticipated. As in all other Pacific and New Guinea versions, the sacred name 'Jehovah' is transliterated, never translated, thus adding immeasurably to the force of the contrast between the ever-living God and the objects worshipped by the heathen. The English rendering of 1 Kings xviii. 21 is tame indeed in comparison with the Rarotongan.

The original translators of the Rarotongan Bible caught the real genius of the language, and gave it a permanent embodiment whilst it was as yet utterly untouched by outside influences. The rendering of the patriarchal portions is simply perfect, the language of the islanders being so well adapted for the purpose. Indeed, Polynesian life, at its best, is strictly patriarchal. The Gospels lend themselves very readily to translation ; but in the Epistles a difficulty was evidently felt by the translators in obtaining exact equivalents for the key-notes of the Christian system. Too great praise cannot be given to the Rev. H. Nott, of Tahiti, and his coadjutors, who, in making the Tahitian translation, unconsciously fixed the theological terms for several other groups.

In the Rarotongan version the translators use *akava--ngakau* = 'heart-judge,' for 'conscience.' In preaching or rapid speaking we simply say *ngakau* = 'heart,'[1] which is beyond question the strict equivalent in the Eastern

---

[1] Literally 'the bowels.' These islanders, like the Hebrews of old, place the seat of the affections and intellect in the bowels.

Polynesian dialects, 'heart-judge' being an invented phrase, but now current. 'Faith' (*akarongo*) is '*to listen* to God speaking,' the native preacher being always careful to add, 'with the ear of the heart.' 'Trust in God' is '*leaning* on God.' The pious are those 'who dwell in the shadow of God.' 'Heaven' is 'the day, or light of God.'

In a literary point of view it is remarkable that it should be possible with an alphabet of thirteen letters only to render faithfully the Word of God into the language of savages. In transliterating proper names a few other letters are used; but, in the language proper, as above stated, only thirteen. No book speaks to the heart of man —whatever be his race, home, or speech—as the Bible. Its voice is sure of an echo from the human heart. The islanders in reality possess but one book; hence the anxiety of the brethren to make it a perfect image of what its Divine Author intended. Each edition issued by the British and Foreign Bible Society has been a distinct advance upon the preceding in regard to clearness of sense.

The educational power of the Bible is great. Portions of the sacred volume that to us are of little interest may be most attractive to savages listening perhaps for the first time to Bible story. I never cared much for the genealogical portions until my own converts put me to shame by evincing an intimate acquaintance with them. In Polynesia, other things being equal, the chief with the longest pedigree is most respected. These pedigrees usually carry with them lands and titles. The adaptation of many parts of the Old Testament to their simple, patriarchal mode of life is very striking. Thus the jealousies of children born of different mothers under the old system of polygamy have their exact counterpart in these islands; for although the system has long been abandoned the evils generated by it in former years are but slowly eradicated. The stories contained in such books as Joshua and Judges exercise a marvellous fascination over the minds of brave savages, who are astonished above measure to find that their most famous war-stratagems were long ago anticipated in far-off lands. The awful vengeance exacted upon whole families and tribes is the exact counterpart of what they practised themselves in times of war. The native intellect is interested in tracing the striking parallel which exists between numerous Mosaic institutions and the unwritten laws of *tapu* in Polynesia. It is probably on this ground that all the Christian Polynesians I have met with believe themselves to be Shemites. The histories of Elijah, Elisha, Daniel, and Jonah are of undying interest. After all, the great point is to give to the natives the entire New Testament, the Psalms, and Proverbs, with Genesis, Job, and Isaiah. The lesson of my missionary life is this—I would give to every race, if practicable, the entire Bible. But if this may not be, I would omit as little as possible. There are races that can never hope to get more than the New Testament and the Psalms. Others must rest content with the four Gospels. Let no tribe, however, be without a loving message from the Father of Spirits.

At first the heroic portions of the Scriptures tell most upon a warrior race emerging into the light; then the miracles and parables of the New Testament captivate. But as the spiritual life deepens, interest is centred in the character and work of Christ and the teaching of His apostles. The Bible is read, studied, and quoted by the Polynesians of to-day in place of the heathen songs and myths of bygone ages. In fact, it is moulding the lives and characters of the entire race.

I subjoin a few specimens of idioms used in the Rarotongan Scripture : ' The life we live '; ' the sin we have sinned '; ' the death we die,' etc., etc., etc. For (Rom. xii. 8) ' he that sheweth mercy, with cheerfulness,' we have (instead of ' cheerfulness ') ' with the heart in touch.'

In 2 Cor. iv. 15, for ' abundant grace,' we have ' grace great (even) running over.' So in 2 Cor. viii. 2, for ' abundance of joy,' we have ' joy running over.'

Col. ii. 2, ' knit together in love,' becomes ' fitting into one in love.'

' For ever and ever ' (1 Pet. iv. 11) is ' time on, on, still on.'

The Rarotongan of Heb. xiii. 5 has four negatives : ' I will never leave thee, nor forsake thee ; no, never—on, on, on !' How many dying Hervey Islanders have been comforted by these beautiful words, the final clause showing that the negation goes on for ever !

In Polynesian, as in Greek, the definite article is always placed before ' God ' (Atua). In Rarotongan for ' saying,' six words are needed (*i te na ko anga mai*), and for ' I write ' (1 John ii. 12, etc.), eight words are required (*te tata atu nei au i te tuatua*) ; but ' you and I ' are expressed by a single word (*taua*), etc. So that, after all, the Rarotongan Bible is about the size of the English of the same type.

The manner in which the Rarotongan New Testament was originally received is deeply interesting. ' The eagerness with which they received it would have cheered your heart, could you have been eye-witness to the scene. The countenance of a successful applicant glistened with delight while he held up his treasure to public view ; others hugged the book ; many kissed it ; some sprang away like a dart, and did not stop until they entered their own dwellings, and exhibited their treasure to their wives and children ; while others jumped and capered about like persons half frantic with joy.'[1]

In 1846 an excellent translation of the *Pilgrim's Progress* was made and printed at Rarotonga by the late Rev. A. Buzacott. After the lapse of forty-seven years, this little book—so highly prized by the islanders—has been reprinted by the Religious Tract Society. Three thousand copies of a translation of *Peep of Day*, and *Line upon Line*, by Mrs. Gill, have been sold to the Hervey Islanders. A small library of useful books has been translated and circulated ; but most of these publications are just now out of print.

In 1872 the sole care of the mission devolved upon the Rev. G. A. Harris, as the writer went on furlough to England, and then succeeded the Rev. James Chalmers (now of New Guinea) at Rarotonga.

The good work has experienced many vicissitudes, yet still prospers in every respect, under the indefatigable efforts of our brother. The church at Tamarua having been destroyed by a cyclone, a new stone building was erected. A number of devoted young men and women have gone to labour in New Guinea, after a four-years' training in the London Missionary's College at Rarotonga.

In 1888, as we have already noticed, at the request of the native chiefs, Her Majesty's Government assumed a protectorate over Mangaia and the other islands constituting the Hervey Group. Frederick Moss, Esq., the British Resident, has his headquarters at Rarotonga, the principal island of the group.

The plain old church at Oneroa has just been replaced by a new and handsome edifice.

<hr>

[1] *Life of the Rev. J. Williams*, p. 541.

'On Wednesday last, August 12, 1891,' writes the Rev. G. A. Harris, 'we celebrated the opening of our new Oneroan Church, which has taken two years in building.

'It has cost the people several thousand dollars, as well as incessant and arduous labour. The edifice is a very lofty and commodious place of worship, with immense rafters, all of which are very tastefully covered with plaited sinnet. The walls of stone and plaster are also very high, and, for native workmanship, very evenly built. All the windows and doors are of stained glass, and look very pretty. In fact, the interior is so European in style and comfort that were it not for the bright sun and tropical surroundings, we might imagine ourselves in an English church, erected by properly trained artisans. There is a half-circular gallery at one end, where the singers and the school children with their teachers sit. Altogether, it is far in advance of any church previously built in Mangaia. The many designs drawn out by myself for wood and stone work have been very wonderfully and beautifully executed by the native workmen, all having been done with the chisel, saw, and axe.

'The day of opening was a lovely day, and we had a very interesting service. A large number of visitors from Rarotonga, Aitutaki, and Atiu were present, including some kings, chiefs, and deacons. Mr. Moss, our Resident, with his interpreter, Mr. Nicholas, was also present, and several other Europeans living on the island.

'Our opening service commenced with a new hymn which I composed for the occasion, and for which the young people made up an excellent tune. Native teachers and deacons conducted the entire service with the exception of the sermon, which I myself preached from the words, " How amiable are Thy tabernacles, O Lord of hosts! "'

The Rev. G. A. Harris, writing under date of May, 1893, says :—' I am happy to tell you that the Mangaians have done remarkably well this year in relation to their contributions and to their giving generally. It has done my heart good to witness both what they have contributed and the spirit with which they have given their money to God's cause. I can testify that they have in these their offerings denied themselves many things, especially new clothes, for a large number of the natives. My own seven students, who are to be transferred to Rarotonga when the John Williams arrives (expected here on May 14), with their wives, have been dealt with very kindly by the church, each receiving a substantial present of clothing and other things ere they leave their island home. I have also two boxes filled with pieces of European prints bought by the church to send to the teachers in New Guinea, and I have just had collected a very large quantity of yams from the three villages for the John Williams when she arrives. It is nice to see the people engaged continually in planning work and deeds of *aroa* to aid us and our Society in our good work. Our contributions this year amount to $1,656.00. This is clear to our Society, all the native pastors and internal expenses being paid from a separate fund collected by the classes of the three churches. . . . I have this day (May 24) admitted sixty-seven persons to church fellowship. We had this morning a most glorious gathering at Oneroa. All the native pastors and deacons of the three villages were present. I am happy to say that fourteen of the sixty-seven were unmarried, and very young persons. This is very unusual with us. I have never admitted more than one or two at a time in the past. I sincerely trust that these youthful confessions of Christ will be the beginning of good things among the young on Mangaia.'

The Islanders receiving Gifts from the British Government.

The Board of Trade asked Sir J. B. Thurston, the High Commissioner of the Western Pacific, to expend £30 in the purchase of gifts for the natives of Manihiki, as a return for the hospitality shown by them to a portion of the crew of the ship Garston, who spent several weeks on that atoll. Sir J. B. Thurston requested me to act on his behalf. The goods were forwarded per Lubeck to Samoa, in time to catch the mission barque John Williams. Captain Turpie took great interest in the affair, and landed the goods in good order. The Rev. J. J. K. Hutchin, of Rarotonga (my successor in the Mission), explained the thing to the wondering natives. The following is a literal translation of a letter of thanks sent to me for transmission to the High Commissioner, Sir J. B. Thurston, K.C.M.G. :—

'Manhiki, November 4, 1891.

'O Gill the Second [my native designation]! May you live through the grace of our Lord Jesus, the Messiah!

'Do you make known to [our Queen] Victoria and the British Government, also to the Governor of Fiji, that their valuable gifts have safely arrived, and thus the natives of Manihiki have ocular proof of the goodwill which British rulers entertain towards us.

'The inhabitants of Manihiki are delighted at these gifts. The chief, the under-chiefs, the native ministers, and the entire community desire to express their gratitude for the same.

'Yes; we *did* feel and show sympathy with those shipwrecked seamen in their great distress. Yet, any kindness we manifested was only becoming those who have received the light of Christ's Gospel. It was our duty to assist those who were overtaken by calamity.

'Great is the pleasure felt by all the dwellers on Manihiki in accepting these useful gifts from the British Government.

'This, then, is the message from Manihiki. Witness my signature—Abela, pastor; Apolo, chief's son (on behalf of his father, Jese, who happened to be absent at Rakahanga); Putaura, pastor.'

In reference to the lovely sister island of Rarotonga, the Rev. J. J. K. Hutchin wrote (under date of July, 1893)—

'The population amounts to 1900 people, with a church membership of 693. There are five villages, each having its church, school, and manse, which they keep in good repair. The people pay the salaries of their pastors, and contribute an average of £100; and in 1891–2, the contributions to the London Missionary Society of the Hervey Group district amounted to £783 11s. 2d.

'In connection with the Mission at Rarotonga, an Institution for the Training of Native Teachers was founded in the year 1839, and since that year the work has been carried on up to the present time, and 490 men and women have been trained there. Pioneer teachers from Rarotonga took the Gospel to Samoa, to the Loyalty Group, to the New Hebrides, and to the south-east part of New Guinea, in 1872. From 1872–91, fifty-two couples were sent to New Guinea, and of that number, up to the year 1891, seventeen men and twenty-three women died of fever; three men and three women returned home; four men and three women were killed, leaving thirty men and twenty-five women at work for Christ. Since the compilation of these statistics, several others have been called home. Ebera has lost his wife and child through the terrible New Guinea fever; and yet in his loneliness and sorrow he wrote to me the other day and said: "It is a work of joy to me to be here in New Guinea, doing the work of Christ our Master." These noble men and women are the flower of our churches; and their simple faith and whole-hearted devotion to Christ are worthy of all praise. They have their faults, doubtless, but the same may be said of the ministry in other parts of the world.

'As regards the people of our charge, we believe that great good has been done. These are times, however, when changes rapidly take place. The people are intelligent, and thirst for information. They wish that their children should be taught English, and we are thankful that the London Missionary Society has recognized this want by appointing a lady missionary to commence a school for the higher education of intelligent children. There is much need for improvement also in their mental, moral, and spiritual condition. The people are also coming more and more into contact with the outside world, with its evil as well as its good. Yet as long as they continue to be a Bible-reading and a prayer-loving people; as long as the Gospel is preached, which is "the power of God unto salvation to every one that believeth," we do not fear for the future, being assured that broken-hearted sinners will ever look to a crucified Saviour, and the Church which is founded upon Christ, the Rock of Ages, will survive all the malice of the Evil One and the terrors of the judgment day.'

The London Missionary Society contemplates the early establishment of a central training school in the Hervey Islands for the teaching of English; eighty boys and girls

will be selected from all the islands, and taught in the school
free of charge. It is proposed that the buildings shall
be put up by subscription in the islands; the necessary
teachers will then be sent and paid by the Society, and
a contribution from the Federal revenue not exceeding
$1000 = £200 a year will be made towards the main-
tenance of the pupils in the school when it is established.
—(Signed), MAKEA ARIKI, Chief of the Government,
Rarotonga, July 5, 1893.

In 1872 the writer, associated with the late Rev. A. W.
Murray, located the first Christian teachers on New Guinea.
Of the thirteen dusky pioneers then distributed about,
several, alas! with their wives, were subsequently slain by
the heathen; others returned home; whilst Ruatoka—the
father of the mission—still lives and works for the Master
in New Guinea. In 1883 I again sailed in the John
Williams from the Hervey Group to New Guinea, with
thirteen married teachers and their families, who were all
landed in good health at Port Moresby on February 6,
1884. Blessed be God, despite great loss of life and much
suffering, the mission has taken root, and in the hands of
Messrs. Lawes and Chalmers and other brethren has
proved a great success.

Of the first band of teachers, the most remarkable were
Ruatoka and Piri. They were much respected by the
natives, and were untiring in their labours. It is an
interesting fact that whenever the teachers were prostrate
with fever, the wives conducted Sunday and week-day
services, preaching most appropriately. The natives were
as much pleased as though the teachers themselves took
the services. Schools went on just as usual under the
charge of these good women. Both these women acquired
a singular hold of the natives. They were at the same

time good housewives, and scrupulously clean and neat. Piri's wife could fearlessly steer a boat through the boiling surf with perfect safety. Both these women were natives of Mangaia; their immediate ancestors took part in many of the stirring scenes related in this volume. They grew up in the writer's family, and were there taught and trained previous to their entering the Rarotongan Institution. 'Faithful unto death,' were they. 'The Lord giveth the word : *the women* that publish the tidings are a great host.'

The Rev. H. M. Dauncey related to me the following incident. On one occasion, being temporarily (with Ruatoka) in charge of the principal mission station, Port Moresby, he had—although suffering badly from an attack of fever—to preach. With great difficulty he got through the earlier part of the service and gave out his text. At this point he had to sit down from sheer exhaustion. After a pause, he made another effort to proceed ; but to do so was impossible. He then asked Ruatoka to dismiss the congregation with prayer. Instead of doing so, Ruatoka preached a most impressive sermon from Mr. Dauncey's text. The curious thing is, that Ruatoka had, previous to the announcement by Mr. Dauncey of his text, no notion what the subject would be ! ' Yet,' said Mr. Dauncey, ' a more appropriate sermon I never listened to.'

Ruatoka has just built an excellent dwelling for himself. He was his own architect and builder. Said Mr. Dauncey, ' Sir William McGregor—the Administrator—would be very glad to exchange residences with him.'

The Resident in his report to the Governor of New Zealand writes with regard to Rarotonga, the port of entry for the group :—' The shipping for 1890 was as follows : Arrivals, 71 vessels, with a total of 13,315 tons ; departures,

70, with a total of 13,302 tons. Of the arrivals 52 were British, 12 American, 4 French, and 3 native vessels. The imports were £50,541 for 1890, and exports £20,373 ; but it is believed they could be increased to £150,000 in a few years, with care and cultivation. The bulk of the trade is with New Zealand. A differential duty in favour of island coffee, or its admission duty free, would bring all of this staple to New Zealand.'

CHAPTER III

REMINISCENCES OF NATIVE PREACHERS

IN the Christianized islands of the South Seas the Sabbath is strictly observed, and the churches crowded with devout worshippers; in fact, in most places nine-tenths of the population may be found inside the house of God on the Lord's day. No congregation in Europe or America could hang with more earnestness on the lips of the preacher. It is quite a common practice to take down the outline of the discourse on paper or slates, or even rudely to scratch it on the leaf of the banana or the coco-nut. The people converse on what they have heard in their homes; the usual course being for the husband first to call upon the wife for the text, and, if she fails to remember it, to appeal to the eldest son, and so on, proceeding in the same manner with the successive divisions of the discourse. I have known sermons to be well remembered even ten years after their delivery. Their reverence for the Word of God puts to shame the unbelief of many born in Christian countries. In the letter, as well as in the spirit, they fulfil the ancient precept: 'These words, which I command thee this day, shall be in thine heart: and thou shalt teach them diligently unto thy children, and shalt talk of them when thou sittest in thine house, and when thou walkest by the way, and when thou liest down, and when thou risest up.'[1]

[1] Deut. vi. 6, 7.

The services of the Sabbath begin with a prayer-meeting at dawn ; this lasts about an hour. A deacon usually conducts it. Sabbath-school is held from 8 to 9 a.m., when the full morning-service begins, and from 1 to 2 o'clock in the afternoon ; full service again follows from 2 to half-past 3 p.m. The day closes with catechising and prayer in each family. The early sunset, and the absence of artificial lights, make any later service impossible.

At dawn on Monday (at Mangaia and Aitutaki, at least), a large Bible-class of all the church-members is held ; the aged coming to hear only, the younger to read and ask questions. Similar exercises are repeated at intervals during the week. They go to their secular duties with the more zest for having spent an hour with God. Saturday is the only day entirely free from services or Bible-classes for adults and children.

Some of the following illustrations were from the lips of Mamae, late native pastor and evangelist in Mangaia, whose portrait we give. Mamae was only one of his names ; for the natives use many names, associated with divers events in their lives. It means *sorrow*, referring to the loss of a loved child. His original name was Koroa-the-younger, after his grandfather Koroa, the author of many of the finest songs in the earlier part of this volume. Koroa was a noted warrior as well as poet.

Mamae was no ordinary man. He was well versed in Scripture, which he expounded with great originality and power, bringing his illustrations not ·from books or commentaries, but from Nature, and from events familiar to those whom he is addressing. He had much wit and humour, as well as true pathos ; and, best of all, he was a devout and humble follower of Jesus. Mamae died on

September 22, 1889, after spending forty-one years in the Christian ministry, leaving a spotless reputation. I knew him for thirty-seven years ; and the more I knew him the more I had cause to esteem and love him for his own as well as his work's sake. I regard him as a fine example of the transforming power of the Gospel. For the first half of his life he was an untaught heathen, a worshipper of idols. The very idol which he and his tribe worshipped— a rude carved human figure made of ironwood, named Motoro—is in the museum of the London Missionary Society. The following notes do not represent the substance of his teaching, but are merely given as specimens of the racy and characteristic illustrations with which he enlivened his discourse.

'*They crucify to themselves the Son of God afresh.*' Our weapons of war were all made of ironwood. Supposing one of you should plant a young ironwood tree. It would require much care at first to make it grow at all. And then it has a trick of growing crooked ; little branches all round would require to be lopped off from time to time. After a great amount of pruning and constant care it becomes a stately tree. Imagine that lofty tree [1] to be cut down by a pretended friend, and adzed into a spear, and that spear to be used in piercing your heart! To be slain by a spear made of the tree you planted, nurtured, and cherished!

This is just an emblem of what Christ feels. The very creatures He formed and loved crucified Him! The Jews did this of old ; let us not crucify the Son of God afresh. The love of sin and all ungodliness—these are the spears, these are the nails which pierce the soul of the

---

[1] Generally speaking, spears did not exceed twenty-four feet in length ; the spear wielded by the famous warrior Ngauta was thirty feet long.

Redeemer! The torn flesh and the pain of death are as nothing compared with the anguish of enduring the sins of the world.

Hollow Professors. Some professors are just like empty calabashes. When a man wants a new calabash, he selects the biggest green one he can find, bores a hole in the top, and carries it to a stream, where it at once sinks to the bottom. After a few days he comes back, and finds the once heavy calabash light and floating, the soft pith and seeds inside all decayed, and easily got rid of.

Alas! that the religion of many should too much resemble the green calabash. They cannot endure temptation. Ere long their profession proves to be hollow. Are they not like empty calabashes floating down the stream?

Sometimes, when a fisherman walks along the reef, peering into every pool and crevice in the coral for fish, he sees what seems to him to be a lobster, so perfect is its form even to its eyes, spines, and claws. No defect can be discovered. Cautiously he makes a grab at the supposed prize, when, lo! it proves to be but a cast-off shell! The lobster has gone.

Let us not be mere shells, but real living Christians.

'*Kings and priests unto God.*' In the olden time, the only persons who might bathe at Marua in the interior, or at Vairorongo on the sea-shore, were the kings, who were high-priests of Rongo. These streams were thought to be wonderfully efficacious in driving away disease and pain. The fountains of Divine mercy are free to all; laving our sinful souls in them, we are at once cleansed, and live for ever. Strangely enough, we are made kings and priests to God, and may therefore drink without fear of the river of His pleasures.

'*My son, give Me thine heart.*' To the major gods our fathers never offered tiny minnows, or any of the many kinds of shell-fish. Even small fish like the *avini* (about four inches in length) were accounted unworthy. The best and largest only were considered to be fit offerings, so as to secure their favour.

Shall we offer to the Maker of heaven and earth imperfect service, lip-praise, and heartless prayers? He requires one thing—your heart.

'*Kill not your foes as Teata killed Rangai.*' In the famous night attack upon Rautoa and his clan, Rangai rushed through the back door of the fishing-hut; Teata chased him through the darkness with his uplifted club. The fugitive happened to stumble into a hole on the reef; but, in falling, his head was partially sheltered by a projecting rock. Teata, exulting at this opportunity of wreaking his long-cherished vengeance, again and again struck at his prostrate foe. Instead, however, of hitting his head, as he intended, he only struck the rock!

Having (in imagination) secured this victim, he hurried off in quest of a new one. When he eventually came back, with the intent of battering the corpse, he was astonished to find no trace of Rangai. The intended victim, finding himself unhurt, had long since rejoined his friends in the interior. Hence the proverb, 'Kill not your foes as Teata killed Rangai.'[1]

Take care that, in waging war with sin, you make no mistake. Strike hard, and strike home. See to it that after you have proclaimed the extinction of your old foes they do not, like Rangai, survive to proclaim your folly.

'*Dying in Christ.*' In the terrible famine which depopulated the island in the reign of Makitaka, Rangai

---

[1] *Auraka ta tatou tainga ia riro ei tainga na Teata.*

—now a very aged man—felt his end approaching. Without saying a word to his children, lest they should prevent the execution of his wish, with extreme difficulty he dragged his feeble limbs towards the sun-rising, to the *marae* of his god Tanè. But the dying man had not strength to climb on the shrine (*patu*) itself. His moans at his successive failures attracted the attention of a passer-by, who proved to be his son-in-law, and who at once lifted him on to the sacred spot. Overjoyed at this, Rangai, gathering up his remaining strength, shouted, *Aiaa! kua tae au ki te rua poro!* ('Oh, joy! I have attained my desired resting-place!') Thus Rangai passed away.

This was the model death of our heathen ancestors—'dying in the embrace of the god' (*akamate atua*). They were deceived by Satan. Let us, who know the Gospel, die in Christ. 'Blessed are the dead that die in the Lord.' Thus dying, we shall attain to the rest remaining to the people of God.'

Forgetful Hearers. When the sea-side king was installed in office, and took up his residence near the *marae* of Rongo, the most sacred spot on the island, a large basket was hung up in the neighbourhood, so that all who passed to or from the sea might deposit an offering to the goddess Ruatamaine,[1] the revealer of secrets. Going, it might be only a bit of cooked taro ; on coming back it must be an entire fish. If nothing whatever had been obtained, a white coral pebble should be put in the basket instead. Ruatamaine was a very exacting divinity : if the accustomed offering was omitted, no success in fishing could be expected.

'Now,' said the preacher, 'some of you are continually

---

[1] 'She who speaks through a woman ; ' the goddess being supposed to be incarnate in a royal female whose home was near the sea.

coming to the house of God, and yet carry away nothing! The memory retains scarcely anything beyond the text; and even that is sometimes forgotten. Why so? *Ina! kua vare te kete o Ruatamaine* = "I suspect you have forgotten to put something in the basket of the Revealer of Secrets!" Did you first ask God's blessing on the services of the sanctuary and on the preacher? And upon your return home, did you thank God for the words you had been listening to? Had you done so, your memory would doubtless have been strengthened, and your own basket filled.'

Church Kites. In times of peace kite-flying was a favourite amusement of the Hervey Islanders. Kites were egg, club, or bird-shaped. The first flown was sacred to the gods. Each kite bore a name and heraldic device. Only chiefs and aged men might indulge in this pastime. Tears of joy would be shed by the victor, to whom was given the largest share of the grand feast which followed. During the flight of the kite (or 'bird,' as the native name imports), it was customary to chant a song, composed for the occasion, which was supposed to aid its ascent.

In these days, teachers labouring amongst the heathen are universally called 'kites' or 'birds.' Some churches boast of having three or four 'kites' flying at one time in New Guinea or elsewhere. A church that has not even one 'kite' abroad flying is looked down upon as having failed in duty to the Master. It is incumbent on those who stay at home 'to hold on to the end of the string,' that is, never to forget these messengers of the churches in their prayers to God. Teachers in the field often write pathetically to their friends: 'How can we be expected to fly, if you at home let go the string? If you cease to plead before God on our behalf, we fall and perish.'

Help for New Guinea. Timoteo, of Samoa, ere starting for New Guinea on missionary work, remarked—

A stump-tailed heron once pathetically said to a delicately graceful tropic bird, 'Pray give me one[1] of those handsome red feathers in your tail, for I have none.' The proud beauty disdainfully replied : 'Be satisfied with what Nature has bestowed upon you ; I will not part with my adornments.'

Now Papua is the stump-tailed heron ; Samoa with its Christian privileges is the handsome tropic bird. New Guinea is asking Samoa to spare some of her feathers (sons) to adorn (instruct) her ; but, unlike the stingy beauty of the ancient fable, Samoa is now freely parting with her most prized feathers to beautify the stump-tailed heron of Papua.

'*Ye are the Light of the World.*' Tamarua remarked, 'We are lamps in a dark world. Now the lamp is composed of three parts—the stand, the wick, and the oil. Our heart is the lamp ; the oil the Word of God ; the burning wick the Holy Spirit, setting the whole of our nature in a flame. See that we burn brightly. The darker the night, the brighter the light ; then all will be well.'

The Gospel Trumpet. 'In the old cannibal times no one dared to live in the level land near the ocean. Our fathers therefore built their huts on the spurs of hills, so that if they were attacked there might be a chance of safety by hiding in the recesses of the mountains. Our chief, Makea, was wont to send swift-footed messengers along the crest of the hills, halting near human dwellings to blow the triton shell and deliver the warning to the

---

[1] The tropic bird is furnished with two red tail-feathers, fifteen inches in length, much prized by Polynesians for head-dresses. This bird is unquestionably the most beautiful sea-bird of warm latitudes.

clan. As the shrill sound echoed through the valleys, every one was on the alert to hear the message.

'In these happier days,' said Anguna, 'the servants of the King of kings are running through all lands, blowing the Gospel trumpet. Let us listen and wisely heed the Divine warning.'

Sphinx Moths. In the Hervey Group, as soon as the evening torch is lit, great sphinx[1] moths (from outside) rush down from the ridge-pole—their wings producing a loud humming noise—wildly endeavouring, as it seems, to extinguish the light. Will they succeed? Will they not rather scorch their beautiful wings and perish?

'Now,' said Mamae, 'Christ is revealed as the true Light of the world. Once we were in darkness. Yet, sad to say, as soon as the light has been introduced, things of darkness—great moths of attractive appearance (*i.e.* evil customs from other lands)—come in to extinguish the Light. It has ever been thus. Has the Light of life been put out by them? No; but the foolish perish by their own folly.'

Ear-ornaments. In the Hervey Group in the olden times the ear-lobes of the men and women were universally pierced and greatly distended to admit fragrant plants and flowers. The gardenia and *Fagræa Berteriana* were the most prized. But chiefs inserted these plants and flowers in tiny elongated coco-nut shells (the ends rubbed off) known as *vaao*, which were placed in their ears.

In allusion to this, native Christians continue to speak of Christ as 'the ear-ornament of His people' (= their pride and their joy). Canticles ii. 1.

An Ancient Proverb Applied. 'The eyes of many may be blinded by the dust that one man can beat out of a mass

---

[1] *Chærocampa crotus* of Cramer.

of coco-nut fibre' (intended for the platting of sennit). 'Even so,' remarked Tevori when expounding Joshua vii., 'Achan's covetous heart occasioned the destruction of many in Israel who knew nothing about his sin.'

Sin. The spiny lobsters of Mitiaro and Mauke are entirely poisonous,[1] although in the other five islands of the group they are excellent eating. In allusion to this, the native pastor of Mauke said—

'Sin, lobster-like, has many legs (= devices), each deadly. Our wisdom is to avoid it altogether.'

The Gospel Feast. At Aitutaki a native will sometimes throw a couple of split coco-nuts—unhusked—on the sandy beach and retire. In half an hour he returns to find them covered with land-crabs so intent upon enjoying a feast that they are easily caught by the hand. As many as thirty may thus be secured at a time. Hence the remark of Ngativaru—

'As hungry land-crabs hasten to the opened coco-nut, so should famishing souls feed on divine truths;—not one at a time, but in crowds.'

Clinging to Christ. A deacon prayed that we 'might cleave to Christ as closely as the valves of the *kai* mollusk adhere to each other when touched by a foe.' This simile is often used in preaching.

This *kai* is the *Asaphis deflorata*, Lin., one of the most common bivalves in the Hervey Group. It is impossible to force open the upper edges with a knife; the shell, strong though it be, will break first. It is needful, then, to insert the point of the knife into the side aperture through which the byssus—by which it attaches itself to the sea-weed or coral—protrudes.

---

[1] Arising from the species of seaweed on which they feed. The *Palinurus vulgaris* is the lobster referred to. Our *Homarus vulgaris* is not found in these waters. The spotted ibacus is very common.

'Jesus died a sin-offering on our behalf. Let us all cling to His cross as *bats* do to their favourite tree; fathers, mothers, children—none absent.' (I have seen a living rope, of great length, of bats suspended from a stout branch of *Casuarina* growing over a fearful precipice—a most favourable position for taking to the air.)

The Figurative Language of the South Seas. Upon the accession of a new chief on the island of Mangaia, it was customary for ' the wise men ' to charge him to rule well in the following terms :—

Auā ei vvu te rango = 'Let not the flies (= the serf population) be swept away.'

Auā ei ngaae te rauika = ' Let not a banana leaf be split,' *i.e.* Let not the State (symbolized by a newly-opened banana leaf[1]) be rent by a breath of discord.

Should the paramount chief hear of any trouble, he would visit in state that district and, after the usual feasting, address the under-chiefs in the following terms : ' Prop up my rule, not with rotten sticks, but with ironwood. Let this palm grow tall, and not soon be felled. Therefore have I come, with your help to make peace,' etc. At the commencement of each reign the paramount chief planted coco-nuts, as a visible token of his authority. The hope was that these young palms would be permitted to grow on and bear fruit for many a long year. By the phrase, ' Let this palm grow tall,' he means, ' Let my rule over you long endure.'

In a letter lying before me Ioane pathetically says : ' My chief food as I live here day by day is tears, as I am compelled to watch the unchecked growth of evil.' This is not, as some might imagine, a reference to Psalm xlii. 3, but a very ancient proverbial expression, denoting intense

---

[1] Of exquisite delicacy, split by the gentlest zephyr.

grief. In their classic laments for the dead, this phrase is of frequent occurrence.

At Rarotonga a dying man will say to his friends, ' The reef is nearly dry,'[1] *i.e.* ' death is near.' The idea is, the tide is running out, leaving the coral reef dry.

When a serious quarrel is being composed, a friend of both parties will exhort both the aggrieved ' to bale out the canoe,'[2] *i.e.* ' Out with all your grievances, so that peace may be made.'

At Rarotonga a tenant-at-will is called an *unga*, i.e. a tiny tuber of the indigenous arrowroot, or of the *teve* plant ;[3] the big tuber or corm being the chief or real owner of the soil.

In the olden times at Rarotonga, if a man were killed, an inquiry would be instituted by the elders of the tribe, the slayer being required to confess by whose authority the deed was done. The interrogator first demanded, By the *loins* (slapping that region), *i.e.* common people ? The answer would probably be, No. The inquiry would next be, By the *ribs* (slapping his sides), *i.e.* lesser chiefs ? The reply would again be, No. Lastly it would be demanded, By the *head* (touching his head), *i.e.* the supreme chief or king ? If the reply came, ' Yes, by the head,' no further notice would be taken and no vengeance exacted.

Queen Makea once said to me, ' Your word is medicine. Should any sickness (= evil) grow in any part of the island, go quickly and cure it. If I myself become sick, heal me ' (= if I err, set me right).

In preaching to Polynesians it is well to imitate the example of Him who ' spake unto the multitudes in parables ; and without a parable spake He not unto them.'

---

[1] *Kua rikiriki te tai.*   [2] *Kua tata i te riu i te vaka.*
[3] *Amorphophallus campanulatus.*

Christ's Death.　Marctu, descanting on the story of the crucifixion, broke out thus: 'Alas! Alas! that the Great Chief's Son should be slain by the vilest of serfs.'

Hypocrites.　'As the lobster forsakes last year's shell, so does the hypocrite abandon the ways of godliness—without a thought or an atom of compunction.'

The Judgment.　Pi said, 'Sinners at the judgment-seat of Christ will helplessly tremble, like the *kokiri* (= trigger-fish[1]) at the approach of the fisherman's hand about to seize it in its coral hiding-place. Alas, for the doomed one!'

Faith.　Said Pi: 'If our attachment to the Son of God be not firm, eternal life will elude our grip as does a slippery eel.'

Ingratitude to God.　Marctu remarked, 'Let us not thoughtlessly enjoy the bounty of our Great Chief, subsisting on the good things off His land, yet never yielding to Him the just tribute of prayer and praise.'

'*Should Christians Fight?*'　On the occasion of the visit of H.M.S. Turquoise to Rarotonga in 1880, Captain Medlycott inquired of Makea whether there had been any fighting of late years between the three different tribes in Rarotonga. The queen was surprised, and asked for an explanation. Captain Medlycott reiterated, 'Have you had any fighting, say within the last ten years?' Turning to me, her uncle and spokesman said, 'Tell the captain that when our fathers embraced Christianity fifty-seven years ago, we gave up fighting altogether. Should Christians fight?'

'*The Prince of Peace.*'　Numangatini, the aged king of Mangaia, once said to me when very despondent, 'Missionary, don't be anxious about me. As long as I

---

[1] *Balistes conspicillum.*

breathe I will cling to the Word of God. Until *that* was brought here, the heavens above were the only roof over me, as I hid myself night after night in the tall reeds or fern of the mountains through fear of being slain. Ere it was dark we, in those sad days, hastily despatched our evening meal, so as not to be overtaken by darkness ere a place of shelter and security had been provided for the night. On no account could I sleep in the same place two nights successively. Our wives and children alone slept in our homes, as they would not be slain. *Now* one may sleep without fear on the sandy beach, or in sequestered valley, or in one's own dwelling, and yet be unhurt. Brief were the intervals of peace; war and bloodshed the rule.'

Yet this same king, in times of peace, was so sacred that even the 'lord of Mangaia' approached him, not without an offering, *on all fours !*

It may not be out of place to give the story of Numangatini's installation as king (A.D. 1814). The morning star had just appeared, when the loud call *E tama* = 'O sir !'[1] aroused him. Coming outside he found Tamaine and Vaipo, deputed by 'the lord of Mangaia' as representing the victors. Two curiously platted coco-nut leaves were placed on the ground ; he was desired to plant his feet on them. His legs were then carefully anointed with scented coco-nut oil. Then the sacred girdle (*maro aitu*) was adjusted by them on his person. Six stout white garments (*tikoru*), beaten out from the inner bark of the *Broussonetia papyrifera*, were next placed on his shoulders. Finally these vestments were removed and hidden in a sacred cave. This was the secret ceremony. The public

---

[1] Kings were never addressed by their proper names, but as above, *E tama !*

installation of the new king took place a day or two later. He was on this occasion formally seated by the temporal lord, in the presence of the leading under-chiefs, upon 'the sacred sandstone' in Rongo's *marae* on the sea-shore, facing the setting sun.

During the many years of our close intimacy I saw very much to admire and nothing whatever to blame in the character and Christian profession of King Numangatini. He was always in his place in the house of God. Never was a ruler more sincerely lamented at his death at a very advanced age in 1878. He passed away in possession of all his faculties, and left a beautiful testimony of the power of Christianity.

' *The darkness is past, and the True Light now shineth* ' (I John ii. 8). When visiting the Rev. Dr. Geddie, of Aneitcum, in 1863, he told me that his late chief had been an inveterate cannibal. An incident related to me by the doctor (who was the first missionary to the New Hebrides) is worth preserving. One day in the early history of the mission he remonstrated with Nohoat, and begged him in future to exact pigs from his people instead of human beings. At this the old fellow became very angry, and said, 'Am I not a king ? Only human flesh is fit for *me* to feed upon. You white men—do *you* go and eat pigs. They are good enough for *you* ! '

Nohoat belonged to a class of chiefs regarded with religious veneration while they lived, and worshipped after death. Eventually he abandoned heathenism, and exerted all his influence in favour of Christianity.

On two successive Sabbaths I listened with pleasure to addresses by his son Lathella at the close of Dr. Geddie's sermon, founded upon verses in St. Matthew's Gospel—the first complete portion of Scripture translated into the

Aneiteumese language. Lathella was an elder of the church. The entire Bible is now translated, and is lovingly read by these islanders. Can Rationalism produce a change like this?

'After *my words they spake not again*' (Job xxix. 22). This is exactly descriptive of Polynesian etiquette. At a meeting of chiefs in the Hervey group, it was customary for the king to speak last of all, it being deemed excessively rude to speak after so dignified a personage, except in assent. The usual formula of assent is, 'Thou hast spoken, O king!' or, 'With thee rests the word, O father!'

When Christianity rooted itself in the island of Mangaia, and the great warrior chief Parima, in the presence of the assembled clan, divorced his five superfluous wives, portioning each off, he proposed to his cousin Tetonga that he, being a bachelor, should marry one whom he named. Tetonga looked up and quietly said, 'Are you not my elder brother?[1] Have you not spoken?' At this Parima requested a deacon to take the pair off at once to the native pastor to be married; which of course was done. Very happily did Tetonga and his wife live together the many years I knew them both. They were consistent Christians.

On my first visit to New Guinea in 1872, I noted that Sauai, the heathen chief of Tauan, sent his twelve wives to church first, whilst he—leaning on a spear—brought up the rear. No one dared enter by that door after the chief; the rest of the congregation having entered by another door. Service over, the chief alone made his exit through the same door. His wives slunk out (they would not stand erect) through the open casements near their home. Why thus? The doorway was *tapu, i.e.* sacred, that day,

---

[1] Cousins in Polynesia are called and treated as brothers and sisters.

Sauai, the much-feared warrior-chief, having passed through it !

Nothing is so revolutionary as Christianity. Women, so utterly downtrodden in heathenism, are to-day quite able to hold their own in Christian Polynesia. And doubtless the same will take place in New Guinea as the Gospel wins its way.

CONCLUSION.

Since I went to the Pacific, in 1851, the light of the Gospel has spread over all that vast expanse. War, infanticide, human sacrifice, and idolatry have almost disappeared. The Sabbath is better observed in the Christianized islands of the Pacific than in London.

Heathenism separates and sets at enmity, individuals, families and tribes. Christianity unites, and heals ancient feuds. The *lex talionis*, or law of blood revenge, was one of the chief reasons why the South-Sea Islanders were rapidly degenerating when Christianity arrested their downward progress. In order that the duty of revenge might not be forgotten, it was customary to make tattoo marks on the throat and arms. If the person or persons escaped during the offended man's life-time, he gave strict injunctions to his children at his death ; thus it was handed down from generation to generation, until the lust of revenge was satiated.

Contrast with this the blessed doctrine of forgiveness, as illustrated by the life and death of Him who expired praying for His murderers. That grand doctrine gave new life to the race. But for Christianity, all other attempts to elevate the natives of the Pacific would have utterly failed.

I once remonstrated with an incorrigible heathen thief on the peril to which he exposed himself by his tricks. He naïvely replied, 'The day I was born my father dedicated me to Hiro, god of thieves. His servant I am. I know no other god. Why rebuke me for serving Hiro?' This was in the Eastern Pacific.

In 1862 I first visited the Loyalty Islands (in the Western Pacific), and found a mission family with their converts in nightly expectation of a threatened attack from a host of cannibals. Years afterwards I again called, and found a well-clothed, industrious, law-abiding population, kind and courteous to strangers. A beautiful church (of large blocks of white coral) had been erected by these islanders for their own use. And, strangest of all, there was a band of twelve ex-cannibals, educated and 'mighty in the Scriptures,' ready to go with the Rev. A. W. Murray and myself to instruct the heathen of New Guinea.

THE END.

LONDON: PRINTED BY WILLIAM CLOWES AND SONS, LIMITED, STAMFORD STREET AND CHARING CROSS.